Sing Soft, Sing Loud

by Patricia McConnel

Logoría

1995

This is a work of autobiographical fiction. Most of the events depicted herein are real events which the author either experienced herself or personally witnessed. However, in order to protect the privacy of persons other than the author, all the characters herein are invented, and details have been changed.

Originally published in hardcover by Atheneum, 1989.
Published in France by Editions Fixot, 1991.
This edition has been slightly revised.

Logoria
2700 Woodlands Village
Bldg. 300-417
Flagstaff AZ 86001

520-525-1225
logoria@infomagic.com

Library of Congress Cataloging-in-Publication Data:
McConnel, Patricia.
    Sing soft, sing loud,
    1. Title.

PS3563.C34355S56   813'.54   89-259

ISBN 0-9643253-0-6

10 9 8 7 6 5 4 3

For the women I lived with in various jails and in prison, who, though barely hanging on themselves, always seemed to have at least a little to give. That little bit of something — a story, a song, sympathetic listening, a good laugh, a spirited fight, truth, consolation, a lie told to protect me, a gift of food, a bit of contraband shared, jail-wise advice — was often all that saved my sanity.

If this book is a song, it is sung for them. And this time, gals, I'm singing loud.

Contents

I. Iva

The Difference It Makes Where You Sit   3
The Tourist   9
The Virgin Ear   19
Ho Toi's Luck   27
And Then They Take Out All These Taxes   34
Sing Soft, Sing Loud   59

II. Toni

Blind Corner   75
Esperanza   89
Standing Up for Leon   108
Getting Oriented   131
Prior Convictions   156
All Through the House   170
The Floor   181
Twenty Minutes of Freedom   188
The End   214

Afterword   239
What Can You Do?   245
Organizations for Women Prisoners   250
Acknowledgments   253
About the author   255

I. Iva

The Difference
It Makes
Where You Sit

I'm back in the San Rudolfo City Jail again, same tank, same tier, but this time Millie ain't here. It ain't that I wish her back in jail or anything, but every morning I go down and look over the first tier to see if she come in during the night. She's liable to show up any time – we both spend half our lives in this stinking place, me for hustling, Millie for booze. But she ain't here, and after cleanup I go on up to the second tier and look out the window for a while.

It's a lousy window as windows go, no more than a foot and a half wide and maybe two feet high, and it's set in the wall near the ceiling, too high to see anything through and too small to let much light in, but it's the only window in the tank and at least it's a window. Over in A tank there's no window at all. I wonder sometimes why they put one in this tank and not in the other. This one don't even have any bars cuz it's twenty feet off the floor and the only way to get out of it is to fly.

I hang over the rail on the ramp of the second tier and try to figure out ways you could get out that window. I think maybe they put it there just to make us miserable. It's like a flag of the Free World, a little brilliant blue patch of sky and sun to make sure you don't forget what you're missing. We don't ever get no sun around here. I'm fair-skinned to begin with, and after I been here a month my legs look like fish bellies. But every morning

3

for just about a half hour there's a little patch of sun comes through that window and hits the second tier, and I go sit in it when I can. There's a palm tree growing outside the building, and if you get in just the right place on the ramp you can see the tips of its branches through the window. When it's windy the branches sway back and forth and because they're something alive and swinging they make me feel good. If the screws knew about that tree they would surely have it cut down, so I never open my mouth about it.

I'm standing there thinking about that (I guess I think about it just about every morning) when I hear the tank door open and slam. I lean over the railing to see which screw is on duty this morning. It's that carrot-top chicken-woman Cavanaugh – she's got a potbelly and you can't tell where her boobs end and her stomach begins, and she's got a nose like a beak and when she walks her head bobs back and forth just like a chicken, no kidding. She tramps in like she's mad, and when she stops she stands with her feet planted wide apart, a sure sign she's about to give a Order.

"Get your gear together, girls, you're all moving to A tank."

There's no way I'm going to A tank, so I holler, "The hell you say!"

"You heard me, Iva," the screw says, and starts to leave.

"I ain't going nowhere!" But Cavanaugh keeps going and I hear the tank door open and clang shut. I'm spitting nails. I spend a lot of time here, like I said, and I know how this goddam place is run. There's no way I'm going to A tank. A tank is the holding tank, where they put people when they're just busted, until they go to court or get out on bail, and so there's a ton of drunks in there every night and even the screws call it the Drunk Tank, and it's a snake pit at night. I mean you ain't never heard nothin' like half a dozen alkies all having d.t.'s at the same time. People who been to court and got their sentence are transferred over to B tank, where I am. It's a lot quieter.

So I figure they can't make me go to A, cuz it's against the jail-house rules. I decide I just ain't about to move, and I sit there and watch the other women get ready. There's not much to move, really – just a blanket and a mattress cover, your aluminum cup and toothbrush if you're lucky enough to have one, maybe a pad of paper and a pencil if you got someone to write letters to.

I begin to feel good about holding out. I turn around and let my feet hang over the side of the ramp and swing them back and forth. It don't matter to the others which tank they're in. But it matters to me cuz I got three months to do, and I know the rules and this time the rules are on my side. They think so much of their goddam rules and regulations, well this time let them mind their own fucking rules.

Cavanaugh comes back in twenty minutes. "Everybody line up by the door." The others are all downstairs waiting and I can hardly keep from laughing out loud as I watch her count them. The count don't come out right, of course, and I watch her figuring out who's missing. "I mighta known," she says. "Where's Iva?"

"Here I am, darling," I says, in a sweet high-pitched voice.

"Iva, why the hell aren't you ready?"

"Cuz I'm not going, darling," I says, and some of the women giggle.

"Iva, for god's sake don't give me any trouble today. The feds are sending in twenty wetbacks we got to make room for. You gotta go to A until we get rid of them."

"No."

"Goddam it, Iva, get your stuff and get down here."

"No, I ain't going. The book says I belong in B tank and this is where I'm sitting 'til my three months runs out." I figure mentioning "the book" will get her cuz all these rules gotta be wrote down in a book somewhere and I want her to know I ain't ignorant of it.

"If you don't get down here I'll be back for you in ten minutes with two guards. And you know what that means, Iva. Now move fast!"

I can see the rules don't mean a thing to this asshole. I blow my lid. I yell, "Then get the fuckin' guards, you cuntface!" and I spit, aiming for her head, but I miss.

She looks up at me like she hates me more than her own poison self. "I hope the day you get out you get hit by a truck," she says, and leads the other women out of the tank. I ain't so mad that I don't notice the looks of admiration I get from the other women. I feel pretty good.

I fold my hands on the railing and rest my chin. I know the screw will be back with the guards as soon as she gets the other women settled. I decide to hold my ground right where I am. I look back at my window. The palm leaves are whipping back and forth – there must be a storm brewing. I start picking at the paint on the railing. You can actually smell the lead they make these bars out of. They put a dozen coats of paint on 'em and it always chips and you can make these little circles with different colors by picking through to the metal and then making widening circles around the hole. I mean, that's how bored you can get around here.

It sure is quiet with everybody gone. Nothin' moving but those palm leaves whipping back and forth, and the sound of my fingernails chipping paint. But I get tired of that pretty soon, and I decide to see how many choruses of "Cocaine Blues" I can whistle before they get here.

Two and a half.

The three of 'em – two men guards and the screw – come quiet but fast. The guards never order, never argue, they just come fast and quiet and carry you out. I should know, I been through all this before. As they come up the stairs I stand up to meet 'em. I don't think I can win – don't get me wrong. I ain't crazy. It's just a matter of the rules of war. I have to make it as tough for them as I can – this is in *our* rules, the prisoners' rules, I mean, that ain't wrote down anywhere.

I start swinging as soon as they reach for me. The trick is to keep moving so fast they can't get a good grip on you. Then you get in as many blows as you can with your fists and your feet. I used to try to get 'em in the balls but I finally learned that these guys are trained to protect themselves against that. I usually figure it's been a good fight if I leave one with a shin bruise to make him miserable for a couple of weeks.

The whole thing is silent except for shuffling feet and grunts. The screw watches from the foot of the stairs. Finally one of the guards gets a arm behind my back and the fight is over – if you pull against that you're liable to have your arm tore outa the socket. They keep my arm twisted to keep control and push me down the stairs and over to A tank.

It don't bother me none that the women in A all see me

dragged in like this. What I know is that I fought and they didn't, and they know it too. "Atta girl, Iva!" they shout. "Give 'em hell, Iva!" The guards push me into flatbottom and slam the door. They leave, and they never said one word, or me either, from beginning to end.

Flatbottom don't have a bunk or a toilet. It's where they throw you for punishment. But it don't bother me much cuz I've learned to squat close to the bars and pee so it runs out in the corridor. They ain't allowed to keep you in here over twenty-four hours and I can hold my bowels for that long. But what I hate about A tank is the nights – alkies screaming and the door clanging every half hour as they bring in new bookings. It's impossible to sleep. I figure I better sit down in the corner at the back of the cell and snooze while I still got a chance.

At four o'clock the swing-shift screw comes in. It's Rupert, not a bad person for a screw. She don't wear a scowly expression like some of the other screws, and she don't stomp around like she's looking for a fight. And you gotta raise quite a ruckus before she'll write you up. And she never calls the male guards. She's strong and fast, and if she's gotta hold somebody down or break up a fight she can do it herself. She's got a rep around here for being tough but fair, so we give her less trouble than we give the other screws. She carries herself nice and has an easy way about her. Reminds me of a teacher I had once, before I dropped outa school, that I liked a lot. She's got a sense of humor too. Teases me a lot. Anyway, she stops at flatbottom and looks at me with make-believe shock. "You in there again, Iva? What was it this time?"

"I'm supposed to stay in B tank. I got my rights."

"Iva, if you'd quit hustling you'd never lose your rights."

Well, I like ol' Rupert, but she picked the wrong damn time to come on all righteous like that. So I says, "Where do you get off lecturing me? Ain't it bad enough you're looking at me sitting on the cement floor of a bare cage like a dumb animal? Goddam it, Rupert, don't tell me how losing my rights is my fault. It ain't my fault I got no fucking money."

Now Rupert's irritated too. "You're in jail for hustling, Iva. Lots of other people need money and they don't hustle to get it."

"That ain't what I mean and you know it. Do you see any of

them five-hundred-dollar call girls in here?"

Rupert don't answer. She looks like she wishes she never said nothin'. But I'm mad and I see I got her in a corner.

"Well, do you?"

Rupert sighs. "No."

"And why do you think that is, Rupert?"

She don't answer. She's looking around, anywhere but at me.

"I'll tell you why, since you don't seem to be able to figure it out for yourself. Because they're tricking with the mayor and the D.A. and the city council and the whole fuckin' vice squad, and if by some accident they get busted by mistake, their hoitsy-toitsy la-de-da escort service madam is down here with their bail in two seconds, and then those maggot-eaten cunts just forfeit bail and don't never go to jail, cuz what the hell is a couple hundred dollars to them? Don't tell me I'm here cuz I'm hustling. I'm here cuz I got no goddam ass-sucking freedom-buying money."

Rupert just stands there looking at the floor. I can tell she feels bad, cuz she knows what I'm saying is the truth. So I sit there and she stands there and neither of us says anything. But she's a screw – what can she do, agree with me? I expect her to just walk away, and now that I got all the steam blowed off I feel bad for dumping all that on her. Like I said, she's pretty decent for a screw, and it ain't her fault, but I can't think of what to say to make it right. You can't take back the truth once it's said.

But she don't walk away, instead she finally looks at me and says, "What's so great about B tank, anyway?" I guess she wants to try to fix things too.

I think about the window and the palm tree waving in the wind. For just a split second I consider telling her about it. But I see real clear it can't be fixed, and besides, I can't tell nobody about that tree. War is war and us is us and them is them, and one of my rules is never trust a screw, not even ol' Rupert. So I says, "Nothin'. I'm just not gonna sit out my three months in this fuckin' snake pit."

Rupert sighs again, and this time she looks irritated. "What difference does it make where you sit out your three months, Iva?"

"It don't make a bit of difference at all," I says. "Not a goddam bit," and I close my eyes to shut her out.

The Tourist

They bring this woman in after lights out, which is nothin' unusual cuz they bring drunks in all night long on weekends. I wake up for a minute when they slam the cell door shut but usually I go right back to sleep again, even if they have the screaming d.t.'s, cuz I'm so used to it. But this one keeps me awake cuz she's moaning "Oh my god, oh my lord, ooooh," and pacing the floor. Click-click-click – sounds like her shoes have taps on 'em, or those little spiky heels. D.t.'s I'm used to, but not this clicking and moaning. The whole thing has a maddening rhythm to it: click-click-click . . . oh my god . . . click-click-click . . . oh noooo . . . click-click-click . . . etc., etc., etc., on and on and on. I just come back in here myself, and I was only on the street about a month since last time. So I ain't in too good a mood, and after about a hour of this click-click-click business I get so riled I yell, "Hey, Moaner! If you're gonna pace all night take off your goddam shoes!" The click-clicks stop and I go to sleep.

In the morning the Moaner is still locked in her cell when they let us out for breakfast. Usually the only people they don't unlock in the morning are drunks that ain't sobered up yet, but I sneak a peek at her and she don't look drunk to me. To tell the truth, she don't look like she's *ever* been drunk. She's dressed like a fashion ad, a creamy-colored blouse looks like it's real silk, and she's got one of them spray-can hairdos, and it's pretty obvious she ain't the type for bunko, dope, boosting, hustling, or any of the other things you end up in city jail for.

Another thing I notice about her is they took her belt and stockings. They do that sometimes with people they think are gonna try to off themselves. She's the type for that – a skinny bag, real nervous, and she has these great big eyes with sacks under them sunk way in her face, kind of wild looking, staring out at us like if anyone went near her she'd claw them to death.

When the screw comes in with the trusties to take out the breakfast trays, she yells, "The new woman in the end cell is incommunicado. Anybody who talks to her gets isolation for twenty-four hours."

Very mysterious. Long as I been coming in and out of this place they never had nobody incommuni-whatever except Toni – she's the one got busted on a big dope charge and been sitting up on the second tier over two months with nobody to talk to. Except me. I sneak up there sometimes, I feel so sorry for her.

So anyway now we got two of 'em. But this one don't look like no drug runner to me. Although, come to think of it, if she's a cokehead, that would explain why she's so nervous.

Well, hell, I ain't about to go to isolation. I end up there often enough anyway, and this time I got Millie to talk to, thank the devil, so who wants to talk to some ding-a-ling? So after that I don't pay her any mind and Millie and me start our jailhouse rummy game. We always start off on the table downstairs but we move around depending on what's going on in the tank. For instance this morning one ol' alkie keeps hanging around watching the game and breathing over my shoulder. Her breath is so rank I give Millie a look and when we finish that hand we get ready to move up to our bunks on the second tier.

All this time the Moaner is pacing up and down in her cell. She looks pretty nervous, and I guess Millie notices it too cuz she walks over and offers the woman a smoke. The Moaner glares at her like she's some kind of bug. Don't say nothin', just glares, so Millie sticks her cigarette back in her pocket and comes on upstairs.

When we come down for supper the Moaner is still locked up. She's stopped pacing though, and is lying on her bunk staring at the springs of the bunk above her. They put a tray in her cell but she don't touch it. Can't say I blame her. This stuff is crap. It takes a while to get used to.

The morning of the second day they unlock her cell, which means she ain't isolated anymore and she can come out for breakfast, but she don't. Millie goes over and says, "Don't you want any breakfast?" Millie's a big softie, see. She even looks soft, build like a Teddy bear, and a sweet round face, and frizzy brown hair sticking out in a circle like a halo. The Moaner gives Millie a slimy look and says, "If I wanted some breakfast I would go and get it."

Millie says, "Well, pardon me all to hell," and that's the end of that. But later, when the candy wagon comes around, Millie buys a candy bar and lays it on a crossbar of the Moaner's cell. Millie don't ask her if she wants it, just goes over there and leaves it. After a while we hear this slap on the floor, and we don't have to look to know the woman throwed Millie's candy out. One of the alkies runs over and picks it up. Since Millie ain't looking in that direction she can act like she don't know what happened, but I know Millie, and I know she's got her feelings hurt.

That afternoon they come and take the Moaner out again and she's gone for a couple of hours. While she's gone, I find out from a trusty that she's booked for attempted murder. This is serious news. We may be a sorry lot around here, a bunch of hookers, junkies, boosters, and alkies, but most of us never did no harm to nobody but our own miserable selves. The word gets around fast, and when the Moaner comes back it gets very quiet in the tank. I mean, murder is pretty high-power stuff.

That night she don't come out for supper again, and when ol' Blodgett comes with the trusties to take the trays away and sees the Moaner didn't touch her food, she goes over to the cell with the tray and says, "See here, you. You better start eating. If they have to haul you out of here to the hospital it's me they blame. Now eat this or I'll have to ram it down your throat."

The Moaner looks at Blodgett with the same cold glare she gave Millie and says, "Save your theatrics. Do you think I really care whether you get into trouble or not?"

I really like that. "Right on, sister!" I shout, and everybody starts laughing except for the Moaner and ol' Blodgett, who ain't used to having anybody call her bluff, and she turns red in the face and gives us early lockup to save face. But it was worth it for the laugh.

Later on they come and take the woman out again. They must really be grilling her. When they bring her back this time, she's crying. Once she starts she keeps it up all night and the next morning she looks worse than ever, and she never looked too good to begin with. She don't eat breakfast again but after the trays are gone she comes out of her cell and sits down at the table where Millie and me are playing rummy. She's watching us play, but she don't say a word and nobody talks to her – we're quick to learn around here. But after a while Millie, who don't know any better, offers her a cigarette. This time the woman takes it and I notice her hand is shaking so bad she can hardly hold it. She says, "Thank you so much, you are very kind."

"Don't go overboard," I says, and Millie snaps at me, "Leave her alone, Iva."

"That's just what I been trying to do. It's you oughta learn to leave her alone. Jeezuz." The Moaner busts into tears and runs back in her cell. It's a wonder she don't slam the door shut after her. Millie and me shrug our shoulders at each other and go on with the rummy game. But after a while the woman comes out and sits down. Millie keeps feeding her cigarettes but no one wants to talk to her in case she falls to pieces again. We don't like people falling to pieces around here. It makes everybody do hard time and besides, sometimes it triggers a chain reaction, y'know what I mean?

We're still sitting there when the bell rings for sick call and Millie and me start to get up. The Moaner says, "What's the bell for?"

"Sick call," I says, "get in line."

"I'm not sick."

"Nobody said you was. Get in line and ask for two aspirin and a laxative. They make you take 'em right there while they watch, but you just pretend to swallow and palm them instead. Then give 'em to me after."

"What for?"

"A good cause. There's no time to explain right now. If you don't like what it's for after, you don't have to give 'em to me.

Now get in line, quick. "

She does what I say, which surprises me. I didn't expect her to go for it. But when she gets up to the sick wagon and tries to pretend to swallow the aspirin and the shit pill, she drops 'em on the floor. The screw behind the wagon says, "Try again," and the Moaner is so shook up she swallows the whole business. After the wagon leaves she tells me, "I'm sorry."

"That's something you don't say around here," I tell her. "If you go around telling people you're sorry you ain't gonna survive two days in this place."

She looks like she's gonna cry again, so I tell her real quick, "Come on and I'll show you what they're for." She follows me up to the second tier where Tiny's cell is. Tiny is rolled up under a blanket, shaking. "Tiny's sick," I says. "If they find out, they'll know she's got a habit and she's bound to be sent up for a cure. She was just picked up for pills, and if that's all she gets bagged with, she'll only do ninety days in County, maybe."

The Moaner's eyes are getting bigger while I say all this. "You mean she's a dope addict?"

"A dope *fiend*, lady. A real dangerous evil person." I give Tiny's shoulder a push through the blanket. "Hey, Tiny, Millie and me got aspirin and shit pills." Tiny reaches a hand out of the blanket for the pills and puts them in her mouth, sticks her hand out again for some water. Millie fills her cup at the sink and helps her sit up to drink it.

The Moaner is standing in the door of the cell, watching. She says, "Do the aspirin and laxative really help her?"

I can see she's fascinated and revolted all at the same time. "Not much," I says, "but it's something. If you can get your guts moving again it helps. You get all bound up when you're shooting smack."

The Moaner looks like she just bit into a worm. She says, "She's so quiet. I thought addicts scream and roll around when they're withdrawing."

"You watch too much TV. You'd keep quiet too if you was trying for ninety days instead of who knows how long."

The woman goes over to the sink, takes the towel there and wets it, and leans over the bunk and puts it on Tiny's forehead. "If you don't beat all," I says, disgusted. "This kid is cold. She don't want no cold wet rags on her head."

The Moaner grabs the rag and turns her big wild eyes on me again. "I'm sorry," she says, and I wince. "Oh, I mean. . ."

"Forget it," I says, and she runs out.

On the Moaner's fourth day, Millie and me are playing jail-house rummy on Tiny's bunk. Tiny is over the worst of her shakes now, but she still needs company. She's humming this godawful tune she hums all the time. She gets the tune all wrong and I can't even recognize the song, and on top of that she has this little squeaky voice that gets on my nerves. I tell her to shut up once but she says if she don't hum she'll bite her nails.

Anyway we're sitting there playing rummy and Tiny is humming, and the Moaner appears in the door of the cell. She stands there a minute waiting for someone to speak to her but no one does. She starts to turn away again, then changes her mind and says, "I came to apologize to you girls." She waits a few seconds to see how we take it but Millie and me just keep on picking up and putting down cards. She goes on: "You all tried to be nice to me and I wouldn't let you. The truth is I really thought I was better than you, that I really don't belong here and you do." Her voice is shaking really bad but she keeps talking. "I haven't slept since I've been here and I've had time to think about a lot of things. And one of the things I've had to face is that no matter how justified I may have been, I took a shot at my husband and I do belong here. And that means I'm no different than you and you're no different than me."

"I bet that's hard to take," I says.

The Moaner's eyes get full of tears. "If you don't like me, I deserve it, but I wanted to tell you I'm sorry."

"Sure you are," I says.

Millie looks up and says, "Why don't you come in and sit down?" I give Millie a dirty look but she pretends she don't see it. I don't know why she can't see what a phony broad this woman is, prolly got poison mushrooms growing in her cunt.

The Moaner sits down on the edge of the bunk and watches us play. She takes out a pack of cigarettes and offers us one. Millie takes one, but not me. The woman says, "My husband came this morning and brought me a carton." She offers the pack to me again.

14

"Okay, I'll take three packs."

Millie glares at me. "Back off, Iva," she says. Then to the Moaner: "Your husband ain't mad at you?"

"No. We had a long talk. He says he knows he had it coming to him, that perhaps it's a good thing it happened because it brought him to his senses. He's humiliated me time and time again. He drinks too much and he always has some woman on the string and he's not even discreet about it."

"Dearie me," I says, "the least he could do is be discreet about it."

"Shut up, Iva," Millie says.

"Maybe I shouldn't burden you with my troubles," the woman says, looking hurt.

"You go right ahead," says Millie. "It helps sometimes to talk about your troubles a little bit. Right, Iva?"

Now, Millie knows I don't talk to nobody about nothin', and she knows I don't like this society creep, so why is she asking me that? Then I figure maybe she means to get this woman talking and making a ass of herself just to pass the time. You get a certain type started and they talk for hours. It's better than a confession magazine cuz you can play on how sorry they feel for themselves and you can get 'em to tell you just about anything. They think they're getting sympathy and all the time you're just fuckin' with their minds. Besides, like I said, it passes the time. So I says, "That's right. Don't pay no attention to me, I'm uptight cuz I got troubles too. You go ahead and talk." Millie gives me a peculiar suspicious look but I just study the cards in my hand.

So the Moaner goes on about how this whole thing happened. "At first I didn't think I had really done it. I still find it hard to accept. But I know I did. He came home drunk again and began abusing me and all of a sudden I was just tired. It happened in London and he swore he'd change when we came home and now it's happening all over again here. So I just went in the bedroom and got the gun. I don't remember feeling anything. That's what bothers me. I was just tired and numb."

Tiny says from under the blanket, "I tried to shoot my old man once."

The Moaner's eyes get big and she leans toward Tiny. "What happened?"

"He took the gun away from me, kicked my ass out of the house and wouldn't let me back in for a week."

Millie and me crack up laughing but not the Moaner. She's dead serious. "How did you feel when you shot at him?" she says.

"Hell, I was mad."

This breaks me up so bad I drop my cards all over the bunk and the woman looks hurt. "You're not taking me seriously," she says, just about whining.

"Yes we do, yes we do," says Millie, although she is red in the face from laughing, "go on!" But Millie and me are both having a hard time controlling ourselves. It's funny how when you get a chance to laugh at something around here you tend to go off the deep end. You take all the screaming and crying you got bottled up and you let it out laughing, but of course the Moaner ain't been here long enough to understand about that. She ain't sure how to take us at all, but she goes on.

"Well, when he came this morning we decided it had all happened for the best. He says it really woke him up to what a strain he had been putting on me. He went to the D.A. and dropped the charges against me."

"If he dropped the charges, why ain't you out?" I says.

"It seems the city can prosecute on its own if they see fit. The district attorney said it would be a matter of routine for them to hold me a little longer, but that there is no doubt I'll be released. I suspect it's really because they want to make sure I've cooled down. Anyway, my husband says he is going to be a different man from now on."

"He don't have no choice," I says, "he's liable to have his balls shot off" and this sets us all off again. Even Tiny is shaking under her blanket. The Moaner looks like she's gonna laugh too but can't make up her mind about it. Finally she just smiles a little.

"But guess what else he did," she says.

"Took a plane to China!" I holler, and at this point I'm laughing so hard I'm about to piss my pants, but Millie says, "That's enough, Iva!" so I shut up, but I'm just about choking.

"He went and bought me a new Porsche to go home in."

Well, the rest of it I can swallow but this is too much." *Sure* he did," I says, scrunching my nose at Moaner.

"He really did!" the Moaner says and looks like I've insulted her.

"You mean you expect me to believe you took a shot at this bum and he buys you a new car?"

Millie says, "Iva, he just wants to show her he's sorry."

"That's a helluva way to show her *he's* sorry *she* shot *him*."

"I didn't shoot him! I missed!" The Moaner is almost yelling and looks like she's gonna go all to pieces again.

Millie is pissed off. "Iva, goddam it . . ."

Just then ol' Blodgett comes in. "Hey, Society," she bellows (like the cow she is), "get your things. You're going out."

The Moaner turns into a cyclone all of a sudden. She don't know which way to turn so she turns all directions at once. Millie helps her gather what little stuff she has, and when she's all set to go she gives Millie a hug. I think, If she tries to hug me I'll flatten her. But she don't. She tells Millie, "Take care of yourself, and take care of Iva too."

"Shit," I says, and she is gone.

Millie and me go back to our rummy game. After a while the screw comes back in and hollers up at us, "Iva and Millie, what kind of a con did you lay on that woman?"

I holler back, "We told her you was a angel of mercy!"

Millie says, "Shut up, Iva" – I'm getting a little sick of her telling me to shut up – and then she yells at the screw, "What do you mean, con?"

"You know damn well what I mean. She left fifty bucks for each of you."

Millie looks like it could be a million dollars. The screw goes out without saying nothin' else and Millie says, "Don't that beat all?"

"What a sucker," I says. "You gonna play this hand or not?"

"I feel sorry for that lady," says Millie. She draws from the deck and discards a eight of clubs.

"I hate a goddam tourist," I says. I look at the stack of discards and figure there are only three cards in it I can't use. I pick them all up, lay down a book with the bottom card, and discard.

"Well, maybe she don't know from nothin' but I think she tries hard." Millie draws, and lays down three books. "I'm out."

"I dunno. I figure she'll forget the whole thing the minute she sets her skinny ass in that Porch." I throw my cards down on the bunk.

"Porsche, Iva. You gotta count the points you were holding and subtract them from your score."

"Listen. The only thing I gotta do is serve my time. I don't like this silly-ass game. It's stupid." I'm almost yelling.

"All right, Iva, don't get sore."

"I'm not, I'm not." I pick up the deck and lay out a game of solitaire. I like that game better. Nobody can sneak up on you.

The Virgin Ear

I'm holding ten cards and it's my turn to draw. I pick up a card from the deck and discard. Not a single book. While I wait for Millie to make her move I'm thinking. Eleven down, twenty-nine days to go. God, I'll go crazy it's so goddam boring around this stinking jail. Nothing ever happens around here. I wish we had something to do besides play cards and talk. We sing a lot, but you can't sing all day and all night. So mostly we save the singing for night and play cards all day. One thing we do all the time is tell stories, cuz there's no life in this damn place, and stories are all we got to substitute for it. The biggest punishment about being in jail ain't being behind bars. Hell, that's nothin'. The worst thing is they take *life* away from you. I get to feeling so dead that I'm glad when the tension gets high and someone has a fight. I mean at least if you're fighting, you're alive. That's what I need, a good argument.

I love the hell outa Millie, but it's easy to get her goat. And she's got a real soft head about her brother and her son. I know just how to get to her. I says to myself, Don't do this to poor ol' Millie. But I answer right back, It'll do her good, get her juices flowing. Besides, if she don't know by now not to take me serious, she's got it coming.

I says to Millie, "All men are evil sonzabitches."

"Aw, c'mon, Iva, you know that isn't true," says Millie. She draws a card and lays down two books.

"It is as far as I'm concerned. I was just going over the men I known in my head. There's not a single fuckin' one didn't do me dirt one way or another."

"You tole me yourself 'bout some men that've been nice to you."

"I just didn't tell you how after they was nice they stuck a knife in my back. Every time. Any time a man starts acting nice to me, I say 'uh-oh.' Like that guy said he was gonna get me a job and then it turns out it's a whorehouse."

"Iva, you tole me yourself about men that've been good to you. Remember you said one time you and Tommy were hiding in that freight car in Tucson and you were afraid to get out while it was in the station in case it took off without you, and this yardman found you and instead of turning you in he went away and came back with a bag full of groceries?"

"Yeah, well the part I didn't tell you is that he was trying to look up my skirt the whole time."

Millie sighs and lays down her cards. "Iva, you change things to suit the mood you're in. I don't know what's bullshit and what isn't."

Hot damn. I got her going now. "All I know is, every man I ever known done more evil than he done good."

"It sounds like you're saying that if a man does evil things, the good things he does don't count for nothin'."

"Yeah, that's right."

"Then there's no good in the world."

"You said it, not me."

Millie picks up her cards and studies them. I can tell she ain't really thinking about the cards though. She's quiet and I wait to see what she'll come up with. Millie ain't gonna let it go all that easy.

Finally she starts talking. "The first time I was ever in jail, Iva, I was sixteen years old. I had run away from home and was picked up for shoplifting in El Paso. I was scared to death. The other women in the tank scared me, they were so much older and seemed so tough. I wanted them to notice me but I was too shy and scared to make the first move. So I spent my days sitting by the window looking out over the city, and I passed the time singing. In those days, before I burned my throat up with smoke and booze, I had a sweet voice.

"It was summertime, and El Paso was really hot. But we were on the shady side of the jail – this was the old jail, y'know, before they tore it down – and in the morning the doves used to come and sit on this concrete ledge outside the window. They made these pretty cooing noises, and strutted up and down like they thought they were really something. I'd save my coffee from breakfast and sip on it, making it last as long as I could. I'd sit there with my face pressed against the bars and sing to the doves."

"What was the other women doing?"

"The other women in the tank were busy playing cards, reading, or telling each other lies about their lives outside, just like we do here. I kept myself apart from them, partly because I was so much younger than any of the others, partly because it was my first time in jail, and partly because of what happened the first day. One of the women asked me who I worked for. 'I don't have a job,' I said. She said, 'Very funny. I mean who do you hustle for? I thought I knew every hooker in town, but I don't remember you.'

"That really upset me, that she figured I was a hooker. I thought hookers were pretty awful. I glared at her and said, 'I don't know why you think I'm a hooker. I happen to be here for shoplifting. And I'll have you know I'm a virgin.' I thought I had put her in her place, but she just laughed, and all the other women were watching and smiling. Then she says, 'Sure you're a virgin, honey – in your left ear!'

"I could feel myself turning red and the other women all laughed. They dubbed me the Virgin Ear and from that day on I had nothin' more to do with them.

"But I was awful lonely, and the doves were company. Like I said, I spent every morning in the same window. We were on the thirteenth floor, and no noise reached there from the street. It was so quiet that the flutter of the doves' wings as they came and went from the window ledge was like – I don't know, I can't think of a word, but it was loud and soft at the same time. I sang to them, and to tell the truth, I liked the sound of my own voice floating off into the sky."

Millie is so carried away with her story she starts singing. "Let me sigh, let me cry, when I'm bluooooo, let me leeeave this lonesome town. Won't be looong 'til my sooong here is throughooo, and I know I'm on my laaast go-round." She sings the blues like a goddam cow mourning a dead calf.

"Millie, spare me! Jeezuz. What does all this have to do with men? I only got twenty-nine days left to hear the story, y'know."

"I'm getting to that. You got to know all this other stuff to understand the story. Anyway, one morning I was just finishing a song and this voice comes from outside and above me somewhere. 'That sho' was pretty, honey. Ah'd like to hear some mo'.' You know – that slurred, heavy drawl that only Southern Blacks have. For a minute I thought of not answering him. Black men had always scared me – all those stories I heard when I was a kid. And where I grew up I never saw a black person 'til I was fifteen years old. They might as well be from another planet."

"I don't believe you. Where'd you grow up that there's no black people?"

"Blanding, Utah. It's a Mormon town. Stop interrupting, Iva."

"Jeezuz, if I didn't interrupt I'd never talk again."

Millie ignores that. "So anyway I figure here I was safe behind bars, and besides, I was really lonesome and he was somebody to talk to. So I said, 'I didn't know anyone could hear me.' He says, 'Folks don't sing like that if they figger somebody gonna hear 'em. You pretend like Ah ain't here and sing some mo'.' His voice was soft and careful, like someone talking to a bird, coaxing and soothing so as not to frighten it away. I looked at my doves and they didn't seem to mind him. So I said, 'Any special song you like?' He says, 'Anything you sing gonna be all right wif me.'

"I sang him a country song about a man who is drunk because of a two-timing woman. When I finished, he says, 'Do you have any smokes?' So *that's* it, I thought. He wants to bum cigarettes. So I lied and said I didn't have any. He says, 'Well, you push that window open all the way and I'll give you the ones Ah got. Ah ain't got but two but you welcome to 'em."

"Oh, Millie, he gotcha!"

"Yeah. I was really ashamed. I wanted to refuse 'em but I was too confused to do anything but what he said. The window was outside the bars and opened down and out like a transom. So I put down my coffee mug and pushed the window out until it lay almost flat. I finally got it together enough to say, 'I don't want to take your last cigarettes.' He says, 'Don't fret yo'self none 'bout that, sugar, Ah ain't stayin' here noways. They just stuck me in here 'til the next train upstate, and Ah can get some mo' in the station. I hear the man comin' now. You keep singing , you hear?"

"Two cigarettes dropped on the open window. I tilted it 'til they rolled down where I could reach 'em through the bars and called up to him that I got 'em. Then I said, 'You're very nice. Thank you.' But I felt so funny I think I said it too soft for him to hear."

"You was smoking when you were sixteen?"

"I was smoking when I was thirteen. There's nothin' else to do in a Mormon town. Anyway, there wasn't any answer from the guy. I stood back from the window and looked around for a match. The women were playing cards so I kinda strolled over and picked up a book of matches from the table. 'What's on the next floor up?' I said, trying to sound real casual because I didn't really want to tell them anything. 'The hole,' someone answered. I didn't know what that was so I had to ask. They tole me it was where they put the bad actors and loonies from the men's section. That didn't make any sense so I decided to tell them what happened. I said, 'I was just talking through the window to some guy up there. He didn't sound like a loony. He was nice, he gave me some cigarettes.' One of the women snickered. 'Yeah? Did you make a date for outside?' I said, 'Of course not. He's a black man.' "

"Oh god, Millie. Are you sure this was you?"

"Yeah. Anyway all the women stopped playing to look at me like I was a bug. 'You took cigarettes from a nigger?' That's what they said. It gets worse. I tried to get out of it, see. I said, 'He didn't really give 'em to me. It was a sort of trade. I sang him a couple of songs.' I knew as soon as it was out of my mouth it was a mistake. This one old harpie says, 'What did you sing him, dearie, a love song?' Some of the women tittered. 'Now we know her hustle. Little Virgin Ear hustles cigarettes from niggers.' Everyone laughed and went back to the card game and acted like I wasn't there anymore. I felt like I had been erased, y'know?"

Millie stops and looks like she's fighting not to cry.

"So?" I says. "A bunch of turkey-twats. Why are you still crying about it?"

"I haven't finished the story. I felt humiliated. I went back to the window and looked out so they wouldn't see how upset I was. All the doves had gone but one, and it was sitting there looking at me with this shallow pink eye. I stared back at her, thinking her eye looked as lifeless as a button. She sees everything that goes on but don't understand any of it, is what I thought. She began to irritate me. I picked up my coffee mug and rattled it against the bars. 'Get out of here, you stupid mindless bird,' I said. I scared the poor little dove, of course, and she flew away."

"What does this goddam bird have to do with the story?"

"I didn't know myself at the time. But then I pressed my face up to the bars and I couldn't hold the tears back. And you know what I did then? I started cussing that black man. 'Stupid nigger,' I said. 'You goddam stupid nigger.'" Millie hangs her head and starts sniffling.

"Jeezuz, Millie. That was a long time ago. And you was real upset. No need to go to pieces about it now. He never knew you done that."

"That's not the end of it, Iva. You know how fast stories travel around the jailhouse. That same day we got the news through the grapevine that the man up there was on his way to the state prison and he was gonna be executed. He had killed his wife. He had done time for manslaughter before, but this time it wasn't any hotheaded fight or anything. He planned it all out ahead of time. That's why they gave him the death sentence."

"Jeezuz."

"Yeah. I thought about the whole thing a lot after that. I just couldn't get it straightened out in my mind. How could a man who seemed so gentle and kind murder his wife? No matter how much he hated her, no matter how bad she might've been. I could understand if they had a fight and he got crazy and killed her by accident. But they proved he planned it all out, went out and bought the gun just to do that, set himself up an alibi in another city the night he killed her. It all fell apart in court though. The whole thing scared me. If someone who seemed so sweet could be a murderer, who could I trust? Nobody. I worried about the other thing too."

"What other thing?"

"My cussing him, calling him a goddam nigger. And the things I caught myself saying to those women. And him on his way to his death. Maybe I was the last woman he ever talked to. I never did that before – called black people names. I didn't think I had that in me. I couldn't understand why I did it. But after a long time I figured out the reason was two things mixed up together. One was I was mad at him because the women made fun of me. They rejected me because I was friendly with him. I blamed it on him instead of the women because I needed them more than I did him. They were my cell mates.

"The other part was I thought that to be friends with those women I had to do like they did and hate black people. So I did. After I figured that out I understood how hate keeps going. You got to survive among your own people, and you choose your own people even if you know they're wrong."

"I never done that. I been fighting with my family all my life. If they're wrong I don't stand with them."

"Well, you're stronger than some, then. Anyway, the reason I'm telling you this whole thing isn't because of that, but because I never figured out how such a kind and gentle man could also be a murderer. What I did find out was that I was the same. One minute I was singing my sweetest for this prisoner upstairs, the next I was cussing him and selling him out."

"Jeezuz, Millie, that don't put you in the same league."

"Yes it does. I turned on him just like that, the minute I had some reason to. Ever since then I see everybody that way. I never been able to say anybody's good or bad. I'm not ever surprised when a nice person does me dirty, and I'm never surprised when a mean person turns around and does me a kindness. So don't tell me men are all bad because they do evil things sometimes. Tell me you never done an evil thing."

"Nope, I never did." Millie gives me her Iva-you're-full-of-shit look. I laugh. I says, "If you're such a philosopher, how come you're still in jail?"

Millie giggles. "I didn't say I figured out how to live. I just said I figured out every single living person got two sides. Once you know that, you know you can't ever predict what anybody's gonna do, so you might as well stay drunk."

"What about the bird? You made such a big thing about the bird while you was telling the story."

"The bird was me."

"The bird was you? That don't make no sense at all. Play cards, Millie. And remind me not to cuss on your left side."

"What?"

"Your virgin ear, y'know."

"I knew I shouldn'ta tole you that."

I grin. "Millie, you're easy. Play cards."

Ho Toi's Luck

The reason the judge suspended Ho Toi's sentence and paid her bus fare home out of his own pocket is cuz there just ain't room to put any more people in here. This jail wasn't never meant to hold all these people. All the cells are full and people are sleeping on the goddam floor on the ramps. It was built back in the forties, and since then the city's grown a whole bunch, but the jail ain't grown none. They keep talking about building a new one, but it keeps getting put off cuz nobody wants to spend no money on prisoners. "Coddling," they call it. Why should they put less than three people in a six-by-nine cell? These people are criminals, let 'em sleep on the concrete floor, they deserve it. Don't get me started.

Anyway, I just got busted again myself, so I'm still in the holding tank when they bring Ho Toi in. Ho Toi, she's this little tow-headed thing with a body like a little box. No waist, and no tits either. Everything about her is flat, even her face. She has a tiny little button nose and her face looks just like a pie, no shit. She has pretty blue eyes though. But the funniest thing about her is, she's wearing one of them real thin see-through blouses, and nothin' underneath it. The blouse is dark blue, and underneath you can see her white skin, the whitest person I ever seen – she don't look like she seen the light of day for years – and her flat

27

chest with nipples like little walnuts showing plain as day.

The trusty tells me she was busted for hustling in the bus station. So, seeing as she's a member of the trade, I go over to talk to her. She tells me she works in a real elegant house in San Francisco, and that she come down here to see some people and lost her purse with all her money in it, and so that's how she come to be hustling in the bus station. And she tells me her name is Ho Toi, which is Chinese for "good luck," and that she is one-quarter Chinese, and that her mom was a high-class half-Chinese hooker who got shot down in Chinatown by the feds while she was running from a bust with a suitcase full of cocaine.

Well, quarter-Chinese don't make much sense to me, what with her nearly white hair and blue eyes, but maybe it's the other side of the family came out in her. And I like the story about her mother getting shot by the feds. It's just like a movie on TV. Nothing like that ever happens to anyone *I* know.

So after supper, when everybody's out of their cells until lockup time, me and a couple of other gals gather round where she's sitting and start asking her questions about this house she works at.

"It's a special house that caters to rich people who have all kinds of kinky trips."

"Like what kind of kinks?" I says.

"Almost anything you can think of. One of our regulars is a guy who wants you to dress up like a little girl and then he pisses all over you, and you have to squeal and say, 'Oh, Daddy, don't,' but all the time acting like you really like it."

"God, I thought I had some weird ones, but I never had one ask me to do nothin' like that."

"Oh, that's nothin'. A lot of guys like that. We call it the Golden Shower. There's another man, really rich, and he wants six girls to dress up like Victorian times and go out to his house. The place is all dark when you get there, see, and you have to knock on the door and no one answers. Then you have to go all around the house and peek in the windows. Finally you end up at the back door and try the knob, and it's open. So then you all tiptoe into the house, whispering and giggling – you got to do all this exactly like I say, or he won't pay – and finally you come into this big room with candles lit and sitting all over the room, and in the middle is this big coffin with the lid closed. So you creep all around the room for a while, and you whisper to each other how scared you are, and then suddenly the lid of the coffin pops up and the guy sits bolt upright. He's made up all white like a corpse and then you all have to scream and pretend to faint."

"That's it?"

"Yeah. "

"You mean he gets his rocks off from that?"

"Like I said."

"Jeezuz. What does he pay for that?"

"I don't know. They don't tell us."

"Well, what do you get paid?"

"I get paid five hundred bucks a night, whatever."

"So with six girls it must cost him at least three thousand bucks just for the girls."

"Yeah. Well, it depends. We get bonuses sometimes if it's really weird or a lot of trouble. They gave me a thousand dollars for the duck man, and I didn't have to take any other tricks the same night."

"What duck man?"

"Well, this guy called and wanted a girl with very light yellow hair. He wanted her to be naked and powdered so she was very, very white. And he wanted her to lie on this platform kind of thing in the middle of an empty room, and she wasn't to move no matter what he did. Her eyes were supposed to be closed. In other words she was supposed to act like she was dead."

"This was some guy that hadn't been there before?"

"Right."

"Hell, I wouldn't like that keep-your-eyes-closed-and-don't-move-no-matter-what-he-did thing. Some guys can get pretty mean."

"Oh, there's usually no danger. See, all the rooms have little peepholes. The johns don't know it, but somebody's watching them every second. If they start beating up on you or something, a guy will be in there in a second."

"Okay, so what happened?"

"Well, they picked me because I'm so fair anyway, and they fixed me up just like the guy wanted, and I laid down on this thing in the center of the room, and pretty soon the guy comes in.

I peeked a little. You know how you can open your eyelids just a tiny bit so no one can notice? Well, he had a little airlines bag with a zipper, and he unzipped it and took out a live duck."

"A *duck?*"

"That's what I said. And he puts the duck down on the floor and it starts waddling around. Now the guy takes off all his clothes below the waist and he starts chasing after the duck. He's still got his jacket on, see. So the duck is quacking and trying to get away from this guy, and he is after it all over the room. He could have caught it anytime he wanted, really, but chasing it around seemed to be part of the trip. But get this – as he chased the duck, his thing got hard. I was just thinking What does he need me for? when the guy swoops down on the duck, picks it up, and then so fast I don't know what's happening, he pulls a knife from his pocket, slits the duck's belly, jams his pecker into the duck, and falls on top of me, duck and all. I was screaming bloody murder, and Jerry comes running in and grabs the guy. They threw him out, of course."

Millie's been sitting back all this time, her mouth hanging open, taking it all in. She ain't a hooker, see, so all this stuff is blowing her mind. Now she says, "I don't get it."

"What's there to get?"

"Why did the guy want you there at all?"

"Well, we figured the duck was a substitute for me, see. He really wanted to slit my gut and plunge his dong into it."

Millie just sits there looking like she don't believe it.

"Jeezuz," I says, "one day he's gonna just skip the duck."

"That's what we figured. So they wouldn't let him back anymore, and we warned everybody in the trade about him. But anyway, they gave me a thousand dollars that night and I didn't have to take any more tricks."

"How did you end up working in a place like that?" Millie says.

"It's not easy to get in. I got in because of my mother. She was about the classiest hooker in San Francisco while she lived. She never got less than a thousand dollars a trick. She was so beautiful! Her skin was like chalk and her hair and her eyes were black as volcano glass. And she was supposed to know secrets about pleasing men that came with her mother from China – I come from a long line of hookers. But my mother never liked you to call her a hooker. She said she was a courtesan. She was loved by everybody in the trade. When she died, I was raised by the madam of this house I'm telling you about. She was a good friend of my mother's. And so when I got big enough I went to work there."

All this is a lot to think about, and everybody is real quiet. Jeezuz, I thought the guy who wanted me to sing the "Star Spangled Banner" while he marched around the room naked was strange. Finally I says, "Sounds like the more money people got, the weirder they are."

"Well, I tell you what I think. I think everybody's got something real weird inside themselves, but it doesn't ever come out until you got so much money it doesn't matter."

So that's something else to think about too, and the conversation just kinda winds down and people drift off to play cards or lay on their bunks.

The next morning is Monday, and me and Ho Toi and a half a dozen other women are marched off to court. Ho Toi is called up before I am, and she's charged with soliciting, and she's asked does she want the court to appoint her a lawyer and she says no, and the judge asks her how she pleads and she says guilty. I mean, she propositioned a vice, so what's she gonna say? The judge looks a long time at this rap sheet he has in front of him, and he says to her, "You're from Barstow, it says here."

I says to myself, Barstow?

She says, "Yes."

The judge says, "You have a long line of arrests for soliciting. But I'll give you thirty days and suspend the sentence if you leave town today and go home. We don't need any more of you girls here. Tell that to your friends in Barstow." Everybody in the courtroom giggles.

"Yes, sir, that would be fine, your honor, except I can't go back to Barstow because I don't have any money."

"What is the bus fare to Barstow?"

"Seven dollars and sixty-eight cents, your honor."

The judge digs in his pocket. He pulls out a five and a one and some change. "Who's got a dollar to put in here?"

Everybody in the courtroom is surprised and so for a second nobody moves, but then one of the cops standing by steps up and hands the judge a dollar, grinning.

"All right, young lady," the judge says. "Here's your bus fare. It's cheaper than keeping you in jail here, and we don't have the space. But if I see you in here again I'm going to give you the maximum sentence for the offense, do you understand? You are not to come back to this city."

Ho Toi nods her head, but she don't move. She seems scared to walk up to the judge's bench.

"Well, come on, come on," he says, looking real impatient.

So Ho Toi moves up to the bench with a little hop, and takes the money. A screw takes her out of the courtroom.

Barstow? *Barstow?* What happened to San Francisco? Arrested a bunch of times for soliciting? What about this high-class house she worked in?

Then I feel like some kind of goddam fool. Nobody who makes the kind of money she was bragging about is gonna get stuck hustling the bus depot just because she loses her purse. She would just call somebody to send her some money. And no high-class hooker is gonna walk around the street with her tits hanging out like that. Now I wonder if she even lost her purse. She just prolly come over from Barstow to see if she could hustle a few sailors. Shit.

About this time they call me up, and I get my thirty days, and they take me back to the jail. When I see they're putting me back in the holding tank, I says, "Hey, I got my sentence. What're you putting me in here for?"

"No room, Iva. We'll shift you over to B tank when someone gets out. You're gonna have to stay here a few days."

Well, that's how it is, just like I was telling you. But once I get to my bunk my mind is back on Ho Toi. I can't think why we was all so gullible to believe all that stuff. We oughta been able to tell just looking at the kid she never seen the inside of a dime-store house, much less a thousand-dollar-a-trick one. Hell, she prolly ain't even Chinese. She prolly made up her name too. Why didn't I ask her to talk some Chinese? Why didn't I say, "Oh yeah, how do you make chop suey?"

About the duck, though, I dunno. How could you make up something like that? It's too weird to make up, unless Ho Toi's got a real twisted mind. It gives me the willies just thinking about it. If her name really means "good luck," then she's got the wrong damn name, from the looks of things. I been hustling four years and the weirdest trick I ever had was the guy who wanted to suck my toe while I read a book. What if Ho Toi runs into another duck man, y'know, and she's not in no house where somebody's watching out for her through a peephole, like I know she never was the first time it happened?

And Then They Take Out All These Taxes

For once I'm more scared getting out of jail than I was going in. That's because I made up my mind about something, and I have to tell Arnie and he ain't gonna like it. That's what I'm thinking about while the screws check me out. They're making me go over the stuff in my brown envelope. "Personal property," they call it. Ha! If you call a key ring and a empty wallet and a heart locket with the gold plate wore off and no pictures in it personal property.

When they're all through I call Arnie to come pick me up. Lucky it's still in the morning cuz Arnie never gets up til noon. After that I'd never get hold of him, cuz he hits the street and don't never get home 'til three or four in the morning. But it's 1 a.m. when they finish all their little procedures and when I call Arnie he is there.

"They're cutting me loose," I says. "Come get me."

"I thought you wasn't getting out 'til Saturday."

"If you ever come to see me you'd know I got two days good time."

"Aw, well, you know it ain't easy for me to go near that jail, honey."

"Ain't that a shame. It's real easy for me to be *in* it, y'know."

"Hey, you ain't even out yet and you're giving me a hard

time. Look, it'll take me an hour to get ready and come down there. Why don't you take the bus home? You'd be here before I could get there."

"You asshole, I ain't even got bus fare. You didn't send me no money."

"Aw, Iva, I meant to. I just forgot."

"Well, maybe you should forget me altogether."

"Now, sweetheart, don't be mad. You know I love you. I'll be down to get you soon as I get straight, and I tell you what – we'll go out on the town and celebrate tonight. Big dinner, a show, anything you want to do."

"Yeah, okay, but hurry, will you? I don't think I can stand even being in this building one fuckin' more minute."

"Okay, okay, I'm on my way, baby."

Well, it's a hour before he shows up and I'm sitting there on the steps of the jailhouse thinking. The more I think, the more my mind is made up. I don't never want to see this stinking jailhouse again.

When he finally pulls up in his white Lincoln, though, I'm so glad to see him I almost cry. God, he's a fine-looking man. Silvery blond hair and big grey eyes with dark lashes – what a combination. He's got long legs and thin hips and big shoulders he got from working on the docks, but he moves like a dancer. It seems I can't ever get mad enough at him that he don't turn me on just to look at him.

That night Arnie takes me to dinner at the Swashbuckler. Hot damn. It's the fanciest restaurant in town, down on the tourist part of the docks near the marina. It's got real palm trees growing everywhere and a fountain in the lobby and big aquariums along all the walls with crazy-looking fish you couldn't make up if you wanted to, and they put some special kind of light on the fish that makes 'em look like neon. Really pretty, every color you can think of.

After two months of beans and turnip soup and cold oatmeal I am ready to eat everything on the menu, but I settle for steak and lobster and one of them fancy Hawaiian drinks in a pineapple with a little paper umbrella. Arnie talks a lot about things going down in the street while I was away – I'm too busy eating to talk

– and it's the same old shit: who got busted, whose ol' lady left him, who got wasted by somebody over dope. Hearing all this just makes me feel more and more like I made the right decision. It's always the same, it ain't never gonna change. But I want my night on the town before I tell him. The shit is gonna hit the fan and blow right back in my face. I'll be lucky if he don't beat me up. Not that he ever has, but he's acted like it a bunch of times, twisted my arm and stuff, and I never really stood up to him all the way like I'm gonna do now. Might as well get my first-night-out celebration before it all comes down on me.

When dinner is over, Arnie says, "Well, baby, let's go check out the Seven Seas."

That's the last place I want to go. It's our usual hangout on the waterfront, over near the docks where all the seamen hang out, where Arnie does his dealing and I do my hustling. It's a dump. You can't go right from the Swashbuckler to the Seven Seas without getting depressed. I says, "I want to go to the Trade Winds."

"Now, baby, that's out of our league. I can't afford it. I already spent fifty bucks on dinner."

"Arnie, I just got out of jail. You promised me a celebration, and I got it coming anyway. I want to go to a decent place and dance to real music and be where nobody knows us. The Trade Winds is right down the street and it's real nice. They got live music and it's pretty, just like this place."

"Hey, what's wrong with the Seven Seas? You go to jail, you come out with high-class notions? You got it backwards, don't you? Besides, I gotta see a guy there in a while. And maybe you can score a john while we're there."

"I can't believe you, creep! I *thought* that must be the idea. I ain't even out of jail one day and you want me working already. I got a celebration coming. I don't have to work tonight."

"Now, honey, it was just a suggestion. See, the reason I don't want to go to the Trade Winds is I can't afford it. You been gone sixty days, remember. That's been hard on me. Look." He opens up his wallet and shows me sixty dollars, just enough to get us out of the restaurant and ten dollars for drinks at the Seven Seas.

"Poor darling. Sorry *my* being in jail is so hard on *you*. Arnie, this is Iva, remember? I know you don't keep your real money in your goddam wallet. If you don't take me to the Trade Winds you can just forget it."

I got him now. He knows I know he has money stashed inside his belt. So we pay the bill and go to the Trade Winds, but he looks unhappy and he's nervous, I can tell, cuz he always jingles his keys in his pocket when he's nervous and he's jingling his keys. I'm thinking it's just because he's such a goddam cheap-skate, but we ain't been there ten minutes when some girl comes over from the bar and greets him like a sweetheart. "Hi, Arnie." She bends over and plants a kiss on his forehead. She's a tacky-looking fake redhead in hot pants and spike heels from Frederick's of Hollywood – I know cuz I seen 'em in the catalog. It don't take any thinking at all to know what's going on. Arnie looks miserable. He should, the shitmouth coyote.

"Who's your friend, Arnie?" I says.

"Uh, Iva, this is Nancy. Nancy is an old friend. She just got back to town while you were gone."

"I bet."

Arnie says to Nancy, "Iva and I are celebrating something tonight. I'll see you later, okay?"

Nancy looks like she don't like being brushed off too good, and she looks at me hard before she turns and walks away. She prolly thought she's Arnie's only filly.

I'm just sitting there glaring at Arnie. Waiting for him to start his rap, trying to get out of this one.

"Look," he says. "You were in jail. Money's tight. It was just 'til you got out."

"She sleeping in your bed?"

"Just 'til you got home, sweetheart. You know a man's got to have it or he goes crazy, right?"

"Aw, don't talk to me like I'm a idiot. So that's why you didn't want to come here. Jeezuz. How come you never had me work the Trade Winds? How come you don't have her at the Seven Seas?"

"Now, Iva, this ain't your kind of place. The johns that come here, they want, uh, you know, a debutante kind of girl."

"Debutante? You call that two-bit maggot-cunt hooker a debu-tante? What am I, a alley cat?"

Arnie laughs. "You hit it right on the head. If I had to say what kind of animal you was, I'd say you was a alley cat. Scrappy and beat up and always hungry and digging in the trash. I'm sorry, babe, but you ain't Trade Winds material and Nancy is."

I'm crying now and I never cry. It makes me ashamed, and I'm trying to choke it down and I can hardly talk but I manage to say, "Is she staying at our place?"

"Well, I was gonna talk to you about that pretty quick. See, I thought you weren't getting out for another two days. So I haven't had a chance to tell her she has to move out. So just for a couple of nights, Iva, maybe you could get a room at the Roosevelt."

"Me go to the Roosevelt? How come you don't send *her* to the Roosevelt?"

"Now, Iva . . ."

"Aw, you shrivel-dick creep. You're making it a lot easier for me to tell you something."

"Tell me what?"

"I don't want to hustle no more."

Arnie laughs. "What brought this on?"

"I'm tired of being in and out of jail. All the vice knows me now. It ain't you that goes to jail, Arnie, it's me, and you know how bad it is in there. You won't even come near there to visit me. And this time when they sent me to the clinic I had the clap again, and all those antibiotics are messing up my system. The doctor tole me the reason I have pains in my gut is a reaction to the antibiotics. They killed off these bugs I'm supposed to have that keep me from getting yeast, and I have yeast all the time. He says even if I don't end up with AIDS, if I keep going like I am I'm gonna have this pelvic inflammatory disease that you can't cure and I'll be all eaten out inside."

"You dumb shit, they just tell you that to make you stop hooking."

"All I know is I'm sick down there all the time. I got a discharge and I get sore when I trick and I get these pains in my gut when I take the antibiotics, and what he said made sense to me. But mostly I just don't like it. When we started this four years ago it was supposed to be just 'til you got on your feet. But you never even tried to get on your feet. You just hang around dealing and I don't even know what you do with the money from that, and you take my money too and I never have anything, I never get ahead at all. I can make five, six hundred a week and I'm always broke. That's no way to live, Arnie."

"Now whoa there, girl. One thing at a time. Since you bring up that stuff about being sick, I got something to tell you. While you was on vacation . . ."

"On *vacation?*"

". . . the word came down that all the girls got to be examined once a month by ol' Doc Barnes. If you got something he'll fix you up and if you're clean he'll sign your card. You got to have a card. It costs a hundred bucks. Then when the vice checks you, if you got your card and it's signed off, they won't bust you."

"Like a goddam union card? How can they do that if hooking ain't legal?"

"Well, they're doing it. It's this new police chief's idea. They figure this being a seaport town they can't stop the hooking but this way they can at least make sure the girls are clean."

"Clean, my ass. They make sure they get a hundred bucks off everybody. You got to pay this every year, or what?"

"Every month. When you go get examined. It's to cover the expense."

"Every month? Jeezuz. Doc Barnes is a falling-down knee-walking lush and a creep. All he does is sell prescriptions to dopers. Mona tole me she went to him once and he put her feet up in the stirrups and then spent five minutes pretending to look for that thing they stick up your cunt to look at you with. All the time he was sneaking peeks at Mona's pussy. She says she finally tole him he'd have to pay her if he was gonna do that. That old slimy-balls pervert gets a hundred bucks for that exam?"

"Of course not, stupid. He just collects it for the city. It's for the card. The word I got is that he does the exam for free. He's been about to lose his license for years, y'know. About all he's good for is to patch up the fighters over to the ring. But what I heard was they're gonna leave him alone if he does these exams for the city."

"So what it adds up to is we're paying a hundred bucks a month to the city so we don't get busted."

"Well, you know, hon, it's a good idea to have a regular exam anyway."

It seems to me like my whole goddam world has changed and turned upside down while I was in the can. My mind is set more than ever. "That does it, Arnie," I says, "I'm quitting."

Arnie laughs. "Yeah? What're you gonna do, toots, become a lawyer?"

"I'll figure something out."

"Yeah? Were you figuring something out the night I picked you up in that bus station? You was sitting there like a lost puppy, didn't know which way to go."

"I can get a waitress job."

"You're too hot-tempered. You won't last two days. You'll end up throwing a bowl of soup on some guy says the wrong thing. That's why you can't work the Trade Winds. You got no class, no control."

His insults are just rolling off me now. I'm already as mad as I can get. "I can do it," I says, "and you can keep your goddam red-head twat. But I need some money. Give me a couple hundred bucks so I can get a room and eat 'til I get a job."

Arnie is laughing again. "A thousand bucks ain't enough to keep you 'til you get a job, cuz you ain't gonna get one, alley cat. And even if you con somebody into hiring you, you're gonna get sick of working on your feet for eight hours a day for thirty or forty bucks, when you can work four hours on your back and make two hundred. But here." He slips his fingers in the pocket inside his belt and takes out some bills, counts me out a hundred bucks. "I'm so sure you'll be back crawling in a week, I'll stake you to your little crazy spell. But I'm giving you a hundred bucks, not two. Don't forget you owe me a hundred bucks. And when you come back, Iva, things will be different. I been treating you like a friend and you don't appreciate it. So I'll treat you like a pro. When you come back, you turn over everything you earn to me, and I give it back to you when I think you need it. Understand?"

"I won't be back, creep. And I don't owe you no hundred bucks. You owe me about ten thousand, all the money you took off me." I don't try and get the two hundred cuz I know he ain't gonna give it to me. I grab the money off the table and leave. I can hear him laughing as I walk across the room, and it's all I can do to not go back and belt him, or bust into tears, either one.

The first thing I gotta do is rent a room. I don't like the idea of going to the Roosevelt. It's a crummy place near the bus depot. It's mostly a hotel for transients and a lot of the street hookers use it for tricking and it ain't exactly the kind of place I want to live in, but I know it's the cheapest hotel in town and a hundred bucks ain't gonna take me far. If you trick there, they charge you twenty bucks for the night. But it's gotta be cheap by the week, since nobody lives there but alkie-dopies. So that's where I go, and they charge me fifty-six bucks a week for a housekeeping room, a hot plate and sink, but no refrigerator. "You can keep your food on the windowsill," the clerk says. Jeezuz. How do all those bums come up with that much money a week?

Next I go over to our apartment – well, it ain't ours anymore, it's Arnie's – to get my clothes. I find my stuff all shoved down to the end of the closet to make room for carrothead's things. At first I can't find my favorite purple skirt, but it shows up in the hamper in the bathroom. I know I just got that skirt out of the cleaners right before I was busted, and I didn't wear it even once. That maggot-twat has been wearing my clothes. So what I do is, I pick out a nice hot-pink blouse of hers that fits me, and take it with me. I also go over the place good for money, but I can't find a cent. I don't know where Arnie keeps his cash. Not here, that's for sure. I even look for bills taped to the bottom of the dresser drawers and in the toilet tank. I find a shopping bag I had stuck behind the dresser and I put all my toiletries in it and my shoes, and the Walkman I bought for Arnie for his birthday. The hell with him.

At the hotel, it takes me a long time to go to sleep. I keep going over things Arnie said at the restaurant. How I'm a alley cat, beat up and digging through the trash. It hurts a lot, remembering that. I was too mad and upset at the time to let it sink in just how bad I been took. I mean, Arnie and me was a team. I thought he loved me. He never *said* he loved me, but I just figured he was one of those guys don't say things like that. But now I see real clear that I'm just a piece of merchandise to him. Dime-store goods. And I really believed I was only gonna hustle until he got set up some way. He told me he was gonna be a bookie, but he needed some money to get started. All that was bullshit and I believed it. He never meant to do nothin' but live off me, and now he's got another woman and maybe more, for all I know. I never seen myself as such a goddam fool in my life, and it hurts more than anything ever hurt me before.

I cry so much that finally I'm too tired to cry anymore and I go to sleep. I wake up just once, when whoever is in the next room throws up in the sink right on the other side of the wall from me. Well, I put up with a lot of that in the drunk tank in jail, so it's nothin' new to me, and I go right back to sleep.

In the morning I feel better. The sun is coming in and making even the old piss-colored wallpaper look cheery. I think I was lucky to get a room on the east side of the building. I get up and go down the block to Melba's for a cup of coffee and a paper. I feel good. On my own, starting over.

Sitting at the counter, I look over the want ads while I drink my coffee. Three ads for waitresses. Good. It's early yet, not even nine o'clock. I got a good chance if I get to these places first.

One place is close, just over on Kilroy Drive, not more than ten blocks, in the business section of town. I tuck the paper under my arm and walk over there. It's a nice little place, the kind that serves breakfast and lunch to folks that work in the neighbor-hood. It's called the Bluebird and it's got plants in the windows and it's nice and clean and cheery, everything yellow and blue. I get excited when I see it. I know there's gonna be decent people here. I ask for the manager and a nice-looking man comes out of the kitchen. "Have you got any experience?" he says. I'm all ready for that question. I thought about it last night. Waitressing can't be hard to pick up. I mean you just take people's orders and carry stuff to the table when it's ready. I can fake it. So I tell the guy, "Yeah, I worked in a restaurant back home."

"Have you worked anywhere locally?"

I'm afraid to lie about that because he might check. "No," I says.

"Well," he says, "I need somebody pretty bad. Tell you what. If you can start today, I'll try you out. We have people coming in on their ten o'clock coffee breaks in about ten minutes. You help Jessie, and if you do okay, you can stay. But if you don't do okay, no job. I give you a couple of bucks cash for the time you work. Okay?"

Wow. This is terrific. Wait'll Arnie hears this. He'll shit. So while we wait for the coffee-breakers, Jessie shows me where things are and tells me to cover the counter, it's easier than the tables for a newcomer. She seems nice and I'm feeling good. I know I'm gonna do okay.

The first wave of people I take care of fine. But when they get ready to leave I find out I been forgetting to write them tickets, and so I have a bunch of people lined up at the register which Jessie can't ring up cuz they got to have tickets. So while I write them tickets more people are sitting down. Well, I want to give them quick service so I take their orders right away, writing the tickets right then, but I don't clean the stuff away from the customer before, so when I bring their coffee and donut then I got no place to set it down, and I gotta take the dirty dishes away. That gets me even more confused and I forget people's orders and by the time 10:30 comes, the boss is standing in the door of the kitchen glaring at me. When it finally calms down and the place is near empty, he says, "You told me you were experienced."

"I am," I says. "It's just a new place and all."

"You never waited table in your life," he says.

I feel ashamed, cuz he seems like a nice man. "Look," I says, "I really need a job. I can learn, honest."

"I'm sorry," he says, "but I just don't have time to train you. You can see how hectic it gets. Lunch hour is worse. Jessie and I are too busy to teach you, see?" He goes to the register and gives me five dollars for my forty-five minutes' work. I guess I look pretty dejected, cuz just as I'm turning to go out the door, he says, "Come back for lunch. I'll tell Jessie there's no charge."

"Thanks," I says, but I know I'm too ashamed to come back.

The next place is much farther downtown, in the middle of all them big buildings. Monique's, it's called. One of them places charges a whole lot for things. You can tell cuz it's dark in there. I don't much like the feel of it, but I ask the hostess for the manager and she takes me to a little office where there's this buffalo of a woman stuffed into a maroon suit and a ruffled blouse that makes her look like she got no neck. You know the kind: too much makeup and a hairdo that's made of plastic. She don't smile at me or nothin'. When I tell her why I'm there she says, "You're too short. How tall are you?"

"Five foot two," I says, although the truth is I'm five foot one. "What does that have to do with it?"

"What that has to do with it is, you are too short to reach across a table well and too small to carry a heavy tray."

"Hell, I can reach," I says.

The buffalo frowns. "We don't swear in Monique's. Let me see your hands."

I put out my hand. "You bite your nails," she says. "We can't have that. Monique's customers don't want food served to them with hands that look like that."

"I can let them grow out," I says. "In the meantime I can get me some of them fake nails that glue on."

"Young lady," she says, "you're making it difficult for me. You won't do at all. You don't speak good English, and you don't have the, uh, presence for Monique's. Now good day."

"Good day yerself," I says, and I stomp out. What the hell does she mean, presence? How can I be here if I ain't present? And how good does your English have to be to bring some jerk a hamburger? I'm starting to feel discouraged, but I climb on the Northtown bus and go on out to the other place, a spaghetti joint out near the university. It takes me half a hour to get there, and then I don't even get to talk to nobody. The job is took already, the hostess says. All of a sudden I feel tired, and hungry too. All I had was coffee this morning. I figure if I got to keep pounding the streets for work I better eat something, so I stay there and have a pizza and a beer.

While I eat, I'm thinking. I decide my best bet is to go down to the Department of Employment.

Department of Employment – ha! They oughta call it the Department of You-Can't-Get-No-Employment. They make me fill out all these forms, and then I sit there in a stiff chair with fifty other people for thirty-five minutes waiting to see somebody, and then this woman looks over my forms and tells me they don't have nothin' for me. "It's very hard when you don't have any experience," she says.

"Well," I says, "how can I get experience if I can't get no job?"

44

"I wish I had a dime for every time someone asks me that question," she says. "I might be able to get you into one of our training programs. Would you like to be a clerk-typist? You go to school for three months, then we can place you as a trainee."

"Lady, I got about forty bucks between me and forever," I says. "I got to get a job right now."

"Oh dear," she says, and she looks like she really is sorry. "Look, I'm going to send you over to the Department of Social Services. Maybe you can get some emergency relief." She is writing down a address on a slip of paper.

"You mean welfare?"

"Well, I think it takes a while to get ongoing assistance. But I believe they'll try to see to it that you don't go hungry."

"You mean they'll give me money?"

"I don't think it's quite as simple as that. You just go over there and ask for Ellen Wright. Tell her your situation and I'm sure she'll be able to help you."

"Okay," I says, but I know I ain't going. Welfare! Wouldn't Arnie love that? No way. Besides, I can tell by the way she's beating around the bush and not giving me no straight answers that they put you through all kinds of aggravation and make you feel real low and give you a peanut and then expect you to feel grateful. I heard about that, and I ain't going through it.

So I leave, and buy me a cheap bottle of wine, and go back to the Roosevelt. I can't do nothin' 'til tomorrow's paper comes out, and I'm beat anyway. Pretty soon the wine puts me to sleep.

The next couple of days is just more of the same. Riding the bus all over town, chasing down jobs that take me half a hour to get to, and ten seconds for them to tell me no. I get pretty sick of hearing how I got no experience. "I got plenty of experience," I tell one fellow, "but it ain't what you want." For one afternoon I think I got me a job at a self-serve gas station. They ask me if I got experience running a register, and I says – and this is the truth for once – "Yeah, I helped my poppa at his gas station back in Winslow all the time I was growing up. I took the money most of the time." So they put me in this little glass cage and I think I got me a pretty easy gig, but then they got this computer that shows how much gas each pump is doing, and the money, and that's okay, but between watching the computer and trying to learn to run the damn credit-card machine and turning the pumps on for people and folks piling up four and five deep waiting to pay, and they gotta leave their credit card or some money in advance and then when they come back I got to make change and remember who is who, I get confused and blow the whole gig. They won't even pay me. They say it was just a tryout, they didn't really hire me yet.

But the fifth day, Friday, I get me a job at the lunch counter in Walred's Drug Store. This time I just tell the guy right out I ain't got much experience, but he says he'll train me, he needs somebody real bad who can start right away. It's pretty much like the blue-and-yellow place, though. I can get the orders and write the tickets but I get nervous and forget to pick up the dishes and pretty soon I got a whole counter full of people sitting with dishes stacked in front of them and no place to set their food down. I try hard cuz I'm plumb desperate, and after a couple of hours I'm doing a little better. When the shift ends I tell the manager, "I know I didn't do too good, but I'll get better." He surprises me by saying, "That's okay, you'll learn." How about that? A nice guy, I think. Then he says, "How would you like to drive up to the mountains with me tonight? We'll be back in time for your shift tomorrow." Well, hell, that's just exactly what I took this job to get away from. So I says no thank you as nice as I can, but I can see he ain't too pleased. Anyway, the next day I do a little better, but at the end of the shift he tells me I'm laid off. I'm real upset. "I'm doing better," I says. "Give me a goddam chance. I'll have the hang of it in a day or two."

"You misunderstood," he says. "I only needed someone for Friday and Saturday. Go down to the personnel office on Monday and maybe they can place you in one of our other stores."

"What about my money?" I says.

"They'll give you your check at the personnel office."

Shit. I only got about six bucks left and my rent runs out Monday. Well, six bucks will feed me 'til Monday, and two days' pay oughta just about cover another week's rent. By that time I oughta have something. Hell, I had three jobs already this week. Nothing to it. So Sunday I lay around in my room and read the

Sunday paper. And what do you know, I'm having a good time. Maybe this room is only mine 'til Monday, but today it's mine, and nobody around to hassle me, and I'm my own boss and don't have to do nothin' I don't want to do. That's about the first time I can ever remember it being like that. Even when I was a kid I had to cook and clean house for my pop, and he kept me home from school to help him in the gas station. I knew how to fix cars before I was twelve, when he was too drunk and I didn't want the customers to know and maybe lose their business. Then when he done what he done to me when I was fourteen, I figured there just wasn't nothin' at all that's mine, nothin' that people can't take when they want it. And it seems like someone else been running my life for me ever since, and if there's no one else around to run it for me, I don't know what to do. That's why it was so easy for Arnie to pick me up in that bus station. I had the gumption to get out of Winslow, but when I got to the city and there wasn't nobody to tell me what to do, I just set there and give up. So Arnie comes along and says, "You look like you could use a friend," and I just kinda fell into his arms, and from then on Arnie was telling me what to do, and I was grateful, even when I didn't like what I was doing. But this last week ain't been like that. I been running my own life! And I like it, and I like my room. It's sleazy, man, but it's mine.

In the afternoon I says to myself, "I think I'll go take me a walk." And I do, and I go where I want, and I buy me a can of beer to take back up to the room, and I sit drinking it at the window, looking at all the people passing by in the street below. When it gets dark I don't turn on the light, and the red neon hotel sign blinks on and off and throws red lights on my walls, and I think, Shit, people uptown got to pay money to decorators to get a light show like that, and I go to bed only a little worried about tomorrow, and otherwise happy.

In the morning I go down to Walred's personnel office. It's a crummy-looking place upstairs over one of their drugstores. Since it's Monday, there's a bunch of people there. I'm number six in line, so I sit down by this other chick about my age and we start rapping to pass the time. It turns out she's been working for Walred's regular for a year, as a relief cashier. They move her around from store to store wherever they need somebody temporary. She's in here to get a new assignment. I tell her about what happened to me, how weird it was to get laid off after two days, and about how this guy Maddox asked me to go to the mountains with him. Turns out she knows the store, and she says Maddox is famous for that. If you don't sleep with him you don't work there. I says, "I didn't think that was the reason he laid me off. In fact, I didn't even think of it. To tell the truth I didn't do so good waiting counter."

"He doesn't care about that. He's got some kind of conquest thing. He only wants you to do it once, and then you can work there. It isn't really the sex he's interested in. He just wants to feel like he owns the girls, like a harem or something. You shoulda gone with him, you wouldn'ta had to do it again. He's actually real nice to work for. Generous, you know. It's part of his trip, see. You're his girl, and he treats his girls nice."

"Naw, I didn't want to do that. Did you?"

"Hey, you're not supposed to ask things like that. But no, I didn't. I just heard about him from other girls that worked there."

But she looks away while she's saying this and starts fumbling in her purse for a cigarette and I can tell she's lying. She makes it sound easy and simple, and now I wonder why I didn't go with him. I mean, here I am a hooker – well, a former hooker – and I don't want to sleep with a guy even one time to get a job. I guess it's because I like that feeling of running my own life. If I slept with him, the job wouldn't be mine, it would be his. I been liking this feeling of things being mine for a change. I don't say any of this to her, of course.

Pretty soon she's called up to the counter, and she gets her assignment, and smiles at me as she leaves. She calls clear across the room, "Good luck, Iva. I hope I see you in one of the stores soon." I notice she has a sassy kind of walk. I like her.

Then it's my turn, and I tell the woman at the desk how I been laid off, and how I come down to see if they got another opening and to pick up my check. She writes down my name and goes in the back somewhere. In a few minutes she comes out looking mean. "Why did you tell me you were laid off? What makes you think you can get away with that? Don't you think we check?"

I'm flabbergasted. "What do you mean?" I says. "I told you the truth. I was laid off."

"You were fired for general inefficiency. I just talked to Mr. Maddox on the phone."

I feel myself turning hot and red. "He told me I was laid off and you would give me a job someplace else."

She looks at me like I'm a criminal or something. "I just spoke with him, I told you. We're very busy. You'll have to leave."

I'm about to cry or scream, I don't know which, but then I remember my money. I gotta have it. I blurt out, "What about my check?"

"It takes about two weeks for payroll checks to come through. It will be mailed to your home."

Then she walks away. Home? What home? I was counting on that check to go back and pay some rent on my room. I turn around and see that everybody in the place is staring at me. I run out, cuz I'm scared I'm gonna blow into a million pieces right there.

On the street I stop cuz I don't know what to do next. I didn't expect any of this. I feel mixed up. And scared. More scared than I ever been before. Everything's run out on me. I don't have more than a couple of bucks in my pocket. My room rent is run out. I gotta go get my clothes. I left them there cuz I thought I'd be back with my check and pay some rent. But on the way back to the hotel I realize I don't have any place to keep my goddam clothes. I don't even have a suitcase so I can put them in a locker somewhere. I carried them over from Arnie's on hangers, with my shoes and underwear in a shopping bag. I don't even remember if I kept the goddam shopping bag.

At the hotel I collect my stuff – I find the shopping bag folded up and stuffed behind the dresser mirror – and go down to the desk. "Jimmy," I says, "I got me a apartment so I won't need the room no more. But can I leave this stuff here until I can get my friend to bring me over in his car to pick it up?"

"Sure," Jimmy says. He takes my things and puts them in a closet in the lobby. "Don't leave 'em too long," he says, "we need the space."

"Okay," I says, and I go out on the street. Well, the only thing for me to do is get a paper and keep trying. I look in my pocket and count my money. $2.34. And the paper will cost me half abuck. Shit.

The day don't go any better than any of the other days. I even try one of them temporary agencies, and they say they can use me for inventory taking and stuff like that, but those jobs don't come up every day. They'll call me. I don't have a phone, I says. Then give us a call every few days, they says. Okay.

Shit.

By late afternoon I'm so hungry I'm weak, and I gotta spend some money to eat or I ain't even gonna be able to look for work. Then I remember something. There's this big cafeteria downtown that has a sign in their window that they won't turn away anybody who is hungry and can't pay. I remember they got a lot of plants in the window, and a fountain, right there in the window, and it looks different from any cafeteria I ever seen. Shifton's, or something like that. I get all excited, and being excited gives me the energy to walk all the way down there. I'm half scared it won't be there anymore, but there it is, fountain and all, and the sign is right there in the window like it was. I don't even remember noticing that sign before. Funny how, when you really need to remember, things come back to you that you didn't even think you noticed.

I go in and walk up to the cashier, who's the only person I see that ain't behind the counter serving food. "I seen your sign in the window," I says. "I'm out of work and out of money. Can I eat? "

"Sure," she says. "You see that stairway over there? You go on up and you'll see a waiting room. Have a seat there and Mrs. Shifton will come up and talk to you."

Now what does that mean, she'll come up and talk to me? But I go on up the stairs. The room is just like a doctor's waiting room, all right. Lots of chairs and coffee tables with magazines on them, and everything made of plastic. There's a big picture of Jesus on the wall, the one where he's holding his hand up giving the Boy Scout pledge or something, and sort of simpering out at you, with rays coming out of his head. I sit down and pick up one of the magazines. It's a religious magazine, *The Soul's Sunshine Gazette*, so I put it down and pick up another one. The same. I rifle the stack, and they're all the same thing.

I look around and see that there's these printed things hanging all over the walls, and I get up to read one. It's a long quotation from the Bible. All of 'em are. I start getting uneasy. Then I see one that says, "Shifton's Feed-the-Hungry Program." Now that's what I want to see. I don't remember now everything it says, but it boils down to this: you fill out a application and they interview you and if you demonstrate "real need" they give you a can of fortified protein powder!

Jeezuz. I gotta prove I'm hungry? Then it hits me that what goes with the interview is a religious lecture. I hightail it down the stairs – no sign of that Mrs. Shifton yet – and out on the street. I feel like I barely escaped with my life. Every day in every way I'm getting stupider and stupider. What made me think there were these nice folks running this cafeteria that when you go in and say, "I'm out of work and I'm hungry," they'll say, "Sure, just go through the line and get what you want and you don't have to pay"? There's no such thing as a free lunch. That's what they always say, and I shoulda known.

I'm so mad at myself I'm walking down the street pounding myself on the head until I notice people are looking at me, so I quit. But I can't stop thinking about it. I can picture this Mrs. Shifton, all dressed up cuz she owns the place, and because you're hungry and desperate you got to sit there while she lays her religious trip on you, and to get your protein powder you know you gotta say from now on you'll be good and love the Lord. Then when you crawl away with your can of protein powder, which you can mix up with water in a paper cup I guess, she can turn to that picture of Jesus and say, "See, Lord, ain't I sweet and good?" Man, I'd rather be hungry.

But speaking of hungry, I gotta do something. So I go in a liquor store and buy a fifty-cent candy bar. I figure that's the most energy I can get for the least money. The sugar gets into my system pretty fast, and I start feeling a little better. But now I gotta start thinking about where I'm gonna spend the night. I pass a phone booth and Millie pops into my mind. Good ol' Millie, she's got a good heart. I know she'll let me stay at her place a night or two 'til I figure out what to do. I step into the phone booth and start looking for her name in the phone book. Moser, or Mozier, something like that. But while I'm looking I remember that Millie's married, and that her ol' man beats her up sometimes, and that she's a lush. I only known her in jail, where she's sober. She's prolly really different when she's drunk, like my poppa was. And how would she explain me to her ol' man? "This is my friend Iva, I met her in jail"? I drop the phone book and go on down the street.

I notice I ain't far from the bus terminal, and I think, Well, I can sit in there for a few hours and think what to do. I can always pretend I'm waiting for a bus, or a friend coming in, or something. So I go on over there and sit down on a bench. It's rock-and-the-hard-place time, kid. What the hell am I gonna do? I know I can go to one of them missions, but that's about a mile lower than Shifton's. I know they make you listen to a sermon and sing hymns before they'll feed you, and I picture myself standing in line with all them winos. I ain't ready to admit I'm that low yet. What the hell kind of a world is it that people will only help you out if you let them mess with your head? Well, anyway, I can sit in the bus depot all night if I have to. It seems like there ain't nothin' else I can decide about at this point, so I just sit there thinking for a long time. For the first time I gotta consider tricking, just as a way to hold on 'til I get a job. I hate the idea. It feels like to do that I'd admit being whipped. But I tell myself it ain't being whipped if you're doing it so you can stay away from Arnie, doing it so you can get a job. You keep looking for a job every day, and only trick enough to stay alive. That ain't being whipped, that's surviving. It's winning if you find a job and quit. Just think about going back to the old neighborhood and spitting in Arnie's face. "I got me a job as a secretary, pig-prick. Ptoooey!" Right in his smug ugly kisser.

The thing is, it's scary trying to hustle a neighborhood you don't know. I gotta make a plan, find a bar that looks likely. I'll be damned if I'm gonna walk the streets. I never been a street hooker. That's the bottom. When you gotta do that there ain't no hope. But just then I notice that some guy that's been watching one of them pay TVs gets up to catch his bus and leaves the TV going, so I scoot over and sit down. It's early yet, I'll just sit here a while and watch TV and think about what I'm gonna do. But I guess part of me don't want to think about it, cuz I get all caught up in watching the Jeffersons, and I'm not thinking about anything at all when a voice right beside me says, "You know when the bus leaves for Terminal Island?"

I turn around and here's this sailor, a pimply-face kid, grinning at me. The board with the bus schedule is right behind him, half as big as the whole wall. What luck! He can't be vice, neither, cuz they ain't allowed to dress up in sailor suits. So I says, "No, but I can look it up for you on that schedule on the wall there."

So he looks around and acts like he's surprised when he sees the board. "Well, what do you know about that," he says. He studies the board for a minute, then he says, "Say, the bus don't leave for an hour yet. You want to go have a beer?"

"Sure," I says. What luck! What dumb fuckin' luck!

He says his name is Eddie, and he takes me to some sailors' hangout on the same block as the bus depot. We drink a couple of beers and shoot a game of rotation. I wait for him to make his move. Even though I know he can't be vice, I always let the guy make the first move. Besides, I figure it gives you more bargaining power if they ask you, instead of the other way around.

Finally, he says, "Look, I don't really have to be back at the base so early. I can catch a later bus. How about it?"

"Sure," I says, "but it ain't free."

"I figured it wasn't. But look, I don't want to insult you or anything, but all I got on me is about twenty bucks."

Jeezuz. Is this what I come to? A twenty-dollar trick from a sailor in the bus station? I almost tell him to forget it, but something stops me. I think of starting over, spending my last couple of bucks for a drink so I can hang out in a bar and always the chance I won't score, or that I'll hit on a vice. A bird in the hand, I says to myself. Then I get a idea.

"Normally I'd laugh in your face," I says, "but I got a problem. I need a place to stay tonight. If you'll pay the rent on a room at the Roosevelt, you can stay there with me for a hour. But I get to keep the room overnight."

"How much is the room?"

"Twenty bucks."

"I think we can do better than that around the corner."

"It's the Roosevelt or no deal. I got a reason."

He thinks a minute, but he knows he can't score with a donkey in this town for twenty bucks. "Okay," he says.

When we get to the hotel I tell sailor boy to ask for room 213, and luck is with me that it's still empty. Corky the night clerk don't act like he knows me. That's just the way they do things at the Roosevelt, in case you wanna tell your john some kind of story.

Up in the room I start to strip, but Eddie just unbuttons hisself and says, "What I'd like is for you to blow me."

"I charge extra for that," I says.

"Aw, c'mon. That's all the money I had, you know that."

"Well, okay," I says, "I'll do it cuz I like you." But to tell the truth I'd rather blow him than fuck him. For one thing it's quick. Guys don't usually last long when you blow 'em, specially since I'm a artist at it. And then I don't have to douche or nothin'. Just wash my mouth out. It's kinda hard to get past the first part, cuz the idea turns my stomach and sometimes I almost retch, but once I get started it's okay. Anyway, I tell him I gotta wash him first, and I squeeze his cock to see if he's got a discharge and he's okay. Then he goes over and sits in the chair and I start to kneel down in front of him, but he says, "Finish taking your clothes off. I want you to be naked." So I do.

Of course he's been hard ever since I washed him, so I just take his prick in my mouth and start doing the tongue work that drives 'em crazy and makes 'em come fast. But after just a few seconds he takes hold of my head with both his hands and starts pumping my head up and down on his prick like he was fucking me. He's hurting my throat something awful, and making me gag. I try to push his hands away but he's strong and he's got a good grip. There's only one thing to do. I come down on his cock with my teeth. He gives a big yelp and next thing I know he's clobbered me on the side of my head. I fall backwards on the floor. He jumps up and he's yelling, "You cunt! You goddam sonuvabitch cunt!" Well, I didn't bite him *that* hard, just enough to warn him to stop, but he's in a total all-out rage. As I start to get up he kicks me in the shoulder and I fall over. I see him coming at me and I'm scared he's gonna kick me in the tits or the stomach so I roll up in a ball and tuck my head in my arms, and he kicks me in the back two, three times. It hurts like hell and I'm scared, so I'm crying and too scared to get up cuz then I'll be all exposed. If I was on my feet I could go for his groin or something but he's got me in a totally helpless position.

He's standing over me, buttoning up his sailor suit, and he says, "You bitch. Get your clothes on and get out of here, because I'm going downstairs and get my money back. And if they don't give it to me, I'm coming back up here and take it out of your hide." He goes out and slams the door.

Boy, I'm scared to death, and I scramble around getting my clothes on and figuring how I can get out of there before he comes back, cuz I know the Roosevelt don't give nobody their money back, specially not for a trick room. I don't even know if there's a back way or not. Then I figure, wait a minute, if I lock the door he can't get in, cuz the key is laying over there on the dresser, and Corky ain't likely to give him another key if he's down there making a big scene. And if he comes up here trying to bust down the door Corky will be up here in two seconds flat and throw him out. All I gotta do is stick it out and I'll have a place for the night.

I'm nervous as hell, though, and I wish for the first time that Arnie was around. One thing about a pimp, if he's a good one he ain't never very far away in case you get some nut. I get dressed and sit down on the bed to wait it out. I can't stop crying and I'm so scared I'm shaking like I got the chills. The red light from the hotel sign is flashing on the wall, only tonight it looks like something awful and spooky, like the revolving red light from a cop car, or a ambulance, when something terrible's happened. It even starts looking like blood to me and I don't like my room no more. I want to get out, but I know I gotta stay. I don't remember that I ever been this scared in my whole entire life.

After a while there's a tap on the door and I feel something like fire shoot all the way through my body. I stop breathing and I don't answer. There's another knock, and a wait, and then Corky's voice says, "Iva, I want your ass out of here."

Corky! I'm so relieved I'm almost laughing. I go open the door. "Corky! I been so scared. That guy tried to stomp my ass."

"I want you out of here right now."

"Why, Corky? The room's paid for the night. It ain't my fault the guy's crazy."

"He says you tried to roll him."

"He lied! I never rolled nobody."

"He's one mad sonuvabitch. If you didn't try to roll him, how come he's so mad?"

"He started roughing me up and I bit him."

"That's not what he says. He said he'd call the cops if I didn't give him his money back, so I had to give it to him. I want you out of here, and don't come back here anymore. We can't afford any trouble."

"Aw, Corky, there won't be no trouble. He left, didn't he? He got his money and he's happy. Let me stay here, I got no place to go."

"Yeah? Jimmy says you got an apartment and that you'd be back after your clothes. What are you trying to pull?"

I don't know what to say. I forgot about what I tole Jimmy. I decide to play my last card. I move up close to Corky and lay my hand on his package. "C'mon, Corky. I'll make you a trade."

Corky steps back toward the door. "I'm not interested, Iva. C'mon down and get your clothes and get out of here." He turns and walks out the door. I got no choice but to follow him.

Out on the street, all my clothes on hangers slung over one shoulder, my shopping bag in the other hand like a goddam bag lady, I know I got only one direction to go. It's about twenty blocks, and a damn uncomfortable walk with the hangers cutting into my fingers. I walk slow, too, cuz I never been so depressed in my life, and the idea of facing Arnie and having him gloat all over me cuz I had to come back is almost more than I can stand to think about. And I got twenty blocks to think about it. Even though I don't want to, how can I think about anything else?

As I get farther down into the waterfront bar district, I attract a lot of attention, walking along with all my clothes slung across my back. Anybody but a fool can see I'm cut adrift. I get propositions all along the way, but I don't pay no attention. I know now it ain't no use trying to make it on my own without no money and no pimp. Anybody who wanted to could just cut me up in little pieces and dump me in a trash can. It happens, and it could happen to me, I come that close tonight, for chrissake. So I gotta go back and eat Arnie's shit.

The closer I get to the Seven Seas the more miserable I feel. I'm almost at the door before something hits me. This don't have to be forever! It ain't easy to hold out money on Arnie, but if I'm careful I can do it. I'll just start me a little stash and when I get enough money to live a month or two, I can cut out again. Next time I'll have enough money to carry me 'til I get me a job. Or enough money so I can go take one of them clerk-typist courses the lady was talking about. Shit, I can be a secretary.

But even while I'm saying all this I know it ain't so. There's a voice in me somewhere says I'm kidding myself. I never went no further than the eighth grade and I don't talk good English and Arnie was right, I'm too hot-tempered. I'm a alley cat, just like he says. Beat up and hungry and digging through the trash and no damn good for nothin' but whoring. And my insides are gonna be all rotted out before I ever save enough money to get my ass out. I know when I'm licked and I'm crying when I get to the door of the Seven Seas. Maybe Arnie ain't even here. If I'm lucky, I can sit down and have a beer and pull myself together some before I have to see him.

I hate the sight of this place. It reeks of cigarettes and stale beer, and it looks like every sleazy waterfront bar you ever seen. Everything is so old it's all turned the same color of maroon brown, and I bet there ain't one bar stool or booth seat that ain't got a tear in it. The pictures on the wall are all faded and the glass over them is so greasy you can't even see what the pictures are of.

But in spite of how sleazy it is, the Seven Seas is a favorite seamen's hangout, and a lot of money changes hands in this joint. Those guys come in with thousands of dollars in their pockets when they get off a ship, and they can get whatever they want here. Arnie's got some of what they want, me and some other working girls got the rest of it.

I take a deep breath and walk in. I spot Arnie right away, sitting in the back in his regular booth, facing the front so he can see whoever comes in. He's sitting slid down with his hips on the edge of the seat and his legs stuck straight out, in that cocky way of his, like he's just laying back waiting for the world to come to him. He sees me. Carrying all my clothes. He grins, stares me right in the eye, and waits.

It takes all the strength I got to walk the whole length of that fuckin' bar to get to his booth. When I get right up to him he looks up in my face and grins, waiting to see what I'm gonna say, looking like he expects whatever it is to make his day. I see all of a sudden that I hate this guy more than I ever hated anyone in this world, except maybe my poppa, but I got no options left. But one thing about my profession, I got a lot of practice acting like I want what I hate, and I says to him, "Hi, Arnie. I guess you was right. I got me a job as a secretary right off, just like I said I would, but jeezuz, you got to work the whole goddam day for forty bucks, and then they take out all these taxes and stuff, and it just ain't worth it." I dump my clothes on the seat opposite Arnie and slide in beside them. "So I decided I could do better back here, just like you said."

"Is that so," he says, in a snotty voice, grinning at me bigger than ever.

"Yeah, that's so," I says. "But I proved I can get a job if I want, smart-ass. It just didn't pay, that's all. So tell me, where is it I gotta go to get this goddam union card you was telling me about?"

Sing Soft, Sing Loud

You gotta understand what it's like in here at night. We can start with black. Here, when they say "Lights out!" they mean lights fuckin' *out.* They don't leave *nothin'* on. There's no windows, so light can't even filter in from the street, and when they throw that switch, you're just lost in a black hole. The first guy who said "You can't see your hand in front of your face" was talking about this here jail. That's why when they come in here in the middle of the night and throw the lights on, you're so blinded you can't see nothin' for a couple of minutes, and you feel like somebody threw a spotlight on you.

The reason all this is going on is this is the receiving tank where I'm at, cuz I ain't been to trial yet and I can't get out on bail cuz Arnie's holding all the money and he won't go my bail cuz it's a felony this time. I'm gonna do some real time behind this one and he figures I'm just a lost cause, even though I got busted on accounta him, holding his shit, me that never yet stuck a needle in my arm. So here you are trying to sleep and a bunch of things happen all at once: you hear the creak and groan of this giant metal door opening, blinding lights go on in your eyes, some woman is screaming all kinds of bad shit cuz she's drunk and they're dragging her in here, and the metal door gets slammed shut hard cuz the screw is pissed off with the drunk giving her a bad time, and if you happen to be deep asleep when all this goes off you wake up thinking the world blowed up in your face.

But that ain't all. When they bring the drunks in they're hollering and cussing, mad to be busted if they even know what the hell is going on. But more than likely they got busted cuz they been wrecking some joint or beating up on their ol' man or their kids, and they was mad to begin with. So they raise hell for about a half a hour before they conk out. Then along towards three in the morning some of 'em start with the throwing up and the d.t.'s. Them that's sober enough to think of it tries to find the toilet to throw up in, but it's so dark they can never find it, and in the morning you wouldn't believe the smell and the mess. Some of them has fell down and bruised themselves. Anyway, when they start with the throwing up and the d.t.'s you'd be glad to go back to the lights and the cussing. These women are snake-pit crazy. They think someone's trying to kill 'em, or they think they're eating poison food, or someone's coming at 'em with a knife, or they're being thrown in a pit of fire, or there's rats and snakes coming out of the walls – that's a favorite around here. Weekends are the worst of course. When five or six of 'em get to going at once it's like being in a insane asylum in hell.

One night all this stuff is going on and I'm just layin' there trying to be cool and stay sane through the night, and I hear this one woman with a strong clear voice and she ain't seeing rats or nothin', what she's seeing is flying saucers full of enemy aliens, and they're landing in her backyard and eating up her children, and she's taking charge of everything and she's telling someone to put on his radiation-proof suit and get the ray gun. And then I guess they're going out there to save the kids, cuz she's shouting, "Watch out for that radioactive puddle!" and shit like that.

There's something about that voice that gets to me. I feel like crying, I feel like I know that person, and after a while I realize I *do* know that person. That's Millie's voice. I sit straight up on my bunk and listen hard. Maybe it's somebody sounds like Millie, but it's not, it's Millie; she's got just this certain combination of small-town Western accent and cigarette husky in her voice that ain't like nobody else's.

Jeezuz god on a fuckin' bicycle, I never been here when Millie come in before. I never knew she got that crazy drunk. After I'm sure who it is, I can't even lie down again I'm so freaked out and miserable. First I try not to listen and then I *have* to listen; this is *Millie* talking crazy here. I feel embarrassed, like I'm someplace I ain't supposed to be, like I walked in on somebody masturbating or something, but worse. But I can't help listening, this is *Millie* for chrissake, like I never knowed her. Fuckin' bonkers, jeezuz.

So I'm sitting bolt upright on my bunk, staring out into the black, when the lights go on again and the tank door whocks open. In a few seconds I hear the screws stomping up the steel stairs to the upper ramp. They must be full up on the first tier. And in another few seconds they go by my cell with a black chick who looks like she can't hardly walk, like her legs are gonna buckle under her any second, and there's two screws with her instead of one like usually, and they're holding her up and pushing her along by her arms. I only see her for a couple of seconds, but you know how it is when something's knocked you for a loop. All your circuits is blowed wide open and it don't take you long to take in a whole lot, and that's how I am when they go by with this chick. I get a good look at her face, and in the condition I'm in, all upset about Millie, this chick's face hits me hard. She's got a look people only get when they been down and out a long time, usually they been in and out of jails a lot, and so that's why I call this look *jailface.*

Partly, jailface just happens when you been under everybody's heel too long, but after a while you learn to do it on purpose so you never let on that you're scared or feeling pain or worry or sickness. What you do is, you freeze your face so nothin' moves. Your eyebrows don't scrunch together in a frown, your mouth don't twitch or smile or sneer. Freeze ain't exactly the right word cuz it makes it sound like the face goes hard, when actually it goes limp and you don't let it tighten up over nothin' at all, ever. The real mark of jailface, though, is the eyes. They don't never look straight at nobody and they don't even focus half the time. You can't look into the eyes of somebody with jailface cuz your look bounces off a glassy surface of eyeball that's so hard it would bounce bullets.

Jailface ain't necessarily a bad thing to have, cuz the minute a certain kind of screw knows you're scared or weak she's got the upper hand, and she jumps on you with both feet and don't let up 'til she's had her satisfaction, which in most cases is to see your spirit dead. But if you're walking around with jailface she can't tell if something is still stirring in there or not. Most likely she thinks by your look that you're already dead, so there's no challenge, nothin' in there to kill, see. But people ain't really dead 'til they're really dead, if you know what I mean. Maybe you've given up, maybe you're a fuckin' zombie, but just about anybody got a little life left in 'em that can spark up the minute they latch on to a little piece of hope, and if you got jailface you can keep that hid from the screws so they can't stomp it out of you.

Well, anyway, in this second or two while this chick is passing my cell I decide she's a junkie, cuz a junkie going to jail is about the most given-up person you ever seen, and cuz she's black, cuz funny thing is, black chicks don't get jailface as a general rule. I mean they can, but not usually. I get in trouble saying stuff like this cuz you ain't supposed to say Black is like this and White is like that, but I can't help it, it's the truth. Black women just seem to do their time different. They sing more, goof around more. They don't zombie out like the rest of us. They even get mad more, fight more, and when they turn funny in here, they fall in love harder. I figure the singing and the goofing around is how black chicks cover up, something they use instead of jailface. I don't know for sure – I never been black. But all I know is, when a black chick has jailface it's gotta be something very very bad that's going on, like being a sick hype.

When the screws put her in the cell next to mine I think, Oh great, now I'm gonna have a sick junkie screaming right next door, on top of everything else. As the screws leave, ol' Blodgett sees me sitting up on my bunk and she says, with this nasty grin on what she has the nerve to call a face, "What's the matter, Iva, can't you sleep?"

"Ha ha ha," I says, but they already gone by.

There's a lull in the alkie olympics downstairs. Maybe they was shocked silent by the lights. I'm glad I can't hear Millie no more. But in the quiet I can hear the chick next door moaning, "Oh sweet Jesus, I'm sick, I'm sick."

"Don't you start too," I says. "It's bad enough around here. I don't need nobody moaning and groaning right next door." She don't answer and I don't hear another peep outa her. Millie seems to be quiet now too. In fact, they all quieted down now, finally wore out and passed out, I guess. But I'm too shook up about Millie to go to sleep. I just sit there staring into the dark for a while, and then I start hearing the junkie next door breathing. She's breathing funny, not regular like you're supposed to, catching her breath and trying not to cry or something. I start to feel bad about yelling at her. "You want a cigarette?" I says.

She says, "Girl, I'm too sick to smoke."

So I just sit there staring in the dark, and I wonder what Millie's gonna be like in the morning, and then I don't want to think about it so I don't think about nothin'. I just sit there staring. It's about twenty minutes later when the junkie begins to sing. Real soft, real tender her voice is, and I like listening to a sweet voice singing soft like that. She sings sad dreamy songs, like "Me and My Shadow" and "Down in the Valley." She's gonna sing herself to sleep and me with her. It don't feel so much like being buried alive in the dark with her singing sweet like that. What a relief from all that screaming and crying.

But in a while her songs start getting more upbeat, 'til finally she's singing stuff like "I Can't Get No Satisfaction," and some Aretha Franklin and Tina Turner and Janis Joplin – jeez, I didn't think nobody even remembered ol' Janis no more. She's singing a whole lot of stuff I'm really into, and I just can't help singing with her. When she hears me chiming in she starts clapping her hands, and so I clap too, and when the pace wears us out we go back to old funkies like "Frankie and Johnny" and "Bye Bye Blackbird." Finally somebody hollers, "For chrissake shut up!"

We stop singing and I ask her, "How you feeling?"

"I think I better sing some more. It helps to sing."

"Don't they give you nothin' to help you through it?"

"Girl, they don't know I'm sick. I got busted for soliciting and they never checked me for no marks. If I can keep them from finding out I'm sick, maybe I'll get thirty days for soliciting 'stead of having to take the cure. What's your name?"

"Iva. What's yours?"

"Angora. What you in for?"

I do some fast thinking. I don't want to tell her I'm here

for possession for sale, her being a junkie and all. It don't matter that the stuff wasn't even mine – everybody says that. So I says, "Same as you – soliciting."

"And you don't got a habit?"

"No."

"Good for you, girl. Does your old man treat you good?"

"He's all right."

"Uh-huh. I hear you ain't saying he treat you real fine. Listen, don't let him give you no habit. They like you to get hooked so they can control you. You stay clean. There ain't nothin' worth this misery."

"I managed so far. Listen, you said you want to sing some more. Do you know the slow version of 'Cocaine Blues'?"

"How do it go?"

I sing, "Early one morning while a-making the rounds/ Took a shot of cocaine and I shot my woman down/ Shot her down cuz she made me sore/ I thought I was her daddy but she had five more."

"Naw, I don't know that one. I never heard it."

So I teach her all the words I can remember, then she says, "Do you know the peaches song?"

"No."

She sings, "If you don't like my peaches/ Why do you shake my tree?/ If you don't like my peaches/ Why do you shake my tree?/ Get out of my orchard/ And leave my fruit tree be.

"Let me be your little dog/'til the big dog come./ Let me be your little dog/ 'Til your big dog come./ When the big dog come/ Just tell him what the little dog done."

We giggle over that one, and then I think of "C. C. Rider," and she knows it too, so we sing it together, and then she asks me if I know "Gloomy Sunday," and I says, "Yeah. You know, when that song first come out thousands of people committed suicide all over the country, and they tried to outlaw the song."

"Yeah, I heard that too."

So we sing "Gloomy Sunday" and "I Shall Be Released." These are all songs you learn if you spend a lot of time sitting around in jails, and she's pretty impressed that I know all that stuff. We're having a real party considering the circumstances. Then we hear the tank door clang open and heels clunking on the concrete floor. That can only be Blodgett. She's built like a buffalo and wears size-thirty shoes with lead in the heels. The footsteps stop somewhere under us and Blodgett yells, "Cut out that singing up there or I'll throw you in flatbottom." Then she stomps out and I tell Angora, "A screw can't stand to think there's ever ten minutes you ain't doing real hard time. If we was crying or moaning with pain or screaming with the d.t.'s she wouldn'ta said nothin'."

"I need a cigarette now."

We have to grope in the dark for each other's hands and when her hand touches mine it's ice cold and she's shaking. I pass her a book of matches and when she's lit up she says, "What's flatbottom?"

"It ain't a nice place. Ain't you been in jail before?"

"Not this one."

"I thought all jails had flatbottoms. Anyway, it's a cell on the first tier with nothin' in it. No toilet, no cot, no water, no nothin'. If you piss, you piss on the floor. If you shit, you shit on the floor. Then you sleep in it 'til they let you out to clean it up. They ain't supposed to leave you in there more than twenty-four hours but they keep you there long as they want. It ain't supposed to be for punishment but that's what they use it for."

"What's it for, then?"

"Protective custody, they call it. Somebody's crazy, trying to commit suicide or something, they put 'em in there 'til they cool off. Sort of like a padded cell without the padding."

"I don't see what good it do to make a person shit on the floor."

"I seen people try to stuff their heads down the toilet. Anyway, the screws use it mostly to keep people in line, and it works pretty good that way. So we better not sing no more."

But Angora says, "Girl, if I don't sing, I'll scream. Now I don't mind if I have to go to flatbottom, but I don't want to start screaming cuz once I start I won't be able to stop." And so she starts off again. At first I keep quiet, but after a while I think, Oh, what the hell, I strung along with her this far, I can go to the end. So I sing with her, but softly now. And pretty soon the screw comes back and this time the lights all go on and she comes upstairs and marches straight to Angora's cell. I hear the cell door open and then shut, and then she pushes Angora past my cell and Angora is singing "Won't You Come Home Bill Bailey" and she's doing a little dance step as the screw drags her along the ramp to the stairs. This time I notice how skinny she is.

I hear the door to flatbottom open and then slam shut. Even though I know I was singing too soft for Blodgett to hear me this time, I wait for the sound of her boots coming back up the stairs to get me. Instead, the lights go out and the tank door clongs shut and it's deep pit black again.

At first I feel relieved, but in a few minutes I feel bad. I know this chick is really hurting now, and lying on a cold cement floor. So I start singing a Dinah Washington song, and in a couple of minutes Angora chimes in and away we go again. But when we sing a couple of songs she calls up to me, "You better cool it, girl, or you gonna be down here with me."

"Hell, I don't care. I got a lotta time ahead of me anyway. I might as well do something."

"You ain't gonna do a lot of time for soliciting."

I forgot I tole her that. I think fast. "I been busted a bunch of times before. They're gonna give me a habitual this time."

"That's too bad, and maybe you don't care 'bout coming down here, but I do. Think how it gonna smell in here in the morning with two of us in here."

"You got a point there."

I don't sing no more, but she keeps right on. I never knew one person could know so many songs. Blodgett pokes her head back in once to tell her to shut up, but the kid is already in flatbottom, what more can they do to her? So she don't pay no attention and keeps right on singing. I lie down at last and I'm almost sung to sleep when I hear the tank door open again. This time the lights don't go on. Angora keeps on singing like she don't even hear the screw coming, but over the song I can hear the heels clunk-clunking and they don't stop 'til it sounds like she's all the way to the back of the tank. I sit up on my bunk and listen close cuz I can't figure out what she could be doing in the dark. Then the faucet goes on and I can hear water filling up a bucket and I think, Oh shit, she's gonna douse her, and then I think, Christ, she's gonna have to sit in water all night and her sick as a dog already. I'm gonna call out to tell her to shut up but what's the use? She's gonna get it now anyway, and right then I hear the splash.

Angora screams like someone knifed her in the gut, a awful wail that bounces off the walls and breaks over me from all sides and I think for a second that she's shattered the walls and the jail is gonna cave in on us. I'm so scared I can't move, and then the scream dies away and it's quiet except for the women whimpering, scared out of their gourds, and I can hear Margarita praying. Then I hear the clunk-clunks working their way back to the door and the clang and the click that mean we're locked up tight again.

From flatbottom I hear Angora moaning and crying, and the whole damn thing is finally too much for me, Arnie and Millie and Angora and this fuckin' snake pit, and I scream, OH JESUS LET ME OUT OF HERE! and I cry loud enough for myself to drown out the sobs of the sick hype in flatbottom and the chorus of women crying and praying and after a while I just give out and go to sleep.

In the morning I wake up when they bring the breakfast cart in, but I don't want to get up. I must not've slept more than a hour or so, but mainly I don't want to go down and see Angora. I don't want to see Millie. But we don't get enough to eat around here and if I skip breakfast I'm gonna be awful hungry the rest of the day, and besides, I remember that I got floor-scrubbing detail after breakfast. I got to get up anyway. So I go down and look in flatbottom but Angora ain't there, just a puddle of water. She ain't in any of the other cells either, but Millie's asleep in number 8. She smells awful and she looks sick. And old. Millie's about forty, but today she looks sixty. Just smelling her makes me feel sick too, and I think of all the mornings Millie and me has moved our card game upstairs to avoid the stinking alkies and I wonder, Don't Millie know she smells like that when she comes in? I wonder should I wake her up for breakfast but I decide she's not gonna feel like eating, just the smell of food will prolly make her sicker, so I leave her there sleeping.

I ask Elsie, the trusty who comes with the breakfast cart, if she knows what happened to the chick in flatbottom. "They moved her to the other tank," she says. "What happened, anyway? Her face and arms are all blistered, like she got burned."

"They throwed a bucket of water on her."

"It musta been boiling, then. They brought her over there at five in the morning, and it woke me up, is how I happened to see her."

"I never knowed tap water could be hot enough to blister you."

"Well, I guess it must be."

I'm depressed and ain't had enough sleep and all I feel like doing is hiding in my bunk, but if I don't do my floor I'll get hassled by the screws and maybe go to flatbottom myself, so I figure I better get to it. After I eat I go to fill my bucket and I can't find the box of lye we use for scrubbing the cement, and it only takes a second for it to hit me what become of it. Oh jeezuz. I sit down on the floor against the wall and hold my knees and put my head down on my arms and cry, but when I hear the tank door open for the screw to let Elsie out with the cart I jump to my feet and start working.

All morning I keep checking Millie's cell, waiting for her to wake up, but she's totally zonked. I want to talk to her, even though I know when she wakes up she ain't gonna be in no shape to talk to. But I want to talk to her anyway. I never been so depressed in here like I am today.

When the lunch wagon comes, Elsie hands me a kite. She says, "The spade chick you were asking about give it to me." I stick the kite in my pocket 'til the screw that comes with the food cart is gone and the tank is shut up tight. Then I go to my bunk and read it:

> *Dear Barbera Strysand,*
>
> *They took me out of flatbottom cause they was afraid I'd catch cold and give there nice hotel a bad name. I got some frends gonna come bring me some loot today and i'll send you the cigs I owe you. Hang in there, girl. I'll sing loud enuf tonight so you can hear me over there.*
>
>

Very truly yours,

Angora
>

I feel a whole lot better after I read this, and I write her a note back saying I hope she's feeling better and she better not sing if she knows what's good for her, and maybe I'll see her after I been to court and get transferred out of the holding tank. I gotta hold the kite til supper time and give it to a trusty, so I stick it in my pocket and go on downstairs.

Millie is up at last, sitting on a bench just staring, and I see now she has a big black eye and bruises on her arms. But when I walk up to her she busts into this big happy grin, and I see right away why she looks so old. She got no teeth in her mouth. She looks so pitiful I just about cry to look at her, but she says, "Iva! Fancy meeting you here!" And she laughs.

"Millie, if I wasn't so sorry to see you all beat up I'd be glad to see you. What happened to you?"

"Oh well. I fell down, I guess." Millie looks down at her feet, cuz she's lying, of course. I shouldn'ta asked. I know perfectly well that her ol' man beats up on her when they get to drinking. Jeezuz. What the hell else is gonna happen around here? But I know he didn't knock every one of her teeth out. She musta had false ones. So I says, "What happened to your teeth?"

Millie puts her hand over her mouth, all embarrassed, like she just now realized she don't have 'em. She says, "Well, to tell the truth, I don't know. I mighta lost 'em somewhere along the line, but sometimes when I come in they take 'em away from me so's I won't break 'em or something. If they got 'em, I'll get 'em back later. You got a cigarette?"

I hand Millie a cig and when I go to light it her hand is shaking so bad I can hardly connect. The stench coming off her is sickening, and I'm having trouble with the fact that my friend Millie looks and smells just like all them alkie hags I bitch to her about all the time.

Millie says, "What day is this?"

"Sunday."

"Well, we don't go to court 'til tomorrow then."

"I got no trial date yet, Millie."

"What do you mean?"

I sit down and tell Millie what happened, about holding for Arnie, about not having no bail money, about for sure I'm gonna go to the joint since I got all these priors for hustling. She listens to all this just sitting there shaking her head and looking real sad. I want to talk to her about Angora too, about how I lied to Angora about being busted for possession for sale, like somehow it was my fault she's a junkie, and about everything that happened last night, but somehow I just can't get myself to say nothin'. Millie says, "It's a little late to say this, Iva, but I don't think you should have anything to do with that Arnie when you get out. I shoulda said that to you a long time ago maybe."

"Millie, you don't always have a choice about who you got to do with."

"Yeah, I'm a fine one to talk, huh? Me with my Merv. Listen, I gotta take me a nap."

"You want me to wake you up for supper?"

"Naw. I won't be able to keep anything down 'til tomorrow prolly. "

I figure I got a nap coming myself, and so I go upstairs to my cell and zonk out.

I don't know the trusty that comes with the dinner cart, and you gotta be careful about trusties around here since half the time they only get to be trusties cuz they're the screws' little stoolies, so I hang on to my kite and wait 'til the next morning to ask Elsie about Angora.

"Christ, she's a mess," she says. "They won't let her go on sick call cuz of the way it happened, and she's got a fever and stuff running out of her ear."

Like a dope I ask, "Is she singing?"

"Singing? Have you flipped out? What's she got to be singing about? She don't even sit up or eat."

At lunch time Elsie tells me they let Angora loose, just like that. Just turned her loose. No court, no bail, no nothin'.

I try not to think about her after that, and I got plenty of my own miseries to keep me busy for a while. But after I go to the state joint, sometimes I sit up at the window after lights out and sometimes someone is singing out a window across the mall in one of the other dormitories and my heart gets a catch in it and I think for a second it's Angora. Or sometimes there's not even any singing and she just comes into my mind and I start singing for her again, only this time I sing as loud as I can. But I never keep it up very long cuz I know it don't matter how much I sing, I can never sing loud enough or long enough to change what happened to her back there. It was singing that got her in that fix in the first place, anyway. I just wish I had sang louder at the time, that's all, even though it wouldn'ta done no good then either. Or maybe I coulda got all the women in the tank to sing with us. Just suppose I coulda got 'em to do it. Feature this: all them alkies and junkies and hookers and boosters raising the jailhouse roof with song, and Angora singing lead. Wouldn't that be something? What could the screws do – throw scalding lye on all of us? Of course I know not even all of us singing at the top of our lungs woulda changed a goddam thing in that goddam jail, but it tickles me to think of it. Them screws – it woulda blown their friggin' minds.

II. Toni

Blind Corner

L ook," Tuffy says, "you don't have to do a goddam thing. He's just an ol' man who likes to pat pretty girls on the ass. All you have to do is act like you like him, let him pat you on the fanny, and collect twenty bucks. What's wrong with that?"

What's wrong with that is I don't want to do it, but I can see that Tuffy is getting mad. The muscles in his jaw are twitching. It's the first time I've seen all that power and muscle in his body as anything but beautiful, and he scares me. Something tells me I'd better not say no. "All right," I say, "but I'm not doing anything else."

Tuffy smiles now and takes me in his arms. He kisses my eyes. Softly he says, "I wouldn't let you do anything else. I want you all to myself, sweetheart."

I want to believe him, and I guess I do believe him. "Okay, where do I go?"

"He's got an office down on Beacon Street. Near Shanghai Red's. There's a sign by the entrance, E. Radevich, Accountant. just go on upstairs. He'll be waiting for you."

"You mean you got this all arranged already?"

"Aw, c'mon, sweetheart. It's so easy, it never occurred to me you'd mind. Frankie asked me if you'd do it and I said yes, because if I said no he woulda got somebody else. And you know we need the money."

His fixing it up for sure before he even asked me makes me mad again, but I've already agreed to do it, and besides I'm scared to back out. I comb my hair, and then Tuffy walks me to my car, holding my hand. He leans through the window to kiss me before I drive off. "We'll buy steaks with the twenty bucks, sweetheart." I want to say, "Let's eat pasta and forget the money," but I don't dare.

I park on Beacon Street and walk toward Shanghai Red's, like Tuffy told me, looking for the sign that says E. Radevich, Accountant. All the bars are quiet because it's still early afternoon, but the smell of beer comes out of every door, and from some come loud voices talking drunk. I feel nervous. It's a rough street. I wonder why an accountant has an office down here with nothing but bars and pawnshops all around.

I find the sign by a dark stairway and go up. The second-floor hall is dark too. It's a very old building with octagonal-tile floors and dark wood doors. E. Radevich is the last office at the end of the hall. His door has a white glass pane with his name on it in gold letters. It looks like there's no light inside, but when I knock, a man's voice says, "Come in."

The office is almost as dark as the hall, and a burly man about sixty is sitting at a desk. He has a big bulbous nose and hands like hams. He's wearing a Hawaiian shirt. He doesn't look like an accountant to me. There are some file drawers, and a chair in front of his desk, but there's lots of space with nothing in it. The man is as moldy-looking as the building, but he's smiling at me and it's a nice old-man kind of smile, and I feel a little better.

"Are you Toni?" he says.

"Yes. Are you Mr. Radevich?"

He grins. "You can call me Eric, honey. Have a seat there." He points to the only chair, in front of his desk.

I sit down. I don't know what to say or do next. He looks at me like he's expecting something, and I know I have to speak.

"So you're an accountant?"

This strikes him as hilarious, and he laughs so hard I'm irritated. I'm just making conversation, damn it. When he calms down he says, "Are you a San Pedro gal?"

"Yeah."

"You're Tuffy's girl, aren't you?"

"Yes. We been together three months now."

"I see."

I figure he'll be coming around the desk to get his pat on the ass, but he doesn't make a move. I wonder how long I have to make conversation before we get the business over with. He says, "You're a very pretty girl. How old are you?"

"Twenty-one." I think of asking him how old he is, and this thought tickles me and I manage to smile at him, but I'm getting nervous. He's looking at me very intently, and waiting. Am I supposed to do something? I figure if he wants to pat me on the ass he'll come around the desk. That's what I'm waiting for. But he doesn't make a move. What if there's a misunderstanding? I'm not going to bring it up if he doesn't. While I'm thinking about all this, he's staring at me, and his expression begins to change. He looks irritated, and finally he digs in his pocket for something. "Well, you're a nice girl. Here, go buy yourself a scarf or something." He throws a dollar bill on the desk.

I'm humiliated, confused. But he looks so mad I'm afraid to refuse the dollar. I pick up the money, mumble "Thank you," and bolt out the door.

Tuffy's fist catches me on the bridge of my nose. I fall against the wall, and while I'm trying to gain my balance he hits me again. "You stupid twat! You're gonna make me a laughingstock on the street! One fucking dollar! For what? You shoulda told him to shove it up his ass." I'm leaning against the wall shaking, scared to say anything and scared to move. Tuffy starts pacing around the room, slamming his fist into the palm of his other hand, and I'm sure he's gonna slam it in my face again. But his raving seems to be letting the steam out, and in a minute or so he's not shouting anymore. He stops slamming his fist, and he paces slower, but he still looks awful goddam mad and he's still raving at me. "What did you do, asshole, ask him how he likes the weather?"

"I didn't know what to say. I thought he was supposed to do something."

"You jerk. You gotta go pet him, sit on his lap. Are you just hatched out of an egg?"

"I didn't know what to do. You didn't tell me. I thought he was supposed to do something." I notice that Tuffy's sweating, like he does when he starts to get sick. That's why he's so mad, I bet. He's mean when he starts needing a fix. That gives me an idea. "Tuffy, you want me to go get your 'fit?"

Tuffy throws himself down on the bed, like I just let the air out of him. "Yeah," he says. "But I got a lot more to say to you when you get back, bitch."

"Okay, Tuffy." I go out the front door and turn like I'm going to the street. Tuffy's dope and his outfit for shooting up are hid in a clump of weeds by a power pole down the street about four houses. But my VW is pulled up right in front of the apartment. I walk past the window in case he's watching, but once I'm on the other side of it I double back and jump in my car. There's no way I can close the door without him hearing it, so before I hit the ignition I punch the buttons down on both sides and roll up my window. As I turn the key the front door of the apartment opens. I back up as fast as I can and turn to go out the drive, but Tuffy lands a hand on the hood and vaults over the front of the car, and as I'm pulling away he's running alongside and pounding on the window. He's yelling, "I'll kill you, bitch. Your life ain't worth nothin' if you don't stop right now!"

I think, My life already ain't worth nothin', and I keep going, and I'm shaking so bad I can hardly drive. I know he's on foot and he can't follow me, yet I'm so scared I feel like I can't stop until I've got a hundred miles between us. I head down to Gaffey and the freeway entrance, and once I'm on the freeway my shakes slow down a little. It's then I realize I don't have any money or ID. My purse is in the apartment. At least my cigarettes are lying in the passenger seat, but my hands are still shaking too much to light one. I pull off at the Wilmington exit and park.

Now it really hits me what a spot I'm in. No money, no clothes, no place to go, not even a way to eat. I know some people in San Pedro but when I got mixed up with Tuffy I stopped going to see them. I can't very well go to them now and ask them for help. I can't explain how I got in this fix. They don't know I'm living with a pusher, and I just can't handle listening to everything they'd probably say. And I'm too panicky to think up some plausible lie.

There's one person I can call, though. Tuffy's supplier in East L.A. Leon. Quesos, they call him. What the hell is his last name? Oh yeah, Fuentes. This thought scares me, because Tuffy says the guy is a real bad dude, has knocked off a bunch of people. Tuffy took me up there a couple of times, and the guy even *looks* bad. Beautiful but bad. The blackest eyes and hair I ever saw, and pearly white skin. He always wears black and that makes him look even badder.

But Tuffy said Quesos likes me, asked Tuffy if I was hooking for him, because he wanted to go with me, but of course Tuffy said I wasn't available, I was his girl. Tuffy told me I should come on to him at least a little bit, though, because he's a big important dealer and we want to keep him friendly.

So I think if I call Quesos he might help me out. He'll want to sleep with me of course. But what else can I do? I don't even have the price of a cup of coffee, and now that I think of it, I don't even have the change to call him either, unless there's some under the seat. I rummage around and all I find is a dime, but I'm desperate and I look in the glove compartment. There's a quarter and another dime in there. I pull up the floor mat and I find a nickel, another quarter, and a penny. Total take for four years of never cleaning out my car: seventy-six cents. But that should be more than enough. I start my car and drive along Lomita Boulevard until I spot a 7/Eleven with a pay phone outside. I've pulled up and parked by the phone before I realize I don't have the guy's number. Oh god. Now what. I can't believe a big dealer would have his name listed with information but to my surprise and good luck they've got it: Leon Fuentes.

I'm sure it must be a different Leon Fuentes, but when he answers the phone I recognize his silky voice. "Quesos? This is Toni, Tuffy's girl."

"Hey. How's it going?"

"Not so good. Tuffy just beat me up. I ran out of the house and I don't have any money or any clothes. Can you help me out? I mean, I'd pay you back."

"Where are you?"

"In a phone booth in Wilmington."

"Okay, baby, just come on up here. I'll wait for you at Jerry's.

You know the bar where we met last time? You remember how to get there?"

"I think so. It'll take me about an hour though."

"Okay, mama. I'll be there waiting for you. Don't you worry about a thing."

"Oh god, Quesos, thanks. I'm just desperate. And I'm scared."

"Nothing to be scared of. I won't let that prick hurt you. No te mortificas. Okay?"

There's so much sureness in his voice I feel better right away. "Okay. I'll see you in about an hour."

"Ay te wacho."

I hang up the phone and get back in my car. Now that I'm not so scared I can feel my nose throbbing, and I notice that my right eye is swollen. I look in my rearview mirror and see that my eye is purple and yellow and all puffy. Fine. Just fine. Well, at least Quesos won't think I'm lying about Tuffy.

On the freeway again, I start feeling better and better as I put more miles between me and Tuffy. The panic lets up some, and I begin to think about the spot I'm in. The main thing is I'm having trouble even believing this is me. I mean, three months ago I was working temporary in a bar while I looked for a better job. I even liked working nights because I could spend the mornings job hunting and the afternoons at the beach. When I figured out that Frankie, the guy who owned the bar, was a waterfront money lender and the bar was just a cover for him, I thought it was exciting. Although the word never got said, I knew he was mixed up with "the Mob." I wasn't involved in any way, and so I thought I had a safe place I could watch the action from. I felt like an extra in a gangster movie.

Then Tuffy showed up in the bar one night. Scotty the bartender told me he was Frankie's brother, and just out of the joint. While Tuffy waited for Frankie to get there, I had time to talk to him a while and he seemed like a sweet guy, and very sexy. Heavyset, all natural rippling muscle, not like a weight lifter, more like a Greek statue. But dark, like Frankie. Sicilian. But when Frankie got there he yelled and swore and made Tuffy leave because he's on parole and he'd get busted just for being in a bar. I didn't see Tuffy for a while after that, but Scotty told me one night that Frankie found out he was shooting smack again and tied him spread-eagled to his bed for three days, until he was over the worst withdrawals, and then set him loose.

A couple of weeks went by. I wasn't having any luck finding a job and I was getting worried, almost scared. What I made at the bar just wasn't enough to get by on.

Then one day I ran into Tuffy on the street. He seemed really glad to see me, and asked if he could come over that night. Sure, I said. We smoked some grass and talked and listened to the radio, and he told me how his brother didn't believe he was clean, and it hurt him that his own brother didn't have any faith in him. He seemed so sincere, and he said he didn't have any friends, and I felt so sorry for him that I didn't think twice about making love to him. He screwed me a long, long time, and he never came, and I felt bad, like it was my fault somehow, but he said it wasn't, it was because he had so much on his mind, and he asked me that very night to move in with him. So I did, the next morning. And one of the first things he asked me to do was quit my job at Frankie's Place because he didn't like me working for his brother, who as soon as he knew we were living together would be giving me the third degree about what Tuffy was doing all the time. I forget what Tuffy told me he was doing to make money, but, again, I didn't think twice when he said he had enough money for both of us.

Now I can't remember how many days it was before I realized Tuffy had a habit. Not only that, but he was dealing. It didn't take long. It's hard to hide something like that. It turns out that the reason he can't come is because of the habit. He can't shit either, and stays in the bathroom an hour at a time and gobbles laxatives like candy. And he pulls my dog Brandy's ears. Slow and steady, until the dog whimpers, and then he lets him go. Now Brandy's got pus running out of his ears and I don't know what to do for him. He's back at the apartment too, and I got to figure out a way to get him out of there.

There was a lot of good stuff though. Tuffy is short but he's a street-tough guy – that's how he got his nickname – and he made me feel safe, like I'd be taken care of, and I didn't have any money or a job anyway. He told me he loved me, and he held me at night, and he said he didn't want me getting a habit. He said he was going to get a job on the docks, that he knew a guy who could fix it for him even though he had a record, and when that happened he'd taper off and quit. He said it was hard to get a job when you had a record, and he needed somebody to have faith in him. So I had faith in him.

He taught me to make spaghetti Sicilian style. He showed me how important it is to use real olive oil and fresh garlic, and he said if you gave a Sicilian spaghetti sauce made with hamburger he'd throw it in your face. We bought sirloin tip or veal and cut it in tiny little pieces, and bought grated cheese at a special Italian deli out on Pacific Avenue. He taught me how to throw dope out the window as you went around a corner so the cops chasing you couldn't see you throw it, and we went out and practiced in my VW. I loved the cops-and-robbers part of it. It all seemed very easy. I liked ducking around trees in the park to dig up stashes, and the people who came to buy dope from Tuffy didn't seem like bad people, and I'm wondering now what the hell was into me that I thought like that. Because I'm caught now in something I don't know how to get out of. It seemed so sweet and simple to quit Frankie's Place and move in with Tuffy. I'm always happier if I have a man to live with. I don't even feel like I exist unless I have a man, but it was a blind corner and I had no idea what kind of street I was turning onto. And now I'm moving up the freeway, going around another blind corner at sixty-five miles an hour. Shit. But what else can I do? Nothing.

Quesos takes me to one of his stash pads, an apartment he rents just to store dope in, and it's empty except for a kitchen table and chairs, and a bed. I've been telling him all about the scene with the old man, and how mad Tuffy got, and I'm crying off and on. Quesos is listening, shaking his head from time to time, looking serious.

"Don't you know that's the oldest way in the world to turn a girl out?"

I don't know what he means, but I don't like the sound of it. I look at him and I guess he can see I'm puzzled. "Toni, if you want to put a girl on the street you start by telling her there's this old man who doesn't want to do anything, he just wants to be petted. She goes and lets the guy feel her up a little and she scores a few bucks. It seems so easy she's ready to go the next time her boy says the old man wants to see her. But the next time, the old man goes just a little further. And it goes on like that until one day he's all the way in. See? Tuffy was setting you up."

"I don't believe that. The old guy didn't even try anything."

"Of course he didn't. You got to make the first move. He don't want you screaming rape or anything like that. He maybe didn't trust Tuffy, didn't know what you'd been set up for. So when you didn't do anything he figured he'd be safer to just opt out."

I don't believe this and I don't want to believe it but I start crying really hard and I guess somewhere inside I do believe it because otherwise why am I crying like this?

Quesos doesn't say anything, he just puts an arm around my shoulder and leads me to the bed. Oh god, can't he see I'm in no shape? I feel like I'm in the bottom of a pit and if I fight Quesos I'll be out on the street in this condition with no place to go. Quesos makes me sit on the bed, and takes my shoulders and lays me down. I've given up all the way because I got no choice and I don't even resist. But I'm not volunteering either, and I'm about as limp as a piece of wilted celery. And I can't stop crying, and I just keep crying harder and harder so I can barely breathe.

But then Quesos walks away and goes in the bathroom. I hear the water running. In a minute he's back, and he's wiping my face with a cool washcloth. "Shhhh, shhhh," he says. "You're all wore out, mama. You need some sleep. Look. You go to sleep, and I'll be back in the morning and we'll think about what you want to do. Okay?" I'm so surprised I stop crying. He pulls a quilt up over me, takes the rag back into the bathroom. When he comes back, he says, "You need anything? You got some money to go eat if you want?"

"No. I told you, I don't have anything."

"Okay, baby, here's some money, and here's a key. Don't lose your way, okay? And I'll be here in the morning. You don't have to worry about a thing." He hands me forty bucks and leans over and kisses me on the forehead, like a daddy. Then he leaves.

I'm so relieved and grateful that all the fear and tension go out of me. I lie there marveling at my good luck until I go to sleep, which is in about five minutes.

In the morning when I wake up Quesos is sitting on the edge of the bed looking at me.

"How long have you been there?"

"About twenty minutes."

"Why didn't you wake me up?"

"I like watching you sleep."

Like a lover. I'm embarrassed and don't know what to say. But Quesos doesn't wait for me to answer. "You slept with all your clothes on."

"Yeah, I went to sleep as soon as you left."

"You must be pretty hungry. You want to go to breakfast?"

"Sure. I need a shower, though."

"Okay, go ahead. I'll wait in the other room."

In the shower I marvel again at how nice he's being. I mean, I'm completely at his mercy, and I know from Tuffy he's a pretty tough guy. He turns me on – the bizarre combination of tenderness and respect and toughness excites me. When I come out of the shower I hear him singing to himself in the other room: "Weeping willow tree, weep in sympathy / Bend your branches down along the ground and cover me. . . ." That's the bit that's too much for me. I wrap myself in a towel and go into the room where he's waiting. I stand in front of him and drop the towel. He doesn't act surprised, he doesn't change his expression, he just sits up on the edge of the chair and pulls me over to him. He leans his head forward and probes my slit with his tongue. When he finds my clit he begins licking it. My god. Nobody ever did that to me before. It scares me but it thrills me at the same time. Wow. Before I know it we're on the bed and he's got my buttocks cupped in his hands and he's really licking at me now, and I never felt anything like this in my life and I've never been so hot before and I feel myself getting so wet and sloppy it's embarrassing, but he doesn't seem to mind, he's licking it up like honey, and I begin to feel this hot spot somewhere down there that grows and grows and finally explodes like a star, and I realize, my god, I've had my first orgasm ever.

Quesos gets up now and unzips his fly, he gets on me without taking his clothes off and somehow that's very exciting to me, and he fucks me and because of the orgasm my cunt is so sensitive that it feels like it must be giving off sparks, and as he fucks me I come again and again and then again, and at last he comes too and hugs me to him and gives me a hickey on my neck. "Now you're branded," he says, and there's no doubt about it: I belong to this man now, I'm safe, I'm in bliss.

I've got to go get my clothes and my purse," I tell Quesos over breakfast. "Will you go with me?"

"Sure, baby. We can go right now."

"Maybe it's better if we go tonight. Tuffy hits the street at night and it would be easier if he's not there. I want to get my dog too. I can't leave him there."

"Sure. We'll do that."

Quesos gives me a hundred dollars, tells me to buy some clothes to change into, the rest is to eat on. He'll meet me at the pad about six. He's got business to do and it will take him all day.

A hundred bucks like it was nothing.

It's about nine o'clock when we come into San Pedro. Even though Quesos is with me I've got a fluttery stomach. There's no doubt in my mind he can handle Tuffy but still it'll be ugly. I'm praying Tuffy won't be there. He shouldn't be, but on the other hand he might just be waiting for me to come back. He knows I'm gonna have to have my ID and some clothes. I'm thinking about all this. Quesos has been quiet for the last few miles. Now he says, "Babe, I think it would be better if you leave me off at a bar downtown while you go to the apartment."

I can hardly believe what he's saying. "I thought you were gonna go with me. That's why you came down!"

"I don't want no bad scene. It's not good for business, you know? I'll be right there in the bar, waiting for you."

I feel confused, and I'm scared again. But I don't know what to do. Quesos isn't a guy you argue with. That's always been clear. He's a dangerous man. Tuffy always said so, but more than that, I can feel it. I don't want him mad at me, I don't want to blow things just when they're looking so wonderful. He can tell me to forget it in a split second if he wants to. So I drive him down to Sixth Street and drop him off in front of a bar.

The driveway at the courts seems so familiar to me, so normal, it's strange to feel so scared. I can see that the apartment is dark, but it occurs to me that Tuffy could be in there waiting for me. I park and leave the car door open and the engine running, ready to run for my life if I have to. I unlock the apartment and reach in and throw the light switch that's right by the door, and poor ol' Brandy comes bounding over and nearly knocks me down. He's whimpering, poor ol' thing. "Hey, I wouldn't leave you here, you know that," I tell him. I still feel nervous and I check out the bathroom and the kitchen and finally the closet. Tuffy really is out. But he could come back any minute and I know I've got to move fast. My purse is right where I left it. I don't try to pack my clothes, I just grab them and throw them in the back seat. Brandy jumps in back without my telling him. He can't wait to get out of here either. I know I should double-check to make sure I didn't forget anything, and I should get some food for Brandy, but I'm sure I'm pushing my luck. If Tuffy showed up he'd be between me and my car, and I wouldn't have any way to get away. So I jump in the car – I don't even close the apartment door – and I'm gone.

Brandy's pushing his head over the back of the seat to lick me and his tail is going so hard his whole body is waving around, and for a minute I'm so glad he's safe that I just keep talking to him, reassuring him. But after a block or two the whole thing of Quesos copping out on going to the apartment comes back and I feel double-crossed. What if Tuffy had been there? What good was Quesos sitting in a bar downtown? I can't fit this together with how good he's been to me, how sweet and generous, and I just don't know what to do. I say to Brandy, "You and me can cut out and go to San Francisco." But I know we can't. I gave Quesos the change back from his hundred when we went to dinner. I didn't want him to think I was on the take in any way. I got zero, zilch, nada, I don't even have enough gas to get anywhere but L.A. There isn't any money in my purse because Tuffy always kept the money. It never mattered because we were always together and he paid for everything, even the groceries. I never worried about it. What a mistake that was.

Well, maybe I'm making a big deal over nothing. "Brandy, we got a new friend. He's just wonderful. He didn't want to come up with me to get you, but I guess there's just something I don't understand, because, Brandy, he's been wonderful to me."

We pick up Quesos and he kisses me when we get in the car, and the best part is Brandy loves him right away, he slobbers all over him. He never did that with Tuffy, not even before he pulled his ears. "Hey, pooch," says Quesos, and roughs him up the way dogs love to be roughed up. "How did it go?" he says to me.

"Fine. Tuffy wasn't there."

Quesos smiles. "See? I told you there wasn't any reason I should go up there."

The anger flares up in me again, but because I don't have any choices and because I'm so relieved that I got my stuff from Tuffy's without any trouble, I keep a lid on it. The worst fear and pressure are off me now, anyway, and I can start my new life. But I don't feel at ease and completely trusting with Quesos like I did before we got to San Pedro, and I don't have much to say.

He doesn't seem to notice though, and he starts talking about our plans. "Tomorrow we can look for an apartment, baby. And we'll buy you some clothes. I'm gonna dress you up like a queen." He pulls a wad of bills about two inches thick out of his pocket. He peels off five twenties and stuffs them in my purse. "I don't want you to ever have less than a hundred in your purse, okay? For food and gas, or if you want to have a drink or buy something pretty, okay?"

Okay? Is he kidding? I've gone from not knowing how I'm gonna get my next meal to a hundred dollars pocket money in one day. How could that not be okay? I smile and nod my head.

"You seem a little tense, babe. Is everything all right?" He lays his hand on my thigh, then slides it between my legs. I remember how we made love this morning and I feel a surge of desire that's almost painful. I'm getting wet and my cunt is swollen and throbbing. I've never responded to a man so intensely before. I've been silent while I notice these things, and Quesos says, "Babe?"

"Yeah, everything's all right. I'm just tired. This has been a lot of strain."

"When I get you home I'll rock you to sleep, mama." He squeezes me and works his fingers deeper into my crotch. I'm so hot I can hardly keep my attention on driving.

Quesos keeps talking. He tells me he has five brothers who are all in the business with him. He says, "When you keep it in the family you don't have to worry about getting double-crossed, man." Then he tells me the story of how he got his name.

"Quesos means cheese. Cheeses. You know those little round white cakes of cheese that come in a cellophane package?"

"Yes, I've seen them in Mexican delis."

"Those are called quesos. And my mother used a package of those almost every day, to put in things she cooked. So when I was a little kid I went everywhere on roller skates, and I always skated as fast as I could. I was a demon on skates, man. But I went so fast I couldn't stop unless I crashed into something. So my mother would give me a quarter – you can't buy those cheeses for a quarter anymore – and she'd say, 'Leon, váyate a la tienda y compre un paquete de quesos.' So I'd go racing to the store, which was also run by a Mexican man, see, and I'd be going so fast I'd sail right through the door and slam into the counter and I'd be all out of breath, so all I could say was 'Quesos!' and the old man would give me the quesos and take my quarter and I'd turn around and race home again. So the old man started calling me Quesos, and everybody in the neighborhood picked it up, and I can't get rid of it. It follows me everywhere."

Brandy is looking at Quesos like this is the best story he ever heard in his life, and I'm pretty tickled myself, because I never forget for one minute that this is one of the biggest dealers in East L.A., and that he's got a rep as a really bad guy, yet he's got a nickname from being a little kid tearing around the neighborhood on roller skates. I'm smiling, and Quesos says, "I want you to call me Leon, though. To you I'm Leon."

And so I say "Okay, Leon," and it *is* okay. I've got a hundred dollars in my purse and tomorrow I'm gonna get a hot new wardrobe and I don't have to worry about what I'm gonna do and I've got a man who turns me on more than anybody ever has. I take one hand off the steering wheel and lay it over Leon's hand in my crotch. I'm hot and happy all the way back to L.A.

Esperanza

In my dream I'm still driving that godawful road from Tijuana to Mexicali, six and a half ounces of pure uncut smack stuffed in condoms and hid in my bra. The headlights are behind me all the way from Tijuana. No car attached to them, just headlights floating along, following me, always the same distance behind, as if they were attached to me in some way. I know if I don't get away from them something terrible is gonna happen, but something keeps me from even trying. I just drive on and on like some mindless robot. It doesn't seem like I have any choice, even though I know I'm driving to my own doom.

I drive for a long, long time. The country has been black all the way, no moon, and I can't see anything but the road where my headlights hit and the lights following me in the rearview mirror, and then, high in the mountains I have to cross to get to Mexicali, all of a sudden here is this little guard station, like a sentry box, glowing bright in the night with a soldier inside. He watches me coming, watches me pass, and then in the side mirror I see him pick up a phone and as he talks into it he points after my car, the big yellow Cadillac Leon bought me.

When I get to Mexicali and come up to the border the feeling of doom gets stronger and stronger, and then I'm not in the car anymore, but running down an alley, trying to throw the shit away in every trash can I pass, but it sticks to my hands and all I can do is change it from one hand to the other. Trying to get rid of it I get more and more frantic, and then suddenly a hand grabs my shoulder and the feeling of doom is so strong it feels like death, and just at that moment I wake up.

I'm lying on a cot in a jail cell and a Mexican girl has hold of my shoulder, shaking me. "Levántase, levántase, todos a trabajar." Somewhere in my sleep I forgot I was in jail, and I feel so confused I just lie there stupefied. The girl keeps shaking me and talking her gibberish and suddenly I'm mad. "Stop that, goddam it."

She lets go of my shoulder now she sees I'm awake, but she keeps talking. "Everybody up. Everybody work."

"Everybody but me. I came in at five this morning and I haven't had any sleep for about four days, so I gotta sleep now. Savvy?"

"No. No sleep. Everybody work."

The girl is wearing a thin white blouse and a full purple skirt. I can see she's just another inmate. Where does she get off ordering me around? I roll over with my face to the wall. She shakes my shoulder again and says, "No work, no eat. Is better you come." I turn over to tell her I'm gonna punch her if she shakes me one more time, but she's on her way out of the cell and down the hall. She's not wearing any shoes, and doesn't make a sound as she moves.

No work, no eat, huh? I look around me. There are two bunks in the cell. I'm on the bottom one. There's a sink and a toilet at the rear wall. The space that's left is just enough room to walk from the front of the cell to the back. The mattress I'm on is the skinny kind you use for cots. It has a thin muslin cover and nothing else. No pillow, no blanket. But I sure don't need a blanket. Everywhere my body touches the mattress I'm wet with sweat. Where was it they told me they were taking me? Oh yes, El Rincon. No wonder it's hot.

No work, no eat, huh? Makes me notice that my stomach is churning with hunger. When did I eat last? Can't remember. Been running on bennies for weeks, hardly eating. It's all gonna catch up with me now. Why am I thinking about these things when what I have to think about is that I'm in jail and I don't know where Leon is and I don't know what's gonna happen to me? Don't know? Of course I know. It's all over for me, that's what.

The girl shows up again and hands me a towel, embroidered in blue with "County Jail." She waits, without saying anything, while I wash my face. No soap, no washcloth. She's getting on my nerves, but part of that's because I'm coming down off the bennies. "You come," she says when I'm done, and she leads me down the corridor and around a corner into a big room with some wooden benches and tables and a row of cells that are back-to-back with the row I'm in.

The room is crawling with women, all Mexican, as near as I can make out, and talking in Spanish, fast and all at the same time. I wonder how they know what each other is saying, all talking at once like that. Maybe they don't care. They seem excited and happy as they make up their faces and comb each other's hair, as if they were on a holiday. It's not what I expect in jail and it throws me a little off balance.

A big steel door at the other end of the room opens and two men in denims wheel in a big cart with six shelves. Each shelf is full of aluminum trays. A tiny uniformed woman is with them, holding a big ring of keys. She has a friendly face – not my idea of a jail matron, either. The women swarm over the food cart like bees. I wait for the rush to be over before getting a tray, and by that time all the benches are full, so I find a corner and sit on the concrete floor with my back against the wall.

My tray has oatmeal and toast. There's no sugar or milk any-where, and what's worse is, the oatmeal is cold, gummy, and cooked without salt. The toast is cold too, and there's no mar-garine, but it's better than the oatmeal so I eat it and feel full. My stomach has shrunk from not eating for so long.

My self-appointed keeper comes over and sits down beside me. "You no want your oatmeal?"

"No. This stuff is garbage."

The girl looks at me as if she's waiting for something. Oh god, don't tell me she wants this crap. "You want this?"

"Cómo no?" she says, shrugging her shoulders as if she doesn't care one way or the other. But she eats the oatmeal like it was some kind of treat, and I wonder how she can stomach such trash.

I ask her name.

"Esperanza. You?"

"Toni. You been here long?"

"Some days. What you do?"

"I tried to bring some stuff – you know, dope – across the line. You understand me okay?"

"Oh yes. I speak English very good."

"Okay. So what did you do?"

"We jump wire. All these women here. They put us in big truck and bring us here. Last time they just put me back across line and tell me no to come again. And two time before. But now they know me, the immigration, and when you come too many time they bring you to the jail."

"It sounds like they give you a break when they can."

Esperanza laughs. "The break is the jail have too many. No room for all of us, that is all. Everybody who want to come here from Mexico know this. We know we have good chance they just send us back if we get catched. But we know too if we get past the immigration, if we get to Los Angeles everything okay."

"Yeah, but here you are in jail. What happens now?"

"Maybe they give me three month, maybe one year. Then I go back and try again."

"You can't be serious. What's so good over here you don't mind going to jail?"

She looks at me with a puzzled expression, like it was a dumb question. But she sees I am serious, so she says, "I have two niños, two children, in Mexicali. If I get job in restaurant or cannery I live here on fifty dollar a week and send the rest home. I have a prima – how you say, cousin? – who is a whore in Los Angeles, but she have to spend many dollar on clothes and sometime she get beat up and sometime she get sick and have to have shots. I think this is too hard so I think I work in cannery even if I don't get so much money."

"But why can't you work in Mexicali? Doesn't it cost more to live here and have your children live over there? And don't you miss your kids?"

"Is no work for me in Mexicali. In Mexico are many people for every job, and I have no school. I do not read and write." She hangs her head as if she is ashamed. "In Mexicali there is nothing to do but be a puta and then you no get money, the pimp take it all away from you, and sometime you end up in the Mexicali jail. Is better to be in jail here than in Mexicali. This is very nice jail, you think so?"

"No."

Esperanza laughs. "That's because you never in the Mexicali jail. Anyway, my sister keep my niños for me. She can live and her children and my children on what I send her. You see?"

She has laughed at me twice like I don't know anything. I never asked her to talk to me, and my nerves are raw from not sleeping and coming down off the whites. "No, I don't see," I snap. "I don't see how you're gonna live on fifty bucks a week in L.A., or how your sister is gonna support herself and all those kids on what's left over. If you're a wetback they won't even pay you minimum wage. You'll be lucky if you get eighty or ninety bucks a week. Somebody's filled you full of pipe dreams and you're gonna come down hard."

She just goes on as if she doesn't notice I'm being testy. "I can live on fifty dollar in the barrio. My other sister is there now and that is what she does. She live with our aunt. When many people share it is easier. And my sister in Mexicali, it is easier for five people to live on what is left over than three people to live on nothing, do you think?"

I feel a little ashamed for snapping at her. "Yeah, I suppose it is." I wonder what life is like for this girl on the other side. Maybe I should call her a woman, since she's got two kids and is old enough to be in jail, but she doesn't look a day over sixteen. I can't imagine having two kids and no money at all. "Don't you have any relatives to help you?"

"How can they help me? They must take care of themself. My cousin Graciela is here with me. That's her over there combing Lilia's hair. She have niños in Mexicali too. She have husband. He came across a few months ago and she have not hear from him. She thought maybe he is in jail, but she get a letter from our aunt in Fresno to say she saw him picking oranges. He haven't send no money, so Graciela is going to find him and kill him."

She says these words as if this was a natural thing to do to a husband who doesn't send money home. I study this girl

Graciela. She doesn't look capable of murder, but there is something hard about her eyes. While I'm thinking about this the big door opens and another cart is wheeled in. Esperanza jumps to her feet. "Come, Toni, you and me will pass out the rags."

"What rags?" But Esperanza is already at the door, waiting beside the matron. As I come up to the cart, the matron says, "Are you Antonia Bagliazo?"

"Yeah."

"I'm Mrs. Webster. I take it you're going to help Esperanza." She's smiling like we're meeting at a tea party. But this isn't any tea party and she's got the keys in her hand that lock me up and I'm not about to smile back. "I guess so," I say, and look away.

She turns and walks across the hall to a big closet. Esperanza follows her and disappears inside, and after some rattling and banging comes out loaded with mops, rags, and cans every whichway in her arms. I step inside and grab what's left.

In the tank we pass out the cleaning gear and Esperanza explains to me, "Everybody clean her own cell. You wash toilet with desinfectante, do sink with cleanser, then you put mattress out in hall and wipe spring with desinfectante. Then you wipe bars, and last you mop floor with desinfectante."

"My luck to get here on cleaning day."

"Cleaning day? We do this every day. That is why I like it. So clean here."

"When will I get to sleep? I'm dying." My eyes hurt, and every noise is like an axe blow to my head.

"You sleep later. Everybody work." There she goes with that "everybody work" business again. The way she seems to relish this place gets on my nerves. Maybe she has a rough time getting by and I feel sorry about that, but she doesn't have a long prison rap hanging over her like I do. They're gonna throw away the key on me for six ounces of pure H. Let her tell me how nice it is in this place if she has something like that to think about.

I clean my cell because that's what I have to do, but then I start thinking it really is pretty comforting to have everything so clean. No telling who or what has been here before me. If I catch anything here, it sure as hell won't be because of filth.

When we're all done and the stuff is back in the closet, I collapse on my bunk. It occurs to me I didn't even ask the matron if I can make a call, or what happens next and when. But I'm too sick to care. I need sleep before I need anything else. At least being here will break that cycle of bennies. Always want to stop, never can – coming down just wrecks you. I can hear the voices going on and on in Spanish, and it seems like they don't ever stop for breath, all talking at once, like marbles clattering in a can. I wish they'd shut up so I can sleep. I wonder where Leon is, and how he feels. Then the sound of the women talking turns into a drone, and my head has a buzz in it, and my mind is drifting, drifting, and I'm in the customs building at the border again. They have taken Leon someplace to search him, and I am in the women's head, stripping, while the woman marshal they called down from El Rincon to search me waits in the other room. She leaves the door open and keeps me in her line of vision, but she looks at a magazine and doesn't watch me. I guess she thinks I'm gonna be embarrassed undressing in front of her, or maybe she's embarrassed herself, but anyway I got plenty of time to throw the package out the window, which is open because of the heat, or stash it in the pipes under the sink. Flushing it down the toilet is out of the question, not only because of the noise but because the package is just too big. Of all things to pop in my mind at this of all times is that the brown heroin in condoms is the shape and size of turds, and I wonder if that's how heroin came to be called shit. Anyway, if I throw it out the window, will the package make a big plop on the ground that the marshal or someone else could hear? It's so damn quiet! If I stash it under the sink it can be seen real easy. Will she spot it, or will she be so intent on searching my body, fuddled with her own embarrassment, that she won't notice it? I'm paralyzed. I stand there, like a fool, in my birthday suit, holding the package in my hand. The marshal asks, from the other room, if I'm ready.

"Yeah."

She comes in and says, "I'm sorry, I have to ask you to bend over." She doesn't even see the package in my hand. Miserably, I hold it out to her. "Is this it?" she says.

"Yeah."

She lays the package on a little table by the sink. "I'm sorry, I have to examine you anyway. To see if there is anything else. I have to do it."

"Yeah." I turn my back to her, bend over.

"Please spread yourself."

I do what she says, she peers up my crack. I expect her to stick her fingers up me – I've heard that's what they do – but she doesn't. "Okay," she says. I wonder why, since she has to do this, she thought it would make any difference not to watch me undress. It doesn't make sense. But that's how people are, I guess. Now, in my bunk, I wonder for the first time why I didn't chuck the package out the window. I was caught dead anyway. What difference would it have made if someone heard the package fall and found it? At least that way there was an outside chance no one would've heard it and I might've got away with it, and they would've had to let us go. I can't believe I did that. I'm cooler than that. Maybe the bennies. Too long without sleep. Maybe being scared. But I been scared before and thought my way out of bad fixes. Why didn't I think my way out this time?

I have a headache and I feel like I have a fever. I'm glued to the mattress with sweat. My head throbs and my throat aches. When I open my eyes Esperanza is sitting on the floor of my cell staring at me with her enormous brown eyes.

"I think I'm sick," I tell her.

"Is no good to lie on mattress. Is too hot. The thing that makes the cool breaks the first day I am here and it is not fix yet. We sleep on floor, is coolest. Señora Webster say it is 110 outside."

I sit up and try to pull my wet clothes away from my skin, but when they come apart in one place they stick somewhere else. Even though my head hurts my mind feels a little clearer. I must have slept a little. I remember that no one has told me yet what happens next. My god, no one knows where I am. How do I make a phone call? When do they tell me when I go to court? How do I get a lawyer?

"Is there some way I can call the matron?"

"She come soon to bring the vegetables. You can talk to her then."

"What vegetables?"

"The señora go every morning to the market. They give her things they cannot sell and she bring them to us. We make our salsita from them."

"You mean rotten vegetables?"

"They are not too much rotten. We cut out the bad place and there is much left we can use."

I'm opening my mouth to say "Not for me, thanks," when I hear the tank door being opened. I jump up and race over there to be sure I catch the matron. Some male prisoners are carrying boxes of produce into the room and putting them on the tables. The women are clustered around the boxes, still chattering. What the hell do they find to talk about for hours on end?

I go up to the matron, who is standing by the door. "Hey, when do I get to make a phone call? And I want to talk to my husband so we can arrange to get a lawyer."

"Your bond hearing is set for later this morning. They just told me. Didn't they let you make a call when they booked you?"

"No."

She doesn't look too pleased about that. "I can't take you down right now but I'll come back for you as soon as I can. If I can't make it back, you can make your phone call when you go to court. You can't talk to your husband. You'll see him in court anyway."

"What do you mean I can't talk to him? We got arrangements to make. We have some rights, you know, and nobody's gonna get anywhere until we've seen a lawyer."

The matron sighs. "I wish that everyone who comes through here didn't feel obliged to tell me they have rights, as if I didn't know. You don't need a lawyer for the bond hearing. It's just a reading of the information and setting of bond. Your lawyer can even get your bond reduced later if you don't think it's fair. You don't have to enter a plea until the arraignment, when your lawyer is present. The sooner you get this hearing over, the sooner you have a chance of getting out, in other words. Take my advice and make your phone call to someone who can post bond for you."

"But why can't I talk to my husband?"

"You'll get to see him in court, I told you. It would be very convenient if we let prisoners visit back and forth, wouldn't it?"

The trusties are waiting for the matron in the hall. She turns and closes the door. I walk over to where Esperanza is standing. She's been watching and listening.

"That woman is a bitch." I'm so mad my eyes are all teared up.

"Señora Webster? Oh no! She is muy simpática, very nice. She bring us Mexican magazines to read, and the vegetables almost every day."

"She was pretty bitchy to me." The effort to keep from crying is making my head feel like it's gonna explode.

"Maybe you are not so nice to her?"

"Whose side are you on, anyway? But forget it. What do you do around here while you wait for something to happen?"

"In the morning we make the salsa. Come, I show you."

I follow Esperanza to the tables. There's a lug of tomatoes, another lug about half full of yellow chiles, and a box full of the outer leaves of lettuce, the bruised ones they usually throw away, and a few onions. Two women are cutting the rotten spots out of the tomatoes and chiles while another is chopping up onions. For the first time I notice a hot plate on a smaller table in the corner. Esperanza's cousin Graciela is heating a large frying pan on it.

"You're allowed to cook in here?"

"We are not suppose to have that. The señora bring it and say we must keep it hide in the afternoon when the big boss of the jail might come."

"How do you hide a thing like that? There's not a corner of this place you can't see into."

"Adelita sit on it when someone come. She is the fattest one."

In spite of my bad mood I have to laugh. "So what are you gonna cook on it?"

"I show you." Esperanza gathers up some of the chiles that have been cleaned of their bruised spots and drops them in the pan.

"Don't you put any grease in it?" Then I realize there is no place for them to get grease and I feel stupid, but Esperanza doesn't seem to notice.

"No grease for peeling chiles. Mira." The chiles are beginning to make little popping noises, and blisters are rising in their skins. "You see? You cannot peel raw chiles unless you blister them like that. It make the skin separate from the meat." Esperanza jiggles the pan like she's popping corn, until the chiles are blistered on all sides. Then she dumps them out on the table and several women begin peeling and chopping them up with spoon handles.

"How can they do that with spoon handles?"

"We sharp them on the cement floor. We are not allow to have knife."

"I never would have thought of that."

"Yes, I think you do sometime. Plenty time to think here. You think good when you need something."

I suppose she's right. "So what next?"

"We chop tomato and onion and chile all together, add a puñito of salt. With lettuce we make a little salad if tomatoes not too bad."

"All very interesting, but not very appetizing, to tell the truth. Look, I've got to sleep now. Don't wake me up for any more work, okay?"

"Is no work to do now, unless you want to help with the salsa."

"No, I don't want to help with the salsa."

In my cell I take Esperanza's advice and lie on the concrete floor. Even so, it's too hot to sleep, even if I could get comfortable. I wonder what Leon is doing. Probably scheming and dealing with the men prisoners for privileges. He wouldn't let any of this get to him. He'll be cool. Wherever he is, he'll run the show. But the one thing he can't do now is rescue me from what I'm gonna have to go through. Somehow it always seemed like Leon could do anything. I always felt so safe, I just left everything to him and did what he said. Now look at me. But that's ungrateful. Remember Tuffy! Leon picked me up and hid me after Tuffy beat me up because I wouldn't put my ass on the street. I was heartsick and bruised and hopeless and Leon washed my face and told me I didn't have to come out of that room until I wanted to. And he made such sweet beautiful love to me, morning, noon, and night. Oh god, I can't think about that now. How can I be getting all horny in the spot I'm in?

I comfort myself with thinking about making love to Leon and the men he brought home to "worship at my shrine," as he put it. But you can only keep something like that up for so long, and my mind begins to wander to other things. The dream comes back to me. Funny thing about that dream. It's almost like what really happened, except in the dream Leon wasn't with me, and when I was really making the drive I just didn't notice things. There really were headlights behind me when I drove out of TJ, but they stopped when I got to the part of the road – oh god – they stopped when I got to the part of the road where you can't turn off any more until you get to Tecate. They just sat there a while and then turned around and went back. I saw all that. I was watching them in the rearview mirror, because when you're carrying shit of course you're righteously paranoid. When they stopped and went back I figured it was nothing. But the sentry, or whatever he was, did pick up the phone after we went by. He did look at our car. And it made me feel funny, but I figured it's because I'm paranoid.

Something else flashes on me, but it wasn't in the dream. About an hour before I left TJ I was in the apartment taking a shower and someone knocked on the door. I figured it was Leon. He has his own key of course but he always has me bolt the door because in TJ you never know. So I grabbed a towel and wrapped it around me and went to the door and opened it with a big smile, because I had this big plan to act surprised and drop the towel. But it wasn't Leon. It was Rogelio, a flunky for the dealer we pick up from. I hung on to the towel of course but it wasn't covering any more than it ought to. He looked me over real good and then he handed me a big can of milk sugar. He said it was for cutting the stuff, which seemed pretty weird to me, because of course I'm not gonna carry a big old can of milk sugar across the border with me, but I took it and thanked him. Before I closed the door he asked me how I liked the Caddy, and I said just fine. Then I closed the door because I figured he wanted to come in and Leon would cut his throat if he found him there. He likes me to ball other men, all right, but only the ones he picks and when he's there. I told Leon all this later and we laughed about it. We just figured he had the hots for me. But now it seems really peculiar to me. Why did he ask about the Caddy?

This is a dead end so I go back to the dream. Of course I didn't run down any alley in Mexicali but I thought about it. It was only for a second, just because I'm always scared when I come up to the border. But come to think of it, this time I considered hiding the stuff in an alley and making a dry run across the border just to make sure everything was cool. Why did I think that? I never thought of it before.

But the strangest thing isn't in the dream. The strangest thing is that I stood there like an ass when I had a chance to throw that shit out the window. I still can't believe I did that. And now that I think of it, all those signals add up to: something stinks. Maybe Rogelio came over on an excuse to check out the car I was driving. It's happened before. The customs pays informers working for a dealer on the other side to tip them off to the big loads coming over the border. Sure. If he tipped them off they would follow me, and there was no point in following me after I couldn't go anywhere else but Tecate or Mexicali. And the sentry called to say I was headed for Mexicali, since I didn't go to Tecate. How could I ignore all that? I guess I didn't ignore it completely, because something told me to ditch the stuff before going over. Why did I ignore that feeling? But the weirdest of all the weird things is that I didn't throw that stuff out the window when I had a chance. I set myself up, is what I did. There's no way to get around it. I set myself up. I knew it was coming and I just kept on going. I just can't believe this, but it can't be anything else. Only an idiot would have missed all those signals. I didn't miss them, anyhow. I picked up on them and kept going. Why did I do that? I need to do a lot more thinking about all this, but the sounds of the door and the food cart bring me back to the present. I realize that my stomach hurts from hunger. The toast filled my shrunk-up stomach this morning, but it didn't last long. I walk to the cart, but before I can pick up a tray the matron calls me. "Get ready to go to court, Bagliazo. I'll wait for you."

"I haven't eaten."

"Shall I ask the court to put off your hearing?"

What a bitch! "My clothes are soaked in front where I was lying down. I can't go like this."

"You didn't have any other clothes with you?"

"No."

"Then there's nothing we can do about it. Get your shoes."

"I don't have any. I was barefoot, and they left my shoes in the car."

"Then I guess you're as ready as you're going to get. Come on."

I'm so mad I'm about to cry again. How fucking humiliating. I follow the matron, my jersey blouse sticking to my belly and my breasts, and I have wet streaks on my thighs and over my crotch. No matter what I do I can't squelch the tears, so I keep smearing them to make them blend with the sweat. They aren't gonna have the satisfaction of seeing me cry, goddam it. But the effort is making my throat hurt.

In the courtroom it's just as hot as in the jail, and the sweat trickles down my legs and leaves streaks in the dust on my feet. It looks like I peed myself. The cops in the courtroom look me over like some slave on the block. They don't make any effort to hide what they're thinking about. Leon likes men to look at me like that. It makes him hot. But right now I just hate it. When they bring Leon in I fasten my eyes on him like lichens to a rock. I feel like I'm gonna go under any minute. I don't think I ever knew what scared was until right now.

I thought Leon would make some sign to me, smile or say something, but his face is a completely blank mask. His eyes light on mine for just a second but they're like marbles, I can't get a thing from them. I take my cue from him, like always, and stifle my emotions and stare straight ahead, just like him. We may be busted, but we'll show them we ain't bent.

The hearing is simple. It starts off a little bad for me because the first thing the judge asks us is if we waive counsel for this hearing, and since I don't even know what's supposed to happen that scares me, but Leon nods his head yes and so I do too, because I don't know what good it would do me to say I want a lawyer. Then the judge reads the charges. We are charged with conspiracy to import heroin without declaring it for the purpose of having duty imposed on it. Strange charge. I wonder if we had declared it and paid duty, could we have brought it across? Then he sets our bond at $250,000 for each of us, and that hits me hard. Who does he think he has here, Al Capone or somebody? I sneak a look at Leon to see how he is reacting, but of course he isn't reacting at all.

Then the judge asks us if we have the means to retain a lawyer, because if not, he'll appoint one for us. I glance at Leon again. He says he will get a lawyer. That makes me feel a lot better. He must have things under control. What was I so edgy about? The judge says our arraignment will be on July 3, and then, before I have a chance to think, the marshal has led me out and they've taken Leon out the other door and I never get to say one word to him.

Mrs. Webster is waiting in the corridor and she takes me to make my phone call. I can't think of anybody to call except David. We ran away together when we were in high school. He's the only person I can think of I could stand to tell what's going on. No one else I ever knew knows what kind of life I'm living. Luckily information has his number, but I don't get an answer. Mrs. Webster says I can try again later, and takes me back to the cell block. There's something very scary about no one knowing I'm here. If they want to they can close that door on me and never let me out and no one would ever know. Who would miss me, anyway? David might wonder about me sometimes. But he wouldn't start looking. I haven't been to see him for a long time.

That damned Esperanza is on my bunk waiting for me. "How it went?"

"It went lousy," I bark at her. "How the hell is it supposed to go, just peachy? And I want to tell you something. I'm sick of you coming around here telling me how great it is in this fucking jail. You can stay here your whole goddam life if you think it's so great. I hate it here, it's lousy, the whole thing stinks, it's like being dead. Nobody knows I'm here, do you know that? And your goddam sister doesn't even know you're here. She maybe thinks you're dead or abandoned your kids, or god knows what. I'm half nuts and I only been here one day. In a week I'll be out of my fucking mind. And I got years to do probably. So stop following me around telling me how much you love this goddam jail!"

Esperanza has been listening to all this with such a look of surprise and grief on her face that before I even finish I'm feeling guilty. She slips off my bunk and glides quickly out of the cell. (That's another thing I can't stand, how she doesn't make any noise when she moves.) How come she looked like that? You'd think she'd never been yelled at before. You'd think I hit her or something. Well, goddam it, I didn't hit her, I just yelled at her, and she had it coming. I didn't ask her to appoint herself my goddam friend. But the longer I sit there, the worse I feel. Her face just won't get out of my mind. After a while I calm down a little, and I think maybe I was a little rough on her. Finally I go to find her. She's lying on her bunk staring at the springs of the bunk above her.

"Esperanza, I'm sorry. It's just the shock of the whole thing, you know, court and all, and being sick from the bennies."

"But what you say is true, Toni. This place is bad place for you. Life was good for you out there, and you have lose much by coming here. With me, is different. Life is better here. I don't have to worry about having something to eat. I have clean place to sleep and I don't have to work hard. Is the same with the other women here. We are born in different worlds, you and me, Toni. We both come to this place and for you is bad and for me is good, yet is exactly the same place. This is what I am think about."

I didn't expect anything like that from her and I don't know what to say. We just look at each other for a minute. Then Esperanza says, "I save tray for you. Is cold now, but there is not much to eat at evening so maybe you get very hungry."

I look at the tray balanced on the sink. Beans and hominy. Esperanza sees my expression and says, "Is not bad with a little salsita." She holds out the salsa she has been saving for me in her aluminum drinking cup. For some reason this makes me laugh, I don't know why. "You and your goddam salsita," I say, but she knows how I mean it and she laughs too.

I pour some of the salsa on the beans and try a spoonful. It's tasty even though the cold hominy gags me a little. I probably couldn't swallow this shit without the cover of salsa. Oh god, I'm gonna cry again. I shove another spoonful in my mouth to gag the sobs. When I'm back in control, I look at Esperanza, who is just sitting there watching me eat. Whenever she isn't talking she has this godawful sad expression on her face. That's all I need. I gotta get out of here. "Esperanza, I'm gonna go to my cell to eat. I just got so much to think about, you know? It was real nice of you to save my tray. I really appreciate it, honest."

"Sure, Toni. See you later."

"Yeah, that's for sure. See you later."

No one is in their cells on my row. They are all over in the big room. It's not quite like being alone, but probably as alone as I'm gonna get for a long time – but then in another way I never been so alone. God I got the weepies. I better just finish this stuff, whatever it is, 'cause that's part of what's wrong with me, I think. Too hungry.

After I eat I feel a lot better. Calmer too. I lie on my back on the floor to think some more about that dream and all that stuff about setting myself up. Funny, it doesn't seem to make any difference now. It must be the food. I feel really relaxed. On the other side of the cell block some of the women are singing "Noche de Ronda." I know that one. You get more than two Mexicans together anywhere with more than one drink in them and they're gonna sing "Noche de Ronda." The women's voices are soft and sweet now. The food must have mellowed them out too. No more high-speed grating yakety-yak. They finish "Noche de Ronda" and begin "Tu Solo Tu." Of course. The first two mandatory songs of any Chicano songfest. I'm only drunk because of you, the song says. I'm only drunk and disenchanted and desperate because of you. Blame the woman. Sigh. The singing is really soothing. But of course the bennies are getting out of my system too. I've been wound up like a twisted rubber band for weeks now. It's good to feel loose. One thing about being here that's good anyway. I'll never touch one of those damn things again.

Funny how Leon was in court. That stone face. He was like that at the border after they stopped us, too. You'd think he didn't know me. The only sign he made to me after they took us out of the car was to nod toward my breasts when the customs guys weren't looking. When I nodded back yes, it was still in my bra, he looked relieved and turned away. He never looked at me again until they separated us. Why did he act like that? Part of it, I know, is just a way of keeping himself secret from the Man, but he cut himself off from me too, and of all times to do it. Here I am going to prison for sure for running dope for him, and he can't even give me a warm look? I feel like I'm drowning in loneliness and resentment, and this time I don't even try to keep back the sobs. I been doing it all day and I'm worn out with it. I roll over on my stomach, bury my face in my arms, and cry until I'm exhausted.

When it's all out of my system I just lie there. I'm getting used to this concrete. It's actually beginning to feel good to me. Cooler than anything else around here, just like Esperanza says. For some reason when I think of Esperanza I smile. Bugging me to death all the time. I wonder how come she likes me, anyway? I been nothing but snotty to her mostly. Maybe she's just a kind person. Yeah, maybe she is just a truly kind person.

It feels good to just lie here. I don't have to make a run to L.A. tonight. I can't believe how glad that makes me feel. But I enjoy those trips! They're exciting, and I feel like some big racketeer, pretty glamorous. And it isn't boring, like every job I ever had. But the fact of the matter is I'm tired. Really tired. Boy, it feels like my body could melt right into this concrete. Driving all night, and then the bennies don't let me sleep even when I have a chance. And Leon with his sex parties, even when I'm worn out. I really loved it at first, and he made me feel like a goddess. He *told* me I was a goddess. And I never knew anything so exciting before, like having two or three guys make love to me. But if he worshipped me like he said, how come he never cared if I was so tired I could hardly talk? Drop a couple of beans, he'd say, and we'd be off again. And then my poor pussy would get so dry from the bennies I'd end up all sore and miserable. At least my pussy can get a rest now. No men around here. I'm surprised how relieved I feel when I say that. No men! I must really be tired. Not just tired from last night and today, but tired from a long time. Tired of being scared all the time. Oh god, did I say that? Scared all the time? Well, I guess I am. Scared of getting busted. I don't have to worry about that anymore! But the fact is, I'm scared when he gets that look on his face, that no-look. He told me once he'd killed thirty-seven men. I never really believed him, it sounded crazy to me, macho bad-guy bragging, but maybe somewhere inside I was afraid it might be true. Did I ever not do something he said? I don't think so. I never had the nerve to find out what would happen if I didn't do what he wanted. Scared. Oh god. Maybe that's why I set myself up.

Where's all this coming from? I feel like I can't handle any more just now, and I try to think about something else. Esperanza. I smile again. Why do I keep smiling when I think of her? Because she's funny, partly. Her and her goddam "nice" jail. She sure surprised me with all that stuff she said about seeing this place different because we come from different worlds. She's right too. She must be pretty smart. In a lot of ways. She's a goddam survivor, that's for sure. At first I thought she was stupid to be happy in jail, but maybe it's a sort of courage. It takes a lot of guts to make the best of things here. It's the pits, and that's the truth. One thing for sure, I'm gonna need a friend like her around here, and I guess I should count myself lucky that she likes me.

I seem to be all thought out for a while, although my thinking sure isn't over yet. When I open my eyes later I realize I been asleep. I feel a little mellower, and empty somehow. It's a good kind of emptiness, like what was filling me up was poison. I need company now. I go look for Esperanza and find her resting in her cell. Naturally, she gets this big smile when I walk in.

"Esperanza, I want you to do me a favor."

"Yes, Toni?"

"Tomorrow I want you to show me how to make this salsita of yours. Maybe I can put it on the goddam oatmeal."

Standing Up
For Leon

We can't promise you anything, but if you cooperate with us a report to that effect will be in your file, and the judge will see it before he sentences you. That doesn't mean you'll be given any consideration because you cooperate, understand? We can't promise you that. I'm just saying the judge will know about it."

"I understand."

"You've been read your rights?"

"Yes."

"You understand you don't have to talk to us without an attorney present?"

"Yes."

"Are you willing to cooperate?"

"Yes. It's the only way I'm gonna be able to prove Leon had nothing to do with this." That Leon had nothing to do with this is an outrageous lie, of course, and I watch the two narcotics men closely to see how they take it. But they have expressionless cop faces and I can't tell how they feel about what I've said.

"Leon Fuentes was in the car with you when you crossed the border and were arrested. Are you claiming he knew nothing about the heroin you were carrying?"

"That's right." This is the one thing I've thought about ahead of time. I made up my mind that I'm gonna stand up for Leon, no matter what. I feel like it's my fault we got busted, that if I had just listened to all the signals I was getting that something was wrong, we wouldn't be here now.

"What was he doing in the car?"

"I was taking him to visit his mother in L.A."

"You were carrying the heroin in your bra, is that right?"

"Yes."

The guy who is asking me the questions writes some stuff on a yellow legal pad in front of him. The other guy is smoking a cigar and staring at me. I think he's trying to make me feel uncomfortable. The hell with him.

"Where were you going to deliver the heroin?"

"L.A."

"C'mon now. Who paid you to bring over this load?"

"A dealer in L.A." My mind is racing. I wasn't ready for this interrogation. It never occurred to me I'd be questioned, because I forgot they don't know that Leon and I are it, there's nobody else involved on this side of the border. When Mrs. Webster came to get me and bring me downstairs I couldn't get her to tell me what was up. I didn't know until I walked into this room and saw the two men in sport shirts, sweating and looking hot and mean, that I was gonna be questioned. Now I realize how stupid I've been. I was so tied up with fright and misery I wasn't thinking. I should have been working on my story. Now I've got to make up for lost time, make things up as I go along, and I have to stall while I think.

The cop says, "What's his name?"

Under the pressure of my panic someone pops into my mind, someone I saw once. They probably won't ever locate the actual guy I'm thinking of. "Pinky."

"Pinky what?"

"I don't know, I never knew him as anything but Pinky."

"What's he look like?"

"He's a light-skinned black man with reddish freckles. He's got light hair too. It's because of his skin they call him Pinky."

"How old a man is he?"

"I don't know. Thirty. Forty, maybe."

"Okay. Where do we find him?"

The words are out before I can think. "He has a little cafe near the railroad tracks down near Salamander Street." I'm describing the cafe that the man I'm talking about actually runs. It's going too fast and I don't have time to make things up.

"He's wholesaling drugs out of that cafe?"

"Yeah."

"How long you been working for this guy?"

"This was my first run, actually." I'm not gonna tell them I'm a pro at this.

"How did this come about?"

"I hang out at the cafe sometimes. He asked me one night if I'd like to make some good money and I said yes."

"What's the address of this cafe?"

"I don't know. I just know where it is."

"We've got railroad tracks and we've got Salamander Street. We'll find it." He gets up and gathers his papers. "We may need to come back and ask you more questions later. Thank you for your cooperation."

"Do I stay here, or what?"

"We'll send someone in to take you back upstairs."

When they walk out of the room I try to get a grip on what's happening. I knew from the beginning I was gonna try to protect Leon. They got nothing on him except that he was in the car with me. If I say he doesn't know anything about it, what can they do? But I meant to give them a description of someone that doesn't exist. God.

Your lawyer is here to see you," says Mrs. Webster. My heart jumps. Leon got a lawyer! I run my fingers through my hair. God, I must look awful. They never brought me my stuff from the car and I haven't combed my hair for four days. Well, I can't do anything about it. I follow Mrs. Webster downstairs to the same room where I met with the narcotics men.

The lawyer is cut from the same mold as the narcotics guys, except he's fat. He's wearing a sport shirt, smoking a cigar, and he's sweaty and blank-faced. "I'm Sam Pendleton," he says, and hands me a business card. "I talked to Leon this morning, and he retained me to represent you both. Is that all right with you?"

All right? God, of course it's all right. "Yes."

"Good. Let's get started. First, you need to tell me everything about your arrest, and what your involvement is, and what your relationship with Leon is, both personally and in terms of this drug business. I need to verify all the information on the arrest report. Okay?"

"Yes."

"It's important that you level with me on everything. I don't want any surprises in court. Tell me what you said to the police, and if any of it's different from the facts, I need to know that or I can't do a good job of defending you. Okay?"

"Yes. The main thing is I've told them that Leon didn't have anything to do with it. But he did. It was his money, and his drugs. But I don't want him to go to jail, and I'm gonna say he didn't have anything to do with it."

The man sits back and stares at me. I'm wondering if I just made a terrible mistake. It made sense to me when he said he needed to know the truth so he can be prepared in court. He's paid to be on our side, isn't he? But he's looking at me now with this blank unreadable look, just like the cop. I start feeling nervous. I feel like I need to explain. "Leon has done a lot for me. I owe him a lot. I don't want to get into details, but he saved my ass a while back. He took me in when I didn't even have a place to sleep, he rescued me from a guy who wanted to put me on the street, a guy who was beating me up. I've got to stand up for him now."

He says, "You want to plead guilty?"

"I don't have much choice, do I?"

"Not if this information is correct. You had the drugs on your person?"

"Yes."

"All right. What we'll do is, we'll plead you innocent at the arraignment so that you'll be held over for trial with Leon. Otherwise, you see, you'll be sentenced and shipped off somewhere and it will be very difficult to get you back as a witness. At the time of trial we'll just change your plea to guilty."

He *is* on our side! I'm so relieved I break into a big smile. "Okay," I say. Then I tell him the whole story, and we go over the police report. He tells me we'll be arraigned in San Rudolfo, since that's the closest federal court. Just as he's getting ready to go, I say, "Our bail is set at $250,000 each. That seems awful high to me. The matron here said sometimes a lawyer can get it reduced. Can you do that?"

"I doubt it. Six and a half ounces of pure uncut heroin is a lot of smack." He picks up his briefcase and walks out the door. People are getting busted with warehouses full of cocaine and he thinks six ounces of heroin is a lot? The judge thought so too, or he wouldn't have set our bail so high. I don't get it.

Well, what am I thinking of, anyway? I couldn't make bail if he got it reduced to a hundred dollars, and I don't think Leon had all that much money on him. He put almost everything he had into the drug buy, and whatever's left is probably going to the lawyer.

I'm sitting in the corridor by the barred door that opens into the stairwell. It's one place where a little air stirs once in a while. Sometimes if a door is opened down below it creates a draft for a minute or two. I'm passing the day by singing, and I have half a hope that Leon can hear me, down there in the men's section. I sing his favorite, "Weeping Willow Tree," as a message of love.

I'm still sitting there when the male trusties come up the stairs with the lunch trays. They don't come in this door. They go around a corner to the main entrance to the tank. Mrs. Webster leads them, as always, and as she passes she says, "Hello, Toni." When she's out of sight around the corner one of the men tosses a small matchbox through the bars to me. He looks at me intently as he passes.

I pick up the matchbox and race to my cell to read it. My heart is thumping.

> *Hey sweetness. I'm doing OK. Did you see the lawyer? Some guy in here gave me his name, said he's a real good criminal lawyer. I think about you all the time, how sweet you taste. I told the guys down here about you. ALL about you. When we hear you singing I say, that's my chick, man.*

What does he mean, *all* about me? Is that why the guy who passed me the note looked at me so hard? God. All the men in the jail know about me. Know what? I know perfectly well what. It's exciting. Exciting that Leon talks about me like that, exciting that he writes me such a risky note. What if the cops got hold of it?

I'd love it.

Someone is shaking me. I have a hard time getting conscious. At last I squint into the light and see that it's the night matron and two male cops. "Get up, Bagliazo, you're moving out."

"What?"

"Get your shoes on. Get your stuff together. Do you need a paper bag?"

"I don't have anything. I don't have any shoes. Where am I going?"

"Your shoes may be in the office downstairs. Mrs. Webster told me someone might drop them off. I forgot about it. We can check on the way out. C'mon, let's go. Do you need to use the toilet?"

"Yes."

"Well, do that and we'll meet you at the door. Make it snappy."

They move out, leaving my cell door open, and I get up and splash water on my face. Where the hell could they be taking me? What about Leon? It's the middle of the night. I don't like this. Why would they be taking me somewhere in the middle of the night? It's very weird and it frightens me badly. But I don't know what I can do about it. I use the toilet and go to the door. The matron is holding a paper bag. She says, "While we waited I went down and checked the office. These were on Mrs. Webster's desk. Are they yours?"

I open the bag and it's the shoes I left in the front of the car. I guess Mrs. Webster talked someone into getting them for me. The matron says, "You have a suitcase down there too, with your name on it. But the shoes weren't tagged and I wasn't sure about them."

"These are them."

"Good. Let's get going then." As we go through the building, I see a clock that says it's a little before 5:00 A.M. Outside, there's a car waiting with its motor running. I'm put in the back seat with a woman marshal and we take off immediately.

There's just a faint beginning of dawn in the sky. I'm not used to such intense heat at this hour. It feels unnatural and adds to my something's-not-right feeling. I huddle against the window and watch the gray shapes in the desert take on color as the sky lightens.

When the matron told me about my suitcase I should have asked about the car. What's gonna happen to it? And what about Leon? Is he being taken somewhere too, or is he still at the El Rincon jail? Not knowing where he is scares me. He's my only anchor in all this. If I lose touch with him I don't know if I can keep my grip.

But I feel a little better by the time the sun comes up. Everything has its true color now, but after only a few days in jail the landscape looks strange to me, like a movie I can see but can't touch. Unattainable and not real. I gobble it up with my eyes because I know it may be a long time before I get to have as much as I want of it again. I never thought much about the outdoors before, trees especially, and now I'm looking at trees with pangs of longing.

Our destination turns out to be the San Rudolfo City Jail. I'm fingerprinted and mugged all over again. They go over my personal property envelope, and tell me I can keep five dollars with me. They tell me that even though they can see for themselves I haven't got a single fucking dime. Just a platinum watch worth over a thousand bucks that Leon bought me. I nearly cry as I watch it disappear into the envelope. Then I have to strip and shower, and they take all my clothes away from me except my underwear and shoes. I'm made to bend over while a matron probes up my cunt – what could I possibly smuggle in here when I haven't been anywhere but in jail? Then I have to wash my underwear while they watch. A matron inspects me everywhere there's hair for lice and crabs, and even though I don't have any, she loads my hair with louse powder and wraps it in a towel. I'm given a faded blue denim jail dress that's almost worn out. Four other women have been processed with me, and we end up all looking alike in our blue denim dresses and with our heads wrapped in city jail towels to keep the louse powder from shaking out all over everything.

They process us like we're filthy animals with no feelings, no self-respect. This is the lowest I've ever felt in my life. The way they talk to me doesn't help either. I ask one of the officers how I can find out where Leon is, and she says, "If they want you to know they'll tell you."

"Who's 'they'?" No answer. I say, "I got to talk to Leon before we go to trial. How do I do that?"

"Your lawyer will arrange all that."

"When do I go to court?"

"Your lawyer will let you know. We don't know, that's not our business."

"I never had any breakfast. When do I get to eat?"

"It's almost lunch time. You'll get to eat then."

I ask to make a phone call, thinking I'll try David again, but they say no. Nobody knows where I am, maybe not even Leon. He might still be in El Rincon, for all I know.

At last I'm taken into a huge room with a ceiling high enough for two tiers of cells along one wall. In the open area along the other wall there are wooden tables and benches, and about twenty women, all in blue denim dresses, are clustered around the tables, playing cards or just talking. The place resembles a dark and dingy warehouse. The walls are cream but turning piss color with grime. They don't look like they've been painted for forty years. The room is lit by electric bulbs in the ceiling. The only daylight comes from one tiny window high up in one corner. No one seems to be locked in the cells.

One of the matrons, a huge stupid-looking woman built like a tank, walks me up the stairs to the upper tier. She holds me too tight by my upper arm, and lifts up on it so that my shoulder is hiked up too high and it's hard to walk. I don't understand what this is about and I glance at her, about to ask her what she thinks she's doing, but she stares into my face with an expression so terrified and dangerous that I know instantly I mustn't say or do anything that will give her an excuse to bash my head in. She takes me along the ramp to the cell at the far end from the stairs and locks me in.

None of the other women are locked in their cells, and I wonder what's going on. But maybe this is something they do with new prisoners. I sit on my bunk and examine my cell. The walls are dirty and covered with graffiti scratched in the paint. The basic design is the same as in El Rincon: a sink and a toilet and two bunks, one above the other. The mattresses are thinner and older, but seem clean enough.

I climb on the upper bunk and try to see downstairs. I'm curious about the other women here. But the ramp is in the way. What a drag. I can't even watch what's going on. I settle into the only thing I have to do: worry.

In about an hour I hear the big door to the tank open – what a clanging it makes! – and some commotion downstairs. In a few minutes I hear someone coming along the ramp. It's a prisoner with a big metal cup and a metal plate with a big chunk of bread on it. She hands it to me through a square hole in the cell door that seems to be made just for passing things through. "Here's lunch," she says.

"When do I get let out of here?"

"I don't know. You're in the isolation cell. If you're in isolation, you don't get let out. I'm not supposed to talk to you." She walks away.

What the hell does this mean? I feel like I'm gonna pop a gasket with not knowing what's going on. If they'd just tell me what's going on I could handle it. It's this not knowing that's making me crazy.

I sit down on my bunk with my food. The cup has a watery soup in it, and one whole turnip. They didn't even bother to cut it up. I hate turnips. Who eats turnips? Prisoners, I say to myself. Ha ha. I drink the hot water, which is all the soup amounts to, and leave the turnip. I eat the bread, which tastes funny and turns to glue once I start chewing it. Afterwards I lie down on my bunk and stare at the springs of the bunk above me. The afternoon goes by, minute by eternal minute. At supper time I'm brought a tray with a big helping of spaghetti and I think, Ah, this is more like it. But the spaghetti is cold and cooked without salt, yet with so much pepper I can hardly stand to eat it. God. I settle for the bread again, and some bad coffee. At least the coffee's hot.

The evening goes by the same way – minute by eternal minute – and I try to occupy my mind by listening to snatches of conversation that drift up to me from the women below. Finally the lights flicker, which seems to be a signal for all the women to go to their cells. In a few minutes I hear cell doors slamming and keys turning in the locks. A matron appears in front of my cell long enough to look in at me, then disappears. The lights go out. It's incredibly dark in this place, but I'm glad for it. I want sleep more than anything, so I can forget about where I am and escape from the minute-by-miserable-minute boredom. In the dark at last I cry easily and long, and finally drift away.

I'm blasted out of sleep with a blare of lights and yelling. I'm so startled I jump out of my bunk. A cell door slams and the lights go out again, but the yelling goes on. A drunk. I'm so pumped up with adrenaline I can't go back to sleep. Just as well, because in another little while the whole thing is repeated, and then repeated again and again, for hours.

I don't know what I expected, but this isn't it. I thought El Rincon was bad. I'd give anything to go back there now.

I'm bludgeoned out of sleep by screechy voices singing at top volume: "The church's one foundation / Is Jesus Christ, our Lord / She is his new creation / By water and the word / From heaven he came and sought her / To be his holy bride . . ."

What the hell is going on here? It must be Sunday. They must have services in here on Sunday. God, I'd even go to services if they'd let me out of this goddam cell, that's how desperate I am.

I have a headache. I couldn't have been asleep more than a couple of hours. I remember I saw a trace of dawn through that tiny window before I nodded off.

I lie back down on my bunk and listen to the hymns. Awful. Some of them I haven't heard since I was a kid.

"Stand up, stand up for Jesus / Ye soldiers of the cross / Lift high his royal banner / It must not suffer loss / From victory unto victory / His army shall he lead / Till every foe is vanquished / And Christ is Lord indeed."

God, these people mean business. Then I hear a woman's voice talking, then some more hymns, and then the normal noise of the tank starts up and I know the service is over.

In a minute three women appear at my cell. "Good morning, sister!" one of them chirps. She's beautiful, in a Barbie Doll sort

117

of way, but wearing a dress that looks like it's left over from the forties – too long and baggy, and with an honest-to-god lace collar on it. She's clutching a Bible. The two women with her are young, probably in their teens, and look frightened. I get up and face them through the bars, not knowing what else to do. "They told us downstairs you were locked up here all by yourself," she says. "We came up to pray with you."

"I'm not really into that," I mumble.

"The Lord will hold you and help you in your time of trial," she says, reaching a hand through the bars. She wants me to give her my hand, but I'm not gonna do it. I just stand there looking at her. She withdraws her hand without changing her bright little Jesus-loving expression.

"Is there anything you need, sister?"

"What do you mean?"

"We have combs, and writing paper, and toothbrushes and toothpaste."

I consider this. If I accept these things, will I have to pray? I decide it's a price I can pay, I'm so desperate to be clean. Maybe I can write a letter to Leon. "I don't have any of those things."

She reaches into a big tote bag and pulls out a comb, a toothbrush and toothpaste, a writing pad and pencil. "Would you like a nice bar of sweet-smelling soap, 'stead of that scouring stuff they give you?"

"Yes, thank you."

So she rummages and comes up with a sample size bar of Camay. She also hands me a miniature Bible. "You'll find comfort in this, sister, if you'll let yourself. We'll be back next Sunday, if you're still here. We're going to pray for you, meantime. May we have your name, so we can recommend you to the Heavenly Father?"

I consider refusing to give it to her. But I've got all this stuff she gave me. I've already been bought. "Toni."

"God needs your last name to know who we're praying for, sister."

"Smith."

"Goodbye and God bless, Toni Smith. We'll see you next Sunday."

God. Talk about a captive audience.

By the fourth day in San Rudolfo I've sunk into a stupefied depression. I thought I was depressed before, but it's nothing compared to this. No one to talk to all the goddam day. Nothing to read. The only diversion I got is trying to listen to the conversations downstairs, but most of the time I can't hear them. When I do hear them it's when they talk loud because of an argument, and it's always over some trivial damn thing.

"Get out of my space, girl."

"Who you talking to?"

"You."

"I ain't in your space."

"You got your elbow in my space at this table."

"I ain't in your space. You taking up the whole goddam table."

"You're in my space, and I say get out of it."

And so on.

But on the fifth day a matron appears at my cell. She says, "We've got a hundred dollars for you, Bagliazo. You can check it out five dollars at a time. I brought it up for you, so I need you to sign this withdrawal slip. And I've got a letter for you."

A hundred dollars! It's got to be from Leon. So he knows where I am, and the letter's got to be from him, and I'll know where he is. My hand shakes and I can hardly sign the slip for the money. She hands me the letter and I see from the envelope that Leon is right here in the San Rudolfo City Jail, and I nearly faint with joy. The matron is walking away before I remember to call out to her, "Hey! Why am I locked up all the time? When do I get let out like the other prisoners?"

"You're in isolation, Bagliazo. You'll get let out when they say you can get out."

Fine. That explains everything. But I'm so happy to have a letter from Leon I can't get upset just now. I sit down on my bunk and open it. The envelope's already open. I guess that means they read all our letters. God.

Dear Babes

How they treating you over here? I sent some money over to you with Pendleton so you can get what you need. Pendleton was here? How come he didn't come talk to me? *I'm playing*

a lot of cards. Doing okay with that. I bet he means he's winning money. He can't say so in a letter. *I think of you all the
time, mama, I remember you in your little apron, cooking for me.*

Oh god. He used to like me to dress up in a garter belt with
black stockings, high heels, and a little maid's apron, and nothing
else. What a lot of nerve he has, writing like this to me in jail
where people read your mail. But they won't know what he's
talking about. I'm all giggly with excitement, and I'm happy
now, and I read the rest of the letter, which is all just a lot of detail
about life in the jail, and then I lie back and close my eyes and feel
happy. If I can just have letters from Leon I can stand this. Not
'til now does it hit me: what good does the hundred dollars do
me? They never let me out of this cage. Leon isn't locked up like
this or he couldn't play cards. What the hell is going on?

I'm lying on my bunk with my eyes closed and I hear this snapping noise real close by. I open my eyes and turn my head and
here's this prisoner standing outside my cell looking in at me.
She's chewing gum with her mouth open, like a little kid, which
is what the snapping noise is. That's not the only little-kid thing
about her. She's not much more than five feet tall, wiry. Her
blue denim jail dress hangs on her like a sack. They must not've
had one small enough for her. She's barefoot, and a little bit
bowlegged, and she looks like a waif. She's got a face that's hard,
but pretty, with big green eyes. The prettiest thing about her is
her black hair, as thick as Little Orphan Annie's, standing up in
ringlets all over her head.

After we stare at each other a moment, she says, "How
y'doing?"

Sitting up, I say, "I'm surviving."

"You want some candy or something from the candy wagon?"

"Yeah! I didn't know you could buy candy. I been living on
nothing but that goddam bread. I can't eat this shit they call
food."

"Awful, ain't it? You got some money?"

"Yeah. How much you need?"

"Tell me what you need, first."

"What've they got?"

"Candy, potato chips and corn chips, cigarettes, combs and

toothbrushes, writing paper, stuff like that. That last stuff, you can get it from the church ladies if you don't have much money."

"I found that out. The price is too high though."

"Aw, they're all right. You don't see nobody else caring if we can brush our funky green teeth or not, do you? That main lady, she's a alcoholic. She says Jesus saved her."

"Well, Jesus isn't gonna save me."

"Me neither. I'm just saying, whatever works, y'know? Different strokes for different folks. So what do you want from the candy wagon?"

"How often do you get to go? So I know how much stuff to get."

"We don't go. They bring it to the tank door every day except Sunday. I'll get something every day if you want."

"God, that's really nice of you."

"No trouble. I go anyway."

"Well, get me two candy bars, I don't care what kind, and a pack of Virginia Slims. Will two dollars cover it?"

"Yeah."

"How do I get a matron's attention? They don't even come to my cell from one day to the next. I could die in here and they wouldn't know."

"Aw, you'd start to smell and somebody would notice eventually, unless they thought it was just the food. We call 'em screws around here."

"Screws?" I laugh. "Why screws?"

"Cuz they're always screwing us, I guess. What do you need a matron for? The less them cow-brains notice you the better off you are."

"I'm constipated real bad. I need a laxative. It's that goddam bread I'm living on."

"I'll tell 'em you need to go to the sick wagon. It comes every day too, like the candy wagon. You can get shit pills and aspirin, mostly."

"They bring a whole wagon just for laxatives and aspirin?"

"Naw, they got all the medication people are supposed to be taking. People take thyroid and insulin and stuff. They can't keep that junk in here, so they got a nurse with a wagon comes every day to give it to 'em. Actually I could get the shit pills for you, unless you just want to get out of here for a few minutes."

"Yeah, I do. Even a minute or two would be a relief. Listen, are you supposed to be talking to me? Somebody said she wasn't supposed to talk to me because I'm in isolation."

"Naw, I ain't. But it ain't a big deal. I'll just shimmy off if I hear the screw coming. You can always hear the tank door opening. How come you're in isolation, anyway?"

"I don't know." I start telling her my story. I mean to tell her just the main things, but I'm so desperate for somebody to talk to I tell her the whole story, about the narcotics cops that came to see me, even that I'm lying to save Leon's ass. So then I have to explain why I'm doing that and I tell her the story about Tuffy and how Leon saved me from that situation, and how I'm committed to standing up for him now.

She says she thinks I'm in isolation because of the investigation. "This is my second home," she says. "I'm in and outa here all the time, and I see a lot of stuff going on. Most of the time if people ain't in isolation cuz of acting up and getting punished, then it has something to do with a investigation. They don't want you to talk to nobody."

"That doesn't make any sense. Who could I talk to in here that would have anything to do with my case?"

"Since when do cops make sense? Take it from me, that's the way they do it. 'Less you can think of some other reason."

"No, I can't."

From this day on, Iva comes up at least once a day. She brings me cards so I can play solitaire, and buys me things from the candy wagon, and sees to it that I get laxatives. The screws won't let me out to go to the sick wagon. Iva has to tell them I want a pill, and the screw brings it up to me.

Iva tells me the jailhouse gossip, and gives me her own crazy version of the biographies of the other women in the tank. Because of her, other women start coming up to talk to me sometimes, I guess because they feel sorry for me, but they don't stay long and don't have much to say. I can write to Leon now that I have paper, and he writes to me, and we both write the limit of three letters a week. The letters plus Iva are all that keep me from going head-banging wall-climbing crazy.

The same day Iva is released, I have my arraignment. I haven't seen Leon since the first appearance we made the morning they arrested us, and I'm on the edge of heart failure with excitement. I'm the first one they bring in the courtroom. When they lead Leon in he fixes his eyes on mine and doesn't look away until they sit him in a chair on the other side of the room. He doesn't smile, and when he sits down he looks straight forward and won't look at me again. But I can't take my eyes off him. I need a smile, a tender look, anything.

Pendleton makes a motion to have bail reduced but the judge denies it. It wouldn't have made any difference anyway. We don't have the money and no way to get it. He pleads us both innocent, as planned. The only surprise is that Pendleton asks the judge to order a probation report on me, since this is my first offense. It never occurred to me I might get probation. The judge agrees, and the hearing is over. Leon is led out before I can find a way to speak to him.

When I'm taken back to my cell I'm even more depressed than before, if that's possible. One glimpse of Leon is only enough to make me miserable, not enough to make me feel any better, especially since he wouldn't even react to me. He looked bad too. Pale and thin. He's not telling me everything in his letters. He probably gets the same food I do, and can't eat it. Maybe it's okay for drunks and other people that serve ten days and get out, but for a long-term diet it'll kill you.

And I'm depressed because Iva's gone. I used to just wait every day for her to come up. How am I gonna cope now?

A couple of days after the arraignment a probation officer comes to see me. He's no older than I am. He's cheerful and real friendly, and I like him. He asks me if I have family or friends that would speak up for me, and I tell him I don't have any family, which is a lie, but my father would disown me if he knew about this, and it would kill my mother. So he says, "What about friends?"

"Well, there's some people in San Pedro might give me a recommendation."

"Anybody who's politically important, a public official or something? Or prominent people in the community?" He looks bright, expectant, as if it would be natural for a drug runner to have friends who are prominent in the community.

That makes me laugh. "About the closest is the high school librarian, Miss Baxter. There's the Rongs, who run a crab-fishing barge, and Mrs. Seigel, the mother of my best friend in high school. That's about it."

"That's all right, we'll make do with that. Do you think these people will say you have a basically good character and that you could be rehabilitated?"

"They probably would."

"Fine. Give me their addresses and I'll go to work on it. We're going to get you probation, Toni. This is your first offense and you shouldn't have to do time."

He's so enthusiastic I get suspicious. "Is this your first case?" I ask him.

"No, no," he says, smiling. "I've had two cases before this one. Don't worry, I know what I'm doing. I'm gonna get you probation!" He grabs my hand and shakes it hard before he leaves.

When I go back to my cell I start thinking. All those people are really nice folks. They're gonna say whatever they can to help me, although they're gonna be shocked to hear about this. They're all clean as whistles too. Maybe he's right, maybe I got a chance. I got nothing in my background against it, and everything for it. I come from a real nice family – my friends will say that.

After the probation officer comes, nothing happens for weeks. I try to read the Bible but I can't. Iva told me once, "There's some real wild stuff in there," but I can't get into it. I'm too set against all that bullshit. I especially hate the story about Eve and the serpent. Everything's the woman's fault, as usual. That number began as far back as creation itself. Then there's all that begat stuff – begat this and begat that. No thanks. I'm bored, but not that bored, and never will be.

But the days are hard to get through. Sixteen hours of solitaire is too much even for someone as desperate as me. All I have, really, are Leon's letters and talking with the other prisoners when they take the chance of coming up to see me. They seem to like the story of how I'm trying to keep him from going to prison and I tell it so many times that it starts to fall into a little script, and when I tell them how Leon rescued me from Tuffy, I make sure I mention Leon's the biggest dealer in East L.A., because it adds to the drama of the whole thing. I don't see any harm in it. But that's maybe a half hour out of sixteen hours. The rest of the time is minute-by-minute emptiness.

One day a cop I never saw before shows up outside my cell and he says, "Would you say that the heroin you were carrying was worth about $250,000 by the time it hit the streets?" Well, I got no idea how many times pure heroin gets cut and resold. I know it's a lot, because by the time the user gets it it's snow white, almost all milk sugar. Users don't even know that pure Mexican heroin is brown. But I never bothered to figure out what the final sales would be on that stuff. The police got experts who figure out things like that, and I figure that if $250,000 is what their guess is, well, that's probably what it is. But mainly, I don't want to appear ignorant, so I say, "Yeah, that's about right." He turns and goes away without saying another thing.

I get some relief from loneliness for a few days when they bring some wetbacks in, and they fill up all the cells. Because they're out of space, they put one of them in with me, a woman who doesn't speak any English. They don't know I speak some Spanish. So for a few days I'm happy. I get to figure out how to tell her the "Romance of Leon and Toni" in Spanish, and she teaches me half a million Mexican songs. We write the verses on the cell wall in pencil so I can memorize them. In five days we've got the wall completely covered. She even teaches me "La Malagueña," my favorite. She's a warm, nice person, and when she's finally released, she gives me the only thing she's got to give me, a tiny gold wedding ring. Wedding rings are the only jewelry you're allowed to keep in here. I say, "How can you give me your wedding ring?" And she says (in Spanish of course), "I'm not married, Toni. It's just for show. I want you to have it so you can remember me and the songs I taught you."

God, I nearly cry when she leaves.

Then it goes back to minute-by-minute misery again. That's why when Iva shows up one day about a week later, I'm ecstatic. I no sooner see her face than I break into tears of joy. "Oh Iva, it's horrible that you're back in jail, but I can't help it, I'm so glad to see you."

"That's okay. I come back on purpose. I got to thinking, I wonder how ol' Toni's doing? and I got myself busted to find out."

That Iva. I just love all her bullshit.

At last one day a screw comes to get me, saying, as she opens my cell door, "There's a federal agent here to see you." It's been about two-and-a-half months since I first talked to them. Are they just now getting around to asking more questions? They can't think this is a very important case if it takes them this long between one session and another. But maybe he'll know why it's taking so long to get to trial.

The man waiting for me in the screws' office is one of the men who talked to me in El Rincon. He says, "I think we've got the man. We're taking you to the federal building to identify him."

If I could volunteer to drop dead right now, I would. I don't know what to do or say. What am I gonna do, identify that poor slob at the cafe who I don't know whether he even has anything to do with drugs or not? I'm struck dumb with fear and not knowing what I should do, and so I don't say a word. He takes me out and puts me in a federal car, and we ride in silence to the federal building. When we get there, in the elevator he says to me, "It took us a long time to track him down. He closed up the cafe, maybe when he heard you were busted."

God. They been all this time looking for him. They really do want the guy I was working for. They don't know they already got the man they want. I'm so surprised by this thought that I realize I never expected them to believe my story. But they did! How did I get myself in this much trouble? What the hell are they gonna do to me when they find out? A two-and-a-half-month investigation. God.

The agent leads me into a big office and to a cell at the far end. He turns and watches me as I approach the cell. The poor guy in the cell doesn't look anything like I remember, but he's light-skinned with freckles, all right, a huge guy though, and he's standing there looking scared out of his wits and hugging his shoes to his chest, of all things. He stares at me with as much fright in his face as I feel myself and I'm just stunned, staring at him. "Well?" says the agent. I can't take my eyes off this poor dude. "That isn't the man," I say, without even thinking twice.

The man in the cell is almost dancing with joy. He's got a smile so wide it could break his face, and he's looking at me, saying over and over, "Thank you, thank you, thank you." I'm so ashamed I can't look at him. The agent says, "Okay, let's go." He's got his expressionless cop face on. He leads me back to the elevator, back to the car, back to the city jail, and all the way he doesn't look at me or speak to me, and I keep my eyes on the ground. He turns me over to the screws again without saying a single word, and I'm put back in my cell. If Iva's right, if I been locked up all this time because of the investigation, maybe now that the investigation is over they'll let me out of the cell. But the screw locks me up just like before.

I throw myself on the bunk and hide my face between my bunk and the wall, away from the light. Right now I don't even want to be me.

You have visitors, Bagliazo." The screw unlocks my cell. I can't possibly have a visitor. "Who is it?"

"Someone else checked them in. I don't know. Two men."

Oh god. I knew it. What are they gonna do to me? I'm sick with fear and my legs will hardly hold me up. I follow the screw and she takes me to a room where two men wait. I don't recognize them, they aren't the same agents. One of them says, "I'm George Prescott and this is Al Ramirez. We're from the Ace Diamond Company."

"The Ace Diamond Company? I don't understand."

"You have possession of a Longines platinum watch valued at fifteen hundred dollars, purchased on credit by Leon Fuentes. Payments on the watch are now three months in default. You have the option of paying the entire balance now or relinquishing the watch."

"You're not cops!"

"No. I told you, we're from the Ace Diamond Company."

I'm so relieved I almost laugh. "Okay, what's this again?"

"The payments on the watch are three months in default. We understand that this watch is in your property deposit here. Is that correct?"

"Yeah. Take the damn thing."

"You have the option of keeping the watch. We've just seen Mr. Fuentes and he said to tell you that if you want to keep the watch, he has enough cash here to pay the balance."

Oh, Leon. God. "Take the damn thing."

"You don't want it?"

"No."

"Would you sign these release forms, please? We need these before the police will release your personal property to us."

Iva says, "If he wanted you to keep the watch, how come he didn't just pay the guys off 'stead of sending them over here to ask you?"

"I dunno, Iva. Maybe he guessed I might not want it. I don't. Whatever money he's got on him is all there is. I wouldn't let him do that."

"Anything a man ever give me I ended up paying for ten times over. I think this hot-lips honey-dick of yours knows you're his ticket outa here and he's keeping you sweetened up."

"That's not true, Iva. He's always been that way with me."

I'm so furious I throw myself on my bunk with my face to the wall and I'm having a hard time trying not to cry. Iva says, "Aw, Toni." Then it's quiet and I think she's gone away. I can never hear her come or go in her bare feet. But after a minute she says, "Just ask yourself why he didn't just go ahead and pay it off if he really wanted you to have it."

I jump out of my bunk to tell her off, but this time she's really gone.

Within a week after the narc took me to see the man they arrested, I get a note from Pendleton that our trial date is set. At last I understand that they held the trial up to see the outcome of the investigation. Why didn't Pendleton tell me that? Three months in this hellhole because of my own goddam stupid lie! I feel like the stupidest creep that ever lived. I'm too humiliated even to talk to Iva about it. All I can do is keep telling myself, Now you got a trial date, it will soon be over.

The night before the trial I can't sleep, but in the morning I don't even feel tired, I'm so hyped up. The screw brings me my suitcase so I can pick out a dress to wear. Iva told me yesterday,

"Wear something that makes you look real innocent, so they'll think you didn't really mean to do it." I grin thinking of it: I didn't really mean to put all that heroin in my bra and take it across the border, your honor. I just don't know what I was thinking about. But she's got a point. I pick out a sleeveless pink dress with a high neck, which is about as innocent as I got. All my clothes fit tight, because Leon likes clingy things that show off my shape. When I get the dress on, though, it's loose. I've lost quite a bit of weight, living on bread and coffee.

I start shaking when they come to get me to take me to the federal courthouse, and I'm still shaking when they lead me into the courtroom. My heart nearly jumps out of my chest when I see Leon already there. Almost three months since I've seen him. I forget everything else, looking at him, waiting for him to acknowledge me, waiting for him to show some joy at seeing me. But when he looks my way his face is expressionless, his eyes are marbles, just like he's been every time we meet in court. Well, just the same, he keeps his eyes on me. I know by now he doesn't show any emotion when the enemy is in the same room, and I have his letters to prove he loves me. He watches as I'm led over to sit by him at the table, and when I sit down I turn to him and he looks straight into my eyes. That's enough for me.

I glance at the jury box. They look like a bunch of nice people, and one young guy is actually smiling at me. Maybe they'll believe me when I stand up and say Leon is innocent. But I'm still shaking, and I know most of my fear is that they won't believe me. I wonder what the investigators put in the judge's folder. Is all that stuff about the investigation gonna come up at the trial? I haven't seen Pendleton since the arraignment, and not to talk to since El Rincon. I don't know what to make of that. I'm furious at Pendleton for not coming to see me and tell me what's what before we go to trial. How am I supposed to know what Leon is gonna say? Or what Pendleton is gonna say?

While I been thinking all this the prosecutor and Pendleton have been making their opening statements to the jury, and I've missed it. Damn! I'm so scared I can't think straight or halfway pay attention to what's going on. I glance at Leon. He's staring straight ahead.

The prosecutor is standing in front of the judge now, and he's saying, "I'd like to read defendant Leon Fuentes's arrest record into the record, your honor."

"Go ahead," the judge says.

Arrest record? I never thought about that for one second. Can he do that? I look at Pendleton. He's not moving. Isn't he gonna object? What does Leon's arrest record have to do with *this* time, with whether he knew I had heroin in my bra or not? Why doesn't he object, damn it?

The prosecutor is saying, "Armed robbery, dismissed. Aggravated assault, dismissed. Assault, convicted. Armed robbery, dismissed . . ."

He's reading the damn charges that were dismissed. How can they do that? The jury's not gonna hear the dismissed part! I look at Pendleton again, frantic. He's just sitting there, doodling on a yellow legal pad with his pen.

"Armed robbery, convicted. Procuring, dismissed. Aggravated rape, dismissed."

He goes on but I don't hear him. Procuring? That's pimping! Aggravated rape? *Rape?* I feel numb now. This is all too unexpected, too unbelievable. There's more talking going on but I can't listen anymore. I'm just sitting there staring. Procuring. Rape. Dismissed only means they couldn't prove it, not that he didn't do it.

Then I hear, "I said, will defendant Antonia Bagliazo please take the stand?"

I start shaking again. I lean forward to get out of my chair, but my legs won't hold me up. I try again, and fall back in the chair. I can't stand up. The bones in my legs have melted.

I can't stand up.

Getting
Oriented

Well, it's over and things are looking better to me. Two to ten years is pretty scary at first, especially since I had talked myself into thinking I'd get probation, but actually, when the judge says two to ten I go numb, and I don't seem to feel anything or even to hear much except that Leon gets five to fifteen, and that he's going to some federal joint for men. I don't even think to get a last look at him as they lead me from the courtroom. I'm like a dead person.

The bailiffs take me to the courthouse holding cell, where I have to wait for someone to take me back to jail. Sitting there waiting, the shock wears off a little and I start crying and I feel horribly depressed, and I think, Maybe numb is better. But after a while I'm all cried out and I feel empty, and then finally I think: All the tension of waiting, of not knowing what's gonna happen to me, is over. At least I know where I'm gonna be the next two years, by god. Maybe the next ten. I start feeling so much better I think something must be wrong with me. I should be more depressed than I am. Then I realize that for the first time in months I'm not scared out of my wits. I must not have really believed I was going to get probation, not deep down where you really believe things or not believe them, because if I really believed it I wouldn't have been so scared. My hope is gone now, but my fear is gone too, because I know what's ahead of me. Hope and fear must just be two sides of the same coin, and when one falls through the crack the other just naturally goes with it, and you can resign yourself and get on with whatever you have to get on with.

I start thinking about all the good stuff that can happen now. Comparatively speaking, of course. Like, I'll be moved out of this goddam jail to a federal joint. They told me I'm going to the Federal Reformatory for Women in West Virginia. I feel pretty sure I won't be kept in a cell all the time like I have been here, and that I'll probably have some kind of work to do. And there won't be any drunks screaming and throwing up all night. That alone will improve life a thousand percent.

It turns out I'm right about good things happening, because when they take me back to the city jail they don't lock me up in my cell. At first I think it's a mistake. But I'm not about to say anything, and I sit downstairs and play cards all afternoon. When the supper cart comes I'm sure the screw will see I'm out and lock me up, but she looks right at me and doesn't say anything, and it finally sinks in that it wasn't a mistake. They've let me out on purpose.

After supper I'm so high I run up and down the tank whooping and hollering, and then I jump up on one of the tables and do a flamenco dance – or something like it anyway – just because I'm not locked up anymore. The women are all laughing and clapping and egging me on. Right in the middle of all this the screw comes in. Usually we hear the tank door open and everything stops on a dime, but we're making so much noise we don't hear her this time and she walks in and stands there watching me make a fool of myself. I'm the last one to see her and I only know she's there when I realize that the clapping has stopped and one by one the women have stopped shouting. I look around and see the screw and I freeze. But she's smiling. Smiling! She says, "Bagliazo, you're shipping out first thing in the morning. I thought you'd like to know." Thought I'd like to know? Since when did they decide I have a right to know what's happening to me?

The screw leaves, but the dance is over and I'm a little shaken. Things are moving too fast. I go up to my cell and spend half the night staring straight up at the ceiling, wondering what it's going to be like at the federal joint, worrying about Leon and how he's going to know where I am, and how I'm going to know where he is, and thinking about the people I'm not gonna see for a long time.

In the morning a screw comes with my suitcase and I get to pick out something to wear on the train. I choose my dark grey dress, the one I bought because it's the color of a stormy sky, with embroidered white dots on it like tiny snowflakes, and white lace on the shoulders and around the neck. It's my classiest dress, and I choose it because I know I won't get to look good again for a long time. I put on my sexy white lace shoes, and pack what little stuff I have in my cell – a pad of stationery, my toothbrush, and my comb – and the screw takes the suitcase away again. I feel like a different person with decent clothes on. Myself again.

I have to sit around for more than an hour, but finally they come for me, and after I sign for my wallet and my earrings – no platinum watch, just a receipt from the Ace Diamond Company – I'm taken to the train depot in a federal car, and there's a woman marshal to escort me. I'm so excited just to walk out of that goddam jail I don't even notice her much at first. I'm taking in the street and the sunlight and the people and the trees because I don't know how much of that I'll see for who knows how many years, but once in the car I look at her. She's not the kind you'd expect to be a federal marshal. She's almost sixty, I bet, and she's got one of those sweet gentle older-woman faces that they stamp out by the millions and slap on everybody's Aunt Martha. She's kind, I can see that.

Well, there's no accounting for what the mind does in any given situation. What hits me right away, when I see how nice she looks, is that I got to tell her what goes on in that jail. If I can just tell somebody decent, they'll see that a stop is put to it. So I say to her, "I have to tell you something. Terrible things go on in that jail. People nearly starve to death on the food in there. Sometimes they put so much pepper in it you can't eat it. They do it on purpose. I saw two cops beat a man in the stomach, and he didn't even do anything. And a girl got scalding water thrown on her because she wouldn't be quiet."

I stop and wait for a reaction. The marshal looks at me with an expression of shock. "That's preposterous!" she says.

"Maybe so, but it's true," I say.

Her expression changes from shock to anger. "Really. What kind of fool do you think I am?"

Now I understand that she wasn't shocked because what I was telling her was so terrible, she was shocked because she thought I was telling her a horrendous lie. I try to think of what I can say to convince her I'm telling the truth, but then I realize that I have let myself be fooled into thinking that just because I put on regular clothes again I'm a regular person. The clothes made me lose my grip on what I've learned the last few months: I'm a bug. What the hell made me think for one split second that decent old Aunt Martha would listen to me, a "big-time" dope smuggler?

At the depot Aunt Martha turns me over to a pair of rougher looking women in civies, and I get another shock. They have two other women prisoners with them, and they put me in leg irons and attach me to one of them. The third prisoner isn't shackled. The two of them weren't shackled when I got there. So it seems clear the shackles have something to do with me. Any fantasy I had of enjoying this train ride is now over. The ankle irons are heavy and they hurt, and to make matters worse I'm wearing high heels.

The chain between me and the other woman is about three feet long. We're handcuffed too, and paraded through the station to the train. I start off feeling ashamed, looking at the ground because I know everyone in the station will be staring at us as we go by, but that little corner of my mind that likes to strut wakes up, and I sneak a peek now and then to see how people are reacting, and I see men giving me horny looks with a little sadness mixed in – poor young woman in chains – and I know I look very very good, very sexy in this dress and my lace shoes, and I straighten up a little and put an expression on my face that maybe says: It's okay, boys, my gang is waiting at the pass to stop the train and carry me away. I mean, if that's what the feds think, I might as well get into the fantasy too.

In the train we're taken to a car that has nothing in it but prisoners – all men, all shackled like I am. It's a scary sight. But I don't get to see much of them because we're moved fast into a room that has upper and lower bunks and a couch. Once we're in the room they take the shackles off – a big relief, because to move around in there at all would be to get tangled up in the chains. I can't even think of how we'd get into that tiny toilet. I volunteer to sit on the floor, partly because I'll be able to look out the door at the men prisoners. I'm sick of nothing but women by now. But once the train is under way they close the door, and we settle into our own thoughts. It's quiet, just the rocking motion of the train and the sounds of the wheels on the tracks. I sink into depression.

The whole day goes by in almost total silence, just the screws say something to each other once in a while, and read magazines. They offer me one but I can't read because my head is in a buzz. It doesn't seem to me like I'm thinking or even that I'm very much alive. I'm in a stupor, sleeping while I'm awake.

When night comes, the screws put on pajamas and we prisoners strip to our underwear to sleep. After we've brushed our teeth and we're ready to climb into our bunks, one of the screws tells me she has to shackle us when we go to bed. I'm so stunned I can't even protest. I guess it's so we can't attack the screws while they sleep, and try to get away. As if we could get anywhere from a moving train, even if we could get past the male guards outside in the men's car. I just watch as the screw puts the ankle irons back on. My shackle mate, Dora, looks furious, and she keeps giving me evil looks, because she wouldn't be shackled if it weren't for me.

Although I'm speechless, everything I'm feeling must be showing on my face, because when the screw has finished she looks at me with a sad expression, and she says, "I've been transporting prisoners for thirteen years and I never had to shackle a woman before. What did you do?"

"I don't know," I say, and immediately feel stupid, because of course what she's asking me is what I'm convicted of, but what I'm answering is why they think I'm so dangerous I have to be shackled. But she turns away and it's too late to fix it. She's written me off as a clown.

It takes me a long time to go to sleep. I'm scared I'll thrash around and yank Dora's leg. I just lie there listening to the rhythm of the wheels. The sheets feel crisp and smell good. I haven't slept on sheets for months. I remember when I was a kid I loved to ride on trains and sleep in a bunk. I liked the gentle rocking motion. I liked looking out the window at the landscape zipping by. The noise of the wheels was soothing and as I got sleepier I used to hear music in the clackety-clackety-clackety of the wheels on the tracks. But now the rhythm is ugly to me. It sounds like I'm on a huge noisy conveyor belt that's carrying me into some huge machine that's gonna grind me up.

I can't help thinking about the shackles, about the screw saying she'd never transported a woman in chains before. Up 'til now, their treating me like a big-time criminal has been bewildering, but at the same time a part of me likes it. If I'm gonna be in jail I might as well feel important, at least. And it's kind of funny that they made such a big mistake. But the leg irons – especially their making me sleep in them – make it clear now that they're scared of me. I know that if I make any kind of funny move – and I could make one by mistake real easy – I'm likely to get shot. It's not funny anymore.

How did they get the idea I'm such a big fish? Six and a half ounces of pure heroin is a lot, but not that much. I remember the cop that came in the tank one day and asked me if I estimated the street value of the heroin to be about $250,000, and I said "Yes," thinking they probably knew better than I did anyway. Now it occurs to me that they aren't gonna see anybody who carries that much cash value in one trip as just an ordinary mule. And then I remember bragging to the women in the tank with me that my old man's the biggest dealer in East L.A. Lord, how can I be so stupid? It was just talk. I don't know if he is or not. He's big, but not that big. If they thought I was such a big fish, all the time they had that investigation going they probably had stoolies in the tank with me, and I just gave them what they wanted, trying to make out I was somebody important instead of a mule.

Now that I let one thought like that rise, more come rushing up. Driving that big brand-new yellow Cadillac. Me with my fifteen-hundred-dollar platinum watch. What do the feds care if we were paying off the Caddie at six hundred dollars a month, and the watch at one hundred? Going flashy, going first class, makes us look rich. I groan and pull the pillow over my head. I did a real good job of playing the part. I got myself two to ten years instead of probation, I got myself in leg irons. I probably won't get parole either, for making fools of the feds, sending them on a wild-goose chase during the investigation, trying to cover up for Leon.

God they're stupid. I never thought they were stupid. I believed all the movies and the TV shows, that they were some sort of supermen. But they're stupid. They believed all my bullshit and now they know I made fools of them and I'm gonna pay for it for as long as they got power over me, and these shackles are probably just the beginning. There's only one person stupider than them. Me.

There's probably nothing more depressing than realizing you've forged your own chains, and the rest of the trip is a very quiet one for me. I'm careful how I move, and careful what I say to the screws. I don't feel like talking to the other prisoners, and they don't seem to want to talk to me, especially Dora. I don't blame them. I don't even want to talk to myself.

We make a layover in St. Louis, and we lose the men. They are put on another train for Leavenworth. Because we have to wait a couple of hours for our train to West Virginia, we get to eat in a restaurant. In chains – nice. The screws tell us we can order anything up to six dollars, which doesn't buy a steak but it buys fried chicken and French fries, and it's like heaven compared to what I been eating for three months.

When we leave the restaurant I see men looking at me again, the same sad horny looks, but this time I'm too depressed to get any charge out of it. And for the first time it hits me that it's the chains that are turning the men on. They're getting off on seeing a woman degraded. I was so busy being Miss Hot-Shit-on-a-Stick I never thought about it before. But now I'm so depressed and disgusted with myself that I see everything different. I decide I'm not going to think about this anymore because I'm scared of what else I might come up with.

The rest of the trip is quiet. We pull into Alderson, West Virginia, about four in the morning. They take our chains off to move us to the prison. All this distance in shackles, and now they seem to think it's safe to put us in a car without chains for the last miles in the middle of the night. None of it makes any sense. Stupid. Everywhere I look now I see stupid.

It's too dark to see much when we pull up to the prison. They take me inside a building that could be a hospital or a dormitory, and lead me straight to a small room with a bunk and lock me in. The depression that has been heavy on me for the last three days is blown away because of the room. It's clean, it's got hardwood floors, and no bars except on the window. The walls are painted a nice creamy white, and they're clean. There's a cot with sheets and a blanket on it, and an honest-to-god pillow. Sheets! I thought that was a luxury that was going to end with the train ride. And there's a chest of drawers, a little table and chair, a toilet and a sink. Coming from that jail it feels like a goddam luxury hotel. The window is open and through the bars I can see leaves. There's plants out there! Everything smells good. Clean. And private. Because the door to the room is solid wood. For the first time since I got busted I'm not in an open cage where anyone can watch me any time they want, even when I'm taking a crap.

It's a relief to know for sure that things won't be as bad as they were in jail, and I fall into the bed and am asleep in minutes.

In a couple of hours I wake up to the sound of a key in the door. A young woman comes in with some things in her arms. I can see a towel and a bar of soap. "Hi," she says, "I'm Bertha. Here's some stuff you'll need. If you'll get dressed I'll take you for your shower." She lays the things on the table. "I'll be back in five minutes."

"Okay," I mumble, and she goes out and shuts the door. I sit on the edge of the bed and the first thing I notice is the window. There's sunshine out there. The window is high on the wall, and I see that I'm in a basement room. Plants are growing right outside the window, green and alive. They look so good I don't even mind looking at them through bars. I smile, and get up. On the table there's a towel, a bar of soap, a toothbrush, a comb, and a washcloth. There's a big piece of cloth too. I unfold it and it seems to be some kind of robe, like a hospital gown. I put on my clothes and sit on the chair to wait for Bertha.

It takes her a lot longer than five minutes to get back. When the door opens this time I see it isn't Bertha who has the key, but a screw in a white uniform who walks away as soon as she has unlocked the door. Bertha, I now notice, is dressed in a plain shirt-dress of a light blue, and brown oxfords. I realize that she's a prisoner and that these are prison duds. "Sorry I took so long," she says, "but I have two other women to shower."

"I get to shower now? That's great. I didn't get to wash very good on the train over."

"Sure. C'mon, Antonia."

"Everybody calls me Toni."

"Okay."

Bertha takes me to a big storeroom that has showers against one wall and a single toilet in a stall, but otherwise it's nothing like a bathroom. There are shelves along the walls holding linens and clothing. The showers have little dressing rooms, like locker room showers, and I go in one of these, pull the curtain, and strip. Bertha says, "Hand me out your clothes, underwear and all. I'll be giving you prison-issue stuff to put on."

"Okay. It's my period. What do I do with my tampon?"

"I'll hand you a paper towel, then give it to me."

"Can't I come out and throw it away myself?"

"No. The c.o. has to check everything. Wash your hair too, and then when you're ready let me know."

"C.o.?"

"Correctional officer."

Correctional officer. I am here to be corrected. I do what Bertha says and hand out my clothes. The tampon comes last. It embarrasses me to hand it to her. When they can strip you down so far they even look at your bloody tampon, then nothing's sacred or private. It makes me feel like I got nothing of my self left.

But the shower feels good and I take a long time in it. Bertha is waiting, but says nothing about how long it's taking me. Maybe she knows how I feel. At last I come out, dry off, and call through the curtain, "I'm ready. You got something for me to put on now?"

"Not yet. Stay there a sec."

I hear her walk to the door, open it, and call, "She's ready, Miss Neuman." I hear someone walk into the room, and Bertha says, "Wrap yourself in the towel and come out now, Toni."

When I come out a woman in a white uniform is pulling on a rubber glove. "Stand in front of that chair, give your towel to

Bertha, and bend over," she says.

"I been in custody for three months," I say.

"It doesn't matter. Bend over."

So I bend, and she probes my asshole with her fingers, changes gloves, and goes up my cunt. I'm embarrassed again that it's my period, but she's about as personal as she'd be with a cow, and I guess she couldn't care less. Maybe does hundreds of these a year.

When she's done, she peels the glove off, drops it in a trash can, and leaves. Bertha puts my towel over the seat of the chair, and says, "Sit down, I've got to delouse your hair."

"They did that in jail."

"You heard the lady. It don't matter."

"If you don't give me a tampon I'm going to bleed on the towel."

"Right." She gets a tampon out of a box on a shelf. "Here you are."

"Can't I at least go in a stall to put it in?"

"Sure. Go ahead. But I need all your sizes so I can get some clothes together for you." I give her my bra, dress, and shoe size and go in a shower stall.

I have a hard time keeping the tears down. I got nothing left of my own, nothing but what they want to give me, for however many years I'm here. At least in the jail I had my own shoes. I never realized how important that was 'til now – some little thing that's my own. But I get in control of the tears before I come out. I don't want to start off being known as a crybaby.

Bertha loads my head up with an ugly-smelling liquid and wraps it in a towel. She has some clothes for me: two shirt-dresses like the one Bertha is wearing, three denim shirts, three pairs of jeans, some shoes just like hers, socks, a sweater, a pea-coat, and the ugliest bras and panties I ever saw. "My god, these are old-lady things." I hold the panties up. They're made out of a weird shiny fabric I never saw before, salmon pink. They look like they'd fit a cow.

Bertha smiles. "You'll get used to them. Besides, you don't have to wear them, you know."

I put on a pair of jeans and a shirt. Not what I like to wear but a big improvement on the jail dresses.

As Bertha takes me from the storeroom back to my room I ask her what happens next. She says, "You'll be in isolation for three days. That means you stay in the room you're in. You'll be locked in all the time and you won't get to talk to anybody but me and the afternoon girl. And the c.o.'s of course. You'll get your meals in your room. You can have some magazines if you want. After three days you can come out but you stay in this building for two weeks. Orientation, they call it. You darn your socks and mend your clothes, which are all hand-me-downs, in case you didn't notice, and they'll give you some tests and decide where you're going to work and all."

"But I'll be by myself for three days?"

"Yeah."

"God. That sounds great."

"You got to be kidding. You'll be climbing the walls before you get out of there."

"Naw, I'm gonna love it. You don't know what I came from. I was in a drunk tank for three months. You can't give me enough peace and quiet and solitude for a while. But what's the idea, anyway? The three days' isolation, I mean."

"I never figured it out. I suppose to see if you're gonna go crazy or something. Or maybe to see if you got some kind of contagious disease."

Bertha gets a screw to open my room, then locks me inside. But she's back in five minutes with a food tray and some magazines. There's three strips of bacon, scrambled eggs, prunes, toast, a small glass of milk and a cup of coffee. "Bacon? We get bacon? Milk? Wow, this is terrific."

"We got our own farm here. Vegetables in the summer, pigs and cows. We eat a lot of pork. You'll get sick of it."

I'm getting more and more excited. "A farm, no shit? Do the prisoners work there?"

"Yeah."

"I'd love to work on the farm. Do we get any choice about where we work?"

"Depends. But you don't want to work on the farm. Sometimes you got to work holidays 'cause the animals have to be fed and the stalls cleaned. It's awful hard work. Most of the women who work there hate it."

"What other kinds of jobs they got?"

"Oh, a bunch of stuff. But listen, I'm not supposed to talk to you any more than necessary. I gotta go."

"Okay. Thanks, Bertha." I dig into the food and can hardly eat for crying with gratitude. If the food is always like this it's gonna be easy to get through this time. All at once I think of Esperanza, the wetback woman in the El Rincon jail who told me jail was better than home for her. I bust out laughing. Esperanza, if you could see me now, wouldn't you laugh? I'm just like you – raving about how nice it is in this goddam prison! The more I think of it, the funnier it gets and I'm laughing 'til my cheeks hurt. When I finally calm down, I wonder where Esperanza is. Wherever she is, she's a lot worse off than I am, and the best thing I can wish for her is that she could be here with me, and this thought sets me to crying and I can't eat any more of my beautiful breakfast.

The next three days are easy. Rest and quiet. I'm only taken out for a short time the first day to be fingerprinted and photographed, and to sign an inventory of my purse. My suitcase has disappeared somewhere but by the time I realize they haven't said anything about it, I'm back in my room.

The food is simple but good. A couple of days there's even home-baked pie at dinner. Bertha tells me the cooks are prisoners and they take as much care as they can with the food, making the most of what comes in from the farm. She brings me new magazines every day, *People* and *Newsweek* and *Seventeen* and *Vogue*. None of 'em is my cup of tea, but they're better than nothing. After not having anything to read but the Bible for the three months I was in jail, I'm glad to have them and read every word of every page, even the ads.

My room isn't any bigger than my jail cell, but it feels luxurious to me because I can see the sun and some plants through the window. If I stand on my chair I can look out over the grounds. There's grass everywhere, and trees, but I can't see any other buildings. That's fine with me. I get to take a shower every day, and the rest of the time is quiet and peaceful. I rarely even hear anything going on outside my room. Just the women singing sometimes as they clean the hall, and that's beautiful to hear. All the stuff I was depressed about on the train seems to have gone right out of my head. I spend my time resting and snoozing, remembering good things, not bad things. I'm not gonna think about the bad things if I don't have to. I can't do anything about them now. Everything's decided for a long time to come. I'm sorry when the three days are over, but I'm interested to see what's going to happen next.

The two weeks of orientation go fast. I spend most of each day in a big room with ten other new prisoners. We're given physicals, and we're assigned jobs to do every day. I have to clean the toilets and showers, but I don't mind. No drunks' vomit to clean up, like in jail. In the afternoons we sew, altering our hand-me-down denims to fit, sewing on name tags, and darning socks. We're given some tests – an IQ test and the one that asks you whether you'd rather drive a tractor, bake a cake, or read a book. There's no choice that says you want to be a movie star or ball your old man, so it's really all set up ahead of time that you'll come out one thing or another and nothing in between. But it's something to do besides sew and I don't really mind. It all boils down to this: this place is so much better than jail that basically I'm happy, or as happy as anybody can be in prison. Something inside me has clicked over into accepting the situation, which is just as well since I can't do anything about it.

So all in all it's going pretty well. I can't find out much about the institution though, because all the other inmates are new, like me, and the trusties aren't allowed to talk to us any more than necessary, and the screws are screws – they got no use for us except to tell us what to do. But in my new philosophical condition I don't let this bother me much. I make up my mind to stay grateful that this isn't the San Rudolfo City Jail.

The last day in Orientation they hand us slips to tell us where we'll live and where we'll work. I'll be in cottage 7, and work in statistical coding in the school building. Cottage? Statistical coding? School building? I've already learned that we don't have any right to ask questions about what's happening to us. I wait for Bertha at lunch time to ask her what a cottage is and what statistical coding means.

"I haven't got time to explain it all to you. Just believe me when I say they're both good assignments."

"They got a school here?"

Bertha laughs. "Sort of. But not really. Listen, the school building is a good assignment. Wait 'til you meet ol' Rupenthal. She's not like the rest of the c.o.'s. She's a sweetheart. And kind of dumb. You'll get away with murder up there."

"We live in cottages here?"

Bertha laughs again. "Words have different meanings in this place. Just be patient, Toni. They'll be coming for you about four o'clock this afternoon. If I don't see you again, stay cool. It's really not too bad once you learn the ropes."

The afternoon seems long, especially since we don't have anything to do, but at last we're sent to our rooms to collect our clothes, and then after another wait, three screws come for us. Each screw calls out the names of the women that are supposed to go with her. I get anxious when the last screw calls my name and no one else's. We leave the building for the first time since we arrived, and I see four big brick buildings that look a lot like run-down college dormitories, and another smaller building down near the gate. The buildings are much smaller than I imagined. But the grounds are fairly nice, and the buildings have flower beds around them, and beyond the wire fence that seems to be the only thing holding us in are fields and woods. We are out in the country.

The first two screws with their little groups of women are walking ahead of us along a sidewalk. My screw turns in at the first building, the others are going on to the farther buildings. Now I know for sure I've been singled out again. I'm in some special building. For a minute I've got a fantasy that I'm gonna be locked up by myself again, but I tell myself that I'm paranoid, there's probably some other reason.

The screw leads me to a room on the second floor of the building, and before she leaves me there, she tells me I'm free to walk around the building, and that there's a recreation room downstairs with a television in it where I can wait until the other prisoners get home from work. She says that a bell will tell me when supper is, that lockup is at nine o'clock and I must be in my room by then, and that otherwise I'm on my own until morning, when someone will take me to my job in the school building.

As soon as she leaves I take a good look at my room. I'm

amazed. It's not much different than my isolation room, except that it doesn't have a toilet and sink, and this one is on the second floor, so I have a view of the woods and fields beyond the fence and I can see the walkways between the buildings. The most exciting thing is that there's no bars on the windows. I notice too that the floor is hardwood, polished to a high sheen, and that the dresser and table and chair are good oak, very sturdy although they're pretty banged up. It would look just like a dormitory room if it weren't so tiny. But it's comfortable, and I feel very lucky, and my spirits lift again. I try the cot. Well, not great, but better than the jail. Who's complaining? No goddam bars on the window!

After I put my clothes away I check out the recreation room downstairs. There's no one there but me. I watch TV for the first time in months. Any dread I had left is falling away. The scene in the shower room is almost three weeks behind me now, and nothing else like it has happened since. I keep waiting for something awful to happen, but nothing does, and maybe nothing will. If I'd come here straight from the outside I'd probably complain about a lot of things, but compared to jail it's comfortable. Now that the anxiety is gone I feel incredibly tired, and before "Love Boat" is even over I'm asleep, and I only wake up when I hear a lot of noise – voices shouting and feet tramping in the halls – that tells me the women are home from work.

I go to my room because I don't know what else to do. There are too many women, looks like forty or fifty. I don't know who to talk to or what to say, and my room seems like a more secure base to watch from. I sit on my bed and wait. It's less than a minute before a dark-haired girl with beautiful hazel eyes appears at my door. "Hi," she says, "I'm Terry. I live across the hall."

"Hi. I'm Toni."

"Yeah, I know. Drug smuggling. Two to ten."

"How do you know that?"

"There's no secrets here. Well, hardly any. You might as well know that right away. Where you gonna work?"

"Statistical coding."

"Lucky!"

"Everybody says that but I don't know why."

"Easy work, and Rupie's a doll." Just as she says this a bell rings.

"C'mon, that's supper. I'll take you to the dining room."

The dining room is downstairs, on the other end of the building from the rec room. I'm astonished to see that the room is cozy, filled with small round tables covered with tablecloths. There's even a fireplace at one end. Five or six women sit at each table. Terry leads me to a table with a vacant chair, and I find myself suddenly facing four of my housemates, who are looking at me with frank curiosity. Terry introduces me to Lee, a woman who might be eighty years old, Concha, a Puerto Rican woman of about fifty, and Edna, thirtyish and hard-looking. They ask me a lot of questions, but there is so much to take in and wonder about that I fumble as I try to answer. They haven't been briefed on me, as Terry obviously has been, and I have to explain again that I'm here for drug smuggling and that my sentence is two to ten years, that I'm from California, that I'm twenty-three years old, that no, I've never done time before. But I don't want to answer questions, I want to ask them.

The table is crammed with platters and bowls. There's a rice dish with diced ham, turnip greens, corn, bread, and margarine. I'm distracted as the food is passed around. But I notice that although the food looks good, there's nothing extra. I have to be careful to take only so much, so that the last person won't get shorted.

Once everybody's served, the women eat and let up on the questions. I get a chance to ask a few of my own. "How come they call the buildings cottages?"

"The same reason they call this prison a reformatory," Terry says.

"The same reason they call teaching you to darn socks orientation," Edna says.

"The same reason they call taking you away from your home and your family and your job, treating you like a dog, and fixing it so you can't get another job when you get out because you got a record, that's rehabilitation," says Concha.

"You're gonna learn that nothing is called by its right name around here," says Terry.

"Oh," I say, a little flustered that such a casual question triggers such bitter answers. But I might as well find out about the other question that's bothering me. "Do you know why I'm the only one in my orientation group that got assigned to this cottage? Seems strange to me. Five or six women went to each of the other cottages."

Everybody smiles. "You're in High Power, honey," says Terry.

"What does that mean?"

"It means they take you serious as a criminal, and they want to keep you away from the youngsters they have some hope for. All of us in cottage seven are serious offenders."

Lee speaks for the first time. "Axis Sally and Tokyo Rose were in this cottage in the fifties. And some women the McCarthy committee sent here for being Communists. And Lolita Somebody-or-other. I never could pronounce her last name."

"Lebrón," says Concha.

"She was one of the Puerto Rican revolutionaries who shot up Congress. Now they got me." Lee erupts into giggles. She covers her mouth with her napkin and her face turns red as she tries to get back in control. She's so giggly I can't help but smile.

"What did you do, Lee?"

"I didn't pay my taxes," she says, but this sends her off into such a fit of giggles that Terry finishes answering for her. "Lee makes hooch and sells it. But she didn't get busted for making hooch, she got busted for not paying the federal taxes on booze."

"They sent her here just for that?" I'm shocked, because she's so old. Terry says, "Lee got probation the first time, and a suspended sentence the second time. When she got busted the third time she not only had to serve her suspended sentence, she had a new offense on top of it."

"How long do you have left, Lee?"

"Three years. Don't worry, I'll make it. If I had ten years I'd make it, just so they wouldn't have the satisfaction of seeing me die in here."

"What about parole?"

Lee acts like she doesn't hear me, just keeps eating, so after a few seconds Terry answers for her. "Lee refuses to say she won't moonshine anymore, so they keep turning her down for parole."

Lee looks mad. No laughing now. "It's the only way I got to

make a living. If I can't make hooch I might as well stay here. Don't have to work as hard. I been making a quilt. If you want to see it, come to my room later."

"Okay, I'd like to. You and me got something in common, Lee."

"What's that?"

"I'm not here for smuggling, I'm here for not paying import duty on six and a half ounces of heroin."

Everyone looks at me, surprised. Terry says, "Say what?"

"That's what the indictment said. Failure to declare for the purpose of having import duty assessed, three and a half ounces of heroin." Everyone is smiling. Lee shakes her head.

I ask, "So what did you do, Terry, to belong here with the High Power criminals?"

"I had a fight with my boyfriend and stole fifty thousand dollars he had in his safe. He's a gambler, so he has a lot of cash around. I got to California with it and realized what a dumb thing I did, and turned around and started back to Las Vegas with it. They caught me getting on the plane. They never paid the least attention that I was getting on the plane to go back to Las Vegas. They didn't believe I was taking it back. So here I am."

"Gee, we're really a dangerous bunch. What about the gals in the other cottages?"

"Mostly nickel-and-dime stuff. They end up with a federal rap if they go over a state line, like I did. Lots of the women here are just hustlers from D.C. If you commit a felony in Washington, it's a federal crime. "

"Are there any political prisoners here now, like the fifties?"

"Naw."

"Too bad. If I got to be here, it sounds like it would have been more interesting in the fifties."

Lee says, "You wouldn't want to be here then. It was a lot worse."

"Were you here then?"

"Yes. Don't look so shocked, honey. I haven't been here all the time since then. That was my first trip. We been talking about this last round. But take my word for it, it was a lot worse then. They could get away with doing almost anything they wanted to you."

"You mean now they don't?"

Nobody answers.

In the morning we line up outside the cottage after breakfast for a head count. When we're dismissed, everybody goes off in different directions to work. The farm women get on a waiting truck. I'm standing there wondering what to do when the screw calls out, "Bagliazo!" "Here!" I holler back, and she says, "Come with me."

She takes me to one of the other buildings that looks exactly like the one I live in, but inside it's set up different, a bunch of offices, and Terry told me last night that there's an auditorium there, although I can't see it on the way in. The screw leads me upstairs and then down a long hall to an office on the very end. We open a door and go into a classroom that has desks with typewriters on them. The only person in the room is a huge woman sitting at a desk writing something. I don't mean fat, just big. She stands, and I see that she's at least six foot one and heavyset in a pleasing kind of way, the way you like to think of farm women. Her hair is white and braided over the top of her head like the Swedes, and I see that she is much older than I expected. She has shiny red cheeks and a little button nose. She looks like Mrs. Santa Claus. For a big woman she looks very timid, and she peeks at us with tiny bright blue eyes over her old-fashioned gold-rimmed glasses. The screw says, "Anna, here's your new coder. Bagliazo, this is Miss Rupenthal. She'll be your supervisor in the coding room."

The screw leaves and Miss Rupenthal stares at me over her glasses. She folds her hands over her waist, and, although she isn't exactly smiling, she looks very pleasant. Her nose quivers a little, and it occurs to me that, more than Mrs. Claus, she looks like an enormous rabbit. Harvey. She says, "Well, now." I'm sure something else is to follow, but nothing does. She just stands there staring pleasantly. I'm about to laugh. Finally I say, "Nice to meet you," and this jars her into action. "Come on, I'll take you in the coding room."

We cross the hall, and as Miss Rupenthal opens the door of the coding room, I hear the sound of drawers slamming and chairs scraping. But by the time we get inside, nothing is happening. I see three women seated at desks, turned to see us come in. I see three windows, two on the long side of the room open wide and letting in a breeze and morning sunshine. Miss Rupenthal says, "Girls, this is Antonia Bagliazo. She's going to be working here now. Please don't fill her up with silly ideas." She introduces me to the women one at a time. There is Rachel, a dark-haired, dark-eyed schmoo-shaped woman of about twenty-five, and her "Hello, how are ya?" is thick with a New York Jewish accent. She offers me her hand, and I notice that it's tiny, extremely white, the kind that looks like it has no bones in it. Her handshake is limp, and I decide immediately I don't like her. Miss Rupenthal says, "Rachel has been here the longest, so she'll show you what to do."

Then there is Grace, a lovely long-legged black woman, younger than Rachel, with huge sad eyes. She only nods at me when Miss Rupenthal introduces us and doesn't offer her hand.

The third person, Sandy, isn't even a woman. She's a scrawny, awkward-looking girl, maybe sixteen, with her hair chopped very short. She has a cowlick that stands straight up, her neck and her arms are skinny and too long, her clothes hang on her all wrong, and she looks exactly like the roadrunner in the cartoons. She too only nods.

When the introductions are over Miss Rupenthal points at the one empty desk. "You sit there." She hesitates, and doesn't seem to know what to do next. After a moment she says, "Rachel, show her what to do." She goes to the door, opens it, and turns back to face us. "You girls have fun, now." She smiles as if she has made a particularly clever joke and leaves the room, closing the door behind her.

I sit down at the desk and Rachel picks up a stack of large printed forms that have spaces for information to be filled in. She drops them on my desk and then brings some other papers with handwritten lists of names followed by columns of information such as race, age, offense, and length of sentence. She explains that we transfer this handwritten information to the larger forms, using numerical codes instead of English words except for the names. From here it goes someplace else to be entered in computers.

"That's it? We just code prison statistics?"

"Yeah. It's really easy. You drew a cherry job. Everybody wants to work up here because nobody bothers us much. Rupie only comes in about four times a day, and we can hear her coming because of those big clumsy shoes she wears. Rupie is easy, anyway. You can do about twenty of these an hour, but Rupie thinks it takes all day to do twenty. So we don't have to work much."

"What do you do the rest of the time?"

Rachel points to Grace, who is reading a book, and Sandy, who is writing a letter. "Anything you want."

"If this is such a cherry job, why do you think I got assigned here?"

"You probably scored high on the tests. Administration thinks it takes brains to put little numbers in little blocks. That shows you how smart they are."

Rachel gives me a list of codes for the various items of information and shows me how to enter them. I start to work, and Rachel goes back to her desk, opens the bottom drawer, and takes out some knitting. She knits without looking at what she's doing, and I'm fascinated with how fast her tiny boneless fingers move.

As she knits, she asks me where I'm from, where my mother and father are, if I have any kids, and a lot of other personal questions that I really don't want to answer. Yet this is my first day here and I know I might be in this room with these women a long time. I don't want to start off seeming unfriendly, unwilling to say anything about myself. At the same time I have an instinct that I shouldn't ask the same kinds of questions of them. I'm the new kid on the block. Grace and Sandy look up occasionally, so I know they're listening, but they don't join in. And Rachel doesn't ask me what I'm here for or how long my sentence is, which tells me she already knows. I feel annoyed even more. What if I didn't want anybody to know? There doesn't seem to be any way to keep people from knowing what's on your record. All in all, I'm feeling squirmy, and I'm relieved when Rachel finally abandons the personal questions and asks me what cottage I'm in.

"Seven."

"Seven! Oh my dear, you *are* on top of the heap. Not only in coding, but in High Power. Who have you met over there so far?"

I say the women whose names I remember.

"Lee is a grand old gal. She's a legend around here."

"Yeah, I really like her. One thing I can't figure out though – and I missed my chance to ask – what was she here for in the fifties?"

Rachel laughs, and Grace and Sandy both look up, smiling. "Then you don't know the best part. She took a shot at a federal revenue agent."

I'm shocked, and I can see they're enjoying the effect of this news on me. "Then how come she got probation when she was busted for moonshining?"

All three of them laugh now. "They didn't know she had a record. She didn't tell them, and when they sent her fingerprints through they didn't come up with anything. Nobody knows why. But, you know, federal records are a mess. My cousin went to apply for his veteran's benefits and they told him he'd never been in the service." Rachel suddenly stops knitting, her face goes serious and she seems to be listening hard. Then she says, "The fuzz!" and quickly stuffs her knitting in the bottom drawer. Grace shoves her book in a drawer too, and Sandy slips her notepaper under the forms on her desk. I laugh as I realize that this was the commotion I heard as Miss Rupenthal and I approached the coding room.

By the time the door opens, we are all coding intently. Miss Rupenthal, a woman, and two men enter the room. Miss Rupenthal is twisting her skirt in her fingers. She says to the visitors, "This is the statistical coding room. These girls are the only ones who work on this floor. They code prison statistics for entry into the computer." The three people look around the room, and the woman visitor says, "What a lovely office! What would I have to do to get a job here?" The two men laugh, but Miss Rupenthal ignores the joke, or maybe it didn't register. She says, "I'll show you my computers. Nobody uses them," and walks out of the room, the guests following.

As soon as the door closes, Rachel snarls, "If one more person says 'What do I have to do to get a job here?' I'm gonna get violent."

"Who are those people?"

"Probably politicians. They're always bringing somebody through here. They like to show off the school building. Makes them think the prisoners are getting educated."

"They won't think so if Miss Rupenthal tells them nobody uses the computers."

"Oh, dear old Rupie doesn't know what she's saying half the time. Nobody takes her seriously anyhow. She's kind of dotty."

"She certainly isn't like any of the other screws. How old is she, anyway?"

"In her sixties, I'm sure. Maybe seventy. Personally, I don't think she knows where she is. I think she wandered on the reservation by mistake one day, and somebody thought she worked here and so she's been here ever since."

It's a mean joke and I know I shouldn't smile, but I do, because Miss Rupenthal seems so distracted it's possible.

Rachel and Grace and Sandy go back to what they were doing before the tour arrived, but I keep coding. For one thing, I don't have anything else to do, but anyway I'm interested in the names. As I do each one, and find out if a guy is black or white, how old he is, whether he's married or not, what his crime was, whether or not he's been convicted before, and what his sentence is, I try to picture the guy. I think of Leon and wonder how close I could come to picturing him if all I had to go on were these statistics. Or me. Not close at all, I decide. But I keep imagining about the names anyway. It keeps the work from getting dull.

After a while Rachel says, "Antonia, if you work like that you're gonna ruin it for all of us."

Before I can answer Sandy says, "Fuzz!" and everything goes in the drawers again. Miss Rupenthal comes in and says, "Antonia, they want you down in Administration."

"Do you know what for?"

"No. Nobody ever tells me anything around here." She giggles. "I think you'd better go right away. Don't get lost!" She leaves the room.

I feel panicky. I ask Rachel, "What do you think they want?"

"I haven't the slightest, dearie-dearie. You'll find out when you get there."

I feel irritated that she thinks I need to have the obvious pointed out to me. But I have to ask her how to get to Administration. She gives me instructions and I leave.

At the front desk in Administration they tell me to go to room A3 in the basement. Again, it's some kind of storeroom, and on a table I see my suitcase. A tall, stern-looking screw from Orientation is waiting for me. "Bagliazo, your suitcase should have been sent home while you were in Orientation. Somehow it got overlooked. We need to know where you want it sent, but we have to go over your things first, make an inventory and have you sign a release."

"I don't have anyplace to send it."

"If you don't send it home we'll have to destroy your things. Don't you have a friend you can send it to?"

"Well, I know some people in San Pedro. I haven't asked them, but I guess they'd let me send it there."

"Very well, let's go over your things."

She opens the suitcase and right on top is a bundle of letters I got from Leon while I was in jail. She picks them up first and says, "You can't keep these."

"I don't need to keep them here. I can send them to my friend."

"No, I mean you can't send them. We have to destroy them."

I can't believe what she's saying. "Those are my personal letters. You can't destroy them."

"I'm sorry, but our regulations don't allow any written matter to be sent to anyone who isn't an authorized correspondent."

"Well, can't they be stored here then?"

"We don't store things for prisoners."

There is a silence while I try to collect myself. I have a lump of fire in my chest, and it's all I can do to keep it down. I feel desperate. I know I deserve my prison sentence and I accept it. But what gives them the right to take every goddam thing away from me? First the Cadillac – probably being driven around by some customs agent now – then my platinum watch, the first beautiful thing I ever owned, my shoes, even my goddam tampon. All I have left of anything in the world is my letters from Leon. I feel like if I let them go there'll be nothing left of me or my life. But all I can think of to say is, "Those are my personal letters. You don't have any right to destroy them."

The screw is mad now. She puts her hands on her hips and lifts her chin so she is looking down her nose at me. "Young lady, I think you need to remember where you are."

That does it. I scream at her, "I know goddam well where I am, lady!" She's shocked. I've been a pretty quiet prisoner so far. I'm shocked too, and I'm scared. I don't know what will happen to me for screaming at a screw. We stare at each other, each thinking about what to do next. I decide the smart thing to do is let her make the next move. I stay quiet, but I meet her eyes without trying to hide how much I hate her. It's the first time I've ever been pushed hard enough to face up to a screw, and I have the feeling that everything will be changed from now on, and that I'm not in for an easy time of it.

At last she takes a step toward me, folds her arms over her chest and says, "The letters go." I know perfectly well there's no answer and no argument. I can't hold my eyes on hers anymore. I lower them, and she starts taking my clothes out of the suitcase, and asking me to verify that I'm choosing to send each item. She has a list already made up, and when we've gone over everything I sign the inventory, give her the address of my friend David in San Pedro, and I'm sent back to the coding room.

On the way back to the school building, I see the two men and the woman who came to the coding room earlier. A screw is with them, and they're all smiling and one man is pointing at a flower bed by cottage 5. I want to yell at them, "You stupid assholes, they're only showing you the goddam surface." But suddenly I get a picture of myself when I first got here, how pleased I was with everything, what a great place I thought it was. No wonder Bertha looked at me like I was some kind of nut. What the joint calls orientation isn't the real orientation at all. No sir. The real orientation takes place in the storerooms. I didn't get it the first time, when Bertha took me to the storeroom, so they had to do it again. Everybody tried to tell me they don't call anything by its right name around here. I smile, remembering my own denseness. But I finally caught on, and I'm all oriented now. Boy, am I oriented. I laugh so loud that the screw and the visitors turn around to look at me, cackling to myself like a madwoman, walking fast back to the school building.

Prior

Convictions

When I open my window this morning I notice that the woods outside the reservation are all gold and red and orange, and there's a little bit of ice in the air. How did that happen without me noticing? I've been so depressed since I got here, and the routine around here is so monotonous, I guess I don't expect anything to change. I look a long time at the woods, and take a deep breath. Time is going by, that's what the turning of the leaves means. All the days being alike made it seem like everything was standing still, that I was stuck in time and my sentence would never be over. This morning I understand that it will be over someday, if I just keep plodding along one day at a time.

This thought has me in a pretty good mood by the time I get to work. But I no sooner get my coat hung up and sit down at my desk than Rachel says to me, "You got the highest IQ of anyone they ever had on this reservation."

"What makes you think that?"

"I don't think, I know."

"You can't possibly know."

Rachel smiles that smug smile of hers. "I certainly *can* know, and I do. You oughta know by now it's not that hard to get into records if you have friends working over in Administration."

156

"What the hell right've you got going into my records?"

"Haven't you heard? You left your privacy at the gate, dearie-dearie. If you want to keep secrets, you better check out of this place." Rachel is looking at me with mock sadness, shaking her head as if I'm a hopeless case. Sandy is getting a real charge out of this. She's sitting back with her feet on the desk and grinning like she just ate a cop. She loves it when Rachel and I fight.

It seems to me like the shocks never end. I just decide I've finally been dealt every blow I'm going to be dealt, and then something else happens that knocks my feet out from under me. All my goddam records are public business. I'm so mad I can't say anything. I just stare at Rachel, wondering why the hell she wants to know these things about me, and she answers the question as if she heard me thinking.

"I didn't think you'd get so bent out of shape about it. I didn't check out your records to snoop. We do it all the time. If we know what the score is, we can be one jump ahead of the screws. I thought I was doing you a favor. I thought you'd like to know your test results."

"You should have asked me first."

"Next time I will, believe me." Rachel looks offended. She starts knitting really fast and looking down at her work, and most of the time she never looks at it. She can knit in her sleep. She's not going to tell me anything else she saw in my file, and now I'm curious, but I'll be damned if I'll ask her. She had no right. Besides, whatever she tells me, Grace and Sandy will hear too, and I have no way of knowing what she might have uncovered. Better leave it alone.

I start coding, but I can't shake my anger. My *IQ*, of all the damn things.

The room is quiet for a while. Grace is reading her book, Sandy's writing a letter, I'm coding, and Rachel is knitting knitting knitting. But soon Rachel says, "So tell us about your old man."

"What makes you so sure I have an old man?"

"Just making conversation. Do you have one?"

"Yeah."

"Is he a spic or a spade?"

What a question! The nerve of this woman. "What makes you

think he's either one?"

"You're the type, honey."

"What does that mean?"

"It doesn't mean anything except you're the type. Is he a spic or a spade?"

"He's Mexican, and don't call him a spic. How do you feel when people call you a kike?"

"Spic is just a term. It doesn't mean anything."

"Nothing means anything to you. Well, kike is just a term. Do you like it?"

"I'm sorry. I didn't know you'd get insulted. So is he in the joint too?"

"Yeah. I don't want to talk about it."

"You got busted behind your old man?"

"I don't want to talk about it."

"How come you got busted if you're so smart?"

"Well obviously I wasn't so smart."

"You got the highest IQ they ever had on this reservation."

"Did you start all this just to come back to that again? Don't you ever say anything about my IQ again, you hear? Just because a person has a high IQ doesn't mean they're smart." The tears are rolling down my face, I'm so mad.

Rachel looks shocked at my tears. She has even stopped knitting. I bend back over my coding to hide my face. Rachel says, "I'm really sorry. I didn't realize it was such a big deal to you. I mean, if I had an IQ like that I'd be unbearable. You're awfully touchy. Where I come from, we say 'spic' all the time and no one thinks anything of it."

I don't know whether to believe her or not. "In L.A. you can get killed calling someone a spic."

"Oh, well, L.A.," she says, smiling. In a soft voice she says, almost crooning, "Friends, okay? I didn't mean anything."

"Okay," I say, but I'm still mad. Somehow I end up saying whatever she wants me to say, telling her whatever she wants to know. Part of the trap is that she seems so sincere, and part of it is she just keeps at it 'til she gets an answer. Why can't I just say no and hold the line? But maybe she's telling the truth, maybe she's really sorry. Maybe I'm too touchy, like she says. Then she says, "So why are you so sensitive about your IQ?" and I decide,

Here's my chance to make her understand. So I say, "All my life someone's been telling me how smart I am just when I'm messing up really bad. As if because I'm smart I got no right to mess up. As if I messed up because I wanted to, or out of meanness. I flunk a test and some teacher tells me, 'You can do better than that, a smart girl like you.' Well, if I could've done better I would have, damn it. And now you're telling me again how smart I am, and here I am in this goddam prison. Just like you said, how come I'm in prison if I'm so goddam smart? So I don't want to hear about my fuckin' IQ."

"Please excuse me if I'm wrong, but maybe the teacher's right. You couldn't have flunked because you're stupid. And anything else, well . . . maybe you just weren't trying."

Rachel's smugness is infuriating. "It's more than that."

"Well, what?"

"It's hard to explain. Doing good at stuff isn't automatic just because you got a high IQ. There's been lots of times when I really wanted to do well and I just couldn't."

"For instance?"

"Well, once I was in a play. I think it was in the eighth grade. We were doing a Shakespeare play, and I got a real important part. I had to die on stage, and while I'm dying I give this long terrific speech on how beautiful England is. I can still remember one of the lines: 'This royal throne of kings, this sceptred isle.' When I read for the part I was so good the teacher didn't even have anybody else read. And all through the rehearsals I knew my lines and never blew them once, and I put a lot of feeling into them and Miss Green, the teacher, was so thrilled she almost cried. But when the performance came I stood up there and said my lines as if I was reading the phone book, and I left out about twenty lines right in the middle of the sceptred isle speech. When I walked off the stage Miss Green was standing in the wings crying. I felt awful, because she was very old." I'm so involved in the memory now I forget I'm mad at Rachel. "I still feel bad about it, because of all the teachers I had in high school, she's the only one who taught me anything I still remember. I can still remember part of that speech: 'Methinks I am a prophet new inspired/ And thus expiring do foretell of him./ His rash fierce blaze of riot cannot last,/ For violent fires soon burn out themselves/ something something something/ With eager feeding food doth choke the feeder. . . .' "

Grace says, "My mother would like that line. She always said I eat too fast."

"And I remember some of the England stuff. 'This blessed plot, this earth, this realm, this England,/ This nurse, this teeming womb of royal kings . . .' "

"Teeming womb?" says Rachel, laughing.

"Yeah. Pretty rich stuff, huh? And guess what else I remember: What Zephirus eek with his swete breeth inspired hath in every holt and heeth the tendre croppes, and the yonge sonne hath in the Ram his halfe cours y-ronne, and smale fowles maken melodye, that slepen al the night with open ye."

"I understood the last part, about the fowls sleeping all night with their eyes open. What is that, German?" says Grace.

"Naw, it's Middle English."

"No shit."

Rachel says, "That's not Shakespeare."

"No, it's Chaucer's Canterbury Tales. Anyway, Miss Green was a good old lady, and I wanted to please her, and then I blew my speech even though I knew my lines perfectly and I wasn't even that scared. I never knew why I did that."

"I think anybody could do that. You were probably more scared than you thought."

I don't know what to say, because I know what I know, but I don't know how to convince her and I can't think of any other examples off the top of my head. I've forgotten a lot of things like that, because I didn't want to remember them. Rachel is silent, knitting away. Her hands move so fast they remind me of little white birds fluttering. I stare at them while I try to come up with another example. But the silence makes me feel like I gotta say something. Even Grace has put down her book and is sitting there looking at me, like she's waiting for me to go on.

Then something occurs to me. "A little while ago you said to me, 'How come you got busted if you're so smart?' Well, that's just what I'm talking about. You got busted, Sandy got busted, Grace got busted. But you aren't asking them why they got busted. By asking me, it's like you're saying you guys had a right to get busted but I didn't, that being smart takes away my right to mess up, but you guys have the right. That's what I'm talking about, see?"

"Oh . . . yeah, I think I do. But you said there were times you wanted to do well and couldn't. I don't see the connection."

"Neither do I." We all laugh.

Grace picks up her book and starts to read, I go back to my coding, and it's quiet again except for the click of Rachel's needles. But only about a minute goes by when Sandy jumps up out of her chair and shouts at me, "You're full of shit, you know that?" She paces the length of the room and back again, slams her chair back against the wall, grabs it and puts it back in position, and sits down. She takes her pencil and goes back to writing her letter.

The rest of us are stunned. Rachel looks at me and shrugs. Sandy's hated me since the first day I got here, and this kind of tantrum is routine, but I can't figure out why she hates me and I want to know what's going on. "Sandy? What's the matter? What did I say?"

"You're full of shit, that's all."

"That doesn't tell me anything, Sandy. Tell me what's the matter."

"I told you. You're full of shit."

There just isn't any way I can answer that, so I don't even try.

About fifteen minutes of silent reading, knitting, and coding pass. But Rachel has pushed my button, and I can't stop thinking about the IQ thing. I really didn't know 'til now that it bothered me so much. Nobody ever asked me any questions about it before. I can remember how mad I got when my mom bragged to people about the A's I got on my report cards. Then next time my grades would go down. Way down. Then she couldn't brag about me and I liked it better that way, but I don't know why. There was another thing too. I wouldn't do anything hard. Like working for my Girl Scout merit badges. If I could do the work in fifteen minutes, fine. But if I had to dig in and do some real work, some real learning, I wouldn't do it. When I ran out of easy merit badges I dropped out of the scouts. I dropped out of everything after a while.

I'm thinking along like this when the door opens – there's the usual panicked scramble to get knitting, books, and letters into drawers – and Rupie comes in. She peers at me over her rabbit glasses and she's smiling. "Antonia, you have a visitor."

I'm stunned. It just isn't possible that I have a visitor. "Who is it?"

"They didn't tell me. They just said to send you down to the visiting room."

I look at Rachel, whose eyes are big. She's looking almost as pleased as if the visitor was for her. She sure loves something – anything – to happen. But I feel scared. There just isn't anybody who could be coming to see me. Not that many people know I'm here, and the people who do know have no way to come this far. Rachel sees my panic and she says, smiling, in her crooning voice again, "Go on, Baggie, you won't find out who it is unless you go."

All the way down the hill to the visiting room I have fear pains in my stomach, just like I did at the trial. At the same time I know I couldn't not go. It's not that often there's any break in the routine around here. When the unexpected happens, even if it's something horrible, you end up feeling grateful for it. It's better than the deadly monotony.

When I walk into the visiting room though, it's much worse than anything I could imagine. It's my father. I stop in my tracks, unable to keep walking. My legs feel like they're melting under me, and if I thought I had fear pangs before, now my insides are being burned out.

My dad is sitting on a couch, grinning at me across the room, enjoying the hell out of my shock. I feel like I can't let him see how scared I am, and I pull up all my strength and walk the rest of the way across the room. But I can't smile. This is too terrible. "How did you know I was here?"

"My agents are everywhere."

Fine joke. Just fine. I sit down in a chair opposite him.

"How are you getting along?" he says.

"I'm surviving."

"You look healthy."

"Yeah, I'm okay. The food's better here than it was in jail."

"Look, Toni, I'll come right to the point. I don't have much time because I have to drive back to Baltimore this afternoon. I know a little bit about what happened. It's clear that you can't go back to California. Those people will be after you . . ." I open my mouth to say "What people?" but my dad keeps right on talking. ". . . they don't let you go that easy. Have you thought about what you're going to do when you get out?"

"No. I don't know. That's a long way off yet." I'm lying. I've always assumed I'd go back to California, but I can't say that after what he just said.

"Well, I came to tell you that I'm willing to sponsor you when your parole time comes around, but I don't want you to think you're going to have an easy time. You'll come to Reisterstown, and you're going to have to grow up. You think you're a woman but you're not, you're a child, or you wouldn't be in this situation. You're going to be responsible to me, and you're going to have to grow up. Is that understood?"

I'm almost too stunned to answer, but I manage to nod. I'm stuck back there at the people who won't let me go. What people? And I'm numb with the dread of being on parole to my father. I'm more scared of him than of anything, maybe even death. But at the same time I see instantly that my dad, with his big business and his high-class neighborhood and all that, is my ticket to an early parole. It seems like I have to choose between the frying pan and the fire, but then . . . the choice has already been made for me, like it always has been. I just haven't got enough guts to say, "I'd rather do more time than be paroled to you."

My dad gets tired of waiting for me to say something – I'm staring at him with my mouth open while all this whirls through my head and finally he says, "Betty and the kids send their love."

"Oh . . . yeah. How are they?"

"Everyone's fine. We live in Reisterstown now . . ." and he goes on like that for a while. I hardly hear him. I have so many awful feelings swirling around in me like a whirlpool I can't even think. Finally my dad gets up and I automatically get up too. He hugs me, and the familiar smell of his pipe and his expensive wool clothes is almost more than I can stand, and tears start coming, but I swallow them back. "Be good," he says, chuckling at his own joke, and then he's gone.

On the way back up the hill to the coding room everything erupts. How dare they contact my father! I'm twenty-three years old, I'm an adult, it should be up to me, how dare they! The main thing I'm feeling, besides rage, is humiliation. It seems my dad shows up every time I'm in disgrace of some kind. He likes to come riding in on a big white horse and do rescues. Where were you when I really needed you, you sonuvabitch? Where were you all the ordinary everydays of my childhood when I was going nuts trying to live with a crazy mother? But there's no white horse to that, is there, Daddy? You were off starting a new family with Betty and to hell with the old family. A child, am I? Listen, children don't run dope over the border. And if you could see the tricks I do in bed, you wouldn't call me a child, damn it. I'm a woman! A WOMAN! Ask Leon! And the worst thing of all the stuff I'm feeling is a small question on the edge of my mind, wondering if he could be right.

I don't want to go back to the coding room. I can hardly stand the idea of facing Rachel's goddam nosy questions. But there's nowhere to go. The screw at the visiting room will check with Rupie by phone in the next few minutes. If I'm not there they'll start looking.

When I walk into the coding room everybody looks expectant, even Sandy, but something in my face must warn them to leave me alone – nobody says anything. I go to my chair and sit down and start coding. After a while I feel more in control, and I'm grateful to them for leaving me alone. But I can't keep this all inside myself. I announce to the room in general, "It was my father."

Rachel says, "It doesn't look like you're too happy about it."

"I'm not."

"You don't get along with him?"

"I'm scared of him."

"You didn't know he was coming, I take it."

"Hell, no. I didn't want him to know I was here. I don't even know how he found out. I haven't seen him for six years."

"How come you're scared of him?"

"It's complicated, and I don't want to talk about it."

"Sorry. I didn't mean to pry."

Is this Rachel talking? I can't believe it.

I go back to my coding, but I'm thinking about Rachel. She's trying to do better, and I'm touched. A few minutes go by. I glance up at Rachel, and she's knitting away even faster than usual. Her face is blank. I can't stand it. "Rachel, my folks were divorced when I was five, and he used to come see me once a year and take me to all sorts of fancy places my mother never took me, and he'd bring all kinds of expensive presents my mother couldn't afford to buy even if she wanted to, which she didn't. So I thought he was some kind of god. But when I got older, I spent more time with him, and if I'd do something wrong he'd get so mad he'd scare me to death, and then he'd just cut me off and have nothing to do with me for years at a time. He was always pulling the ground out from under me, and I got so I was scared to just be around him." I never told anybody this stuff before, and I'm telling more than I meant to. I make up my mind to stop now.

But Rachel says, "You must have needed him a lot, then," and that statement is so right on that I can't help saying, "Yeah, that's just it. My mother was crazy. I mean truly certifiably crazy. I grew up thinking it was normal to put scraps of paper on top of the doors so you could tell if anyone sneaked in your house while you were gone. I didn't understand her and I needed him so bad that I couldn't stand it when he pulled the rug out from under me. So I just preferred to stay away from him."

"So how did it go down there?"

I might as well tell her everything, now. I can't seem to help spilling my guts any time Rachel snaps her fingers. I don't know how to stop. "Not so good. I was so shocked to see him I couldn't think of anything to say. I just sat there like a stupe. He did all the talking. He's going to sponsor me for parole. He's got a business, and he's one of these upstanding Rotary Club-Kiwanis-Jaycee-type of guys, so it'll help me get out, I guess."

Rachel stops knitting and looks at me with a big grin. "Toni, that's just great! How can you look so depressed with news like that? Even if you don't like him, that's great news."

Grace is grinning at me too, and I can't stand it. They don't understand. "In the first place, I want to go back to California. I lie in my bed at night and think about the ocean, and the town where I went to high school. What few friends I got, that's where they are. In the second place, it's gonna be sheer misery living with my dad. I'd almost rather be here."

Nobody is smiling now. Rachel looks at me a minute, then she says, "Then why don't you tell them, Princess Baggie? When you go before the parole board, you tell them, 'Listen here, you send me back to California or I won't accept parole.' Tell them you don't want to go home with your rich daddy. While you're at it, why not tell them you want to go home in a limo? You might as well ask for severance pay too – a few hundred thou might come in handy." She is glaring at me like she hates the fact I even exist. This really pisses me off.

"Rachel, I've had it with you. I've been real patient with your constant questions and snooping and nosiness, and you changing colors one minute to the next like a goddam chameleon. I don't have to tell you my business, I'm just trying to be friendly, and then you get nasty because you don't like what I tell you. Well, I'm not going to put up with it anymore. You don't know what I'm going through, you got no right to judge."

Rachel looks shocked. Her mouth even falls open. Then she puts down her knitting and gets up. She goes out the door without a word. Grace and Sandy are both staring at me; they look shocked too. Finally Sandy barks at me, "Asshole!"

Why is she yelling "asshole" at me? Sandy goes back to her letter writing, but Grace is still just sitting there staring at me. I don't exactly know what to do. Grace says, "Toni, do you know that Rachel is doing thirty years?"

This hits me hard. "Oh god" is all I can say.

"Yeah. She's not eligible for parole for ten years."

"Oh shit."

"You understand what I'm saying, girl? You're coming up for parole next spring. This ain't your life here, you're just passing through. But Rachel's got nothing else for the next ten years. It ain't that she's so nosy. It's just that this is all there is for her. Whatever life she's got here she's got to make. You understand me?"

"Yeah, yeah, you don't have to beat me over the head. I understood all that the minute you said she's doing thirty years."

"Well, keep it in mind."

"Yeah."

I feel really bad when I think back over all the stuff I said, especially about how I'd rather stay here than be paroled to my dad. It isn't true. I was on a bullshit run, and I can't stand to think of how all that sounded to Rachel. And now I feel like no one here likes me, and I got to be in this room for god knows how long.

When Rachel finally comes back in the room, I can't think of anything to say to her. She sits down and doesn't speak to anyone. I pretend to be coding and all the time I'm trying and trying to think of some way to tell her I'm sorry, but everything I try out in my head just seems like more bullshit. I can't take back what I said. But I want to say something to her, and finally I say, "I been meaning to tell you, that's a real pretty sweater you're making. Who's it for?"

Rachel smiles, but she still looks sad. "It's to sell in the commissary. That's how I get my candy and fruit money. You really like it?"

"Yeah, I sure do."

"It will be for sale in the commissary when I get it done. Maybe you can get your rich daddy to buy it for you."

Well, so much for that. She's not gonna let me make up. The rest of the day is pretty slow, pretty quiet.

That night I have a dream. I'm in a courtroom watching a trial, and a whole bunch of prosecutors are showing the judge pieces of paper. They seem to be different kinds of things. Some of them are drawings, some are essays, some are tests. The judge looks at each paper and then throws it back to the person who gave it to him, pounds his gavel and says, in a big mean ugly voice, "Not good enough!" Then I realize that these are all my papers, and it is me that is on trial. Then I see that the judge's face has changed and he has become – my father! I begin to feel terrified because I know I'm going to be found guilty. Then I see my mother running around the courtroom picking up the papers that the prosecutors have thrown to the ground after showing them to the judge. She takes the papers and she starts showing them to the people who are watching the trial. She's grinning and looks very proud. Her mouth is moving but no words are coming out. It doesn't matter because I know anyway that she's bragging about these papers, saying that she's proud of me and that I'm a very smart girl. She passes real close to me a couple of times but she doesn't say anything to me. In fact, she doesn't even seem to see me.

Right then I wake up, and I have this big black hopeless feeling and can hardly keep from crying. Wow.

Later, at work, even though she hasn't spoken to me since that mess yesterday, I tell Rachel about the dream, because I feel guilty about what happened yesterday and I want to offer her something. I want to tell her it's okay to be nosy. She just keeps knitting, and when I'm through telling the dream she doesn't say a word. She acts just like nobody's been talking, and I feel like a fool telling all this to someone who won't even talk to me. But Grace saves things by asking, "What do you make of it?"

I don't know what to do but keep going. "Well, my dad has always been real hard to please. I just never seemed to be able to live up to what he expected of me, and he's always gotten real mad at me for messing up. That's why it was so hard to see him yesterday. I just feel like a big fuck-up every time I'm around him."

Rachel shakes her head over her knitting, and Sandy's bent over her letter and she's making snickering noises I know she means for me to hear. But I've done it again; I'm so deep into it now I don't know how to stop. Besides, I feel a strong need to talk about the dream, and at least Grace seems interested.

"I think the dream came from those two things yesterday. We were talking about my IQ and then my dad came, but they seem to be mixed up together in the dream, and I don't really see any connection between them. One thing I was real aware of in the dream was that my mother never looked at me or spoke to me. She was running around showing the papers to everybody and bragging, but not to me."

Wow. I hear what I've just said. My mother bragged to other people, but not to me. I never got any goddam praise from her, no matter how well I did. It was all for show! Once I say this to myself, I can't help knowing what it means. My mother didn't like me. And once I admit that, I see that it's something I've known all my life, yet this is the first time I ever said it in so many words. My own goddam mother didn't like me! No wonder I hated it when she bragged about me. It was a lie, and some-where in myself, even when I was a child, I knew it was a lie.

I've stopped talking while all this hit me and now I'm sitting there with tears streaming down my face, and Rachel and Grace are looking at me with helpless expressions on their faces. Sobs start coming up out of someplace deep. It feels like my guts are going to come up with them. My face is so twisted with crying that it hurts, and I know I must look ugly. I want to hide, but there's nowhere to go. I put my head down on my arms, helpless to stop the sobbing. I hear a chair scraping on the floor, and I'm afraid someone is going to go get Rupie. But in a few seconds I feel a hand patting my shoulder. It can only be Rachel, and she's saying, "Shhhh, shhhh, shhhh."

My mother never did that.

All Through
The House

I 've just finished painting a Santa Claus on the rec room window
and I'm putting his beard on with a can of spray snow. The
spray snow is old and the can is nearly empty, and the stuff
doesn't even look like the snow it's supposed to be, much less like
a beard or the fur trim on the Santa suit. It looks like whipped
cream left out in the sun. But that isn't my only problem. There
isn't any red paint, so Santa's suit is brown. All in all, it's a pretty
sorry-looking Santa Claus. I'm standing there, depressed, wondering if I ought to just wipe it off and forget about it, when the
truck drives up with the women from the farm. They're bringing
them back at noon because it's Christmas Eve. The rest of the
prisoners have the whole day off, but the farm women had to
work because the animals need to be fed and the stalls cleaned.

Because of Santa Claus I'm looking out the window when
Suzie gets off the truck. Her peacoat is bulging like she's eight
months gone, and I wonder, What's she got, a watermelon? Not
much chance of that in the middle of winter, so I hurry down the
hall to get a look at her when she comes in, because whatever it
is, it has to be contraband or she wouldn't have it under her coat.
Passing contraband is the main game around here. It's about the
only thing to do to keep from going nuts, the only excitement we
ever get. I want to see how Suzie's gonna get past the screw's

office with something that big. The screws always look us over when we come in, and every so often they have a shakedown just for the hell of it. The only way to get into the building with something big is to create a diversion, and I want to see the action.

Sure enough, just as Suzie starts up the steps, Lou and Jody begin scuffling and yelling at each other on the sidewalk. The screw goes running out to break it up and Suzie bolts for the cellar. I'm not far behind her, of course, and when we get down there we duck inside the supply closet and shut the door. Suzie opens her coat and out wriggles a collie puppy.

"Suzie, you're out of your fuckin' mind."

"I know," she says, and starts to giggle.

What a dumb stunt. She's gonna get us all in trouble and fuck up Christmas, if you can get any more fucked up than to be in the joint. But Suzie is only sixteen and not too bright. She shouldn't be in the federal joint at all – she's too young – but since they call it a reformatory instead of a prison they can get away with it. So here she is with all us dope smugglers and revolutionaries and bank robbers, and all she did was take a joy ride with her boyfriend in a stolen car. They went over the state line and that made it a federal offense. Which proves my point that she isn't any too bright. As if this wasn't enough, she has epilepsy. All of us know this and we try to take care of her, but she can be a pain in the butt sometimes and now is one of those times, pulling an idiot trick like bringing a dog into the cottage.

I know why she did it though. They shot a rabid fox on the reservation a few weeks ago and the head screw has given the guards orders to shoot any stray animal they see. We all know the reason for the order. I mean we see the regulation logic – that's what we're supposed to be in here to learn, regulation logic – but we still feel bad about it because we're in the middle of the mountains of West Virginia and there are lots of little animals around here. Like the skunks. If I wake up early enough in the morning I can look out my window and see them trying to get into the garbage cans. The lids fit tight and the cooks put bricks on them for good measure, but sometimes the skunks get in anyway. They stand up on their hind legs and push at the edge of the lids with their noses. They work and work at it until finally the can falls over and the lid comes off. They're pretty little things and they don't really bother anything, just dump over a garbage can now and then and maybe raise a stink once in a while. Every so often I hear a shot in the night and worry that maybe one of our skunks got it.

Well anyway, I don't even ask Suzie how she got the dog, because I can guess. She finds this puppy wandering around the farm, probably strayed from the little town of Alderson down the road, and she figures he's gonna get shot so she hides him and brings him back to the cottage. It's a stupid thing to do, but that's how Suzie is, she can't think ahead. That's how she got in the joint in the first place. And she's goodhearted. But I'm at a loss and I say to her, "Suzie, what are you gonna do with this goddam dog?"

She looks at me with big teary eyes and she says, "Toni, we just got to hide him. It's Christmas Eve and we just can't let him get shot on Christmas Eve. Not on Christmas, Toni, please," just like it was up to me. Shit, it has nothing to do with me. So I walk away, saying, "It's not any of my business, Suzie. I don't want to get caught with contraband and spend Christmas in the hole."

But Suzie calls after me, "Toni, I don't know what to do with him. Help me! I can't leave him in the supply closet. They'll find him."

"Where's your pals Jody and Lou? They helped you get into this mess, let them help you lose all your good time."

Suzie sits down on the floor and scoops the puppy onto her lap. She doesn't look at me anymore, and I think, She'll sit right there 'til they find her because she doesn't know what else to do. Jody and Lou have washed their hands of it or they'd be here by now, unless they got thrown in the hole for fighting, but that's not likely. Most of the time a little scuffle only means early lockup and bad marks on your cottage report, unless someone gets hurt or the screw on duty has it in for you. And Jody and Lou know just how far they can go with a sham fight and get away with it. They're the main diversionary-tactics force in our cottage. No, they're through with it, and Suzie's stuck here by herself with half a brain and a puppy.

I sigh. "Look, Suzie, the screened porches are locked for the winter and nobody goes in them, not even the screws. We can put him out there for the night if he doesn't make any noise, but tomorrow he's got to go, understand?"

Suzie nods, smiling like a cocker spaniel.

"You stay with the goddam dog and I'll go get the lock off the porch. I'll get someone to divert the screw if she starts down here for anything. So just sit tight and don't let him make any noise. If he starts barking, strangle him." God, I'm pissed off.

I go upstairs and find Jody and Lou in the day room. "Hey, you finks, are you gonna leave Suzie stranded with that mutt?"

Jody says, "Hi, Toni, your Santa Claus looks like a banana cream pie somebody shit in."

"There wasn't any red paint so I had to use brown, wise-ass. Now answer my question."

"We told her not to do it," Lou says. "We told her we'd help her get it in and that was it. Nobody wants to spend Christmas locked up."

"Yeah, yeah, tell me about it. So you fixed it so Suzie's almost sure to be locked up over Christmas. You're in it now and you gotta see it through. I'm gonna get the lock off the porch and put the mutt out there, so you guys cover for me."

"Aw, hell, Toni, we . . ."

"You think I want to go to the hole? You fools started it by helping her in the first place. You know she hasn't got the sense of a pigeon. You got no right to back out now. You're already in it. It's gonna take all of us to keep him hid. If Suzie goes to isolation it's your fault and goddam it you're going with her."

They can see I mean it. "Shiiiiit, " says Jody, but she goes on up the hall to watch the screw's office. Lou gets up too, and she says to me, "Come up to my room later. I've got something good for you."

"Something good" can only mean contraband. Lou is making it with some old man who works in the administration building with her – in the supply closet, no less – and now she makes him bring her all kinds of stuff from the Free World. If she ever tells on him, he could do time himself, because it's a felony to fuck a prisoner. So Lou gets about anything she wants: Free World underwear and perfume and makeup and all kinds of food. She's a first-class hustler, even in here. And a genius at finding places to hide her loot. For example, when she washes her Free

World underwear, she hangs it from the springs of her cot at night and puts it on damp in the morning.

When Lou first came here she was a redhead, I mean carrot red, but after the first few weeks you could see the dark roots showing, and then all of a sudden the dark roots were gone and the screws noticed, so they called her down to Administration. Lou claimed she was a natural redhead, knowing they knew better, but what could they say except "No you're not"? Lou just kept saying "I am so," putting on a lot of righteous indignation, and there wasn't anything they could do without proof, so they kept trying to intimidate her. But Lou's a pro and she's already been through just about everything there is to go through and she doesn't intimidate easy. So then the shakedowns started. First it was just Lou's room. They'd dump out all the drawers and tear up the bed and make as big a mess as they could and leave it that way, and Lou had to clean it up. The word spread fast, and everyone asked Lou, "Did they get it?"

"No."

It got to be a big hilarious game, with everybody involved in it. You have to understand that some screws become screws because they want power and the only way they can get it, since none of that type has an IQ over seventy, is with a stacked deck, which in this case is a ring of keys. Just once in a while a chance comes along for the prisoners to hold all the aces, and when that chance comes nobody passes it up even at the risk of going to the hole eventually because it's about the only time you get to rise up off the floor and spit the shit out of your mouth for a while. They're gonna find a way to knock you down again in the end, but for that short while, how sweet it is!

So everybody was high on Lou's little game, especially since it made the screws look so ridiculous, and Lou rubbed it in by walking around with an expression like the canary that out-smarted the cat. It takes a long time to do a dye job and the stuff gets all over the sink and it's a mess you can't hide in a hurry. The screws know that too of course, so it makes them look just that much more stupid. But when it was time for Lou to do a touch-up everybody in the cottage covered up for her. If a screw looked like she was even thinking of going near the bathroom there would be a ruckus at the other end of the cottage. We had so many fights, so many people falling down stairs with freaking-out fits, it's a wonder the screws didn't think we were all coming down with a disease of the central nervous system. They never did seem to catch on.

Next they started shaking down the whole cottage. We'd get back from work and the whole place would be torn up and we'd have to work all evening to get things back in order, but we just got more determined. After every cottage shakedown the question went around the reservation, "Did they get it?" and the answer was always "No." Each time it happened it got funnier and more satisfying.

Then the screws played their last card. They shook down every cottage on the reservation, every prisoner, and the administration building (because Lou worked there) all at the same time. They figured they had to catch it that way.

"Did they get it?"

"No."

It all made life worth living for a while, even though Lou got caught with her Free World bikini underpants on the body shake and lost two weeks good time. They were glad to get her on something but Lou didn't care. The fun was worth it, and she made the old man bring her a new pair of bikinis the next week.

After that the shakedowns stopped. They gave up on it. They had to. Lou is still a redhead and we all feel a little glow of pride every time we see her shining scarlet head. It might seem a small thing to put yourself through all that grief and misery for, but you got to realize that when someone has absolute power over your body, when they have the power to lock you in a cage and to humiliate you in any way their disabled minds can think of (You don't think anybody with a *healthy* mind ever takes a job in a prison, do you? Keeping other human beings in cages?), when they can strip you, make you bend over and stick their fingers up your cunt looking for contraband if they feel like it, well then the only way you survive without going freaked-out suicidal is to stay free in your own mind, and the way you do that is to beat them at their own game. Lou is a master of the game and they never found the goddam dye.

But now I have to think about the dog, so I go and do my trick with the lock on the porch, and it's an easy matter to get Suzie and the puppy up there. Only trouble is there's snow all over and the damn dog starts quivering the minute we put him down, so Suzie puts her peacoat down for him to lie on, and I have to cover him up with mine. It's a good thing he's a quiet mutt. It seems like all he wants to do is lie in the coats looking pitiful – depressed, to tell the truth – and the screens are all clogged with snow and there's a lot of bushes around too. There's a minimum crew working on account of its being Christmas, and all in all it looks like his chances are pretty good as long as he stays quiet.

I get the lock back on so you can't tell it's been off, and that's that. All we have to worry about is whether he'll start barking or whining. If he doesn't, we're home free.

I leave Suzie in the rec room telling everybody about her dog and I go on up to Lou's room. Lou, Jody, and Angie are waiting for me. They all grin like they're getting out tomorrow and I say, "What's the big secret?"

Lou says, "Look around, you fool."

I look around and I can't see anything. "Well, whatever it is you're gonna have it hid anyway, so how am I supposed to know?" I feel irritated because I don't like anybody to make a fool of me.

"Boy, are you stupid. You're stupider than Suzie. Look again."

This time I spot something: four bottles of regulation prison-issue shampoo. Four? I go over and uncap one of the bottles and take a sniff. Whisky! I'm so tickled I bust out laughing. There's nothing I need more tonight than a drink, and I grab Lou and give her a big hug. We each sit down with a bottle of "shampoo" and start the party. Pretty soon we're bragging about our men on the outside, which leaves Jody out because she's lez outside the joint as well as in. Lou and Jody are lovers in the joint – what a pair they make, Lou with her delicate frame, pale skin, and red hair; Jody with her dark-chocolate skin and athlete's build – but Lou's got a man on the outside, and she's bragging that he runs an exclusive racket in Washington, D.C., providing call girls and dope to rich politicians. So then I brag that my old man is one of the biggest dealers in East L.A. and I tell them it was for him that I was running dope across the border. Angie starts in about her pimp in New York and how good he is to her. She says he sent her ten dollars for Christmas and she seems to think that's a big deal. Ten dollars!

Jody has been quiet through all this but I guess the ten dollars makes her mad enough to speak up. "I wrote bad checks to take a trip around the world and you know who I did it for? Me! My own fucking self."

I feel like I've been slapped. I glance at Lou and I can see she's mad too. We both know Jody is saying we're fools since we're in the joint because of some man taking advantage of us. I think, Jody is just sour because she doesn't have a man and she's probably lez because she can't get one, but I really know better and the lie sticks in my chest before I can let it rise up and turn into something ugly to say. And if what she's saying is wrong, why do I feel so ashamed? Before I can think any more about it, Angie starts talking again. Jody's remark has gone right over her head, not because she's stupid but because she's ripped already. She's a tiny thing and I guess it doesn't take much liquor to get her loaded. She goes on and on about how great this pimp of hers is, and Lou and I don't know how to stop her. The more she talks the more I feel like crawling under the bed. I can't look at Jody. Finally Angie says, with her eyes rolling up in her head, "Man, he sure can eat pussy."

There's a long moment of silence, then Lou says, "Angie, you don't tell things like that on your old man."

"Why not?" says Angie. "I can come just thinking about it." Jody and I laugh, but Lou says, "Any guy who eats pussy is a fag. They do it because they really want to be eating the cock of the guy who just fucked you."

It gets stone quiet and we all just sit there, not knowing what to say or do. There's no call for Lou to talk like that even if she could be right. We all know pimps hate women. Besides, any woman likes a man to eat pussy and Lou is probably no exception and we all know that too. And what the hell do she and Jody do at night, hold hands? So it's a mean and crazy thing to say to Angie. Thinking on her old man is all she has to help her make it through her time.

Angie looks at Lou a long time and then she says, "You lie." She gets up and walks unsteadily out the door. I can see Lou feels rotten. I don't know why she did it or why Jody said what she said and probably they don't know either. Maybe we're all just feeling bad because it's Christmas and we're in the joint and you can't fix it by drinking a little bourbon out of a shampoo bottle and someone had to do something mean to someone to get the shit out of her system. I came real close myself when Jody made her remark. So everybody got mean but Angie.

Later we go to the dining room, and when Suzie and I show up for the lineup outside the cottage without our peacoats the screw notices. "Where the hell are your coats?"

Suzie looks panicked and I know I have to say something before Suzie blows it. "We're forming a polar bear club," I holler, trying to sound enthusiastic, and I jump up and down and slap my hands against my upper arms and puff like an athlete. Suzie takes the cue and starts trotting in place. "We're getting in condition," she says, but she doesn't say in condition for what and the screw isn't bright enough to ask her. She just shakes her head and marches us off to supper.

Christmas Eve dinner is a downer. We thought we might get turkey but instead we get ham. We shoulda known. We got turkey for Thanksgiving. They wouldn't do it twice in one year. Anyway we have to take the ham back for the dog so maybe it's just as well because it would have been harder to give up the turkey. But still, I'm cussing him because we don't get ham that often either. We got lots of pigs here but the screws must take all the hams home because all we usually get is the fat.

Since Suzie and I got no coats, we have to pass the ham to some other women to carry for us. They don't like getting greasy pockets and they don't like kicking in their ham too in order to make enough for a meal for the dog, so Suzie and I aren't too popular around here right now.

With Jody watching the screw, we feed the dog and give him water and clean up his mess and he seems happy. He doesn't bark or whine at all, just wiggles anytime someone comes near him.

There's a Christmas program at the auditorium in the evening, some songs and skits the inmates fixed up. It isn't very good but it's something to do. Still, I'm glad when it's time for lockup. I just want to be by myself and the only time for that is in my room after lockup. I sit at the window and look out at the reservation.

It's pretty, with fresh snow all around. But no matter how pretty it is, a prison is a prison, and the key turns in the lock every night. But I love to look out my window at night. In the country the sky is so much blacker than in the city and there are so many more stars. As I gaze at them I try to think messages to people I know back in California. Sometimes I feel like someone comes in the window and is there with me. I pretend it's Leon. I talk to him and convince myself that wherever he is he can hear me. I believe it so much that I spook myself sometimes, but it's all I can do. They won't let me write to him because he's in the joint too.

The reservation is quiet for a long time, and then late, about eleven o'clock, some lonely gal starts singing Christmas carols out her window, and one by one other voices join in. I guess everyone on the reservation is still awake, and I get shivers because those voices are so beautiful echoing across the reservation. I sing too, opening my window like everyone else so we can hear good and sing together even though it's biting cold. We keep each other company, each in our own lonely room – until the whistle blows.

It's an awful wail – if God was a whistle he'd sound like that when he was mad. The only time it ever blows is when somebody makes a break. I guess some poor gal couldn't take its being Christmas and the singing and all, and dropped out her window and took off. The singing stops, of course, and every woman on the reservation is sitting alone at her window wondering who it is that ran for it and if she will make it.

By the time the whistle stops, the hounds have started. The guards track the breakouts with hounds but you never see them. You just hear them echoing back and forth between the hills like the wail of a train down a long tunnel. Then someone hollers out her window, "Make it, baby!" and her voice echoes off the hills and mixes in with the baying of the hounds. It's the way we're set down in the mountains that does it. One by one we pick up the cry. Every few seconds someone hollers, "Make it, baby!" although we know she won't. No one ever does. The legend is that only one person ever broke out successfully. She's supposed to have walked out in a nun's habit she made in the sewing room, but I don't know if I believe it.

The baying of the hounds goes on for a long time. Then it stops and we know they caught her. It's only then I realize that mixed in with all the other echoes is the howling of our puppy from the porch downstairs.

No one sings after that, and I close my window and go to bed. I'm half frozen and I cry a lot before I go to sleep. I don't cry much since I came here. No one does, mostly because it doesn't do any good but partly because once you start it's hard to stop. Yet once in a while I can't help it. This time I'm crying for myself and for the gal who didn't get away and for Angie and for poor dumb Suzie and the puppy and for everyone in the whole world except the screws maybe.

In the morning the lineup for breakfast is very quiet. Suzie and I still don't have our peacoats but the screw doesn't say anything. They get withdrawn and mean when something goes wrong. It's Christmas, so we get Canadian bacon and eggs for breakfast and we take the bacon back for the dog.

But when we get to the porch he's gone. Our peacoats are there but no dog. Suzie starts crying. "They found him," she blubbers, now they'll shoot him." What can I say? We didn't hear any shots during the night. We would have had to turn him loose anyway, and listen for the shot all day, but it won't do any good to tell Suzie that. Another thing I think of which I don't mention to Suzie is that our peacoats have our names in them. The screw that got the dog knows who we are.

All in all, it's a shitty Christmas. I put my coat on to take a walk outside. My last walk, I figure, before they come to take me and Suzie to the hole. As I go out the door I shove my hands in my pockets and I feel a piece of paper. I pull it out and read it. *I took him off the reservation,* it says. That's all.

I never find out which screw it was, because no one ever comes to lock us up. Sometimes I try to tell by looking in their faces, which is hard to do because screws don't like you to look them in the eye – they think you're challenging them. It's safer to keep your eyes on the ground. But I study them whenever I think I can get away with it. Trouble is, they've got expressions so stony you can't tell what is going on in there. To tell the truth, they all look alike to me.

The Floor

Sometimes I think I can't stand it anymore. I know I did a dumb thing, not going to Easter services, and what makes me so depressed is I knew it was a dumb thing to do. Jody copped our cottage reports a few weeks ago, grabbed them off the screw's desk when she forgot to lock them up and went off to get something in the cellar, and we all hid in the toilet stalls and read them and found out what evil thoughts the screws are thinking about us. And right there on mine, so important in the screw's mind that she changed to a red pen to write it down, is: "Does not attend church services."

And now as I sit here with my chin in my hand staring at the goddam beautiful rhododendrons blooming under the goddam unbarred window of this goddam nonetheless prison, it seems unbelievable to me that I didn't go to Easter service, the only woman in this cottage not to go, so that Garth had to stay here and miss the service because they can't leave a prisoner alone in the cottage. I should've known I was asking for trouble. I don't know what came over me. It was almost like reading that cottage report made me more determined than ever I wasn't gonna go, even though I know those reports are read by my parole advisor, and that's all she knows about how I'm doing. She's gonna base her recommendation to the parole board on the cottage reports and one interview with me, and if you want to get out early you play the game and do what they want you to do. What a jerk I am! I maybe just blew it.

I manage to play the game better than most of the women, most of the time. I bow and scrape and say "Yes, ma'am" and never get in fights and when I go to work I actually work. I get good work reports. Some of the women think they're cheating the system by working as little as possible, but I see it as one way to get brownie points for getting out, and besides, goofing off actually makes the time go slower. When I get into my work the time passes much easier, though it doesn't make me too popular with some of the women.

But there's something about that goddam church-service thing that gets to me. We're supposed to have religious freedom in here, including the freedom to *not* go to church, but in practice it doesn't work out that way. No one tells you to go, no one says anything if you don't go, but it ends up on your cottage report in red ink. What are you gonna think? That bothers me more than almost anything else around here, though I can't say why. I was upset when they took away my room and put me in the dormitory because I lost what little privacy I had. But I grit my teeth and accept it. I put up with feeling degraded all the time, and being pushed around and bellowed at and lousy food and loneliness and depression and boredom and a thousand other tortures of this place, but something in me just won't put up with being forced to go to church when I don't believe all that crap, and I won't pretend to believe it, and I won't go even if it means I spend extra time in this hellhole. I can't even say why it makes me that mad. It's just going too far, that's all. Just going too goddam far. I mean, even in prison you got to draw the line somewhere or you can't stay alive inside.

So when they lined up for Easter service this morning I stood out. Garth didn't say anything at all. When they filed out for church I came up to the dorm and Garth went in her office. I lay on my bunk and the sun and the sweet-smelling spring air were coming in the open window, and something came over me that surprised the hell out of me: I wanted to wax the dormitory floor. I mean, it's a helluva crazy idea because of the way we wax floors in the joint, which is the hardest way possible.

But anyway I go down to the office and ask Garth if she'll open the supply closet because I want to wax the dorm. She looks at me like I must be up to something, because nobody ever volunteers for extra work around here unless they're promised some kind of reward. But she doesn't say anything, and she goes and opens the closet for me. I get a pail and paste wax and one of the old socks we use to put the paste wax in and some liquid wax and the buffer and some rags and the steel wool, and Garth watches me as I pick up every single thing, as if she expects me to pull some trick, and she stands there glaring at me as I lug all this stuff to the stairs.

There are five women in our dorm, sleeping on two bunk beds and one cot, and there's three dressers and three chairs and assorted junk. I push everything down to one end of the room and already I'm wondering what I wanted to do this for. Those bunk beds weigh a ton apiece, and the dressers, crammed full of stuff because they have to be shared, aren't any too light either. But I'm committed now. First I wipe up the loose dust with a soft cloth, then I pour liquid wax on the floor and scrub it down lightly with steel wool – that's how we clean the old wax off. Then I wipe it all up good with some rags, and take a cigarette break while it dries. I wonder if I should do the whole floor with liquid wax first, and then repeat the whole thing with paste wax, but then I would have to move all that furniture twice, so maybe I'd better do one whole half the floor to completion and then the other half.

I put a blob of paste wax in one of the old socks and start rubbing it in the wood. The heat from the friction and from my hand melts the wax just a little so it oozes through the sock and comes out just right. The floor glistens where the sun hits it, a glowing apricot color. This must have been fine wood they built these floors with. As many prisoners as have tramped over it, it still looks good. The air is cool and sweet like only early spring air can be, and there are a few birds singing – they can't help it, they don't know they're on prison ground. All these things, plus the motion of rubbing and rubbing, maybe the monotony and the rhythm of it, and maybe the unusual quiet in the dorm, make me feel peaceful. I don't often get to be alone in the daytime where it's quiet and calm. The more I rub the better I feel. Not happy, exactly, just not feeling the pain that usually stays with me. I'm not even thinking, just feeling the sun and the fresh sweet air and the smell of the flowers.

I push all the furniture all the way to the end of the room I just finished, and I go through the whole procedure again on the other half of the floor. Garth shows up at the door and stands there watching me a few seconds like she can't believe it. She goes away again without saying anything.

At last all the hands-and-knees work is done, and after putting all the dirty rags and socks and cans and steel wool out in the hall, I turn on the electric buffer and buff the floor down real nice. I'm in a state of mind I don't remember ever being in before, mellow to a point where it doesn't even matter anymore where I am. The humming of the buffer seems like music to me, and the swinging movement of the buffer and the easy rocking motions of my body melt together and become one movement. We're swaying back and forth, back and forth, together in a rhythm I didn't even try for, but it's rhythm all right, and it's a dance. I'm sorry when I finish buffing.

Now I have to shift all the furniture again and buff down the other end. Then I put all the furniture back in its usual place and buff up the marks I made moving it.

That's it, I'm done. I didn't realize how hard I was working, but now my body aches and the fumes from the wax have made my head feel a little weird. Well, that's okay. The sight of the beautiful floor is very satisfying. I don't get to do many things here that I can feel proud of. Just work well done, you know? I light a cigarette and lean in the doorway, taking a breather and letting my poor bones rest before I put the stuff away, and while I smoke my cig I admire my floor.

Garth appears before I finish my cigarette. "You can't leave that stuff lying all over the hall," she says.

"I'm just having a smoke," I say. I know she knows I wasn't gonna leave it there. She stands there glaring at me with her feet apart and her hands on her hip, like she always does. I know I better put out my cigarette now and pick up the stuff. I reach out my hand for the bucket and Garth says, "Pick up that bucket." I pick it up. I take a step to where the rags are lying, reach for them to put them in the bucket. "Pick up those rags," says Garth, at the very instant my hand starts moving downward.

Garth is a specialist at the power/humiliation game. She knows that every instinct in the marrow of my bones is rebelling. But if I stop reaching for the rags, if I even hesitate too long, that's it. I've been insubordinate and she can throw me in the hole, and there goes some of my time off for good behavior. There's no one around to witness that I hesitated only a second. But if I go ahead and pick up the rags she's won too, because she's stolen my right to act on my own, like a human being. She's ordering my every movement as if I were a robot. I'm damned if I do and damned if I don't. It isn't a decision I can take time to ponder over, and the main thing in my life right now is to get out of here on the earliest possible day. If Garth doesn't get my self-respect today she'll get it tomorrow anyway so what's the use?

But when you're thinking survival, thoughts aren't necessarily in words and they can go through your head like a lightning flash. I've considered the whole situation and made my decision in a split second. Even so, I'm sure there's been a flinch in my movement, a hesitation that she can see and gloat over. I'm so enraged that I want to kill her, but another part of the game is that I mustn't let it show. Don't *dare* let it show, or she'll go after that chink and probe at it until she provokes me into something worse than insubordination. I gather all my will to hold on to my feelings.

I gather the rags together, start to pick them all up. "One at a time," says Garth. I pick up a rag and put it in the bucket. I reach for another rag. "Pick up that rag," says Garth. I pick up the second rag and put it in the bucket. I bend down for another rag. "Pick up that rag," says Garth. Oh god. There are six rags.

Time seems to slow down. Because my mind is racing, I feel like I'm in a slow-motion movie, or stoned, and there's time to think between every frame. I wonder if it would be better to just tell the bitch off and go to the hole. I've never been made to bend this low. It's like licking somebody's shoes. So what if I lose some good time? Some of the women do that. They figure it's worth it. You got to save your self-respect somehow. It doesn't matter about Garth, she's not gonna respect me no matter what. It wouldn't matter which way I choose, not to her. But it matters to me. If I just tell the bitch off and go to the hole at least I'd respect myself. I'm on the brink every second of making that decision, and yet I can't make it. I feel like I'm dangling from a tiny thread that's the only thing holding me from falling into a bottomless pit, and if I even breathe wrong the thread will break and down I'll go. I open my mouth to say something but I choke on my own panic. I can't do it. Yet the more I stall the lower I feel.

Another course occurs to me. I could act like I don't understand what's happening. I could pretend I don't see anything abnormal in what she's doing to me. I could just go ahead and pick up the stuff, piece by piece like she wants, and all the time be smiling and jiving and telling her how nice the sun is and how I enjoyed the quiet and how proud I feel about the floor. I could act like I don't doubt for one minute that she's enjoying the story. I could even say, "Gee, I'm sorry you had to stay in the dorm with me and miss the service." If I don't take it seriously what would she be left with? Herself as a fool, telling me to pick up every goddam thing while I'm already doing it. After all, I don't have to believe what some twisted mind cooks up to make herself feel like God. It strikes me that the whole key is to not believe in any of it, to not believe in humiliation, to not believe that going to the hole can grind my spirit to powder. The trouble is, it isn't that easy to change what you believe or don't believe. I know if I don't give her the satisfaction of humiliating me she'll just go to more and more extremes trying to get her jollies, and I'll end up in the hole anyway. So I've come around in a circle right back to where I started from. Yet I still have a suspicion that some kind of switching around of beliefs would set me free. But how to do that is just out of reach, like a word or song I can't remember. If I could just grasp it something amazing might happen. But I can't convince myself the humiliation isn't real. How can I not believe what I see and hear and feel? It's too scary. All I've got is what I see and hear and feel, and if all that isn't real, then there's *nothing*.

Now I realize I've picked up the last of the stuff and it's too late to change tactics anyhow. I've agonized all my time away. The game is over and Garth is in control. We walk to the supply closet with Garth right behind me, as close as she can get without actually stepping on my heels. Crowding me. I think of swinging the bucket right in her face. Garth opens the closet and I put the stuff away. "Stay in the dorm until the others get back," she says. I start to walk away without saying anything. "Bagliazo," she says.

I stop and turn around.

She waits.

Then it occurs to me what she's waiting for. "Yes, ma'am," I say, being careful to say it with just the right amount of humility.

Twenty Minutes
of Freedom

The rhododendrons are in bloom, the trees shine with bright
green new leaves, Mildred's daffodils and tulips are blos-
soming around the cottages, and the sun is so bright and cheerful
I feel like I'm in a Disney movie about spring. Weird, when I'm
in such a terrible place, to be steeped in so much beauty, walking
down to Administration to get my answer from the parole board.
I remember every terrible thing that ever happened to me happened on a perfectly glorious day and I'm scared this means I'm
gonna be turned down. Seems like it should be rainy and
gloomy when terrible things happen, but I bet people get executed on days like this.

I'm walking slow because I want to make the beauty last.
When I come back up this hill I might feel like dying. I don't
think I can take another year of this place, and they can keep me
for ten years if they want to. I know I wouldn't make it. I don't
know how women with long sentences hang on. I think I'd off
myself. These thoughts make the new spring growth all the
more poignant, and the beauty all around me actually hurts.

When I get into the administration building I begin to shake
and I'm afraid I might throw up. The best thing to do is get in
there and find out what's what as soon as possible so it's over. I
knock at my parole advisor's door, she tells me to come in, and

as soon as I see her face my stomach drops: she looks grim. "Sit down, Toni." I sit.

"Toni, the parole board has granted you parole beginning July 28, on condition that you go to your father's home and stay there for the duration of your parole period."

I was so ready for disaster that I can hardly believe what I'm hearing, and I feel light as a balloon and I want to cry and laugh at the same time. As a matter of fact, my eyes are tearing and I'm giggling. My glee seems to irritate Mrs. Bentley, but fuck her!

"Toni, I want you to know that I recommended against parole at this time. The parole board overruled me, which is very unusual. They rely heavily on the parole advisor's opinion." This sobers me up fast. I wait to see what else is coming. "They felt that your family background and your father's interest and sponsorship were strong factors in your favor. My own opinion is that you psyched out the parole board. I think you're very intelligent and that you figured out what the parole board wanted to hear and that's what you told them. I don't believe you're sincerely remorseful or that you have tried to realize the seriousness of your crime. I'm telling you all this because I think you're going to get in trouble again, and I want to take this chance to caution you that if you break parole and come back, it's a lot harder to get out again. You'll go before the board again and again and again and you won't make it. Understand?"

I nod. Why is this old bitch trying to spoil this for me?

"All right. You can arrange for your father to pick you up any time after ten o'clock on July 28. You'll need to have him send you your release clothing and a suitcase. You'll report to a parole officer in Baltimore. We'll give you all the information when you leave. You understand that any problems between now and the time of your release may result in revocation of your parole?"

I nod again. I don't want to say anything in case I set her off again. I just want to get out of here. All her negative shit doesn't stop my spirit from wanting to jump out of my body with joy.

On the way back to the school building I run and jump in the air and spin completely around before I come down. I haven't done that since I was a kid. The flowers and the trees seem like close friends now and I'm talking to them, telling them over and over and over, "I'm free, I'm free, I'm free." I'm still grinning while tears run down my cheeks, and when I get in sight of the school building I see Rachel and Grace. They're in the typing room, hanging out a window, waiting and watching for me to come back. Of course they can tell right away that I made it, and they yell and smile and wave, and I give the thumbs-up sign. I take the stairs to the coding room two at a time, but halfway up I remember Rachel's thirty years. It seems wrong to be too joyful, and I'm almost ashamed that I'm getting out so soon – one year by the time the parole date comes. Rachel's been here three years and she doesn't even come up for parole for another seven. God.

But Grace and Rachel are waiting for me in the hall, grinning, and Rachel throws her arms around me. There's nothing phony in the hug she gives me, and I start crying again because I'm so touched.

"What's your date?" says Grace.

"July 28. Six weeks."

Rupie comes out of her office and stands there with that funny little smile of hers, looking like a big rabbit and twisting her skirt into little rolls with her fingers. She says, "Well, now, isn't that nice." All of a sudden I realize that she's the only good thing in this whole goddam place, besides some of the prisoners, I mean, and I can't help throwing my arms around her. "Now, now," she says, "let's not get carried away." When I let her go I see her face is bright red. She walks back into her office quickly, saying, "That's not regulation, you know. What would happen if all the prisoners went around hugging the screws? That would be a fine mess, wouldn't it? Dear, dear." Grance and Rachel and I look at each other, laughing. She actually used the word *screws*!

We go back in the coding room and I see that Sandy isn't there. "Where's Sandy?"

"She got a library pass. I don't think she wanted to be here when you got back," says Rachel.

I sigh. "Why does that girl hate me so much?"

"Everybody got to have somebody to hate. For her, it's you. There doesn't have to be any reason. She just picked you, that's all."

"I don't believe that. You gotta have a reason to hate people."

"Don't bet on it. Anyway, forget about it. I have a celebration present." Rachel goes into her knitting bag and pulls out some-

thing wrapped in tissue paper. She unwraps some fancy choco-
lates.

"Wher the hell did you get these?"

"You know better than to ask that," she says.

When I get to the dining room that night everybody's talking
about who got parole and who didn't. Terry's got a
release date only two days after me. We're thrilled to be getting
out almost at the same time. Lee didn't make it again. She
doesn't seem upset. I guess she's used to it, and doesn't expect to
make it. Maybe she's so old it doesn't matter where she is. "I ain't
finished my quilt yet anyways," she tells me. Lou made it, and
has an early release date. She takes off in only four weeks. Jody
is trying to be cheerful about it but you can tell she's hit hard. She
adores Lou.

After dinner I go to the dorm and write a letter to my dad. I
ask for an overnight case, and when I get to the part where I have
to ask for clothes, I balk. I've gained twelve pounds on the
starchy and fatty food here. I know I can't get into a twelve anymore. Terry walks in while I'm sulking about it. "You writing
your dad?"

"Yeah."

"It's quieter around here tonight than I ever heard it.
Everybody's holed up writing their families that they made it or
didn't make it."

"Yeah. I hate it that I gained all this weight. I can't make
myself ask my dad for a size fourteen."

"You got six weeks. You could get some diet pills from the dis-
pensary and take some of it off."

"You got to be kidding. They'll give you diet pills?"

"Yeah, if they think you're serious. They weigh you every
week and if you don't lose weight they won't give you any more."

"Hot damn. I'll tell my dad to get me a size twelve, and then
I'll have to lose the weight or go home naked."

"Sure, why not?"

Later, after lockup, I'm lying on my bunk smiling at the ceiling,
dreaming all kinds of stuff about getting out, like buying clothes
and going to the movies and walking down a nice tree-lined
street to the drugstore to get an ice cream cone. God! If I can just

be free to go to the drugstore any time I want I'll never complain about anything again.

In the middle of all this, I hear crying coming through the wall. It's Donna. She got turned down for the second time. She's got a two-year-old baby staying with her grandmother until she gets out. The grandmother is too poor to travel from Georgia to West Virginia, so Donna never sees the baby. All of a sudden I feet really depressed. I pull the pillow over my head so I can't hear her, but with the excitement for myself and the depression about Donna making war in my head, it takes me a long time to go to sleep.

I float through everything for the next few days. Nothing bothers me. When the usual aggravations start, when a screw talks to me like I'm a cockroach or Sandy acts like I'm Attila the Hun, I just think, I'm getting out of here in six weeks, and shine it on. I go to the clinic, and Terry was right, they give me diet pills and tell me to come back every Friday to get weighed. I stop eating anything with starch or fat in it, which is just about every-thing. But I'm feeling so good I don't care. I can even get into feeling hungry. "Lean and mean," I tell myself. And I start doing whatever exercises I can remember, to tighten up my gut.

But about the fourth day my mood changes. I wake up and think about going to the coding room, and I feel like I just can't do it. But of course I have to, and I do. When I get there I feel all tensed up, wired, and everything starts to irritate me. Rachel's constant chitter-chatter, the click of her eternal knitting needles, Sandy's hateful attitude, Grace's feet up on the desk all day. I've got a book to read, some crazy thing I found in the library, *Gargantua and Pantagruel*. Yesterday I was getting a kick out of lines like "and the pair of them often played the two-backed beast, joyfully rubbing their bacon together," but today I can't concentrate on it, and nothing strikes me funny. Now the book irritates me, seems stupid and silly. I put it down, and think about coding. But Rachel gets all upset when I code a lot. She says it builds up the expectations of the madam, meaning Rupie. So I get up and start pacing.

It's something I never did before, and everybody notices and gets quiet. "Oh-oh," says Rachel. "Short-time fever done struck our home."

"What do you mean by that?"

"I mean you got short-time fever."

"And just how do you come to this almighty conclusion?"

"Because you're pacing, and you never pace. Now you're gonna be unbearable for the next six weeks."

"I don't know what you're talking about."

"Sweety, you'd know what I was talking about if you'd been through parole time before. People find out when they're getting out and once the first high wears off they go crazy. They can't stand anybody or anything and they get mean as grizzlies. You're gonna do hard time for the next six weeks, dearie-dearie. Every day is going to seem like a week, and you're gonna take it out on the rest of us, so we're all gonna do hard time over you."

"Lord, you're smug, Rachel. How do you know what I'm gonna do? And I'm not uptight. I just get sick of sitting at that goddam desk all the time."

But it turns out Rachel is right. Starting that day I can't stand anything or anybody. The chatter in the dining room drives me nuts, the days seem eighty hours long, I can't sleep at night and so I'm miserable all day, and every time I get a little hassle from a screw it's all I can do to not hit her. The worst of it is that Terry and Lou are in the same condition. We snap at each other until we just automatically stay out of each other's way. They've been my best friends here and now I can't stand them.

I get a letter from my dad saying that Betty is shopping for clothes for me, and that my half sisters are excited about my coming there to live, and that Betty is fixing up the front bedroom for me. I try to picture the house in Reisterstown, and I escape from my nerves by fantasizing about life with my dad's family. It sounds like they're truly glad to have me coming and this makes me feel better. I wonder what the girls look like, and what my dad has told them about me.

My diet goes well. Always in the past I used to eat when I got nervous, but now it gives me a feeling of control to not eat. It's the only thing I got control of in this damn place. Even when I get out I'm not going where I want to go. I have to go to my dad's because if he didn't sponsor me for parole I wouldn't be getting out. So when I sit down at that table, I make the decisions about what goes in my mouth, I decide what kind of body I'm gonna have when I leave. Fuck 'em all. When I go over to the clinic on Friday I've lost two pounds, and they give me some more pills, which the cottage screw has to keep and issue me one at a time before meals.

Trouble is, I begin to realize that the pills are part of the problem. The way I find out is one day I forget to take the pill before supper and I sleep like a rock that night. The other thing is that when I get up in the morning I feel like a bag of wet cement until I take my pill. My energy is so low I feel like I can't move. Then I take the pill and I feel fine for a while, and then I get real tense, and I can feel my teeth grinding. I mean, I'm right back where I started. I was taking a roll of bennies a day when I was running dope across the border, and I had a rough time for a while when I got busted. When I started taking the diet pills I thought they were appetite depressants. Well, they are, but I mean I didn't know they were speed. I just thought they'd never give me anything like that in the joint. So here I am again, dammit, back on the same goddam roller coaster. Adding that to my short-time fever, I'm in sad shape.

I decide I got to stop taking the pills. I keep picking them up from the screw, but I don't take them. I stash them away because . . . well, I dunno, just because. Just to be ripping off the joint. My state of nerves is really bad, but I know I just got to go through that to get off them and I'm hanging in there, and about that time they transfer Sandy over to cottage 7. It's bad enough to have to work with her, and now I got to put up with her in the rec room and at meals, always giving me dagger looks. Rachel tells me they transferred her to cottage 7 because she caused so much trouble where she was. So now she's a big-timer in the High Power cottage. Big *shit* is what she is. But even with that extra pressure, I'm determined I'm gonna get out of here, and I keep my cool and hang in. I just avoid Sandy.

Until one day we get yard duty together. We got to trim the grass around the sidewalks and pull up any weeds we see. Sandy doesn't like working with me any better than I like working with her, of course, and we work without talking for a long time. I try to ignore her and think about something else, but I can feel her hostility like little rays in the air piercing my skin.

I sneak peeks at her and she's going after the grass like it's a rat she's killing, and I start to get bugged again about why she doesn't like me, and I feel like it isn't fair that she doesn't tell me, and by god I'm gonna find out. So I get myself all wound up like that and finally I say to her, "Sandy, we worked together all this time and you've hated me from the day I walked into the coding room and I've never known why. I think it's time you tell me what's eating you. So why don't you just tell me what it is."

She doesn't say anything, just keeps ripping at the grass like it was guts she was tearing out of something she hates. What does it take to get through to this kid? "Sandy, if you aren't gonna change the way you feel, at least tell me why you're so mad at me. I never did anything to you and you never gave me a chance. At least you can do that, dammit."

Sandy lets out a big exasperated sigh. She sits back on her heels and glares at me. "You're a big phony, that's all. You think you're better than anybody else."

This surprises the hell out of me. "How can you say that? I never did anything to make you think that."

"Sure you did. You're always talking about how your old man is such hot shit, the biggest dealer in East L.A., and your goddam big Cadillac he bought you, and how much shit you had in your bra when you got busted, and how you're such a big-time pro they brought you here in leg irons, and your rich daddy, and your bullshit fancy school, and bullshit, bullshit, bullshit. I can't stand to listen to you."

"God, Sandy, I didn't tell those things to be bragging. They're just things that happened. I can't help it if my dad's rich, and I can't help it if they put me in leg irons, and all that." But even while I'm saying it I know maybe there's a little bit of truth in what Sandy says. I remember, though, that she already didn't like me before I told any of those things. I'm puzzling on that when she says, "You remind me of my mom."

Oh-oh, here it is. "How can I remind you of your mom? I'm only twenty-four years old."

"You remind me of her all right. She's a know-it-all, like you. A goddam Communist too."

"That's a helluva thing to say about your mom."

"Well, she is. She and my dad, they're organizers. They have

all these meetings at our house, and they distribute all this propaganda. We get all this stuff in the mail and the mailman knows
they're Commies, and my school friends all know, and I'm
ashamed. I'm always telling my folks I'm ashamed of them too.
I say, I'm American. American!"

The five o'clock whistle blows and it's time to quit work.
Sandy and I stand up and we start gathering our tools. Sandy
says, "The part I hate worst is the propaganda. They distribute
all this shit about how the worker is exploited and the capitalists
are robbing them. They're not Americans and I'm really
ashamed."

"Well, it's true, partly, isn't it? I mean big business makes
money off the workers, don't they? If big business didn't exploit
the workers we wouldn't need unions." We're carrying the tools
toward the storage shed behind the cottage.

"I knew it! You're a Commie like them!"

"Oh god, Sandy. A fact is a fact. And Americans spread plenty
of propaganda, it's not such a big deal."

"They do not!"

"Of course they do. What is Voice of America all about?"

I've been putting tools in the shed and not looking at Sandy.
Suddenly her fist crashes into my face. I'm so surprised I just
stand there looking at her, and she yells, "You think you know
everything. You're a bitch, you're a Commie bitch!" And she
turns and walks fast toward the cottage. My first thought is, That
kid is totally crazy. My next thought is that if the screw saw what
happened, I've had it. It wouldn't matter that I didn't hit Sandy
back and did nothing to provoke it. We'd both go to the hole for
fighting, and goodbye parole. I look around, but can't see
anyone. My face smarts over my cheekbone, but it's not too bad.

I finish putting the tools away, close the shed, and I go back to
the cottage and wait in my room for supper, relieved that we
weren't seen by a screw, but scared anyway. I feel really bitter at
Sandy. If I lose my parole over her I don't know what I'll do. I
know I can't keep working in the coding room without killing
her.

Suppertime finally comes, and no one says anything, so I guess
nobody saw us. All I got to hope now is that I don't get a black
eye.

But next morning I see in the mirror in the bathroom that my eye is turning blue. Not much, but noticeable. I try to keep that side of my face turned away from the screws when I go to breakfast, but of course I can't hide it from the women at my table. Nobody says anything. When it's time to go to work, I have to go by the screw's office to get out the door. I see that it's Garth in there. Just my luck. But her head is down, looking at some paper on her desk, and I duck by without her seeing me. Of all the screws I don't want to have to deal with, it's her.

In the coding room, Rachel and Grace can't help but see the bruise, but they don't say anything. In a place where nothing is private, there are some things nobody will ask you about. Sandy won't look at me and doesn't say anything all day long, just keeps writing those eternal letters of hers. I'm quiet myself, and code like a demon whether Rachel likes it or not. It keeps me from having to talk. Rachel and Grace are less talkative than usual too, knowing something's seriously wrong, and suspecting it's Sandy that gave me the black eye, but they make some effort to act like business as usual. I'm grateful they don't ask me anything. Sometimes those gals are all right.

But as the morning goes by, I go to check myself out in the bathroom, and I see that my eye is getting darker and has a bright green border around it. There isn't any way the screws aren't going to see it. Rupie comes in the office once, sees my eye and says, "Oh dear." She goes right out again and doesn't come back all morning. I guess she doesn't want to have to report it. I'm getting more and more tense. I know it's just a matter of time.

When I go back to the cottage for lunch I get by the screw's office okay, but sitting at the table in the dining room, I look up and see officer Taylor looking right at me. I look down again real quick, but I know I've had it. I got no choice but to just go through motions until I get called down to the office. It happens as we're leaving the dining room. Taylor steps over and says to me, "Go to the office and wait for me, Toni." I do like she says, and sitting there waiting for her I figure it's all over. I'm so depressed I don't even care what they do to me. I'm not getting out, and anything else on top of that won't matter.

Taylor comes in and sits down at the desk, rummages in a

drawer, and pulls out a form of some kind. "You got yourself a black eye. I have to make a report on it. How did it happen?"

"I got up in the night to use my pot and I tripped in the dark and hit my eye on the corner of the bureau."

Taylor writes for a minute. Then she holds the paper up and reads: "When questioned about her black eye, Toni Bagliazo stated that she got up at night to use her chamber pot. She tripped in the dark and hit her eye on the corner of the bureau." Taylor looks at me. "Is that correct?"

"Yes, ma'am."

"All right, go back to work, Toni. In the future, you should report such incidents right away. We might have been able to keep it from swelling and discoloring so much if we got you right over to the clinic."

"Yes, ma'am. I thought there wasn't anything you could do about a black eye."

"You should report all accidents immediately anyway. You know that, Toni."

"Yes, ma'am. I just didn't think that much of it."

"All right. Get back to work."

"Yes, ma'am."

I can hardly keep myself under control 'til I get out the door. But as soon as I hit the sidewalk I jump in the air and click my heels. How did I get off so easy? Taylor's one of the more easy-going screws, but still . . . didn't it cross her mind at all that someone may have clobbered me? Well, I'm not gonna sweat it.

The relief is so great that I'm in a terrific mood when I walk into the coding room. Rachel's been anxious; I can tell by the way she looks at me. So I say, "The screw held me up after lunch. She had to make out a report on my eye." Sandy's head snaps up from her letter-writing so fast she could have whiplash. "None of you guys asked me about it this morning. You musta thought I got in a fight or something. But all that happened is I hit my head on the corner of my bureau when I got up to piss in the dark." I look sideways to see how Sandy is taking this news, but she's turned her head and is looking out the window. Jerk.

"You'd better go tell Rupie," Rachel says. "She was just in here wanting to know where you were."

"Oh. Okay." I go across the hall to Rupie's office. "Miss

Rupenthal, they held me over at lunch to make out a report on my eye. I banged it on my bureau last night."

Miss Rupenthal looks at me over her little gold-rimmed glasses. She seems to be thinking. Then she smiles, and says, "It's supposed to be a door you walk into, dear."

"Well, I had to say it was the bureau because I can't exactly have a door open any time I want." I'm smiling as I go back to the coding room. Rupie made a joke! And she wouldn't have made it if she thought I was lying. Everything's gonna be okay. I decide to celebrate by letting myself have a pill. It's been a hard enough day without having to cope with zero energy. I duck into the library and get a dexy from my stash in the magazine section and swallow it on my way back to the coding room. The rest of the day goes pretty much as normal. Except Sandy doesn't talk at all, not even her usual hostile explosions at me. It bothers me a little, her not even looking at me, because I saved her ass. Of course I wasn't thinking about her at the time, I was trying to save myself, but still . . . I'm amazed now that I ever cared whether she liked me or not. What difference does it make what her reason is? She's a jerk. Worse. A little creep. Look at her. The roadrunner.

I never hear any more about the black eye, and life goes on normally. The closer it gets to my release date the more tense I get, and sometimes I take the pills and sometimes I don't. When I don't take them I think it will be easier if I do, and when I do take them I think it will be easier if I don't. One thing I'm consistent about, though, is my diet. There's something in me that says, "I gotta be in control of my body or I won't have anything at all." So they keep giving me the pills, and since I only take them two or three times a week, my little stash in the library grows.

On July 14, Lou leaves, the first one from my cottage to go. She's still got her red-orange hair, by god, and Terry does her a fantastic hairdo for her release day. She's had a friend send in a suit and she looks like a million bucks. She goes out smiling like a Buddha, and for a day or two I do easier time. Seeing her actually go makes my leaving seem less like a pipe dream. I only got two weeks to go and my short-time fever's getting worse and worse, but poor Jody's moping around like a sick puppy, and so

Terry and I spend a lot of our off-time trying to keep her busy and cheered up, playing Ping-Pong and cards, and that keeps me busy and makes it a little better for me. The day after Lou leaves I get my suitcase from my dad and it's got a nice pants suit in it, size twelve, and I can just get into it. Just a tad tight around the waist, but if I keep up my program for the next two weeks it'll be perfect by the time I get out. The screws don't let me keep it. They just give it to me to check that everything's there and fits, then they lock it up downstairs. But just having my clothes there makes getting out more real, and my morale goes up and I decide I'm not gonna take any pills, and be completely clean by the time I get out.

About ten days after Lou leaves and three days before I'm due to go, Rachel says, "You hear about the papers?"

"No."

"Nobody from Washington got their D.C. paper today."

"So? What's the big deal? Maybe something happened to the mail. They'll show up."

"No they won't. They were confiscated."

"How do you know?"

"Like I know everything."

"Why would they confiscate a newspaper, Rachel? There's no reason."

"Yes there is. There's something in the paper they don't want us to know."

"Aw, your mind is too busy."

"Okay, just wait and see. I'm gonna find out."

"I bet you will."

The next day we no sooner get settled in the office than Rachel says, "Toni, come out to the bathroom in a minute." She gets up and leaves. I don't know what to make of this. No more than one person is allowed to go to the head at one time. You get written up if you're caught. My first thought is, I don't want to get written up three days before I leave. But on the other hand there's not much risk of getting caught. There's no screws in the building in the daytime except Rupie, and Rupie's never written anyone up to my knowledge. Rachel's never asked me to do anything like this before. There must be a reason. So I get up and go to the head. Rachel is at the mirror, primping her hair.

"What's up?"

"I know why they confiscated the papers."

"Is that all? You asked me to risk a write-up for that?"

"Wait'll I tell you what it is. Lou got busted."

I have trouble taking in what she's saying. "Lou just got out."

"Yeah. She was home four days and they busted her and two guys on a cocaine deal."

"I can't believe it."

"You better believe it, it's true."

I sit down on the radiator in front of the window. I feel scared, and a little faint.

Rachel says, "Ain't it the shits?"

"It's worse than that. How could she do that?"

"What else is she going to do? She's been in the life a long time. Lou's a pro."

"I didn't know she was into drugs. I thought she was just a hooker. My god, she's gonna have to finish out her old sentence and a new sentence too?"

"You're so naive sometimes, Toni. Hookers are in the middle of it. Even high-class call girls like Lou get involved in everything. You're right about one thing though: she's out of commission for a long time."

"Listen, she's gonna be back here in a few weeks anyway, so everybody's gonna know. Why should they keep the papers?"

"Because sometimes bad news like that starts some kind of reaction. People try to kill themselves or start a riot and do weird things."

"They can do the same thing when they see Lou back here."

"Well, then she's here already. I don't know. Nobody understands Administration logic. I'm just telling you that's why they confiscate the papers."

"God."

"Look, Toni, while we're in here, I never get a chance to talk private to you. But I want to tell you something about Sandy."

"Don't bother. I quit caring. She's a little creep."

"No, I got to tell you this. I think you might change the way you feel. You know all those letters Sandy writes?"

"Yeah."

"Well, Sandy doesn't have any correspondents."

"What do you mean, she doesn't have any correspondents?"

"I mean she doesn't have any correspondents."

"How do you know that? Oh, never mind. Of course you know that." I think about it a few seconds. This is just about the craziest and the saddest thing I ever heard since I been here. Rachel's right. It changes the way I see her. I mean, I can't hold anybody that pathetic responsible for what she does. She really is crazy. Literally. "Rachel, what does she do with all those letters?"

"I don't know."

I smile. "You mean there's actually something about this place you don't know?"

Rachel doesn't smile back. "There's a lot about this place I don't know. Listen, we'd better go back before Rupie misses us."

"Okay. But I want to ask you something. How come you told me about Lou, but you didn't tell Grace and Sandy?"

"Because you were close to Lou, and because you're tough and I knew that even though you'd be upset, you could handle it."

I'm amazed by what I just heard. "I'm tough?. . ." But just then the door whocks open and Grace comes in, looking anxious. "You guys better get back there. Rupie came in and asked where you were, and I said you both had to go to the head, but she went out looking real upset and twisting her skirt."

Rachel and I go back to the office, making a lot of noise in the hall so Rupie will know we're back. I sit down at my desk and pick up my pencil, but my mind is so boggled I can't even pretend to work. Lou busted. God. What a stupid damn thing to do, go right into a drug deal as soon as she got out. How did she set it up that fast anyway? There were two guys involved, Rachel said. Maybe one of them was Lou's old man, maybe it was his deal. I shouldn't feel sorry for her, since she's so stupid, but I can't help it. My heart aches. And then I think of Jody. She's gonna be overjoyed in spite of herself, and that's gonna make it bad between them when Lou gets here. God. And this time, Jody's gonna get out before Lou. I wonder if she'll go.

I glance at Sandy, and there she is, still writing away at her letters to nobody. I can't even bear to look at her. I turn my head and look out the window. I don't know how I can take so much sadness. Going home day after tomorrow, and I feel as if somebody died. Too much shit going down. Too much. How can Rachel say I'm tough? Tough! Me! That sure changes my opinion of Rachel. As much as she irritates me sometimes, I've always thought she was pretty savvy. But if she can't see that I'm scared shitless all the time, that everything that happens just wipes me out completely, then I don't think she's so damn smart. Tough! Huh.

Rupie comes in to make sure we're back. She looks upset still, but it's more because she doesn't want to write us up, I think, than because we broke the rule. She says, "You girls know you're not allowed to leave the room more than one at a time."

Rachel says, "Sorry, Rupie. We both had to go so bad we couldn't take turns."

Rupie stands there for minute. She can't think of a solution to suggest. Finally she just turns around and goes out.

Rachel says, "Poor Rupie."

I say, "I don't think you should call her Rupie to her face."

"I wouldn't call her one thing behind her back and another to her face."

"Oh, come off it. You know she's too soft-hearted to write you up, and you're just baiting her."

"I'm not baiting her. Anyway, I think she likes it."

"I don't think so. I think she feels like she doesn't have any control here. You ought to try to make it easier on her. She's a nice old lady."

Rachel doesn't answer. But she doesn't seem mad at me. Maybe I got some privilege now that I'm going home. Short-time fever and all.

I decide that, as low as I feel, I could use a pill. So I duck out to my stash. When I come back we're all very quiet. Sandy and Grace know they been left out of something, and they're sulking. Sandy doesn't look up from her letter-writing the entire rest of the day, and Grace just sits reading her book. But I feel better when the pill takes effect, and Rachel and I jabber back and forth about this and that. Finally it's time to quit.

The next day is my last day, and I feel like I'm going to come out of my skin. I can't concentrate on anything. People talk to me and what they say doesn't register. I can't eat, and I can't stand time. Every minute is like an hour and I just want to hit my head against the wall or something because the tension is miserable. I go to work but of course I don't do anything. Rupie comes in and out half a dozen times, stands there looking at me like she wants to say something, changes her mind and goes out again, making things worse. Sandy is more compulsive about writing her letters than she's ever been, and she won't talk to anybody, and every time I look at her I want to cry, so I stop looking at her. Grace and Rachel try to act normal, chatting about this and that, but I miss the point of their jokes and my mind drifts away so I don't answer when I'm supposed to, and all this strikes Rachel as very funny and of course this annoys me. I finally decide the only way to cope with this is to stay loaded, so I take two of my dexies. In about a half an hour I'm feeling really terrific and my mind is doing about eighty miles an hour. I can't eat anything at lunch, but everyone thinks it's just excitement, and I'm still sailing when I go back to the coding room. Sandy doesn't come back from lunch – which means she's claiming to be sick and has chosen to be locked into her room. Nobody says so, but we all know it's because she doesn't want to be around on my last afternoon. I'm too high to get depressed about it. Actually I'm a little relieved. I just don't know how to act with her now.

Rachel's been bugging me for weeks about what I'm gonna do when I get out, and I keep telling her I don't know, I have to just go to my dad's house and see what happens. He's probably got it all laid out for me. I probably won't have much to say about it. But with a couple of beans in me I tell her I just been kidding, I got all kinds of plans. She looks interested, and I start: "First I'm gonna take up jogging and get in real good shape. When I'm not training I'm gonna write a book called *My Life of Crime* and in it I'm gonna blow the whistle on this joint, and I'm putting you guys in it, everything you told me since I been here. Then I'm gonna win the New York marathon and get rich. When I'm rich I'm gonna hire me a bunch of hit men and get rid of all the screws in the world except Rupie. Then I'm gonna run for president and shut down all the prisons, and put all the criminals in the police force. Rachel, you're gonna be the head of the FBI." I go on like this for a long time, and Grace and Rachel just listen and grin. Sometimes they throw in a suggestion, until I get the whole country reorganized and everything turned upside down.

But after a while my energy runs down, and goofing around has only made me more painfully conscious that I haven't got the faintest idea what I'm gonna do or where my life is going. Since I'm on parole to my father, they didn't even tell me I have to have a job, so for all I know I'm gonna sit around at his house and watch *Love Boat*. I want to stop thinking about it. One of the things that hits me is, after today I won't get to talk to Rachel anymore, and I search my mind for things I want to tie up with her before I leave, and I remember the remark she made yesterday.

"Rachel, yesterday you said I was tough. What did you mean by that?"

"I meant you're tough."

"C'mon, I really want to know. I don't think of myself as tough. I feel like the opposite, like everybody else is always pushing me around."

"I just get that impression from the stuff you've told us."

"Like what?"

"Well, let me think a minute. You said when you were a kid you had to take care of your mother. You said that one time you went on a trip and your mother got crazy in the train station and you had to buy the tickets and find the right train. That's tough, for a kid. You were eight, weren't you?"

"Yeah. But that's not being tough. I just had to do it. Besides, that was when I was a kid. That doesn't have anything to do with now."

"A lot of kids wouldn't have done it. They would have sat down and been scared until their mother finally did something. But if you want *now*, I'll give you now. You hung in there all through that pretrial investigation, months in isolation, and you didn't crack up. Or even more now than that, you kept both yourself and Sandy out of trouble when she gave you that shiner . . ."

"Wait a minute . . ."

"Oh, c'mon Baggie, give us credit for more than half a brain. We know Sandy clobbered you. Anyway, you were real cool about that. Someone else half crazy with short-time fever would have decked Sandy, or blown the whistle on her, or fucked up in some way or other. But you didn't, and that's being tough. Okay?"

"I was just scared of blowing my parole."

"But you stayed in control. You always stay in control. It's one thing to be scared, but it's tough to stay in control."

"I never thought about it that way. I didn't do so good outside though. Always hanging on some guy who was no good. I never seemed to be able to make it on my own, and I always pick guys who are no good for me, and then I never handle it very well when they fuck me over."

"From what you told me, you weren't ever able to get a decent job."

"No. I didn't even finish high school, and I didn't have any skills."

"Well – so you survive by hanging on to these guys. What else are you gonna do?"

"But what's tough about what you don't have any choice about?"

"People who have choices tell you you're self-destructing if you do drugs or drink or sell your ass or hang on to some no-good thug. They don't understand that when you got no choices, you do what you have to do to survive. When Tuffy beat you up because you wouldn't put your bod on the street, you went with Leon. You were surviving, dearie-dearie. You told us already you didn't have any choice. You had no job, no money, no friends who would have understood what you were up against. Right?"

"Right."

"So was that self-destruction, or survival? Seems to me like if you wanted to self-destruct, you woulda stayed with Tuffy and let him turn you out. But you didn't. And you didn't sit out on the curb and cry, you didn't jump off a bridge, or become a junkie. You did what you had to do to survive, and that's *tough*."

I'm beginning to see it Rachel's way, and I'm almost in shock because now I see all the stuff I been feeling ashamed of as being strong, kind of. Rachel's right, I haven't had any choices for a long time. Maybe going from Tuffy to Leon was jumping from the frying pan into the fire, but it's true, it's the only choice I had at the time. I thought it might be better with him, and it was. For a while, anyway.

All the stuff I ever been mad at Rachel about leaves my head now. She's given me a going-away present worth more than anything I can think of. I don't know what to say to her, and so I stay quiet. Grace and Rachel are quiet too, because it's getting close to five and in a few minutes I'll be leaving and I'll never see them again. I hope.

When five o'clock comes I give them both a hug and we say all the usual things: Take care of yourself . . . I hope I never see your ugly face again . . . I hope everything goes all right with you. They walk out of the office first, and I go across the hall to say goodbye to Rupie. "Goodbye, Toni," she says. "What is it you girls say, 'Hang tough'?"

"We don't say that, Miss Rupenthal, but I know what you mean. Listen, thank you for being so nice. It made things a little easier."

Rupie gets all flustered and starts twisting her skirt, and I want to hug her but I hang back. I can't stand to see her get all red in the face and upset. So I shake her hand and walk out.

I duck into the library and get my little stash of pills. But as soon as I have them in my hand I know I'm not going to take them with me. Everyone says they don't search you on your way out, but I can't take a chance. Besides, I'm starting over now, and I'd better start over without pills. So I stick them back in the magazine box and walk out, chuckling as I think of the surprise on some prisoner's face when she comes across them someday. "Have a high on me," I say, and go down the stairs.

Back at the cottage, I check Sandy's room, and, sure enough, she's locked in. She won't be let out for dinner. They discourage you from being "sick" by barely feeding you. For supper they'll bring her a dry peanut butter sandwich and a glass of milk. I wonder a little if she might really be sick, but I know I'm trying to kid myself. She locked in to avoid seeing me on my last day.

At the dinner table the main topic is my getting out, of course. Although I remind them that I'm not going home to California, I'm going to my father's house, they keep referring to my "going home." In a way, anyplace that isn't here must seem like home. They ask me what the first thing I'm going to eat is, and I say, "The biggest, fattest hamburger I can find, loaded with fried onions."

"What's next after that?"

"A pizza!" Terry is almost as nervous as I am; she goes home two days after me, and I know she feels like I did when Lou left – my going makes it real at last for her.

There's meat loaf for supper, a rare treat, and, though I know better, I wrap up a piece for Sandy in a napkin and stick it in my pocket. After supper I take it to her room and throw it through the transom. I want to say something to her, and I stand there a minute, trying to think what I could say. But nothing comes to me and I go on down to my room. She won't know who brought her the meat loaf. Just as well. She'd probably flush it down the toilet if she knew.

A few women drop by my room to say goodbye because things will be too hectic in the morning. After breakfast they'll be going to work and I'll be getting ready to leave. Saying goodbye makes me more nervous. I feel like it's bad luck. If I believe I'm going enough to say goodbye to people, maybe it won't happen. I know it's stupid, but that's how I feel, and I wish they wouldn't come. But I can't tell them not to, so I go through motions with a fake smile glued on my face, until at last it's time for lockup.

I wish now I'd taken another pill before I left the school building. I've been down for hours now and I feel rotten. Depressed and wiped out. At the same time I'm too nervous to sleep, and I sit up looking out the window for the last time at night, over the woods in the moonlight, and at the sky and the stars and the moon. I've been avoiding thinking about Leon all these last months but now he won't leave me alone. I know I'm not going back to him, not even when my parole is over, because as much as I love him I know I could never go to prison again. It would kill me. Everything in my body connected with emotion aches: my chest, my throat, my face, my brain. Leon is the only person in the world I love but I hate prison more than I love him. I look at the moon and think maybe it's the satellite for telepathic communication. I beam a message to Leon up to the moon, asking it to bounce it back to wherever he is. "Please understand. Please understand. I just can't go to prison again. I'm doing the only thing I know to do."

While I sit there I hear that long lonesome wail from the train I've heard every living night I been here. I'm not ever gonna be able to hear a train whistle again without thinking of this place.

I'll probably get fear pangs in my stomach from it just like I do now.

I sit there a long time after that, thinking about Leon, remembering things, and thinking about the future, which is hard because I can't imagine what it's going to be like. There finally comes a point – it must be three or four in the morning – when I think I can sleep, so I go to bed.

In the morning I wake up feeling better. Today is the day and it did finally come. I can hardly believe it. At breakfast I can barely speak for excitement. I just sit there with a stupid grin plastered on my face while people kid me. They know how I feel and they don't expect me to talk much, or to make sense when I do. The hard part comes when everybody goes out the door to work. A few give me a final hug, and when Terry hugs me I start to cry. Then Angie slips me a kite, and says, "Toni, mail this to the address on the top, will you? It's to Marco. They won't let me write to him. Okay?" But when I go to my room to get ready my mind is only on getting out that gate, and I finger the kite in my pocket, and I think, No matter what they say about not getting searched on the way out, I'm not taking any chances. I go down to the head and tear the kite in little pieces and flush it down the toilet.

The screw brings my suitcase up about nine o'clock, and at last I can take off my institutional duds for the last time. I put on my pants suit, and it fits like it was custom tailored. I really did it! Even not taking the pills all the time, I lost twelve pounds and got down to a perfect twelve. The screw checks in all the prison-issue clothing, and we go down to the administration building. I'm shaking all over and feel like I might lose my breakfast. I wonder, on the way down there, how I can stand the last part, waiting for my dad, but when we get to Administration he's there waiting already, grinning at me like this was all some big joke. I don't know whether to cry or laugh, and I go through the final paper-signing without even knowing what I'm doing. Then I'm walking out the door with my father, getting into his Chrysler, and riding out the gate. Just in time, I think to turn around and watch the gate recede behind me – that stupid wood archway with the paint peeling off of it, saying Federal Reformatory for Women. When it disappears, I turn around and look at my father directly for the first time. He's still grinning. "Well," he says, "we're on our way."

I feel stupid because I can't think of a single thing to say. To tell the truth, I don't want to talk to him, not now or ever, and that's completely crazy because I'm going to live with him and he's my parole sponsor. I look out the window while I try to think of something to say. We pass through Alderson and I'm surprised to see what a crummy little town it is. It was nighttime when I went through on my way in, and I didn't get to see it. It has a depressing air to it. Maybe it spills over from the prison. Then we're out in the country and I just gulp in everything I can see of the countryside. West Virginia is beautiful. Hey, that's something I can say. "West Virginia is sure beautiful, Dad."

"Yes, it is. We've got a nice ride back."

He doesn't say anything else and I'm glad. I guess we're not very comfortable with each other. But I don't want to worry about that now. I'm beginning to feel the exhilaration of being out. The countryside rushes by. I'm in a car, I'm with my father, which is better than being with a screw even if I don't like him much. I can go wherever I want – well, to a certain extent – and the whole goddam nightmare is over. At the very least I can walk to the drugstore anytime I want to, and that thought reminds me of the promise I made in the joint: if I could just be free to go to the drugstore anytime I want I'll never complain again. Okay. I make up my mind to cooperate with my dad. After all, he's sticking his neck way out to sponsor me. He doesn't even know if I'm a goddam junkie or not. If I fuck up totally, a lot would come down on him, with his business and his social life and his community and all. For the first time it hits me that he's gone way out on a limb for me, that I've had some kind of chip on my shoulder and that I haven't been fair. I turn away from the window and say, "Daddy, I'm grateful to you for all you're doing."

"I wouldn't have done it if I didn't believe that you can do something with your life. Have you thought about what you want to do?"

"Yeah. Pig out on hamburgers." I see right away this is a mistake. This is jailhouse humor, not Daddy-just-got-you-out-of-prison humor. My dad doesn't even smile. "I'm just kidding,

Dad. I guess if I could do anything I want, I'd go to college." I don't know where this came from. I haven't thought about college at all. Maybe I just want to impress my dad that I have serious intentions. It works, because he's smiling.

"I think that's a good idea, Toni. If you want to, you can work for me at the plant this summer and enroll in the University of Maryland in the fall."

I'm stunned. I never expected anything like that. And now that he says it's possible, I'm about to cry, and I realize I really do want to go to college. I never thought about it because I never believed I had a chance. I don't even have a high school diploma, and my dad doesn't know that. I'd better clear this up. "Daddy, I never graduated from high school."

"Yes, your mother told me. You can take a GED."

"What's that?"

"A high school equivalency examination. Don't tell me you never heard of it?"

"No. I thought I had to go back to high school or something."

"No. We'll get that all set up."

"Even if I pass that test, I don't think I can save enough money this summer to go to college."

"I'll pay your way, Toni, as long as you do well."

I'm so overcome with gratitude and excitement I can't talk. I sure did underrate my dad. I turn back to the window until I get hold of my feelings and can talk without crying. When I'm in control again I say, "I'll pay you back, Dad."

"If you want to. Did they tell you we're stopping to see your parole officer when we go through Baltimore?"

"Yes. Listen, seriously, can we have a hamburger on the way home?"

My dad smiles. "I think that can be arranged."

I smile too. "I can't wait to go to the movies. I want to go to the movies every night for a month. And dancing."

My dad stops smiling. "Toni, on the way home we might as well talk about the ground rules. The conditions of your parole are very strict."

"I know that."

"You can't associate with felons, and you can't go to bars."

"I wasn't exactly planning to hang out with criminals. I just want to go dancing."

"Don't be flippant, Toni. This is serious. I'm imposing some further rules. You aren't to go anywhere without clearing it with me first. You aren't to drive a car, and you aren't to go out alone in the evening. And you're not to correspond with anyone in California."

"Dad, I'm twenty-four years old!"

"If you were twenty-four years old emotionally you wouldn't have been in prison. You've lost your right to adult privileges. You'll have to earn them back by learning to be mature and responsible."

"How can I do that if you treat me like a kid?" I'm about to cry again.

"You're proving that you're a child by the way you're reacting, Toni. As long as you act like a child you're going to be treated like a child. You have always been irresponsible. You have always rebelled against discipline. But as long as I'm sponsoring you for parole, as long as you are under my roof, I make the rules. Until you learn to respect authority, until you learn to accept discipline, you'll remain a child. I intend to make an adult of you."

Lord, is this ever familiar. I had forgotten that no matter how I react to something I don't like, my dad takes what I say and turns it into evidence against me. I've never won an argument with him and I'm never going to.

My dad gets tired of waiting for me to answer. "You don't want to abide by the rules I gave you?"

"Of course not. I might as well stay in prison."

"Fine. We'll tell that to your parole officer when we get there."

He's got me. I'm so full of rage and hate I can hardly breathe. I turn my face to the window again, struggling with all my strength to get a hold on myself. And he's so calm and smug, just like he's always been. In control of himself and of everyone around him, the sonuvabitch. Power. That's what it's always been, and why was I such a fool I didn't see that right away? He's got me right where he wants me, where I can't rebel because he can do me in. He's got complete control. Great. I've moved from one prison right into another one. I might as well have stayed at

Alderson. But as soon as I think that, I know it isn't true. I wouldn't go back there for anything. I have to find a way to cope with my dad. I have to survive. The word survive brings back, in a flash, my conversation with Rachel. "When you got no choices, you do what you have to do to survive." I'm tough, Rachel says. Maybe I am. I glance at my dad. He's staring straight ahead at the road, grim. Waiting for me to buckle under. He knows I will. I turn back to the window. I picture Rachel at her desk right now, her little white hands making those knitting needles fly. I wish I could tell her what's happening. Rachel! Stay with me, girl. Please, stay with me.

The End

I've been waiting for days for this letter, and so much depends
on it that I haven't been able to do much else but wait. One
minute is a long time when you're doing nothing but waiting,
and a day never ends. But I've learned to do time, all right, that's
one thing prison taught me. Like that guy Siddhartha in the
book, the one that's supposed to be about the life of Buddha. He
said, "I can fast, I can think, I can wait." What a weird guy. But
anyway, I know I can't fast and I'll swear there are times I can't
think, but I sure as hell can wait. That doesn't mean I don't suffer
waiting though.

The letter is longer coming than I thought, and when it finally
arrives my hands shake opening it. I knew my dad wouldn't let
me down in such terrible trouble, but I'm also scared, because I
expect he'll be awful mad at me for running off and coming back
to California without telling anybody. He didn't know I was
pregnant, and that's why I left. I was knocked up and I was too
ashamed to let him know I'd messed up again, after he got me
out on parole and set me up with a job and then paid for me to
go to college. So I just left, and let him think what he wanted.
Dumb. But I doubt anybody could've done better in the same
spot. You get all bound up with misery and don't think straight.

So I came back to California because I told my gay friend David
all about it in a letter and he said come on out, I could stay with

him and we'd even get married if I wanted the baby to be legal, so I came. And it was okay for a while, but David just has this crazy streak in him. He's all messed up in the head from the hassles of being gay, I think. Anyway, he was mean. He'd get vicious over something that didn't matter, like the way I cut up a piece of meat, and we fought all the time. Then I started bleeding and we went to a doctor in Eureka so he could take care of me while I had the miscarriage, and he put me in a Catholic hospital. The next thing I knew I was floating in a dreamy place and I had this idea that days were drifting by and then it turned out days *were* drifting by – he had drugged me, trying to save the baby. He was Catholic and wasn't going to let me lose it.

Finally I stopped bleeding and I went home without losing the baby, and David and I were both in a bit of shock. We had thought my troubles were over. And now I seemed to be awful sick. I got sicker and sicker, but when we called the doctor he said to just stay in bed until I felt better. Then one night I felt like I had to have a BM, so I went in the bathroom and plop, out comes the baby, just like that, and it looks all purple.

So back to the hospital I go, carrying my baby in a shoe box. It's dead, of course. I was only about three months along. They keep me in the hospital while I pass the afterbirth, which is when I have all the pains. It's one helluva trip. One of the nurses tells me, whispering like it's a secret, that the baby's been dead for a long time and that I had systemic poisoning from the dead fetus and I was lucky to be alive myself. I didn't figure out 'til later she was trying to tell me how bad the doctor loused me up. I guess she told me so I could do something about it if I wanted, but what's the use?

Well, once that was over I could move out of David's if I got a job, so I went and applied for typist at a local junior high school and I got hired. But the first thing they told me after they hired me was that all school personnel had to be fingerprinted at the police department, and I should go down there and have that done. My heart dropped in my shoes and I didn't do it of course. I thought I would just stick it out as long as I could and at least I'd have some money.

A couple of weeks went by and nobody said anything, so I thought maybe they forgot about it. I started enjoying my job because I got to talk to these funny little kids who were always running into the office with some big comical emergency. But then one day the vice principal I was working for came out and told me they were getting upset over in personnel because I didn't get my prints taken and I'd better do that right away. That same day I started bleeding so hard a pad couldn't hold it. I kept on bleeding like that all night, so in the morning I called a doctor, a different one this time, and he said I probably needed a curettement and I'd better check into the hospital right away.

I didn't have much money but I didn't tell him that, because I had to have it done, so in I went. When it was over and they released me I was short four hundred dollars. I told them I'd have to get the money and they were pretty nice about it, although you hear lots of horrible stories about hospitals and how they let people die because they don't have any money. These people weren't like that at all, which made me want to pay them as fast as I could.

I didn't know anything else to do but write my dad, because I couldn't keep the job any longer. They'd be sure to fire me if I gave them my fingerprints and they found out I had a record. The doctor told me to take it easy a few days, so I did that while I wrote to my dad and waited for an answer. I told him I was sorry I ran off and I'd explain someday but right now I had been in the hospital and could he lend me the four hundred dollars and I'd pay him back as soon as I got a job. Because, see, I love Arcata, this funky little northern California town near Eureka, and I wanted to stay there and get another job where I didn't have to have fingerprints taken, and try to make myself a new life. And of course I couldn't make a new life if I didn't pay my bills, because it's a small place and that kind of thing gets known around town. I wanted to pay them anyway. They were real nice people, and maybe I ran dope and did a lot of other stupid things, but I never stole from anybody. I don't feel good stealing. Some people have said to me that running dope is a lot worse than stealing because I was victimizing helpless addicts, and look what dope does to people's lives, but even though I don't defend what I did, I say it's different than stealing because, when you get right down to it, junkies are volunteers. Nobody holds them down to stick those needles in their arms. But people don't volunteer to get robbed.

So anyway I wanted to pay that money. I wanted a new life, and to be decent to folks who were decent to me. It seemed possible in this nice little friendly town where nobody but David knew anything about me, and David wouldn't say anything about my past even if he was mad at me, because no matter how mean and crazy he gets sometimes, he's basically decent. Besides, he's got secrets of his own. The bank where he works doesn't know he's gay.

So here's the letter from my dad at last and my hands are shaking so I can hardly open it. I feel a jerk in my stomach when I see there isn't any check in it, and the message is real short. It says, "You have chosen to go your own way, now go it."

I've hit bottom a lot of times in this life, and sometimes I've hit pretty hard. But usually I can see it coming. Usually there's a point where I know I'm sliding and I'm grabbing at handholds and scrambling, trying to save myself, and then I hit, but at least I feel myself falling first. This is like failing off a twelve-story roof one second and landing on your head the next. No time to get ready, not knowing the crash is coming. I just stare at the letter, feeling like I been smashed all over the sidewalk.

All the rest of that day I'm confused, but by nighttime I'm able to think again, and what I think is, Whatever made me believe he would bail me out this time when I've fucked up over and over and over, and this last time I left without so much as a fare-you-well? It seems to me like the dumbest thing I ever believed, and I wonder why I believed it. I guess I had to believe it because I don't have a single friend left in the world, I don't have enough money to live on until I can find another job, much less pay what I owe to the hospital, and I had to believe my dad would help me out because if he didn't it would just be the end. And it is. The end, I mean.

I'm numb with pain, and after thinking these things I just lie on my bed for hours. I don't even know what I'm thinking about. Every time I think about my dad I can hardly stand the feeling of shame I get. It seems like every chance I get I blow it somehow, and every person I ever love I lose, and now I don't even have David. I got nobody.

Well, yes I do. Leon would take me back. Even after this long a time. He'll understand if I tell him. I didn't want to go back to all that, but it seems like I can't make it any other way, and that's all that's left. I messed up in school, I messed up all that nice stuff I had going back east by getting pregnant, I never did anything but mess up all my life, and now I see pretty clear that I'm nothing but a fuckup and the sooner I just accept that, the better off I'll be because then I can get on back to where I belong, with other fuckups like myself. With Leon.

I feel better. Mad, like. I get up and count the money in my wallet. There may be enough to make L.A. I put what clothes I got, which isn't much, in my duffel. I also got a big gorgeous coat I bought on sale at Maison Cher with my first paycheck after I got out of the joint. It weighs a ton and looks like a million bucks although it was two hundred marked down to a hundred. It's the only high-class thing I ever owned in my life except for the yellow Caddie I was driving when I got busted, and the platinum watch the Ace Diamond Company repossessed while I was in jail. Anyway, it isn't ever cold enough in California for this coat, but I can't bring myself to leave it behind, so with the coat over one arm and the duffel in the other hand I go down to the bus depot. There's a bus at 11:20 that will get me into L.A. tomorrow afternoon, and I got enough for the ticket and some left over for food. I don't even think about what will happen if I can't find Leon. He might not even be out of the joint yet, but I have to take that chance. There just isn't anything else left to do. If I can't find him, that's the end.

On the bus I go into a buzz and I don't know where I am for that eighteen or twenty hours. In the bus depot in L.A. I find Leon's mother's name in the phone book – lucky! – and I call her. She sounds strange when I tell her who I am, and says I should wait ten minutes and call back. I don't know what else to do so I do what she says, and the second time I call she says Leon is in Tijuana and that he says for me to go down there.

For the first time since I got that letter I feel alive again. I found him and he wants me! That's all I need to know. I'm so excited I can hardly think to take down the information his mother gives me on how to contact him when I get there. It's like being told I don't have to die after all.

The ticket to TJ takes my food money but that's okay. I'm alive again.

I'm pushing the bus with every nerve in my body, all the way to TJ. I call Leon from the first phone I see after I walk across the border. My stomach just about won't stay in my body as I call. When Leon answers and I say it's me I can tell something's wrong. He sounds cold, formal, and it scares me. He tells me where to meet him, a bar we used to go to, and hangs up without saying he's glad to hear from me or anything. I feel like something terrible is going to happen, and I'm so scared I don't want to go but there isn't anything else to do. I wait a long time in the bar, and when he finally comes all my fear goes up in smoke and I'm so relieved and glad to see him I think I'm gonna melt on the spot. He smiles but is cool, and I understand that I shouldn't try to kiss him. There's some explanation for this, I know it, and he'll tell me when he gets a chance. He doesn't even want to stay and have a drink, which confirms my idea that something's wrong, and we leave.

He's driving an old Buick, an old wreck, and I laugh at it. He tells me he has to be careful not to look like he has too much money in TJ. He takes me to a little apartment, and when we go in I recognize it as a stash pad. Nothing in it but cheap plastic furniture. The couch is orange with a big tear in it. I turn to face him once he has the door closed and right away he says, "Why didn't you get in touch with me when you got out?" He looks mad. Well, he has a right to be, and that's why he's been acting so cool to me. I just have to explain.

"Leon, they paroled me to my dad. There was no place I could get mail from you. If they thought I was in touch with you they would have sent me back. I came as soon as I could." This is only partly true of course. I could have written if I wanted to, rented a P.O. box or called his mother, and I could have come back when I finished my parole, but I need for him to believe it all and I believe it as I tell it. But as soon as it's out of my mouth I realize that of course he knows it's bullshit.

He sits down on the orange plastic sofa and lights a cigarette. "Look, babe, it's complicated here. I got married. I married the daughter of one of the biggest sources in Baja. You understand? I didn't know where you were and I figured you weren't coming back. Because of this marriage I'm sitting pretty right now, but I could blow it real easy. She's very jealous, very suspicious. We've got to be real careful. Comprendes?"

I feel like someone just walloped me in the stomach. So that's it. That's why he was so cool on the phone. That's why he's so reserved. He's really upset. I'm so relieved – it's just a situation! I say, "Sure, Leon, I understand. Just so you want me."

"Of course I want you, baby." For the first time now he smiles. He reaches for my hand and pulls me to him. He pulls down my jeans with one hand while he undoes my bra with the other. He spreads my legs and begins to lick me. In seconds I'm in heaven. It's been so goddam long. Lord, how I used to dream about him eating me out while I was in the joint. Sometimes I felt like it was the only thing that kept me going. Maybe I got a one-track mind, but when something's that good, it's hard not to put all your thoughts on it when everything else in your life is the pits. But here I am and it's so goddam good and I wonder why I waited so long to come back. What made me think I could do without this, without Leon, without a life where I feel wanted and important?

When it's over I feel all mellow and ready to talk and talk and

talk, to tell him all about everything, and I want to hear everything that's happened to him since I last saw him. But he just
says, "I got to go now, babe. It's important you don't leave the
apartment 'til I come back, okay? Someone may be watching the
place. I'll be back as soon as I can, but you understand that I have
to be careful."

"Sure, Leon, I understand." But I feel like something has been
pulled out from under me. What the hell am I supposed to do in
here? There isn't even a TV.

Leon goes and I spend a lot of time walking around the empty
little apartment. I wonder where the dope is – not that I want
any – but I know it's here and I'm just curious about how much
he has. Probably a lot. I look out the blinds. It's your typical
Tijuana street: tacky. And it has that funny thing like all border
towns – the walls are like loudspeaker, you can hear everything
that's going on in the houses. Mexicans tend to talk real loud too.
In Spanish of course, and that gives me a little feeling of being at
home, because the sounds remind me of the apartment we had
here before I got busted. There used to be a bunch of jai alai
players upstairs and they came home with women every night
and partied 'til dawn. I kind of liked their noise because it was
always happy. Different women every night, lots of music and
laughing and jokes.

Well anyway. This is sure different. Hiding out.

I'm hungry. Leon didn't even ask me if I wanted something to
eat, and he didn't leave me any money. It's a lot different than
the first time he rescued me. He probably thought I ate on the
way down, but I don't have any more money, or only a couple of
bucks, anyway. I'm too hungry to sleep, and too excited. I feel
all wound up, so excited to get here and start life all over with
Leon, and after he's with me half an hour he's gone, and I got
nothing to do with my excitement but pace the floor. God, what
a letdown. But it'll be better later. I took him off guard, that's for
sure. He needs a few days to set things up for me, and then life
will be full of excitement again. Yeah.

Leon doesn't come back 'til late the next day. I'm feeling sick
with hunger and cranky and mean. When I hear the key in the
lock I don't know if I'm gonna hit him or fall apart crying. It
turns out I just fall in his arms, I'm so relieved. "I'm starving," I
say.

"Didn't you go out and eat?" he says.

I can't believe this. I scream at him, "You told me not to leave
the apartment! And I don't have any money! You didn't leave

me any and I spent the last I had getting here."

Leon laughs. "Poor babe! I had so much on my mind, I didn't think about you needing food. C'mon. We'll go eat, and then we'll have a celebration, alright? I fixed it so I can stay out tonight. We'll have a good time, okay?" He puts his hand in my crotch and I begin to melt.

"You better feed me fast, or there won't be anything left to celebrate with." I'm trying to stay mad but I'm so goddam glad he's here at last that I can't pull it off.

Leon just laughs and we go get in his funky old Buick. He takes me to the fancy restaurant where his brother Fernando works as a waiter. Fernando deals dope too, but everybody in Leon's family has a job for a cover. Sometimes I think there's not much point in dealing dope if you have to work a shit job anyway, but since they're known dealers the cops watch them pretty close. I guess the cops figure that anybody who has any money whatsoever from any other source would never work as a waiter if he could help it. So as a cover I suppose it works pretty good.

Anyway, we have a steak and lobster dinner with champagne, and of course Fernando serves us like royalty. I have a chance now to take a good look at Leon, and he seems different to me. I can't say how, because he looks exactly the same. But I remembered him as being bigger, and stronger. Not body strong, but something about his face. I remembered that he always looked like he was king of the mountain. He doesn't look like that now. His face is soft, almost like a woman's, yet there isn't anything feminine about him. Or is there? He used to look cool, now he looks cold. His head is smaller than I remember it. Funny thing to notice. The main thing is that he always used to look pleased with me. He doesn't look pleased now and it makes me feel like I did something wrong. But all these impressions come in little snatches while we're talking, between and back of everything else.

From the restaurant we go to one of the clubs. It's too early yet for the show so we just sit and drink Scotch. I start feeling better after a couple of drinks and then Leon has his hand in my crotch under the table and I feel like I used to feel – like a sex queen. I'm hot and I like feeling hot. Leon keeps ordering drinks, saying, "C'mon, babe, this is a celebration. Drink up." So I do. Then the show starts and the dancing. We aren't talking now, just drinking and watching. I'm sitting back enjoying the feeling of being safe again. I belong to the baddest cat in East L.A., and maybe in Tijuana besides.

After a while Leon nudges me. "See that guy over there at the bar? How do you like him, babe?"

"Leon, I want this to just be you and me tonight. I'm tired with all the excitement. I been through a lot in the last few days. I just want to be with you tonight."

"Hey, it's okay, mama! I just asked you how you like him. I like to know you're still my little hot mama."

"He doesn't appeal to me too much," I say, although I know he won't like that answer. He always wants me to say I'm really turned on by someone he points out. It gets him hot. I know he's gonna be irritated about it but something in me feels stubborn. I don't want to party tonight, not with anybody but him.

"Too bad, baby. He's been lookin' at you. I could get him for you if you want him."

"I told you, Leon, I can't handle that tonight." He sees that I mean it and he sits back quiet and listens to the music. I can see he's mad. I wish he'd say something instead of just sitting there looking cold. More drinks come. Normally I don't drink fast, but now I do. I need to relax after all the misery of the last few weeks. I need to numb myself against his anger. My head begins to buzz. Leon takes us on to another club where the music is louder and there are more people. It's a whorehouse, I can tell, because there's so many women and they're all rigged up to look real available, tits and ass hanging out all over the place, and they're laying all over the men at the bar. But I feel okay in here, though I wouldn't have before I was in the joint. I knew a lot of hookers in the joint, and they were the best people there, so now I feel at home. I feel like I could tap someone on the shoulder and say "Hi," and she would smile at me. But I'm getting drunk. Leon doesn't dance, so usually he gets somebody to dance with me, but he must have got the message clear the first time because he doesn't try to get me to dance with anybody.

After a couple more drinks I feel my mind slipping away. The music is too loud, and there's this buzzing in my head that I always know means I'm really drunk, and I can't concentrate on anything around me, not even on Leon. I hear him talking to somebody and then he's telling me to move around to the back of the booth – it's one of those U-shaped things – and I know dimly that somebody has sat down with us. I'm so drunk by this time that I don't even look to see who it is. But then there's a hand in my crotch and at first I think it's Leon but then I realize it's two hands, one from either side of me.

I look up and Leon isn't sitting by me anymore. On one side is a light-skinned black guy, tall and skinny, wearing a hat. On the other side is another black guy, this one dark, with a long scar on one cheek. It's funny how when you're very drunk you may be half gone but the half that's still there sometimes sees things real good. The light skinny guy I don't like at all. The dark guy has a sweet face, but one with a lot of mileage on it. He's been on some long, hard trips. The two of them are feeling me up under the table, and Leon is looking at me to see how I'm gonna take it. He must've got them over here while I was nodding.

Something snaps loose in me, like a little thread that's stretched too tight and breaks. I feel it go, yet I'm not sure what the name of it is. Whatever it is, it's the last thread that holds me to anything in the past. But it's more than that, more like the thread that my will is tied to. I know that this is it, this is all there is for me, I don't have any more choices. In this very moment I truly understand that I won't ever see my dad or Betty or my half sisters again, or my mother, or David, or anyone I ever knew in my entire life. I got nowhere to go but where I am, and Leon is it. Period. And if I don't do what he wants me to do, then there isn't anything left for me at all. Period. The End.

Knowing this, I look at Leon and I open my legs a little. I feel fingers going under my bikinis, playing with me. I let my head drop again. I'll just sit here and they can do what they want. I drain my drink. But Leon is saying, "C'mon, let's go." The guys are getting up and I feel myself being half dragged out of the booth. The dark guy walks with his arm around my waist, half holding me up. I can hardly make it. The skinny guy and Leon are walking ahead, talking. I can hear Leon saying, "She loves cock, man, she just can't get enough." The dark guy holding me up is saying in my ear, real soft, "C'mon, now, you can make it. C'mon now."

I feel so woozy in the car I don't pay attention to where we're going, but when Leon parks I know we're back at the apartment. Great. The Plastic Pits. Stupefied as I am, I notice that Leon is toadying to these two guys, acting excited, saying things like, "C'mon, c'mon, you're gonna love this cunt, wait and see." He hardly pays me any attention at all, he's fumbling with the keys. He's more than a little drunk himself, and talking a blue streak. Definitely not cool now. I never saw him act like this before, but I never saw him drunk before either. He used to drink and drink and it never had any effect on him. But I'm only noticing this with half my mind. The other half is totally occupied with steering a straight course and staying on my feet.

Once inside, Leon lifts my skirt and drops to his knees. He goes after my crotch with his mouth like a starving man. The dark man has his hands on my breasts from behind. Actually he's half holding me up, but the skinny guy says, "Stand back, man; let the man eat that pussy." He's real turned on, watching. But all I can feel is that I have to bend my knees so I can spread my thighs so Leon can get at me and I'm damned uncomfortable and about to fall over without the other guy behind me to support me. I think, If I can do time I can do this. I just have to wait it out. It will be over eventually.

But Leon is eager for the guys to fuck me, so he eats me only for a minute, then he leads me to the bed. I'm so relieved to lie down that I hardly notice my clothes are being taken off. Then the skinny guy is on me. He has a long prick and I'm dry because I'm too drunk and not worked up at all and I'm afraid he's gonna hurt me. He's not any too delicate but it's not too bad and I'm holding on by holding my breath. I don't even know why that helps. I hear the skinny guy say, "She's got a dry cunt, man," and Leon goes to the bathroom and brings back some Vaseline, which helps. I hold my breath as much as I can, and I keep thinking the guy has to come soon, but he goes on and on and on. It doesn't seem like he even enjoys it. He's holding himself up on his hands and looking down at me without any expression at all. I can't look at him. He's a goddam fucking machine. Finally I wonder if he's holding off, waiting for me to come, so I say, "You don't have to wait for me. I'm too drunk." He says, "I never come." Never come? What does he do it for then? But about that time he climbs off and the dark one gets on. But instead of pounding into me like the other one, he lubes me up good first, and kisses me around my face and neck, though I won't let him get to my mouth. I can hear Leon talking to the skinny one on the other side of the room. They are really into it about something. I strain to hear. Leon is saying, "One time she took thirteen men, man, thirteen of 'em. And she still wanted more." That's a goddam lie. What's he telling lies like that for?

The dark man is a relief after the other one. He thrusts slowly, and moves his hips from side to side, and I can tell he's an artist at this, and if I wasn't so drunk and numb, and this was some other time and place, and the situation was totally different, I might like it. He's looking at me, I can tell, though I keep my face turned away. He keeps looking at me so hard that finally I turn to look back at him. He has a tender expression on his face.

Maybe he's thinking of some girlfriend or something. But I don't mind, because he's not just fucking. Even if he's pretending I'm someone else he's being careful with my body, which I appreciate after the other guy.

When I look at him he says, very very soft so the others can't hear, "How did you get yourself in a mess like this?"

I turn my face away and don't answer. What the hell can I answer?

"I can get you out of here if you want to go. Do you want to get out of here?"

I look back at him again. He means it. I can't stand looking at him and I turn away again. He has stopped screwing.

"We can go to L.A. I got a good job. It'll be all right. You want to get out of here?"

"It's too late."

"No it ain't, honey. I can get you out of here. I can handle the two of them."

"It's too late. The thread is broken."

"The thread?"

Just then the other guy comes back. "Hey, man, let me at her again." The dark man gives me a long searching look but I won't look him in the eye and finally he gets off and goes in the bathroom.

I try to shut everything off and just endure while the skinny guy fucks. He's like a machine, pumping, pumping, pumping, and he doesn't seem to feel anything. Finally I hear the dark guy say, "C'mon, man, you ain't never gonna get off. Let's go." The skinny guy gets off and everybody forgets about me, for which I'm glad. I'm thinking that now they're going, I can sleep. I look over at them when they're at the door and I see the skinny guy hand Leon something. Or is it the other way around, did Leon hand something to the skinny guy? For a second I think it's money but then I think, That's ridiculous, and about then I conk out.

But Leon shakes me by the shoulder and says, "C'mon, let's go."

I groan. "Go where?"

"C'mon," he says. I pull myself up and put my clothes on, but I'm arguing while I do it. "I'm tired, Leon. I drank too much and I feel sick. It's late. Why do we have to go out again?"

He kisses me on the cheek. "Tell you what, babe. We'll go for some coffee and get straightened out, okay? I might not get out again for a while. I want to spend all the time with you I can."

He could spend time with me right here. We could curl up and go to sleep together. But I know he doesn't mean that stuff about being with me anyhow. He means something else and I don't quite know what, I'm still too drunk. I know all this and it's the first time I've ever seen things this way and at the same time I don't care. I just goddam don't care. It's partly the thread being broken, it's partly I'm just so damn tired and sick from too much booze. I feel cold too. I pick up my coat. Leon says, "You look real fine in that elegant coat, mama. Some guy buy it for you?"

"I bought it my own damn self."

Leon takes me to a restaurant I've never been in before. There's hardly anyone in it, just some TJ pimpy-looking guys sitting around drinking booze from coffee cups. It must be three in the morning. Leon orders some coffee and when I go to drink mine it's almost pure whisky. "God, Leon, I don't want any more to drink."

"It's just what you need, babe. Straight coffee won't do you no good. Be a good girl, drink up." I don't know why but I do what he says. I don't seem to have any will to argue with him. I haven't finished the cup before there's some guy sitting in the booth with us. He's real young but he has the sure stamp of the TJ pimp on him. Those guys smell or something. Leon leans over the table and his eyes look funny. I never saw him look like that before. He looks a little crazy, to tell the truth. He says, "You like him, honey?"

All my life I've had a sure instinct when I better answer a certain way if I want to stay healthy. I've got that instinct now and I've got it real strong. "Sure, Leon, I like him."

"Let's go then." Leon gets up, and the guy stands up too. He looks like he's bored and above it all. He must think he's stooping pretty low. I get up and by now something in me is more busted than just the thread being broken, something now is completely disconnected. The phone is off the hook. No, the line is dead. Nobody and nothing is gonna get through anymore. I walk to the car like a good little robot and don't pay any attention at all to where we're going. But I'm surprised when we stop at a hotel, a pretty nice one, at that. I wonder why he didn't go back to the pad this time, and something about it makes me uneasy.

When we get into our room Leon takes out a bottle. He takes a big swig from it and says, "Go to it, boy." The "boy" comes over to the bed and starts taking off his pants. He does it like he was going to use the toilet. He doesn't seem interested in me at all.

When he turns to touch me, there is no expression on his face, nothing at all. He's as dead and blank as I am. He's a goddam zombie. Is that what I'm turning into?

I hear my own mouth saying, "I'm not gonna do it." I don't know where this voice is coming from.

Leon's black eyes are shooting icy hate at me. "You what?"

"I'm not gonna do it." The boy looks at Leon, not knowing what to do.

Leon's expression changes. He looks sweet, like he used to all the time. He comes over to the bed and leans down and kisses me on the forehead. "Come on, now, sweetness. Do it for Daddy, okay?"

I know I'm committing suicide. But the voice comes out of me again. "I'm not gonna do it."

Leon's eyes turn to black ice again. Did he turn that sweet look off and on again like that before, when I still thought he loved me? I can't remember that he did. But I never stood up to him about anything before.

Leon tells the boy, "Okay, you can go," and he gives him some money. Leon follows him to the door and for a second the boy turns around facing Leon and me. Over Leon's shoulder, I pantomime desperately, Don't leave me alone with him! But he doesn't register anything although he's looking right at me. He takes his money and goes out the door. Leon locks it and turns around.

"Goddam bitch," he says. "Goddam filthy cunt. All alike." He paces back and forth in a fury, taking swigs out of the bottle. I'm scared to move. Then he puts the bottle down and takes a switchblade out of his pocket. He opens it and starts swinging it back and forth through the air. I know for sure he's gonna cut me up and probably kill me. I start plotting, fast. There's only one way out and that's through the door, and Leon is between me and it. The main thing I see that might help me is that Leon's attention is not all on me. He's walking around the room swinging the knife through the air, working himself up, muttering about goddam filthy whores. He's looking at me about half the time, hating looks that, if I could feel anything but terror, would rip me worse than that knife, or would if I still had any love left for him, which I don't know if I do or not. I don't know anything at this point except that I got to get out that door or this is the end. By moving slow I get on my feet without his noticing. I'm watching him, feeling like any movement I make is gonna get me killed. Yet it's only by moving real fast that I'm gonna save my goddam life. Suddenness. Take him off guard. So when I decide to move I fly like lightning and unbolt the door and am out and running through the lobby and out onto the street and I don't dare even look back until I'm halfway up the block. Leon is after me, all right. But it must have taken his liquor-stupefied mind a few seconds to react. If it hadn't, I'd be dead.

I run like I'm jet-propelled, up the block to the main drag, and I see a cop directing traffic on the corner, one of those guys who stops tourists and says he's going to give them a ticket but if they want to they can pay a fine on the spot and he won't have to make them go to court. I run up to him and point back at Leon, who when he sees this stops running and starts walking like he's not doing anything. I say, "Please help me, that man is trying to kill me." The cop doesn't seem concerned, as if he hears that stuff every day. He stares at Leon a moment, then he whistles and beckons to a car parked on the side of the street, and I see for the first time there's a cop car there.

The car cuts over to where we're standing, and the cop tells them something in Spanish so fast that I don't understand him, even though I know quite a bit of the language. They give me slimy, suspicious looks and tell me in English to get in the car. They ask me a lot of questions: what am I doing in Tijuana, who is the guy who was chasing me, what is my relationship to him? I lie about everything of course. They ask me for identification, and only then do I remember that my purse is back in the hotel room. I ask them to go with me to get it, because I'm afraid Leon will be there. They drive me to the hotel and when we go in the room Leon is standing there going through my purse, taking things out of it and stuffing them in his pockets. Of all the things that have happened this is the weirdness that makes me decide Leon has flipped his lid. As if everything else he did wasn't crazy. It's the complete uselessness of robbing the purse of somebody he knows damn well doesn't have a thing worth having, and doing it when he must have known I'd be back with the cops any minute.

The cops give me the purse and my coat, and one cop leaves with me, the other stays to talk to Leon. I ask the cop if he'll take me to the border. He says we have to go to the police station first and make a report. I tell him I don't care about pressing charges, I only want protection so I can get to the border. He says, "It is required." So we go. But at the police station, instead of taking a report he takes me right through the station to a cell, and I'm locked up with three other women. I haven't been booked, and when I ask him what the hell is going on he acts like he doesn't hear me. I'm more scared now than when Leon was swinging at me with that knife. When he was thinking about cutting me up I had no time to be scared. I was thinking of how to get the hell out of there. But this is different. I don't know why the hell if Leon was trying to kill me they lock me up instead of him. It scares the hell out of me because for the first time I remember that Leon is connected with the biggest dope trafficker in Tijuana and half the police are probably in on the thing and of course they aren't gonna arrest him. I just may have got myself in more trouble than I was in back in the hotel room.

I'm so scared I feel sick, and I sit down on a bunk. The other women look like hookers. They don't talk to me because I suppose they figure I don't speak Spanish and that's fine with me, I don't want to talk to anyone. As I sit there I get more and more scared. I've heard of people being thrown in jail in Mexico without being booked or tried and they just rot for months, even years. In Mexico sometimes you can't get out of jail unless you have money, and that's the thing I've got least of all right now. No one will ever know I'm here, and that's a laugh because who is there to know? Being back in jail is the last thing I ever thought would happen to me, and it seems the nightmare I'm living is getting worse by the hour. When I ran out of that hotel room I had time to think, in spite of my panic, "I made it," and I thought everything would be all right if I could just get out of reach of Leon. And now having nothing to do but think, it occurs to me that if he's in with the local police, they just might give me back to him. Women are nothing here, less than garbage.

Well, all I can do is wait. I look around. The cells are built around an indoor courtyard. There are bars all the way across the front of each cell, so you can look across the courtyard right into the cells on the other side. I notice now for the first time that the men's cells are right across from us. There's no privacy for the toilet, or for anything else. But the men don't seem interested in us. They've got miseries of their own, I guess.

I have no way of knowing how much time goes by. Scared as I am, what I think is an hour may be ten minutes, who knows. But the more time goes past the more I figure my worst fears are right. They've got no reason to hold me unless something is fouled up. There comes a point where I know that even discounting my fear, several hours must have gone by.

Then they come for me. I'm taken into an office where a guy in plain clothes is sitting at a desk. He gestures to a chair. I sit down. Right away I notice that my little bottle of douche powder that was in my purse is sitting in the middle of his desk blotter, with nothing around it, so it stands out. It goes through my mind in less than a second that they think it's dope – the douche powder is a white crystally stuff. I'm too scared to laugh. The same instinct that tells me it's all over if I don't answer a certain way tells me to pretend I don't notice it.

The guy asks me the same questions the cops in the car asked me, and I tell him the same lies again. He looks at me hard, like he's studying me. He looks hard at my coat, which I'm still hanging on to. Once when he's saying something he reaches down and plays with the bottle of douche powder, as if he's just fiddling with it, but he's watching me intently. I pretend not to notice. I'm sure he's gonna ask me about it. But finally he says, "We will let you go, but you must go directly across the border. You must not come back to Tijuana again, you understand?"

I'm so relieved I could fall on my knees and kiss his goddam cop hand. "Yeah," I say, smiling a mile wide in spite of trying to appear cool.

They give me back my purse and turn me loose. No paperwork, since they didn't do any paperwork putting me in. A very simple system. Why didn't somebody in the States think of that? And I notice that this is the first time in weeks I've made a joke to myself or to anyone else.

When I get outside I look in my purse, and they have put everything back except the douche powder. They must have got it all back from Leon. Now I see why they didn't ask me directly about the douche powder. It was probably in Leon's pocket and they didn't know if it was mine or his. He surely said it was mine, especially if he thought it was dope. They planted it on the desk to see if I reacted to it. I feel pleased that my instinct did right for me. Pretending not to notice it was the best thing I could have done. Maybe they'll bust Leon for possession of douche powder. Oh god, it's good to laugh!

I can't travel any farther than I can walk, because I don't have any money. I can't eat, or buy a place to sleep. But these problems seem like nothing compared to what I've already been through, and I'm not even depressed about it. I just put my mind to work on it. If I got this far I can get the next step on down the line. First I got to get some money, and I think of Frenchy, our old connection. He runs a bar called Frenchy's, which is the front for his drug trade. He's not hard to find.

I make a beeline for his place – no, a desperate-woman line, I think to myself. Boy, I'm sure a comedienne now I'm just about home free. In the bar I ask the bartender if I can talk to Frenchy, and he calls a flunky over, who disappears in the back. In a minute or so another guy comes out, all dressed up in a fancy suit, looking like a Mexican version of Super Fly. He looks me over good and says, "What do you want to see Frenchy for?" I tell him, "It's personal. Tell Frenchy it's Toni, that he remembers me from three years ago." He goes in the back. God. Things have changed around here. Before, everybody in the place knew me.

I wait about five minutes, thinking about how much money I can ask for. I figure I've got to ask for some amount that he'll fork over real easy. I don't want to get in the spot of having him turn me down, and then having to make the bad play of asking for less once I've been turned down for more. Then Frenchy comes out. He's smiling, friendly like a snake. But he's my only chance. "Frenchy, I can't explain, but I need to borrow a hundred bucks. You know me, you know I'll pay it back."

"A hundred is all you need? Sure, Toni. Wait here."

A hundred is all you need? Oh god. I blew it. How much could I have asked for before he wouldn't say is that all you need? I can't believe my good luck. Why so easy? I don't know. The flunky comes back in a couple of minutes with the money; Frenchy doesn't reappear. I take the money and fly. I'm so elated now I feel like I can float to the border. It's getting hot and my Maison Cher coat is roasting me but I don't care. It's the only goddam thing I got besides the blouse and skirt I'm wearing.

It's not 'til I'm over the border that I know, really know in my bones, that I'm okay. I'm on the bus before all the tiredness and misery catch up with my body. I crash hard, but I'm too excited to sleep. All the way to San Diego, I think.

I can't believe how different I feel right now than I did twelve hours ago. Twelve hours ago I was dead. I couldn't feel anything, and I heard and saw everything through a thick glass. Now I even notice how bright colors are, how much sound there is and how loud it is – the bus motor, the people talking. When did that change happen? I think it started when I said I wasn't gonna fuck that pimp. But wait a minute. I fucked the two guys before, so what made the difference? What gave me the strength to defy Leon? I don't know. Up 'til the moment I said I wasn't gonna to fuck that pimp I seemed to have just given up. But there was something about that boy being such a zombie. Looking into his face was like looking in a mirror. We were both

Looking into his face was like looking in a mirror. We were both in the same state of dead indifference, and I could see my life as a zombie day after day forever, like his must be. And something in me said: No!

Well, anyway, here I am.

I think about the black guy who wanted to take me out of there. He could be on his way back to L.A. right now too. Wonder what he'd think if he knew I was on this bus? He probably thinks I'm still there in TJ, he'll probably picture me there forever, if he remembers me after a week. I wonder why I didn't let him take me out of there. I can't understand that. I just can't understand it at all. I didn't even have any goddam will to get out. But I had a limit, that's for sure. I'd put up with all that other stuff but not with fucking a zombie hustler, not with being cut up. It's making me crazy trying to think what the line was, why I had no will to get out of the one situation and then something turned and I couldn't do it anymore. He went too far, that's all, too goddam far. But I don't know what too far is. It all looks the same to me. What's the name of the line I can't be pushed over? The border of Zombieland? I don't know. Well, it's nice to know that as bad off as I am, I got my goddam limit somewhere, even if I don't know what it is.

Now it occurs to me that I got thrown out of Tijuana. Tijuana! I laugh out loud. You can't sink much lower than that. What's left, when you've been thrown out of the worst cesspool in the Western Hemisphere? David will sure get a kick out of that. Then I remember I haven't got David anymore. Oh well. It's a sad thought but it doesn't keep me from laughing every time I think, I've been thrown out of Tijuana.

I won't be laughing when this hundred bucks runs out.

I think about Frenchy and wonder why he lent the money so easy. He's got plenty, of course. He could lend me a thousand without noticing it. But I know those guys. They don't give anybody anything without expecting something back for it. But he didn't ask me to go to bed with him or anything. I can't figure it out. Maybe he figured I'd be back. Maybe he just likes me. But I don't waste much time on it because I won't ever see him again. If I ever go back to TJ they'll have to drag me across in chains.

In San Diego I find a cheap rooming house and rent a room for the week. In the room, at last I can let go and rest and think about what to do. That's when the emptiness hits me. I'm empty, my life is empty. There's been hundreds of people in this room probably, and there's not a trace of any one of them. Empty. Empty drawers in the dresser, empty closet, empty wastebasket. I don't even have a goddam change of clothes. All I have is a two-hundred-dollar Maison Cher coat that weighs a ton and ain't worth a dollar at a pawn shop.

I got to get past this. I need a job. I look at want ads in the paper I picked up in the bus depot. There's a few jobs for secretaries and typists, but I don't know how I can take a job like that when I can't even change my clothes. I'd have to wait too long to get paid too. There's a few jobs for waitresses, and I figure that's a better bet because I'll get at least one meal a day free and tips, and that'll carry me through 'til I get paid. I'm going through these motions of thinking about getting a job but I just can't seem to care about it. I can't see any reason to go to the trouble. Why struggle to survive when life is so fuckin' empty?

I force myself to go through some motions: I wash out my blouse and panties and hang them up over the radiator. I take a shower. That feels good, and I wash all the slime of Tijuana off me, the slime of Leon, the slime of those men and those bars. The black guy keeps coming back to me and I wonder why. Maybe just because for a few minutes there I had a friend in this world. What a stupid ass I was to let him go. I must have really wanted to die. But if I wanted to die, why didn't I let Leon finish me off? Well, because I don't want to die piece by piece with a goddam knife, that's why. I want to die slow, so it's hardly noticeable and I don't have to suffer. Fuckin' coward. And as if I wasn't suffering through all that shit. But the fact is, I didn't feel anything.

I lie down on the bed and soon I'm asleep. When I wake up it's dark. Except for the faint buzzing from the neon "ROOMS, Weekly Rates" sign outside my window, it's absolutely quiet. I don't even hear any cars on the street. I have pangs in my stomach. Some of it is hunger, but I feel scared too. Why am I so scared? Because the inside of me is as empty as this room, as my life. My empty stomach is the least of it. But I should get up and go get something to eat. I just don't seem to care. What good is it gonna do to eat? What good is it gonna do to get a job? This room will still be empty when I come back to it. I'll still be empty. I can't face going through all those motions, struggling and struggling and struggling when there's no point to it. Maybe this is the end.

But maybe when I get a job I'll meet some people. Yeah, sure. Like you been meeting people all your life. Either you fuck up or they fuck you up.

I can't stand lying here with my mind going around in circles. I get up and check my blouse. It's damp but not too bad. I put it on, and my skirt and my shoes. I pick up my purse, and I start to pick up my coat. I'm sick of that goddam coat. It may be cool out but I'm tired of wearing that lead coat. I look at my purse and I don't even want to carry it. I dump everything out on the bed, and put my money in my skirt pocket. I look at the rest of the stuff: a lipstick, my wallet with all my IDs, some chewing gum, a comb, the key to this room and the key to my room up in Arcata, the letter from my dad with Leon's phone number in TJ scribbled on the envelope. Ha.

I get the little wastebasket by the bureau and put it in the middle of the room. I take all my IDs out of my wallet and put them in the wastebasket. There's some matches on the bureau; I strike one and light the corner of the letter. When it's going good I drop it in the wastebasket. I wait to make sure everything is burned and that the room won't catch on fire. Then I put the rest of the stuff back in my purse, but at the last minute I drop the purse on the bed and leave it too. I lock the door behind me and drop the key on the desk on my way out.

I don't know where the hell I am going. Someone or something else is driving. I don't feel anything or care about anything. I'm just going where my feet take me. I don't even know why I did what I just did.

I walk a long time, and I don't know the city so I don't know where I am. It doesn't seem to matter. It must not be very late because there's lots of people on the street downtown.

Nobody notices me. Nobody knows me here. I'm nobody. I am really nobody now. I sing, "You're nobody if nobody knows you, / You're nobody if nobody cares. . . ." I don't even have an ID. If the cops pick me up they won't even know who I am if I don't tell 'em. I can tell 'em I'm the Queen of Sheba. Without an ID, Toni doesn't exist anymore.

Whose stomach is this that's screaming for food then? I'm feeling kind of light-headed too. But I'm starting to feel in a good mood. The more I walk the more I think it's great to not have any baggage, not even that goddam coat. I feel light. No ties, no weight to carry. No family, no friends, no belongings. I don't even have a goddam identity. But no Leon either. Nothing, not even a goddam purse anymore. Hey, if you got nothing, you got nothing to lose. That's what they always say, but I never knew how good it felt 'til now. If you're really at the bottom, if you're really down and out, there's no way to go but up. Where'd I hear that? Oh yeah. That loudmouth lady who used to sing in all those Broadway shows, broke your goddam eardrums. "Da dum da dum dum, dum da dum/ remember whenever you're down and out the only way is up . . ." I been singing as I walk along and I realize people are staring at me. It breaks my concentration and I can't remember any more of the song.

I stop to look at myself in a store window. God, I look skinny. I must've dropped some weight the last few days. I don't look like anybody I know. I don't even know my own goddam self. That really makes me a nobody, doesn't it? Hey! If I'm nobody, I can be anybody. Ha-ha.

All this has been kind of a joke up 'til now, but now I think seriously: I am really free for the first time in my life. I am really, truly free. I can't be any worse off, I can't have any less, I can't lose any friends, nobody can take anything away from me, not even my self-respect, because that's long gone, man. I'm not even Toni anymore. I burned everything that says I am. I am really, truly free. Where'd I hear that? Oh yeah, Janis Joplin. "Freedom's just another word for nothing left to lose, / NA na na NA na na NA na na NA," or something like that. Yeah, I haven't even got an identity to lose anymore. The end is the beginning. I can invent a new me from this minute on, and anything is gonna be an improvement on the old one. Maybe I'll be Elizabeth. That's a really elegant name, like a movie star or the queen of England. I start to sing the Joplin song as I walk, mostly the na-na-na-na part because I can't remember all the words. I sing loud. I don't care if people stare at me or not. Who is left to be embarrassed? Nobody!

I don't even feel like eating anymore. Maybe I'll write that guy Siddhartha a letter.

Dear Sid:
I already learned to wait. The hard way, man. Now I'm learning to fast. I'm learning that the hard way too. I'm still not doing too good in the thinking line. I been going around in circles a lot. Mostly I don't understand why I do things or why things happen like they do or why other people do things either. But just now I figured something out, all about having nothing and being nothing and freedom. And I've never been free before in my whole entire life. So who knows? Maybe I'm even learning to think.

Love, Elizabeth

I'm getting a little weak in the knees so I sit down on a bus stop bench. Buses go places. Where the hell am I going? Maybe I'll just get on a bus and go wherever it takes me. Then what? Hey! There's supposed to be one helluva zoo in this town. Maybe I'll check it out tomorrow.

If I make it through tonight, that is.

Afterword

Afterword

About ninety percent of the events described in this book actually occurred. Either they happened to me or I was a witness to them. I have invented characters and fictionalized my experiences for a variety of reasons; one of them is to protect the privacy of other prisoners. Lily Tomlin's character Edith Ann says, "You can make up the truth if you know how," and that's what I've done. You can trust that what little I have invented is nonetheless true to the jail/prison experience.

There are things that burn in my memory but couldn't be developed fully in this book. I remember being in a hallway in a city jail as two policemen came out of a courtroom holding a male prisoner by both arms. When the door to the courtroom swung shut behind them, the prisoner muttered something under his breath. The two cops glanced at each other. Apparently a signal passed between them with no more than a look, and they threw the man against the wall and hit him in the stomach as hard as they could. Then they pushed him on down the hall to the men's tank. This incident is mentioned only briefly, in "Getting Oriented," when Toni tries to tell the marshal what goes on in the jail. In my real experience, as in Toni's, the marshal thought I was lying about that and about a guard having thrown scalding water on a prisoner.

As a culture, we are not willing to believe what goes on in our jails and prisons. We hear about the most extreme atrocities and tell ourselves these are aberrations, and now that such a stink has been made, things will be cleaned up and improved. Sometimes they are. For a while.

It's no wonder we can't believe that prisons are as bad as they are. What we read about them is, for the most part, unbelievable. Jails haven't changed much since the time of Christ, except that they are cleaner and the forms of torture have become more subtle and less verifiable. When we are confronted with the stories that sometimes make their way to the press, we are so shocked that we find ways to tell ourselves we aren't responsible for such horrors. This can't be, we tell ourselves. Prisoners lie. After all, they are criminals. The media exaggerate things, they sensationalize, everybody knows that. And so on.

The first story I ever wrote was an early version of the title story of this book, "Sing Soft, Sing Loud." I was married at the time. Although my husband had "magnanimously" forgiven me for my past, he considered it a shameful thing and he didn't want it mentioned, ever. But my prison experience and the events leading up to it were the most traumatic things that had ever happened to me, and I needed to talk about them. To suppress and deny this part of my past was to suppress and deny a vital part of myself, and so I was crippled by my husband's rule of silence. Above all, I needed to be accepted in toto, warty past and all.

I was like a capped volcano and inevitably I erupted. One day I sat down and wrote "Sing Soft, Sing Loud" in one sitting, shaking and in a cold sweat. I showed it to my husband and told him that it was based on an incident I had taken part in while a prisoner in a city jail. He said, "I don't believe that happened." I said, "Are you calling me a liar?" "No, I just don't believe that happened." The only other thing he said about the story was, "I don't know why anyone would want to read something like that."

My husband's attitude was a bellwether. I had a hard time getting anyone to believe the stories were based on truth. No one would publish them for a long time. Some people said, "Well, you were particularly unfortunate." No, I wasn't. My experiences were extremely tame compared with some. Prisoners are often starved, beaten, and locked in dark isolation cells for months at a time. A lot of them go crazy. If you ever have a chance to watch a rerun of *60 Minutes'* report on the Pelican Bay facility in California, be sure to do so. You will see for yourself that I do not exagerate.

When I visited San Francisco County jail in the spring of 1988, I read "Sing Soft, Sing Loud" to a group of prisoners. After the reading, two prisoners – a woman and a man – came up to tell me, independently of each other, of a cell in a particular California jail (not San Francisco) called the "cold cell". The cold cell is like flatbottom, with a couple of modifications. There is a drain in the center of the floor so you can piss into it. The door is solid rather than barred, and in the ceiling is an air conditioner. When prisoners are sent to this cell for "adjustment", the air conditioner is turned on full blast and left on for as long as the prisoner stays there. No doubt prisoners on the brink of hypothermia become much more tractable.

Another woman, a heroin addict, told me that police officers twisted her arm while making their arrest. While they were booking her, she tried to tell them that her shoulder was injured. They accused her of being a crybaby and insisted that she was not hurt, and they would not send her for medical attention. It turned out that they had dislocated her shoulder, and it was not treated until she was released from jail. In the meantime she was in excruciating pain, as anyone who has had a dislocated joint can testify. At the time I spoke to her she had a lawsuit pending against the police department.

However, many mistreated prisoners are afraid to pursue legal remedies for mistreatment, fearing retaliation from the police. Their fears are justified. Dannie M. Martin, a federal prisoner, wrote about prison life for *Sunday Punch*, the Sunday supplement of the *San Francisco Chronicle,* for several years. He did so at considerable risk to himself, out of a commitment to letting the public know about conditions in the prison. In June of 1988 he wrote an article critical of policies of the current warden. Two days after the article appeared, Martin was taken to "isolation." The officers who took him to "the hole" refused to tell him why he was being cited. He was issued two sheets and a pillow case, but was refused a blanket although it gets extremely cold in the prison at night. (Other prisoners in isolation had blankets.) He was also refused paper and pencil. But another prisoner brought him writing supplies and Martin wrote up his experience and got it to *Sunday Punch*. He told what could happen to him now that he had incurred the disfavor of the warden:

> I could be put on the 'Merry Go Round.' In federal prisons, when a prisoner is en route, he's not allowed phone calls or mail privileges – the reasoning being that he could attempt an escape. So what is sometimes done is that they put a fellow like me on a bus and drop him off at Isolation for a few weeks at every prison they stop at. I've seen convicts get caught up in that for nearly two years, never able to contact anyone. It's known as the Merry Go Round. Old convicts call it 'bus therapy.' If things get really bad, I could be pumped full of psychotropic drugs like Prolixin or Haldol and locked up in IO Building at the Springfield, Mo., prison, which is the final stop for troublesome federal prisoners. . . ."
> (From "A Report from Solitary," by Dannie Martin, *Sunday Punch*, July 3, 1988.)

Martin got transferred, just as he predicted. He was told he could not write for news media under his by-line. The *Chronicle* went to court to challenge the rule and after an adverse lower court decision, the *Chronicle* got around the rule by running Martin's articles with no by-line, saying only they were by a federal prisoner.   Martin was released from prison before the *Chronicle's* appeal on the lower court ruling was resolved and so the court threw out the case, leaving the rule still standing. Therefore federal prisoners still may not write for news media for pay or under their own by-line, nor act as a reporter for any news medium. The whole point, of course, is that the governement doesn't want you to know what really goes on in federal prisons.

Martin and his editor at *Sunday Punch*, Peter Sussman, wrote a book which is a compilation of Martin's writings and accounts of Martin's experiences and the court case. *Committing Journalism: The Prison Writings of Red Hog*, was published by W.W. Norton in 1993.

Nowhere is it specifically written "Thou shalt be cruel to prisoners." It is not a policy anyone would openly condone. But there is tacit approval throughout the system. Part of it has to do with an unconscious projection on the part of society as a whole: through prisoners, we symbolically lock our own dark sides away and secretly believe those selves deserve what they get.

But much of the cruelty results from the perpetuation of a physical format for imprisonment that is essentially medieval, and the inevitable psychological effects of that format. Ask yourself what kind of person wants to take a job keeping other humans in cages, and you will have the answer to why so many prison employess are sadistic and morally corrupt individuals. These people bring their own agenda to work with them, and carry it out without anyone but the prisoners knowing what they are up to, as Garth did in the story "The Floor." That incident, by the way, is a literal account of something that happened to me in Alderson. In fairness I must note that there are also well-motivated and humane people working in prisons, but they are in the minority and can do little to change a system whose very structure is rooted in the concept of sadistic vengeance.

Ask yourself what would happen to your concept of yourself if you were locked in a six-by-nine cage, often at the mercy of people who are your moral inferiors, and at the same time you received messages on every level that you are a pariah, and you will have the answer to why so many prisoners are unable to function in society when they get out.

In 1988, there was a little flurry of interest in women in prison. NBC did a TV special on women in prison, and *Parade* ran an article on women in jail. A central point in both features was that most women end up in prison because of dependencies on men who are involved in crime. There seems no end to the forms sexism can take. Poor helpless little things only got in jail because of some big bad mans. That this simplistic and harmful idea was presented by women journalists, who ought to know better, infuriates me.

The reason this idea is so harmful is that jails and prisons work actively to remove from women every last vestige of autonomy, every self-assertive instinct, every last trace of initiative, responsibility, and self-respect we may have left by the time we get through the court system. Take any well-adjusted, successful woman, put her in jail for a year, and when she comes out she will need permission to put on her own shoes.

And here come the media, saying that now we aren't even capable of being responsible for getting ourselves in jail!

Superficially it may appear, to someone who isn't thinking, that the majority of women in prison are there because of the men we are dependent on. But the fact is that most often the cause behind all other causes for women's crime is that we did not get adequate education and so can't get decent jobs. Many of us are the children of alcoholic, drug-using, and/or abusive parents. A significant number are raised in ghettoes where violence and poverty and despair are so pervasive that we don't even have any hope to lose. We don't have a chance to learn the values on which a healthy productive life is based, the most important of which is an individual's responsibility for her own actions, and we don't have a chance to learn job skills.

Without resources, without skills, without hope, and without self-esteem, of course many of us take the only option we see open to us: we attach ourselves to mates we perceive to be in control of things. That's what Iva and Toni did. That's what I did. But such dependency is a symptom, not the cause. The last thing any of us needs to hear is that we aren't responsible for the mess in which we find ourselves, because *our only hope for change is to take control of our own lives, and you can't take control of a life you don't even accept responsibility for.*

Yet even accepting responsibility for our lives won't help if we still face all the conditions that have left us only desperate, self-destructive choices, such as the one Toni made when Tuffy beat her up and she called the only person she thought it was possible to call – another drug dealer. That's from my own life, but I can give you a current example. Martha and Lindy – I've made up the names but these are real women – have five children between them, no husbands, and they live in one room in a rat-infested hotel in Oakland. Lindy stays home and takes care of the children; Martha supports them all by prostitution. Tell me, if you were Martha, wouldn't you laugh in the face of someone who tells you that you ought to stop hooking and take a job at minimum wage at McDonald's?

It might sound like I am contradicting myself. On the one hand I am saying we need to acknowledge that we are responsible for our actions; on the other I am saying we usually have no options. It sounds like I'm saying that we both are and aren't responsible at the same time. That's right, that's what I'm saying. It's called a double bind, and it can and does drive people nuts.

We don't need excuses made for us. We need programs that are truly rehabilitative, run by sane and humane people. We need education and job training. We need options.

What Can You Do?

Work as a volunteer, teaching literacy and/or your job skills to jail and prison inmates. Call the institution nearest you to find out if they have a volunteer educational program. If they don't have one, ask them to let you start one.

If you own a business, contact your local parole and probation offices and volunteer to hire a parolee, probationer, or work-release prisoner.

Be realistic. If you work with prisoners, expect them to disappoint you regularly. A lifetime of conditioning is not going to evaporate just because someone gives them one opportunity. Reconditioning takes another lifetime. (I know!) Instead of giving up, do what you can to help them learn to correct their mistakes and go on, and do it in a nonjudgmental way.

Support prison reform legislation, especially work-release programs. One of the ways you can keep informed on legislation is by joining C.U.R.E. (Citizens United for Rehabilitation of Errants). C.U.R.E. works for prison reform and concerns itself with a broad spectrum of issues affecting prisoners. A very moderate membership fee will bring you their quarterly newsletter, with news of upcoming legislation and information on action you can take, which is usually as simple as a letter to members of Congress.

C.U.R.E.   202 842-1650
P.O. Box 2310
National Capital Station
Washington DC 20013-2310

C.U.R.E. for Veterans
P.O. Box 86
Boston MA 02122

Call the **ACLU** (American Civil Liberties Union) office nearest you and find out what the most urgent problems are in your local institutions; ask how you can help to solve them. Ask the ACLU for the names of prisoner rights organizations in your state, contact them, and volunteer your help. If you can't find the ACLU office in your state, write the national headquarters:

National Prison Project   202 234-4830
American Civil Liberties Union
1875 Connecticut Avenue N.W.
Washington DC 20009

The National Prison Project seeks to strengthen and protect the rights of prisoners and to improve conditions in correctional facilities. They file class action suits on issues that affect prisoners as a whole. They do not provide legal assistance to individuals. The *National Prison Project Journal* reports on the progress of these cases and publishes articles on prison problems. The Project also publishes a number of useful books and papers, including a *Bibliography on Issues Concerning Women in Prison*, a handbook entitled *The Rights of Prisoners*, and a *Prisoners' Assistance Directory*. Write for a complete list of publications and prices.

The Fortune Society offers a variety of critically needed services to ex-offenders, including one-to-one counseling, ex-offender to ex-offender; a one-to-one tutoring program for those whose

246

reading and writing skills are so poor they can't get jobs; and assistance in entering vocational schools. They also have a public education program, sending ex-offenders on speaking engagements so that the public can learn about prison issues from the people most affected by them. I am more excited by this program than by any other I know because they are doing what the prisons should be doing – helping prisoners to help themselves. A moderate fee will get you a one-year membership and subscription to their newsletter.

The Fortune Society   212 206-7070
39 West 19th Street
New York, NY 10011

The American Friends Service Committee sponsors two programs to benefit prisoners. The **Prisoner Visitation and Support** program finds volunteers to visit prisoners in federal and military prisons who have no friends or family to visit them. The **Criminal Justice Program** helps community based programs advocate for change in the criminal justice system in their communities. They have a particular commitment to finding alternatives to prison.

Prisoner Visitation and Support   215 241-7117
Criminal Justice Program   215 241-7134
American Friends Service Committee
1501 Cherry Street
Philadelphia, PA 19102

For New York prisoners only:

Prisoners' Rights Project   212 577-3300
Legal Aid Society
15 Park Row
New York, NY 10038

The **Correctional Asso. of New York** investigates local prison conditions and lobbies for legislation on prison issues. They have a Women In Prison project.

Correctional Asso. of New York   212 254-5700
135 East 15th Street
New York NY 10003

If you are interested in gay and lesbian prisoners, the **Prisoner Project** of Gay Community News provides a pen pal service and a forum in the paper where prisoners can voice their concerns. The prisoner forum in the paper is the only place I know of where anybody can find out from the prisoners themselves what is going on in the prisons. Subscriptions are free to prisoners:

Prisoner Project   617 426-4469
Gay Community News
62 Berkeley Street
Boston, MA 02 I i 6

Books

Acquire and read *We're All Doing Time,* by Bo Lozoff (Prison Ashram Project, Rt. 1, Box 201-N, Durham, NC 27705), especially Part 3 (letters from prisoners and Bo Lozoff's answers to them). If you agree that this project is doing extraordinarily valuable work, send them money. Call the Project at 919 942-2138 to find out the price of the book. It is free to prisoners.

Other books you should read:
Kind and Usual Punishment, by Jessica Mitford (New York: Vintage Books, 1974).
Part II of *Stranger In Two Worlds,* by Jean Harris (New York: Macmillan, 1986).
They Always Call Us Ladies: Stories from Prison, by Jean Harris (New York: Scribner's, 1988).
Sisters in Crime., The Rise of the New Female Criminal, by Freda Adler (New York: McGraw-Hill, 1975).

Committing Journalism: The Prison Writings of Red Hog, by Dannie M. Martin and Peter Y. Sussman (New York: W.W. Norton, 1993)

When reading other books about women in prison, be cautious about accepting the opinions of sociologists who have studied women in crime in New York City and who then think they know about women offenders all across the country. I'm not referring to Jean Harris. She is a prisoner, not a sociologist.

But you will find the women in Jean Harris's books (New Yorkers mostly) different from the characters in my book. That doesn't mean that either one of us is wrong in her perceptions. It means that we served our time in different parts of the country. An important motivation for writing *Sing Soft, Sing Loud* has been to bring some balance to the public's impression of women in jails. Most of what has been written about women prisoners to date is based on the way things are in New York. New York is a different planet, New Yorkers a different breed.

In many institutions, prisoners have a hard time getting books. A prisoner in San Quentin told me bitterly that the administration there had recently thrown out some four thousand books, saying they "didn't have room" for them. Since self-education is the single most valuable way prisoners can spend time that is otherwise lost from their lives, such actions are unconscionable. We all need to do what we can to get books into the prisons.

Some prisons don't allow books to be sent in by anyone other than the publishers or approved prison book programs. The theory is that it is easy to smuggle drugs in the bindings. (This is one way of denying that most prison drugs are brought in by prison personnel.) Other prisons are more liberal in their policies. The only way to find out is to call or write saying you want to donate books, and see what they say. If you can't donate directly, here is a prison book program you can help. They distribute books to prisoners nationwide. They need books, of course, and they also need money for postage and packaging:

Books To Prisoners   **206 622-0195**
c/o Left Hand Books
Box A, 92 Pike Street
Seattle, WA 98101

ORGANIZATIONS FOR WOMEN PRISONERS

Aid to Imprisoned Mothers   404 221-0092
805 Peachtree Street NE, Suite 300
Atlanta, GA 30308

> Assists the caretakers of children of incarcerated women in Georgia.

Aid to Incarcerated Mothers   617 536-0058
32 Rutland Street, 4th floor
Boston, MA 02118

> Offers many programs and services to incarcerated women in Massachusetts, including legal counseling and help for substance abuse and AIDS.

CLAIM   312 332-5537
205 West Randolph, #830
Chicago IL 60606

> Attempts to keep families together by providing legal assistance and education to incarcerated women and their families.

House of Ruth
2201 Argonne Drive
Baltimore MD 21218

Legal Services for Prisoners with Children   415 255-7036
1317 Eighteenth Street
San Francisco, CA 94107

National Clearinghouse for Battered Women   215 351-0010
125 South 9th St., #302
Philadelphia PA 19107

National Women's Law Center   202 328-5160
Women In Prison Project
1616 P St. N.W. Suite 100
Washington DC 20036

The **Women In Prison Project** works to ensure the rights of incarcerated women in the District of Columbia by answering requests for legal assistance and providing legal education and counseling.

Social Justice for Women   617 482-0747
20 West Street
Boston, MA 02111

Assists incarcerated pregnant women, or those in danger of being incarcerated, with programs that address a variety of problems including AIDS and substance abuse. Tries to arrange alternatives to incarceration.

These are a few programs I happen to know about but they represent only a sampling of the programs available. I have listed them here so you can get a sense of the kinds of assistance available to women prisoners. Because you don't find an agency listed for your state does not mean there is none. A phone call to the administrator of your state women's prison will get you the names of appropriate organizations for your particular interests.

Some of these organizations are able to do only very limited work because of lack of money and lack of volunteers. Most of them work only with one prison or one state. The need is desperate. Please help.

Two Final Suggestions

1. If you know someone who has been imprisoned, don't think you are being polite to avoid mentioning it. Ask her about her experience. She needs to talk about it, and needs to know you care and that you are interested. Just be tactful. You might say something like, "I know you've been in prison. I know that must have been hard and I'd like to know more about it. Do you mind talking about your experience?" That lets her know you respect her right to privacy if she wants it.

2. Don't assume you'll never be there.

Acknowledgements

Works of fiction are usually considered to be produced by a single writer working from within herself, and in the most literal sense this is true. But this book would never have been completed without crucial support from many different quarters. So in a broader sense, *Sing Soft, Sing Loud* is the result of a team effort.

Three people are due more thanks than I can ever express: Bernard Conrad Cole, my friend and patron of twenty-three years; G. Barnes, literary director of the Utah Arts Council; and Ellen Levine, my former agent. I also owe deep appreciation to Judy Kern, my editor at Atheneum for the hardcover edition of this book, and Dan Wright, my dramatic rights agent. All these people have believed unwaveringly in this project, and each has invested generously in me and in my work.

Of institutions, I thank the National Endowment for the Arts for literally putting its money where its mouth is. I enjoy the irony that the same government that locked me up (and nearly destroyed an already shaky psyche) has now given me large sums of money to write about how despicable its penal practices are. Only in America? Probably. We are nothing if not schizoid.

About the author

Patricia McConnel has had a distinguished career. By her sixteenth birthday she had already ridden freights and hitchhiked across the country and had accomplished the first of several incarcerations (her experience in the El Paso County Jail eventually became Millie's story in "The Virgin Ear"). Before she was out of her teens she had been fired from two waitress jobs for general inefficiency, one job as a B-girl for the same reason, and two jobs for refusing to sleep with the boss. Desperate, she joined the WAC (Women's Army Corps), but was discharged in less than a year for general inadaptability. After a series of short-lived jobs in machine shops and cocktail bars (she had learned to quit before she was fired), she turned to a life of crime, which seemed to offer high wages for people like herself, that is, with no particular skills. After failing at that as well, eventually ending up in a federal prison, she tried marriage, the worst disaster of all. When you've failed at everything you ever tried, what's left? To become a writer, of course.

As a writer, McConnel continued the pattern of failure for many, many years, but eventually found an agent, Ellen Levine, who recognized the value of her work. In 1986 her first book was published: *The Woman's Work-At-Home Handbook: Income and Independence With A Computer* (Bantam Books). While working on that book McConnel won her first creative writing fellowship from the National Endowment for the Arts (1983) for work that eventually became *Sing Soft, Sing Loud*. A second NEA fellowship came in 1988. Her short story "The Aviarian" was chosen as one of the Ten Best PEN Short Stories of 1984. In 1985 she was invited to give a reading at the Library of Congress. She has won several other literary grants and awards, but, with few exceptions, literary magazines still do not publish her work. In 1989 Atheneum (a literary imprint of Macmillan Books) published the hard cover edition of *Sing Soft, Sing Loud*.

With two published books in lieu of academic credentials (in fact, she never finished high school), McConnel taught creative writing for a year at the University of Nevada at Las Vegas, but she failed to adapt successfully to the academic environment. She now visits jails and prisons to give readings and teach writing workshops, and, having accepted once and for all that she is unemployable, makes her living at home as an independent contractor doing editing, page design, typesetting, and database programming. She is at work on a novel, *The Quest of Elizabeth Halfpenny*, which is an attempt to write a heroic quest myth that has relevance to the lives of 20th century women.

McConnel lives in southeastern Utah with two cats, Anastasia and Mitzi, and two old trucks, Serafina and Suzie, at least one of which is not running at any given time. McConnel attempts to repair them herself but, of course, usually fails.

Books

Sing Soft, Sing Loud
Fiction, hard cover edition: Atheneum, 1989
Paperback edition: Logoría, 1995

California Song
The French edition of *Sing Soft, Sing Loud*, Editions Fixot, 1990

The Woman's Work-At-Home Handbook: Income and Independence With A Computer
Bantam Books, 1986

Eye of the Beholder
Jumping Cholla Press, 1994

Editor:*Women's Voices Within: An Anthology of Writings from the Women's Correctional Facility, Draper, Utah.*
Utah Arts Council, 1993

Guidebook for Artists Working in Prisons
Utah Arts Council, 1994

Anthologies

"The Floor"
Great & Peculiar Beauty: A Utah Centennial Reader, Gibbs Smith, Publisher, 1995.

"Edna"
Selected Tumblewords, University of Nevada Press, 1995.

"The Way I Live"
Title story of *The Way We Live,* Signature Books, 1994.

"The Floor"
Passages North Anthology, Milkweed Editions, April 1990.

"The Triangle"
Touching Fire, An Anthology Of Erotic Writings By Women, Carroll & Graf, December 1989.

"Sing Soft, Sing Loud"
Wall Tappings: An Anthology of Writings by Women Prisoners, Northeastern University Press, 1986.

"The Aviarian"
The Available Press/PEN Short Story Collection, Ballantine, 1985.

Sing Soft, Sing Loud